# THE CURSED EARTH

# D.T. Neal

# THE CURSED EARTH

N*P

NOSETOUCH PRESS

CHICAGO · PITTSBURGH

ISBN-13: 978-1-944286-70-5

Published by Nosetouch Press
Chicago, Illinois

www.dtneal.com | www.nosetouchpress.com

Cataloging-in-Publication Data
Names: Neal, D.T., author.
Title: The Cursed Earth
Description: Chicago, IL : Nosetouch Press [2022]
Identifiers: ISBN: 9781944286705
Subjects: LCSH: Horror—Fiction. | Paranormal—Fiction.
GSAFD: Horror fiction. | BISAC: FICTION / Horror.

Cover & interior design by Christine M. Scott
www.clevercrow.com

Select elements of the cover illustration by
Artgraris Studio at Vecteezy.

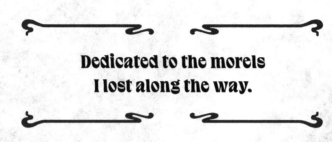

Dedicated to the morels
I lost along the way.

"Good can be radical;
evil can never be radical,
it can only be extreme,
for it possesses
neither depth nor
any demonic dimension,
yet—and this is its horror—
it can spread like a fungus
over the surface of
the earth and lay waste
the entire world."

—Hannah Arendt

# PROLOGUE

**Park Ranger Hunter Charles walked the perimeter, as**
he had a thousand times before within the Forest Preserve
since he'd taken the job. He knew She was somewhere from the
frightened words he'd heard from others, but had yet to find
Her, to even see Her.

Tall enough without being a giant, and lean-built with a
rough-cut sort of face that managed to be unhandsome without necessarily being unattractive, Hunter was content to dwell
within the hundreds of acres that were his to protect and care
for. He made his way through the interwoven trails on foot, listening for the sounds of the forest—the birds and other ani-
mals, the breezes, the rippling of rills, the whispered secrets of
countless leaves, the creak of interwoven branches.

It was Her forest as much as it was his, and in his humility,
he understood it wasn't truly his at all. He was, after all, only its
faithful steward.

And yet, deep within it, far from his wooden cabin and
tower, away from the wounded world itself, he saw the statue of
Her that had been placed by the Foundation when they'd created the Preserve.

How pretty She was, standing mossy on Her plinth in a
pavestone glade, canopied by conifers that gave off the most
pleasant scent. She stood garbed in stony robes, Her lovely face
inscrutable, Her arms outstretched, Her long fingers flexed, as
if She were grasping something he could not, would not ever
see. A small basin flanked Her base, filled with a crescent of
water in which little things swam, where wind-tossed leaves
sometimes found their way and pine needles played.

"Milady," Charles said, tipping his hat in salute.

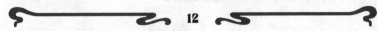
She was, as ever, coldly radiant. What tourists who came rarely got this deep into the forest preserve, and when they had brought Her here, he thought it had been deliberate—only the most determined found this pretty shrine.

As it was spring, he could see the first of the fungi showing themselves the way they always did, comfortable in the dark of the conifers, almost luminous—big, white Puffballs and the glossy orange Witches' Butter upon fallen branches. He knew they were edible, but he never partook of them out of respect, and perhaps even fear.

For he knew She was here in Neverwhere, watching.

# PART ONE:
# BEFORE

# 1

**It wasn't exactly a plan so much as it was a scheme.**
But sometimes, schemes were enough in the right hands. In
this case, it was two men just a stone's throw from the Susque-
hannock State Forest, near the little town of Lynchburg, Pennsylvania, spying on the Nightcap Mushroom Farm.

"It fucking stinks, Francisco," said the younger man, holding his nose, half-pacing behind his older peer.

"It's a mushroom farm, Matteo," said Francisco. "It's supposed to stink. It's all the compost. They aerate it to keep it from
getting really bad."

"Aerate? What the hell are you talking about?" Matteo
asked. "You mean this *isn't* bad?"

"If they let the compost just rot without aerating it, it *really*
stinks," Francisco said.

"Fuck this, man," Matteo said. "If this is it not really stinking, God help us. If Carlos wants this place so bad, he should be
out here himself."

They were Big City men, unsuited to tramping in the
woods. Matteo, the younger one, wore a navy blue track suit
with a black leather jacket. He had black hair he'd shaved close
to his head, and had a petulant scowl on a hard-looking face
that spoke of a rough past that had not left him. Francisco, the
older one by maybe a few years, wore all black—black pants,
black shirt, black leather jacket. His hair was styled in a black
lacquered pompadour he'd picked up in Pittsburgh.

"You can't talk like that about *El Segundo*," Francisco said,
turning away from his binoculars to glare at his younger partner. Carlos Mendoza was the Underboss of their gang, and that

meant he carried nearly as much weight as his big brother, Santino, who was the *Jefe*.

"Meaning no disrespect," Matteo said. "I just don't know why we're even here, man. We should be in Hidden Hollow."

Hidden Hollow was the nearby gated community where they'd been sheltering after catching some heat in Pittsburgh. When things got too hot in the city, they'd slip away to the countryside. A place like Hidden Hollow had its own private security, and the gang had often used it as a kind of safe house. Local authorities had no jurisdiction in gated communities, and it offered them a respite from too much harassment.

For the residents of Hidden Hollow, the appearance of *Las Muertes Rojas* didn't earn more than a furtive glance or two. To be able to live in Hidden Hollow meant having money, wherever it came from, and not asking uncomfortable questions.

"Carlos wants us to shake down these *pendejo* farmers," Francisco said. "Says there's real money in it. He says they're filthy rich."

"Filthy, maybe," Matteo said. "Rich? I don't know."

"Look at the size of the farm, Teo," Francisco said. "They've got money to burn."

Around them was thick woods on a rolling hill that gave them a good view of the farm, which was a dozen big, white buildings arranged in three interconnected circles and lots of trucks and tractors. The trucks came and went constantly. The farm was guarded by a fence and spotlights.

"You see all those trucks, Matteo?" Francisco asked.

"Yeah, I see them," Matteo said over his pinched nose.

"All loaded with product bound for Pittsburgh and Philadelphia," Francisco said. "They haul ass."

"Mushrooms," Matteo said. "Fuckin' mushrooms. I hate mushrooms."

"They got all sorts," Francisco said. He went back to his binoculars and his little red notebook in which he'd been carefully jotting down his observations. They'd been there for two days, tasked by Carlos to get as much information as they could before they made their move to try to extort the farmers. It was a straightforward plan, something Carlos had done in Mexico with avocado farmers. You simply offered protection and then extorted them into subjection and servitude with taxes. The

ones who resisted got killed. Eventually they came around. This would be no different—lean in, lean on, and squeeze.

"All sorts?"

"Yeah," Francisco said. "Like drugs, man."

"Magic mushrooms?" Matteo asked.

"Yeah," Francisco said.

"Down there?" Matteo asked. At the mention of drugs, the younger man's attention was more focused. The prospect of a quick turn of a buck on some psilocybin mushrooms was something any *Las Muertes Rojas* man could appreciate.

"Somewhere down there," Francisco said. Matteo broke into a grin.

"Man, you should have led with that," Matteo said. "Like two days ago. I thought we were boosting grocery trucks or something."

Francisco turned his gaze to Matteo a moment. Matteo was a good kid, but his mouth got ahead of what brains he had.

"You think Carlos would have us out here just for some grocery trucks, Teo?" Francisco said. "You know what? Why don't you, I don't know, guard our perimeter or something? Just let me do my thing here. Go check on the car, make sure that *loco* park ranger isn't snooping around."

Matteo nodded, sticking his hands in the pockets of his leather jacket. They'd driven out there in a black Dodge Challenger with a yellow racing stripe. Carlos had wanted them to be low-key when hiding out in Hidden Hollow, but the joke among the *Rojas* was that the car was so overt, it was practically invisible. People liked their muscle cars in Pennsylvania. It was a sure way to blend in.

"Sure, man," Matteo said.

"Yeah, go check on the car," Francisco said. "And don't bug me. If I can wrap up here today, we can get back to Hidden Hollow and tell Carlos what we saw."

Francisco shooed the younger man away, glancing at the sky around them. It was late afternoon, but in the woods, the shadows got long quickly from the tall trees, and where they were was already getting dark. He could see the orange light of

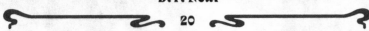
the waning sun painting the tops of the trees at the far side of the clearing around Nightcap.

As Carlos had told him, there was a big Fungus Festival in Lynchburg in mid-September, just days away. It was a big event for these people. That's where they would arrange a meet-up with the Nightcap people.

"It's like their Woodstock, their Bonnaroo, their Burning Man, their Coachella, Franco," Carlos had told him. *El Segundo* was Francisco's age but looked younger. He looked like a man without a care in the world—handsome in a predatory sort of way, with the way a fox or wolf about him. He was fit and agreeable when he got his way, which was very nearly always, with only Big Bad Brother Boss Santino saying otherwise. "We get with their people and we squeeze them."

"And if they say no?" Francisco asked. They had been in the *Segundo's* Hidden Hollow McMansion, an absurdly big, grey-painted house on a spacious plot of well-tended land.

"Then we squeeze harder," Carlos said, holding out a well-manicured hand and balling it into a fist. "You know this dance, Franco."

"I do," Francisco said. That had been three days ago. Carlos wanted them to recon the place as thoroughly as possible, and not to come back until he'd gotten all he needed to know about their operations. As such, Francisco had been taking copious notes. He had not survived in *Las Muertes Rojas* as long as he had by screwing things up or doing things half-assedly. Carlos Mendoza was a good *Segundo,* but he was a *Segundo* all the same, and he wasn't known as *El Martillo* for nothing.

The mushroom farm was a hive of activity. Always moving, always composting, always shipping. Francisco could smell the money in the place over the stink of the compost. The farm was thriving, and, to his eyes, had minimal security. Nightcap counted on its relative isolation out in the middle of nowhere to keep trouble away. And acres of fencing to mark off its property. And a half-dozen big dogs. And some roving guards.

But if the shakedown went as planned, none of that would matter. *Las Muertes Rojas* didn't bother with dogs and foot soldiers. They went right to the top. And if reason didn't prevail, then other measures would be taken. It was why Francisco was taking all those notes. He committed them to paper so there'd

be no risk of some stray bit of information finding its way on the Internet. They all regularly used burner phones, anyway. Paper offered a perverse form of security in the age of telecommunications. The notebook could only give up its secrets if someone pried it from Franco's cold, dead hands.

There was some rustling in the brush around him, and Francisco grumbled to Matteo, not taking his eyes away from his binoculars.

"Did you check the car?" Francisco asked.

He was greeted by silence and peeled his eyes away from the binoculars in the direction of the sound he'd heard. He saw only trees and brush. Maybe it had been a deer or something. They tended to come out either early in the morning or late in the day. "Matteo?"

He knew the kid couldn't shut up, so if he was within earshot, he would have said something. Francisco got up from his hiding place, stretching his legs, mindful of the cracks his knees made, and stuffed his little red book into his back pocket.

Francisco put his binoculars into their case and dialed up Matteo. The kid picked up on the first ring.

"Yeah?"

"Where the hell are you?" Francisco asked.

"I'm heading to the car, just like you said, Franco," Matteo said.

"Alright," Francisco said. "I'll be there in a few. We're done here tonight."

"About time," Matteo said.

"Yeah, yeah," Francisco said. "Just wait for me by the car. I'm driving."

"But it's my turn," Matteo said.

"You drive us out, I drive us back," Francisco said. "That's how we do it."

"You drive me crazy is what you do, Franco," Matteo said.

"Keep running that mouth, Teo," Francisco said. "You'll be riding in the trunk."

Their connection was dropped, and Francisco was really pissed. Had Matteo hung up on him? He dialed him up again, but it rang and rang, went to voicemail.

"Hi, this is Teo. Leave a message, maybe I'll call you back," the voicemail said. Franco hung up, dialed again. Again with

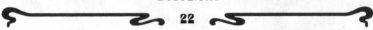
the voicemail. Only Teo would set up voicemail on a burner phone.

He texted the kid. The pecking order in the gang had it that the kid sure as hell better answer when Franco called.

*Teo, you'd better pick up.*

He sent it, waited. A reply came back.

*Teo's unable to take your call right now.*

Was this a joke?

*You'd better call me right now, Teo.*

His phone rang, Matteo's ringtone. Franco answered directly, laid into him.

"You stupid fuck, you answer when I call you," Francisco said.

"I told you, Teo's not able to take your call," a woman's voice said.

"Excuse me? Who is this?"

"This is *La Signora Grigia,*" the woman said.

Francisco drew his pistol, a Glock 20. Having the 10 mm pistol in his hand made him feel somewhat better, although he was wondering how the hell some chick got the drop on Matteo. The kid was an idiot, but he knew better than to just give his burner phone to some babe in the woods.

"Who?"

"You heard me," the woman said. *"La Signora Grigia."*

"I don't know who you are, *Señora,*" Francisco said.

"You will soon enough," the woman said.

"Where's Teo?" Francisco asked. "Put him on."

"He can't talk now," the woman said. Francisco started stomping in the direction of where they'd secreted the car. Whoever this was, she was going to take a bullet or two for this nonsense. Franco didn't hesitate when it came to offing people. It was another thing that had helped him rise within *Las Muertes Rojas.* The willingness to do the bad thing at a good time made all the difference, more often than not. Franco had not ever been squeamish or hesitant. He figured if he could keep *La Signora* on the phone, he could get that much closer to dealing with her.

"And why is that?" Franco asked.

"Because he's dead," the woman said.

Francisco was really pissed, now. Not scared, yet. Just angry. He'd faced down rivals a thousand times. He'd been beaten up,

had been shot at, had been stabbed, had fought his way through dozens of scraps. It's why the *Segundo* trusted him to this stuff. He was reliable, he was ruthlessly dependable. It's how he lived.

"Oh, is that right?" Francisco said. "You know who you're dealing with, *Señora*? We're *Las Muertes Rojas*. I'm going to make a punchbowl out of your skull, hon."

He kept marching through the woods, which was dark and disorienting with the sun gone and only spears of fading light visible between the thick stands of trees. Francisco tripped his way through the dense underbrush, sticks cracking and leaves crunching with every step.

"A punchbowl?" the woman said. "That does sound festive. Just in time for the Fungus Festival."

"Are you insane?" Franco said. "I mean it."

"Oh, I don't doubt that you do," the woman said. "We're having a grand festival this weekend. We can't have you gangland types ruining it for us."

Francisco would put two bullets in this woman's head the moment he reached her. No questions asked, no hesitation. She'd earned both of them.

"Seriously, who the hell are you?" Francisco asked. He was maybe five more minutes from the car, if he hadn't lost his way.

"I already told you," she said. "I'm *La Signora Grigia*. Patron saint of Lynchburg. You should appreciate that, right, *Vato?*"

That jogged a memory for Francisco, as he'd done some research ahead of poking around the mushroom farm. It was something Italian. There was a statue of her in Lynchburg's town square. And portraits of her in the shops, little statuettes and other souvenirs.

"I'll see you soon, *Señora*," Franco said, hanging up, turning on the light of his phone to guide his way to the car. He didn't think for a moment that he might actually be in danger. Thinking that way would have made him not only a poor gangster, but a dead one.

No, Francisco relied on bulling—and bullying—his way through any situation not to his liking. The very idea that Matteo could have been killed by some crazy woman in the woods didn't seem possible to him. The kid was a dumbass, sure, but

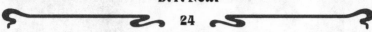
to be caught unaware like that? He knew they were out here for a reason, even if he didn't like it much.

Franco heard something in the woods that wasn't him. He paused in his trudging to listen. The woods was full of evening noises—crickets, maybe an owl or something. But there was something else, something closer. He could feel it.

"Somebody out there? Is that you, *Señora?*" Francisco said. "I've got a gun."

Francisco held out his pistol in one hand, with his phone in the other, shining its little beam of light, which offered a bluish-white glow in its narrow field of view.

"You hear me? I've got a gun," Francisco said.

In the woods, with so many close-packed trees, anybody could be anywhere. The sight lines were poor, made worse in the deepening darkness. The hulking trees just ate up space.

He saw some movement behind one of the trees and headed toward it. Carlos had been very clear that they were to keep as low a profile as possible out here, lest anyone get wise to what they were doing. He didn't want any interference from the authorities messing that up.

"*Señora,* you'd better step out right now if you don't want to get shot," Francisco said. If she'd actually killed Matteo, she was going to be shot, anyway.

Then he saw the figure emerge from behind the trees. It was a grey-cloaked figure, as tall as he was, wearing a grey, stonelike mask. The mask was a woman's face with thin-painted eyebrows and blue-painted lips, and the figure wore one of those Asian conical hats, also grey, which had a grey-white shroud hanging around its neck. The figure had grey sleeves and grey gloves, grey pants, grey boots, even. They were a spectral vision in grey, like a ghost. Almost luminescent in the meager light from Franco's phone. The figure looked like the statue he'd seen in town.

"What the hell are you supposed to be?"

"*La Signora Grigia,*" the figure said. A man's voice, barely more than a whisper.

"Where's the woman?" Francisco asked.

Okay, so it wasn't just some lone crazy woman in the woods. There were more of them. Franco didn't hesitate. He pulled the trigger, and the Glock fired a lone shot, striking the figure in the chest, knocking him to the ground.

"Ghost takes a bullet just fine."

Francisco figured maybe a lone gunshot out in the woods wouldn't draw too much attention. He went over to the fallen figure, figuring he'd put another shot in the crazy's skull just in case.

"Now, you've done it," said the woman he'd been talking to on the phone. She was behind him. Francisco spun around, pistol at the ready. She was dressed as the man had been, identically, in the grey garb, with the grey conical hat. She was as tall or taller than Francisco was and did not seem afraid.

"Okay, *Señora*," Francisco said. "How about you take a step back?"

The woman took a step forward, toward him.

"I'll shoot you dead, *Señora*," Francisco said. "Just like your friend, here."

"You cannot shoot me. I'm *La Signora Grigia*," the figure said, drawing a curved knife from the folds of their robe. It was a nasty blade, polished to a shine, looking almost like a cane knife or a slender machete. It had blood on it, what Franco assumed was Matteo's blood. He saw three interlocking circles etched upon it.

"Glock," Francisco said in a singsong, waving his pistol at the grey woman.

Carlos may have wanted things quiet, but for Francisco, facing down a costumed nutcase with a knife meant that all bets were off. He'd rather drop this clown as well and answer for it later with Carlos than otherwise take his chances. He raised his pistol toward the head of the masked woman.

Then he felt something cold and steely cut across his throat from behind, ear to ear, in one smooth and practiced motion. It had been the man he'd shot. Francisco fired off another shot, a startled shot, missing the woman, who had not even tried to dodge it.

Choking on his own blood, Francisco tried to point his pistol at the woman, determined to take at least one of them with him, but she jumped for him, slashing at his gun arm with her

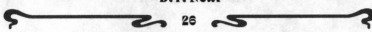
knife, which cut through the tendons of his wrist as if they were twine. The Glock fell from his grasp.

Francisco dropped to the ground in a fount of blood, his world gone from grey, to red, to ever-growing black that was darker even than the dusk-drowned woods around them.

"To the Cursed Earth you will go, *Tio Rojo*. Where we all belong," the woman said, like a whispered, sonorous benediction, repeated by the man, as Francisco died.

# 2

**"I don't know why we had to get here so early,"** Jessica
Jordan said, riding shotgun in the van her brother Jake was
driving. She had long, sand-colored hair she'd been fitfully
braiding on the road trip, wearing denim coveralls and a Fred-
dy Krueger-striped waffle weave sweatshirt of blood red and
swampy green.

Her fraternal twin brother was impeccably casual in his
well-worn blue jeans and black ribbed turtleneck sweater.
Both of them had oval faces and prominent noses, his features
trending toward a scrupulously maintained masculinity, and
hers nestled more whimsically in the realm of the fey.

"We're here early to get ahead of the crowds, Jess," Jake said.

Their passengers were sitting behind them: Austin Adams, wearing a white and red Lynchburg Fungus Festival '18
tee shirt he had picked up online somewhere. Mushy the Mushroom winked at anyone who looked, grinning and vigorous-
ly running his pudgy self through a cartoonlike rendering of
the town. Austin's round, wire-rimmed eyeglasses sat on his
straight nose and his black goatee beard that matched his shock
of Tik Tok-tousled black hair. He wore black jeans and black
Chuck Taylors, and his nearly black eyes were almost blistering
in their contempt for all things that weren't him. The van was
his, but he let everybody drive. That was just Austin's way.

"Crowds," Austin said, peering out the windows of the van
at the endless autumnal rush of trees giving up their leaves.
"Sure, sure."

"They're on their way, Austin," Jake said. "Trust me on that
one."

Sitting next to him was Mallory Tilton, who had told them
about the Fungus Festival in the first place. She'd been Jess's
roommate their senior year at Penn State. She had a mane of

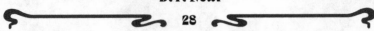
curly red hair she wore to her shoulders and was wearing an ivory-colored jersey tee with a great big zero on it that said No Expectations. She wore some slashed blue jeans so well-worn as to be nearly blue-white, and some brown booties that looked almost new. Her upturned nose was well-freckled, and her lips were full, trending toward smirking looks that played well with her large, moss green eyes.

"Hey, Austin," Mallory said, nodding at his tee. "I was at last year's Fungus Festival. I didn't see you there."

Austin peered at her over the top of his glasses.

"Yeah, well, I *wasn't* there, obviously," Austin said. "But I got the tee shirt. I'm just here for the drugs."

Mallory laughed, an almost barking sound that was more mocking than merry. Austin had the hots for Mallory, and she knew that better than anyone, though not a word of it had been said between them.

"You'll never find the shrooms without me," Mallory said. "The Lynchies are pretty tight about them. This is a family-friendly festival, guys. Don't everybody somehow forget that. Say it with me: Family-Friendly."

They all shared a collegial laugh. They had stayed in touch after college, with Mallory suggesting the road trip as a way for them to get reacquainted after the drudgery of post-collegiate workaday life. None of them would go so far as to call it a reunion, which felt too old and sad. But it was a get-together, at any rate.

"We are hell and gone from everywhere," Jake said. "It's ridiculous to think people trek all this way to this fucking place."

"But they do," Mallory said. "People come from all over the country, all over the world. Not just, you know, druggies like you guys. But, like, chefs and stuff. People who just love mushrooms."

Austin was noodling on his phone.

"Why do they call it Lynchburg, anyway? Did they lynch a lot of people here or what?" Jess asked, fiddling with her braid.

"It's named after Phineas Lynch, the town founder, in 1785," Austin said, quoting from his phone. "He was a Revolutionary War veteran and trapper, apparently. He sold pelts. It was a trading post back then."

"Furs," Jess said, shivering. "Creepy."

"He was probably a cannibal," Austin said, smirking into the light of his phone. "Like Jeremiah Johnson."

"He was 17th president of the United States," Jake said.

"That's Andrew Johnson, Jake," Austin said, making a buzzing sound. "Thank you for playing."

"No, I really think it was Jeremiah," Jake said.

"You're thinking of Robert Redford," Austin said.

"Redford was never president," Mallory said.

"But he played one in *The Candidate*," Jess said. "A politician, anyway. Same thing."

"Most definitely *not* the same thing," Austin said.

"Whoa, guys," Jake said. "Everybody shut up a moment."

Up ahead, they saw some police cars, what looked like Highway Patrol vehicles, their lights flashing. There was a burned-out car crumpled off the side of the two-lane Route 219, having smashed against some trees. A fire truck was nearby, as well as an ambulance. Some smoke was rising from the wreck.

One of the police was waving for them to stop, which Jake did, lowering his window. The patrolman was a middle-aged man, brown-haired and rough-hewn, with a greying mustache.

"Everything okay, Officer?" Jake asked.

"You kids here for the Festival?" the officer asked.

"We are," Jake said.

"Well, you be sure to drive safely around here, yeah?" the officer said.

"For sure, Officer," Jake said. "What happened?"

"Somebody hit a deer," the patrolman said. They could see that there were two bodies being carted away from the ruined vehicle, which looked to be a Dodge Challenger, or what was left of one.

"And their car caught fire?" Jess asked. The officer glanced at her, and Jake gave her a slow head turn.

"Seems that way," the patrolman said. "You never know what'll happen when you hit something out here. You'd best drive safely, now. Enjoy the Festival."

"We will, Officer," Jake said. He drove them around the blockade, past the wrecked and ruined car, and the bodies. Jess and the others watched.

"Jesus, Jess," Jake said. "Don't provoke the cops. You want them to search us? We're in a van, man. Like they need any excuse. We've got a pile of weed in here."

"Yeah, okay, whatever," Jess said, rolling her eyes.

He drove them past the scene, while Jess looked. She didn't see any sign of a deer, only the wrecked car and the two bodies. Not even any blood that she could see. It wasn't her fault that she was inquisitive. Inquisitive people had questions. Did that make her a bad person?

"I'm just saying," Jess said, as they cleared the scene, Jake driving with greater care than he otherwise would have, for the sake of whatever authorities might have still been paying attention. "I mean, seriously—what kind of car blows up after hitting a deer? Only in the movies, that's what. They must think we're stupid."

Mallory went to the back of the van and watched through the tinted bubble rear windows.

"You know, there are a lot of deer out here," she said. "You just never know."

"I neither know nor care," Jake said. "I'm just glad we're on our way. What's the place where we're staying, Jess?"

"The Lynchburg Grand Hotel," Jess said. "Right downtown. We'll be perfectly set up for the Fungus Festival."

Jake laughed. "Still feel like an idiot for coming all this way for this."

"Yeah," Austin said. "Sure. They've got us covered. There's a diner called the Mush Room. And there's a place called The All-Nightclub, like a tavern. We're covered. They're like right across the street from where we're staying. One of the advantages of it being a small fucking town."

"For sure," Jake said, keeping them on the two-lane toward Lynchburg. "This place'll be hopping this weekend."

"Totes," Mallory said, hopping back into her seat and buckling in. "As the only, you know, like, veteran of this, I can guarantee you that. These people take their mushrooms very seriously."

They passed a sign for Lynchburg, which said it had a population of 11,001.

"That's sort of random," Jess said. "11,001. I mean, how often do they update it?"

"Maybe you can check with the Chamber of Commerce on that, Jess," Mallory said.

"Maybe I will," Jess said. "Maybe I will."

Beyond the sign was a big water tower that was painted to look like a giant blue-capped mushroom with white speckles on the top. It had "Welcome to Lynchburg: We're Growing With You" painted on it in big white and gold letters.

"That's one big-ass mushroom," Jake said. The others peered out the windows, looking up at it as they passed it.

"It sure is," Jess said, snapping a shot with her phone camera.

"I can't believe you just photographed a water tower," Austin said.

"I can't believe you didn't," Jess said, sticking her tongue out at him, then holding out her phone to show off the photograph. "It's fabulous."

"It's supposed to be red," Austin said. "Fly agarics are red, not blue."

"Fly what?" Jake asked.

"Fly Agarics," Austin said. "Only the most photogenic mushrooms ever. You know the ones everybody in the world always uses to symbolize mushrooms. Red caps with white speckles."

"Yeah, okay," Jake said. *Mario Brothers.*

"Yeah," Austin said, rolling his eyes. *Mario Brothers.*

Mallory gave Austin a playful poke with her toe, her silver toe ring flashing in the light of the van.

"Look who knows so much," Mallory said.

"I do my research," Austin said. She poked him again, and he brushed her foot away, making her rotate in her spinning seat.

"Nobody's grading you on this trip, Austin," Mallory said. "It's pass/fail."

"Hah," Austin said.

With school behind them, they were all sorting out their various job situations, which meant that Mallory was a barista at Café Loco Rococo in Shadyside, the Twins were working as paid interns for an audience analysis firm their dad owned in downtown Pittsburgh, and Austin was taking a year off because he really wasn't relishing having to even get a job, figured he would tap his trust fund a bit before he got his toes wet and his hands dirty.

"Did I pass?"

"We'll see," Mallory said, locking her chair into place, looking him in the eye. "We'll see."

**2**

**Emily Carver paced from her room in the Lynchburg**
Grand Hotel, looking out the window in walking snapshots,
surveying the street. The hotel room interior was ivory with
forest green molding, and natural wood furniture.

"They're coming," she said. She was tall, more long-legged
than long-limbed, with curly brown-black hair which she
wore shoulder-length. Her eyes were black coffee brown, and
she wore glasses that perpetually slid down her nose, requir-
ing re-setting with a punitive push of her fingertip. Her taw-
ny-hued Creole complexion was freckled.

"Who is?" her roommate asked. It was Ashley Dunn, who
always went by "Ash" when she introduced herself. She was the
opposite of Emily—short, petite, blond-haired, blue-eyed, with
a tan she didn't seem to ever cultivate. Her bearing was athletic
by habit or disposition, perhaps a bit of both.

"Everybody," Emily said. "You know, the Festival people.
They're coming."

"Of course," Ash said. "It's that time. It's going to get worse."

"Certainly," Emily said.

Emily and Ash had become acquainted when their employer, billionaire Jerry Merriwether of Mycopharmix, Inc., had approached the two of them along with a lean-limbed man named
Marquis Allen. Marquis was Black, with the kind of obtuse features that defied anyone to know what he was thinking. His
eyes were large, his face had an angularity to it that spoke to
both a military background and a lifestyle rooted in discipline.
a big man, broad-shouldered with close-shorn black hair and a
strong jaw. He had a well-tended mustache and beard that was
only just beginning to whiten. His eyes were lighter brown, and
he looked like maybe he'd boxed at some time in his life.

Merriwether had invited the three of them to his rather geometric corporate complex in Monterey. Merriwether looking almost cult leader-like in his white turtleneck and black slacks, his blond hair slicked back, his rectangular eyeglasses perched on his arrow-straight nose.

"The future is in fungi," Jerry said. "But we all know this here."

He had a clicker, which he liberally used as he talked them through things. He had wall screens displaying his presentation points.

"At Mycopharmix, we are paving the way toward renewable, scalable pharmacogenetic solutions to everyday problems," Jerry said. "And, at least for me, that means fungi. All mushrooms are magic mushrooms, as far as I'm concerned. Whether for groceries or for their adaptogenic qualities, fungi are the future of farming. Food, medicine, and everything in between. I've put a lot of money behind it. And that brings us to Lynchburg, Pennsylvania."

He clicked through it, showing a map of Pennsylvania, with Lynchburg displayed with graphic arrows.

"More than 60 percent of mushrooms produced in the United States are grown in Pennsylvania," Jerry said, showing pie graphs. "Pennsylvania is brimming with fungi. All types, for all purposes. I want a piece of their action. I want to steal their lunch. I've been working to grow Mycopharmix here in California, but these Pennsylvanian hilljacks still are in the catbird seat. I mean to change that."

Jerry clicked again, showing Lynchburg, an almost painfully quaint town.

"Every year, for the past 50 years, Lynchburg has been hosting their Fungus Festival. They strut their stuff. You get local growers, all of that rot. People come from around the world for that festival. This year, I want to sample what they have for my own use. Species, spores, spawn. I don't care. Any of it."

He clicked through, showing smiling faces of festivalgoers. Crowds of people cavorting about, visiting growers' exhibit tents, sampling mushrooms.

"They get somewhere around 100,000 people there for their Fungus Festival," Jerry said. "The way I see it, somebody could slip in there and sneak away with some samples. I mean, they're mushrooms, for god's sake. You can't tell me there aren't spores all over the place."

"It's trickier than you might think," Emily said. "Knowing what you're getting, tracing it, sourcing it, documenting it."

Merriwether clicked to a shot of a square building, almost Victorian to Emily's eyes.

"This is the Temple of the Lady," Jerry said. "The locals in Lynchburg worship some bizarre cult goddess. *La Signora Grigia*. The Grey Lady, she's called. Italian in origin. I'm not making this up. For whatever reason, this cult religion has run this town. These people aren't Christian. They're unreconstructed pagans. And the roots run deep. Since the 19th century, when they founded the town with Phineas Lynch. The Templetons and Bianchis—those families formed the Nightcap Mushroom Farm."

He clicked and some dour linotypes of Ned Templeton I and Lucretia Bianchi were shown. Ned was an apothecary from Pittsburgh, and Lucretia was his wife, native of Milan. Templeton had a lucrative drugstore business in Pittsburgh before retreating into the countryside with his wife around the time of the anti-Italian immigrant bias that was fashionable in the country then. Mushrooms. Way back then. They grew them, they prospered. Got rich. All under the auspices of *La Signora Grigia*."

He clicked again, showing a statue of the stone-faced woman, blue-lipped, grey-skinned. Emily thought she was beautiful, if mysterious.

"The local Quakers and Catholics didn't like *La Signora*," Jerry said. "But they slowly went away. Nobody quite knows exactly what happened, but by the 20th century, Lynchburg had pulled in Latin American workers—Mexicans and others—and put them to work on their mushroom farms. The Spanish Flu did for most of the holdouts among the locals, and by the time that settled, Lynchburg was a Templeton town. But that's neither here nor there."

"Or maybe it's everything," Ash said. "How does a cult take over a town?"

"The way any religion does," Marquis said. "They just do. Reward the faithful, punish the heretics and infidels. Get rich, let the rest take care of itself."

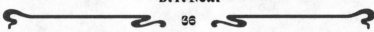
Jerry clicked again, showing some still photographs of people writhing about a beautiful Neoclassical temple.

"Central to the religious practice of the Lynchburg locals are something called 'Lady's Tears'—it's an elixir they serve at their ceremonies," Jerry said. "That's what I'm specifically hiring you three for. Get me samples. I don't care how. The stories are that it's a potent hallucinogen. Like a slate-wiper. Nobody knows for sure because nobody outside of this cult knows what the hell it is. And here's the topper—they hold their religious services and let outsiders attend and partake during their Fungus Festival. With all the tourists in town, they'll have to be on their best behavior, and maybe three enterprising Mycopharmix personnel could acquire some samples."

He clicked, showing people flailing about in ecstasy.

"I want samples," Jerry said. "I'm willing to pay you each two hundred thousand dollars to get me those samples. I'm not picky. You get samples to me, I can get them gene-sequenced. I can capture it and see if there's potential there for production. I would triage it as follows: Primary target: Lady's Tears; secondary target: any specialty fungi available that would be commercially viable; tertiary target: any other fungi you find."

Emily had been as enthusiastic as the other two to take the gig. She'd worked as contract mycologist for Mycopharmix, in their Research & Development Division. The prospect of doing some mycologic fieldwork in Pennsylvania felt like a dream to her.

She and Ash had become acquainted through Jerry, when Ash had revealed that she'd been doing PR consulting work for Mycopharmix. Jerry hadn't minded that Ash moonlit as an investigative journalist.

"I've got nothing to hide," Jerry said. "I'm an honest businessman. I see opportunities and I take them. But I tell you this—you find some bombshells in Lynchburg, I'll help you detonate them. People need to know about these Lynchburg loonies."

"For real," Ash said. She had been only too happy to accept the assignment. For an investigative journalist, that kind of money went a long way. "Only why would you send us? Why not some corporate espionage types?"

"Because I'm sending Marquis," Jerry said, smiling. "And, of course, Emily. Marquis is a top-notch fixer for me. And, you,

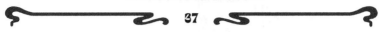
Emily, are a brilliant mycologist. Ash, you're a pugnacious PR person with a journalist's pit bull instincts and an eye for details. Between the three of you, I think you'll be able to get what I need where others haven't."

"What happens if they don't like us getting into their business?" Ash asked. "And you're rich, Jerry. Why not simply buy them out?"

"They won't sell," Jerry said, frowning at the thoughts it brought. He glanced a Marquis, who spoke up.

"I'll keep everybody safe," Marquis said. "We're going to be very discreet. You and Emily provide the cover story—Ash is going as a reporter, and you're going as the mycologist you are. I'm just going as a tourist and sightseer. We'll keep it very low-key and unobtrusive. With all those people in town, the locals will be too busy to bother with us."

"Marquis is team leader," Jerry said. "He'll coordinate the activity as it relates to acquiring and securing the samples and dealing with any problems. Dr. Carver, you'll help provide the expertise as relates to the samples themselves in terms of identification and classification. Ash, you'll document as much as you can and, if necessary, report on it to me. All of this while keeping Mycopharmix's name out of it."

Jerry was used to getting his way, and he was the least surprised person in the room when they all agreed to it. His assistant brought in nondisclosure agreements for them all to sign. Emily read hers carefully, while Marquis just signed his and slid it across the table without a word. Ash was somewhere in between, skimming and eventually signing.

"As a sweetener, if you deliver samples to me that have legitimate commercial value that Mycopharmix can develop, you'll get a percent share in the company profits from whatever products we create from those samples," Jerry said. "More samples, more profit shares for you."

"Bounty hunters," Ash said. Jerry smiled, humoring her.

"I reward success," Jerry said. "I've got more money than I could ever use in a thousand lifetimes. I want you to succeed, too. I'm not greedy. You do right by me, I'll do right by you."

Emily had finished reading the agreement, and slid it to Jerry, who had his assistant take the forms. The assistant left the room, and Jerry clicked through the rest of his deck, showing more images of people having fun at the Fungus Festival.

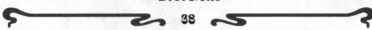
Emily was already excited about it, and this just made her want to go even more.

Emily and Ash had arrived together, while Marquis had gotten in town a week ahead of them.

Ash walked up next to Emily, peeked out the window of their room. They'd booked the room well in advance, since everybody with any knowledge of the Fungus Festival had said that the Grand Hotel filled up fast, and you had to reserve your room months ahead of time. So she had.

"I hope you're okay with crowds," Ash said. "It's going to get crazy."

"Crazy I can handle," Emily said. "I'm a mycologist, don't forget. We're half-crazy, ourselves"

"I haven't forgotten," Ash said. Ash looked Emily over a moment, assessing her. They'd flown into Pittsburgh and had rented a car which they'd driven to Lynchburg. Marquis had arrived on his own and had kept to himself.

"I can't wait to see the samples," Emily said.

"How will you know what's worthwhile?" Ash asked.

"Depends on what Jerry has in mind," Emily said. "Given how much adaptogenic work is being done at Mycopharmix, I'm thinking that'll be the fungi we concentrate on. He's not looking for grocery fungi. Jerry wants things he can turn into drugs. Fungi are potent in that regard."

Ash laughed.

"I've never known a mycologist before," she said.

"I live for the stuff," Emily said. "What about you?"

Ash debated whether or not to tell Emily why she was really here but decided against it. As a journalist, she'd long ago learned it was better to let others fill in the blanks on their own before doing it for them.

"Merriwether's willing to pay generously, so I'm here," Ash said. "A friend of mine was here last year, said it was pretty crazy. I wanted to see for myself."

It was almost the truth, so it came out easily, and Emily seemed persuaded. She watched a purple van roll into town. It had mushroom bubble windows on the back and a psychedelic mushroom pastoral scene painted on its sides.

She and Ash chuckled at the sight of the van.

"Get ready for a lot more of that," Ash said. "Although they'll block off Grand Avenue ahead of the festival. They set it up all

along Grand, which is part of the Historical District of Lynch-burg."

"There's a historical district?" Emily asked.

"Apparently," Ash said, consulting her phone. She'd down-loaded the Fungo Festival App, something Emily had been re-luctant to do. "We're in it."

"Well, alright," Emily said. She didn't think for a moment that Ash was actually intent on the festivities. She had an all-business way about her that seemed at odds with her mas-querading as a festivalgoer. Something about her eyes made her think that, but she wasn't going to push it.

It was okay for Emily, as she was here with her own purpose in mind, above and beyond whatever Jerry had paid them fore. Nightcap delivered top-shelf adaptogenic fungi as well as ru-mors of powerful psilocybin.

"See what you can unearth, Dr. Carver," Merriwether had said, when it was just the two of them. He looked like a quint-essentially Californian tycoon—handsome, tall, with a crin-kly-eyed blue gaze and a gently overwhelming handshake. My-copharmix had aggressively cultivated adaptogenic fungi from around the world. "There's big money being made in Lynch-burg, and I want some of what they've got. That's why I need someone with your eye and expertise there, helping zero in on the prizes."

"Seems like you've got plenty here already, Jerry," Emily said.

"Sure," Merriwether said. "But what they do at Nightcap, I don't know. It's beyond even what we're doing here at Myco-pharmix. The potency, the quick harvest turnarounds. It's un-canny. Almost magical."

Emily shrugged. She'd spent her whole young life studying mushrooms. There was nothing fungi did that didn't impress and enchant her.

Mycopharmix was a very profitable company, but Emily was in it for the research. Growing up in pre-Katrina New Or-leans and landing a scholarship at Berkeley had been a big deal for her family. First kid in college, all of the attendant pressures that came from that. She'd wanted to make her parents proud, even if they didn't understand why she'd studied mycology at all. She'd explained to them that there was money to be made

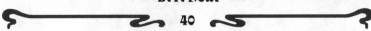
in it if you knew where to look. A few well-placed patents and she'd be at the forefront of something spectacular.

"I don't see why you even want to bother with Nightcap," Emily said. "You're bigger than they are. They're a local operation."

Merriwether smiled at her, his face radiating effortless charm.

"Right," Merriwether said. "I'm bigger, but they're better. They have techniques there that we haven't been able to touch out here. I've heard rumors that they've managed to cultivate porcinis and morels."

"Rumors," Emily said.

Emily was less than convinced. She'd done her research on Nightcap when Jerry had first come to her with the assignment. They were a midsized Pennsylvania mushroom farm operating in the center of the state. They didn't stand out to her relative to the countless other farms.

The family photos from his presentation lingered in her mind. They revealed an American success story, almost mythic. Lucretia Bianchi looked out at her with stern, dark eyes and dark hair, while Ned Templeton exuded a particularly Anglo-Saxon self-assurance.

"Behind every rumor is some truth," Merriwether said. "See what you can dig up, Dr. Carver."

"Alright," Emily said. "Are you going to the Lynchburg Fungus Festival yourself?"

"No way am I going near there," Merriwether said. "I don't want my hands dirty with any kind of connection with what's going on in Lynchburg. That's for you, Ash, and Marquis to unearth."

"Right," Emily said.

"That's why you'll be there, Dr. Carver," he said. "You go, try to find out some special things. Better yet, get some details on their porcini and morel production techniques."

"It's not like I can just walk around unsupervised," Emily said.

"You're smart," Merriwether said. "You'll figure something out. As I said, the Fungus Festival is a great time to go there. There'll be so many people partying there, you can slip right in. Nobody'll notice the three of you."

Agricultural espionage was not why she'd become a mycologist. But she admitted to herself a certain professional curiosity about how Nightcap had done what it had supposedly done. While mushroom farmers had successfully cultivated all manner of species, the wild porcinis and morels were the unicorns of that world—nobody had yet come up with a way of growing them in a controlled setting. If Nightcap had actually done this, it would give them a huge competitive advantage in the industry.

And if Jerry Merriwether was involved, competitive advantage was front and center.

"Hey," Ash said, touching her elbow. "Do you want to get some dinner at the hotel restaurant? Sylvia's?"

"Okay," Emily said. Sylvia's was a nice enough place. They'd already been there a couple of times since arriving, just because it was convenient. Not having to venture out from the hotel was okay by Emily. She was still trying to sort out how she'd gain access to Nightcap.

# 4

**Logan Stephens was in heaven in the Shroom Room.**
The middle-aged, black-haired, Philadelphia-born semi-celebrity chef had driven to Lynchburg for the Fungus Festival, but most of all, for the food. He could hardly wait until the weekend.

He owned a restaurant in Philadelphia, The Chevron, which he'd built up from nothing. American standard cuisine with a Francophile twist and a personal obsession with truffles, he'd gotten wind of Lynchburg when sourcing some mushrooms he'd wanted to fold into the autumn menu he'd been building for the next year. He'd wanted to come out swinging in 2020 and beyond, and thought this culinary safari was just the thing to give him a jump on the new year.

To say that the Shroom Room wasn't haute cuisine was merely stating the obvious. But Logan hadn't been there for that. Looking at the place, which had a round main dining room and peaked roof that called to mind a giant mushroom, the place was more in the Cheesecake Factory school of restaurant design. The tables were arranged in a kind of fairy ring, themselves red with white speckles upon them. The place had a sort of neo-rustic look to it that made Logan think some hobbits might emerge through a diminutive door to serve him. Around the perimeter were colorful booths, one of which Logan had taken.

The waitstaff wore unbleached linens and forest green vests with the Shroom Room embroidered on them in the trippy sort of lettering that was part of the restaurant's logo and overall design motif.

Logan forgave all of this because the menu was extraordinary. The place specialized in mushroom dishes of all sorts. There was a Hungarian Mushroom Soup. There was Wild Mush-

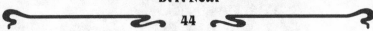
room Chowder with Bacon and Leeks. There was Mushroom Mac & Cheese and a Wild Mushroom Risotto. Stuffed Mushrooms and Braised Pork Chops with a Mushroom Cream Sauce. Fettuccine with Shiitakes and Asparagus. Grilled Porcini-Rubbed Rack of Veal. Mushroom Wellington. The menu went on and on.

He was all for restaurant themes, but he'd never seen a place go so all-in on a theme like this. And every dish he tried was exemplary. Perfectly rendered. His waiter, a lean young man named Colin, kept dutifully serving up the next dish Logan requested.

"I have to know," Logan said. "Can I meet the chef?"

"Maura Templeton," Colin said. "I'll have to check. She's very busy."

"Maura Templeton," Logan said. He'd seen her name on the menu. He'd spotted her online when he'd first zeroed in on the Shroom Room. She was almost witchy in demeanor—strong-featured, dark-haired and ponytailed. She had big brown eyes and a cleft chin. She trended toward a paradoxically smirking severity in her manner.

Maura Templeton emerged from the kitchen, wearing her *toque blanche* and jacket and apron, looking almost like a mushroom to his eyes, the way her hat sat atop her head. She was tall and lean.

"Logan Stephens of Chevron," Maura said, snapping a hand out to him. He shook her hand, a firm handshake from well-tempered hands. "You honor me by coming out all this way to try my food."

Her eyes raked his table, which was covered with plates he was still sampling, since he'd shooed Colin away when the young man had attempted to clear some of them.

"You are a sorceress," Logan said. "Astounding work. Everything is just extraordinary."

"So glad you like it," Maura said. "Any favorites?"

"I wouldn't even know where to begin," Logan said. The restaurant was well-occupied, but not overstuffed. Maura's eyes darted around the room, mindful of the attention she was paying him.

"You were smart to get here before the Festival," Maura said. "It's nearly impossible to get a table then. It becomes very crowded and very, very busy."

"Is everything locally sourced?" Logan asked.

"Yes," Maura said. "Everything comes from my father's farms. The mushrooms, I mean. But we do support local business here. We're firm believers in that here in Lynchburg."

She hovered by his table, and Logan could see the waitstaff covertly monitoring Maura's movements.

"You should be in Pittsburgh, at the very least," Logan. "Or Philadelphia."

Maura's smirk appeared.

"What, like a franchise?" Maura asked. "This is my home. I am comfortable here."

"Sure," Logan said. "But food like this? People would come all over for it."

"They already do come all over for it," Maura said. "Every year."

Logan smiled at her no-nonsense vibe.

"Sure, sure," he said. "But you could have more. I'm imagining Shroom Rooms in those cities I've mentioned. And beyond."

"Is this a business proposition you're making me, Mr. Stephens?" Maura asked. Logan could not tell if she was amused or not by the prospect.

"I'm just saying," Logan said. "There's an opportunity there."

"Enjoy your meal," Maura said, smiling. "I have to get back to work."

He watched her go, watched the staff react to her passing. They looked at her with the awe and wonder any good chef could instill in a restaurant. Maybe a little fear. Fear, he could respect. Fear and good food made sense to him.

Its cheeky name notwithstanding, the Shroom Room was full of fantastic cuisine, thematically narrowcast in the way that would play well in any decently sized upscale urban markets. He could see them in both Pittsburgh and Philadelphia—he imagined the neon sign for the place, the big, trippy letters. He wanted Shroom Rooms to pop up like, well, mushrooms.

Colin returned, now that it was safe with Maura vacating the table.

"Do you need anything else, Mr. Stephens?" Colin asked.

"I'll try some of that mushroom coffee, sure," Logan said.

"It's adaptogenic," Colin said. "We have various varieties of mushroom coffees and teas—Chaga, which is anti-inflammatory; Cordyceps for libido; Lion's Mane, for concentration; Hen of the Woods for immune-boosting; Reishi for anxiety relief;

Shiitake for immunity; Tremella for skin and hair; and Turkey Tail for immunity-boosting and anti-cancer."

"Cordyceps," Logan said. "The coffee."

"Perfect," Colin said, rushing off.

Logan surveyed the plates of all the things he'd tried. He was immensely satisfied, both in terms of actual satiety and in terms of self-satisfaction. He'd gotten in ahead of the festival crowds and had initiated contact with Maura Templeton. From his perspective, the rest was easy.

Colin came back with a little dessert dish upon which a pinkish pyramid sat, dusted with jet-black cocoa powder.

"This is from Maura," Colin said. "It's a black truffle *panna cotta*. She thought you might enjoy it."

"A mushroom dessert?" Logan said. "Of course."

Colin found a spot on his table and set it there with a fresh fork.

"She thinks you'll really like it," Colin said.

"I'm sure I will," Logan said.

Colin told him the coffee was brewing and would be along in a moment. Logan figured he had enough room for the dessert, although he was reluctant to break the lovely symmetry of the pyramid. He chose a corner of it and attacked it with his fork.

Popping it in his mouth, Logan felt transported by the earthy flavors of it. Maura had woven a spell with savory and sweet elements—the cocoa powder playing lasciviously with fresh vanilla bean and hints of honey and the savory bite of truffle. It was magical. It was richly flavored yet delicate. He was so wrapped up in it he hardly noticed when Colin brought the coffee.

"Thank you," Logan said. He took a drink of the coffee and it was extraordinary, too, with a rich and powerful mouth feel that played masterfully with the *panna cotta*. Without exactly seeing evidence of it, Logan could tell some of the Shroom Room staff were watching him. He pretended not to notice what he hardly saw, finished his meal, and settled his bill.

The Festival was going to be a long weekend. He planned to make the most of it.

# 5

**Carlos Mendoza surveyed the ruin of Franco's car in** photographs, had sent someone to reclaim the bodies from the Lynchburg authorities. No way was he going to expose himself by going near that. He reviewed the photographs in his living room, a brutally modernist exercise in willful minimalism that was at odds with his life as a gang leader.

He was a handsome man in a delicate way—big dark eyes, high cheekbones, thick dark hair he wore longer than he needed to, about his shoulders. He was slim and fit from obsessive hours in his private gyms. He was convinced that when the authorities would come for him, he would be ready. He would never be one of those portly, ageing crime bosses who already had a foot in the grave. He would look good when they came for him.

His relocation to Hidden Hollow had been part of that strategy of survival. In a gated community, a rich man could feel safer. Things worked the way they were supposed to, in that he could get and do what he wanted, and nobody would get in his way. People understood him in Hidden Hollow.

So, when confronted by the questionable deaths of two of his men—including one as steadfast, professional, and reliable as Franco, Carlos was less than pleased.

In the room with him was Miguel "Mig" Mendoza, his younger brother, who aspired to fill his big brother's alligator loafers, but was made of baser metals. He had the Mendoza jawline but trended toward doughiness. Not that he wasn't strong. But he lacked the pantherlike frame of Carlos, and the brutal ruthlessness of his big brother, Santino.

Also in the room was his girlfriend and confidante, Lilli Trujillo. She had wild dark eyes and wore her hair up in a high ponytail. She worked out with him in the gym and would always egg him on in her feisty, defiant way. Some bosses didn't

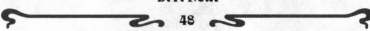
mix business with pleasure, but Lilli had a bloodlust about her that Carlos respected. Her instinct for the jugular was faultless, and he trusted that.

Carlos heard his phone ring, and he picked it up, seeing who it might be. It said it was Matteo. He was grateful it wasn't Santino.

"Hold on," Carlos said to Miguel and Lilli, holding up a hand as he picked up his phone and answered. "Hello?"

"Leave us alone," the woman said.

"Who is this?" Carlos asked.

"*La Signora Grigia,*" the woman said.

"Well, *Signora,* you've got a lot of balls calling me from a dead man's phone," Carlos said.

"Back off or face the Lady's wrath," the woman said. "Leave or we will end you."

"Do you know who you're talking to?" Carlos asked, gripping his phone angrily.

"Of course we know," the woman said. "We know exactly who you are, Carlos Mendoza. And we're warning you away from us. Consider this your only warning."

"Listen, you don't talk to me that way," Carlos said, but the woman hung up. Carlos cursed, wanting to lob his phone away, but instead setting it on the table hard atop the photographs.

"It wasn't an accident," Carlos said, steepling his fingers as he regarded the photos and contemplated the call.

"What did they say?" Miguel asked.

"They threatened me," Carlos said. "It was a woman who called herself *La Signora Grigia.*"

"That's their patron saint," Lilli said, crossing herself. "*La Signora Grigia.* She's all over this place."

Carlos laughed bitterly.

"Or she's some crazy *puta* trying to get in my head," Carlos said. "She called me from Teo's phone."

"These people are playing you for a fool, Carlo," Lilli said.

The challenge in the Lynchburg area was maintaining the necessarily low profile while still applying the necessary muscle to persuade these mushroom farmers to work with him.

"The workers are the key," Miguel said. "Those are the ones we need to reach. Nightcap relies heavily on their Latin workforce, Carlo. They're the ones we need to lean on, to let them know we're here."

Carlos grumbled, thinking of his options. The plan was for Franco to scout out the mushroom farm so Carlos could arrange a meeting with Ned Templeton and offer the services of *Las Muertes Rojas*. He didn't care about *La Signora*. Part of what made *Las Muertes Rojas* who they were was their mythology about their own patron saint, the Lady Red Death they all swore allegiance to, *Dama Muerte Roja*. In their Pittsburgh headquarters, they had a statue of her, a skeleton wreathed in red finery, like a mourner at her own funeral. She was their own home-brewed version of Santa Muerte, and she'd been integral to the *Rojas* instilling terror in those who were in their territory. They simply needed to let these *Signora*-worshippers to understand that *Dama Muerte Roja's* men were displacing their Grey Lady.

"Sure, yeah," Carlos said. "I had hoped to go right to the top."

Lilli sat next to him, pawing his knee.

"Why not both, Carlo?" she asked. "You arrange a meeting with Templeton, and maybe Miguel and some of the others can pressure the workforce."

Miguel didn't like the prospect of being volunteered for a project by Lilli. The rivalry between the two of them was something Carlos valued. Lilli was ruthless in a way that Carlos thought Miguel could never be. Not that Miguel was soft. No one in *Las Muertes Rojas* could ever be said to be soft. But the predatory instinct was stronger in some than others. And while Lilli wasn't specifically a gang member with the accompanying responsibilities, she wouldn't hesitate to stomp anyone in her way. In many ways, she saw herself as a manifestation of *Dama Muerte Roja*, and never let anybody forget that.

"How many people do we have in Hidden Hollow, Carlo?" Miguel asked. "We're supposed to lay low, aren't we?"

"Within reason," Carlos said. "Most of the *Rojas* are back home. But we have three dozen here, beyond my bodyguards. You should know that, Mig."

"Okay," Miguel said, trying to recover. "What if the Nightcap people fight us?"

Carlos laughed.

"Then we hurt them," he said. "Racketeering isn't rocket science, Mig. We just crack the right skulls and they'll knuckle under. They're mushroom farmers, for god's sake. Take Morro and Fleece and go to town. Find out where the workers go. The Latins. Fuck the Quakers."

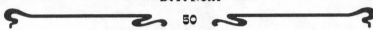
There remained a Quaker community in Lynchburg who were also involved in the mushroom trade. Franco had told Carlos about that in one of his earlier forays. Quaker sects were scattered all over Pennsylvania, however. Carlos didn't pay them any mind. They were like Amish to him. Just particularly insular fanatics, and pacifist in all the ways he needed them to be. Pacifists never put up a real fight.

"Fuck the Quakers," Lilli said, laughing. Her laugh was nasty, sharply rendered, marinated in mockery. Carlos loved to hear her laugh, and to make her laugh. Miguel laughed along with them, although his nervousness galled Carlos.

"What's the matter, Mig? No stomach for a little strong-arming?" Carlos asked.

"There are tons of workers tending those mushrooms," Miguel said. "An army."

"They're sheep," Carlos said. "You, Fleece, and Morro will be like wolves among them."

Miguel wasn't happy about Morro coming along. Another thirsty lieutenant like Franco, he was ambitious and eager to prove himself. Fleece was his right hand, would do whatever Morro required of him. They were both proper thugs. Carlos would have them along with him to deliver the needed muscle Miguel might need.

"So, Carlo," Lilli asked. "If it wasn't an accident that killed Franco and Matteo, who did it? Shouldn't we find that out?"

Carlos frowned at the thought of it.

"Maybe Lilli can find that out," Miguel said, earning a glare from Lilli. Miguel just smiled at her as smugly as he could.

"Lilli stays here with me, Mig," Carlos said. "But you can have Morro do some digging to try to find out what happened. Someone out there killed my men. Nobody gets to lay a hand on *Rojas* without consequence. If he finds out who did it, you bring them to me."

Carlos didn't like thinking about that. Not that it was at all unfamiliar to him. But rather, because Franco and Matteo were experienced gangsters. Anyone in the *Rojas* worth the name understood how to take care of themselves. That somebody got the drop on them both, killed them, and had the presence of mind to make it look like an accident was something concerning. Carlos didn't think any of their rivals were operating in Lynchburg.

But the other possibility was more distressing—that whoever offed Franco and Matteo knew they were *Rojas* and didn't care. Or they cared only enough to make it look like an accident. Maybe that was part of it, too. Lynchburg was a little town. Two murders of known gang members would raise flags and call attention. Whoever had done it didn't want more attention paid to Lynchburg, especially ahead of the Fungus Festival.

That had to be part of it. They didn't want anyone or anything spoiling their big weekend. Whatever Franco and Matteo had been up to, they had gotten information that somebody wanted kept secret. That made Carlos confident that he was onto something with Nightcap, something worth taking.

He snatched up his phone and dialed Matteo.

To his amazement, the Lady answered.

"Yeah?" she asked. "What do you want?"

"I want you to know that I'm coming for you, *Signora*," Carlos said. "And when I find you, there won't be enough prayers in the world to save you."

# 6

**The Lynchburg Grand Hotel did not disappoint Jess and** the others. They walked around the folksy hotel lobby and surveyed the Quakeresque austerity of it with amusement. It looked clean and rustic, without ostentation. But clean was good. Its colors were blue and white—blue walls, white floor, white trim.

"It's like a meeting hall," Austin said, taking pictures. "I feel like they could be voting on which witches to burn in a place like this."

"We don't burn witches in Lynchburg," the hotel concierge said, smiling. She was a pretty young woman with "Cloris" on her nametag. Like the other lobby hotel workers, she wore a crisp white blouse and a black vest. Her hair was black and slicked back into a utilitarian ponytail, and her eyes were as black as her hair. Her features were strong and fresh-faced. She looked to be Austin's age.

"That's a wise policy," Austin said. "I'm Austin Adams."

"Yes, Mr. Adams," Cloris said, clicking on her computer monitor. "We were expecting you. So glad you and your friends were able to make it to the Festival."

He plunked his credit card on the counter, which Cloris took.

"We're very excited," Mallory said, appearing at Austin's elbow. "I was here last year. It's my fault they're here. When I told them about how great it was, they just couldn't help themselves."

Cloris smiled at Mallory, and Austin thought it was a beguiling smile, almost V-shaped.

"You were wise to arrive a little early," Cloris said. "It'll be packed here this weekend."

"So I keep hearing," Austin said, watching Jess and Jake amble goofily around the lobby, taking pictures and unashamedly gawking. "We shall see."

"I see you got the tee shirt," Cloris said, her eyes flitting over his chest.

"He's a poseur," Mallory said. "He bought that on eBay."

"This year's design is even better," Cloris said. "We have a competition each year for the Fungus Festival, like trying to outdo what we did the year before. Mushy's really going to blow you away this year."

"Mushy," Austin said. "I feel like there could be a better name for a mascot."

"Don't mind him," Mallory said, rolling her eyes, talking over her shoulder as she corralled the Jordan Twins. "Austin always thinks his ideas are better than anyone else's."

"Mushy's always been our mascot," Cloris said, handing back Austin's credit card, which he tucked back into his wallet. "Mushy's cute. That's the whole intention. Intention is everything, you know."

"Sure, sure," Austin said, as Cloris slid the key cards to him. They had two adjoining suits, with balconies overlooking Grand Avenue, at Austin's insistence. He wanted them to be able to hang out on their balconies and watch the Festival from a comfortable vantage point.

"I'm still waiting to hear your names for our mascot, Mr. Adams," Cloris said, her smile unbroken. Austin wasn't about to let the challenge go unanswered.

"How about 'Cappy' or 'Shroomer' or 'Puffins'?" Austin asked.

Cloris shrugged.

"'Puffins' is pretty cute, Mr. Adams," Cloris said. "I'll give you that. Maybe I'll bring it up at the next town meeting, although I wouldn't hold my breath if I were you. We've had Mushy for a half-century or so. We're very attached to him and his wife, Mushette."

Austin smiled, pocketing the key cards.

"Mushette," Austin said, shaking his head.

"They're very close," Cloris said.

"Mushy and Mushette. Heh. Well, I had to try," Austin said. He could see there was a little shrine to the Grey Lady off to the side, in a little alcove—a little grey statuette of the robed wom-

an, wearing her conical hat, her arms upraised. Five candles burned in little glass jars at her feet—one white, one blue, one orange, one brown, one grey. "I see you have *La Signora Grigia* represented."

Cloris glanced at the little shrine and grinned at Austin.

"Somebody's done his research," Cloris said. "Yes, we honor *La Signora Grigia* throughout Lynchburg. We owe our prosperity to Her guiding hand."

"That sounds positively pagan to me," Austin said. "And here I was thinking we were in God's country out here."

"It's all god's country, Mr. Adams," Cloris said. "It just depends on the god, and the country, I suppose. Here, we are in Her hands."

"Right," Austin said. "Where can I get one of those statuettes? I'd love to take one home with me."

Cloris smiled at him, pointing to the little gift shop at one side of the lobby, tucked into a corner.

"We aim to please at the Grand Hotel," Cloris said. "But you should get one soon, because once the Festival starts, they sell out quickly."

"I'm on it," Austin said. "Nice talking to you, Cloris."

"And you, Mr. Adams," Cloris said, watching him go to the gift shop, which was tended by a young man with 'Brewster' on his nametag. He was curly-haired and pug-nosed, with light brown eyes and a frowny face.

Jess and Jake joined Austin, while Mallory fiddled with her bags. The gift shop was really more of a gift stand, but there were, in fact, many statuettes of the Grey Lady there, as well as stuffed Mushy and Mushette dolls—the red-capped mushroom mascots grinning at them. There were also some white conical hats, as well as some Lynchburg tour flyers.

"Hey, Brewster," Austin said. "I'd like two of those hats, one Mushy doll, and one Grey Lady figurine."

"It's a statuette," Brewster said. "Figurines are mass-produced from molds. Our Grey Lady statuettes are hand-carved by local artisans."

"Ah," Austin said. "I stand corrected. One statuette, if you please. Don't worry, guys, I'm buying. Jess and Mallory, you get the hats."

Jess squealed and quickly donned her hat, while Mallory took hers and gamely fitted it atop her mass of hair. Brewster

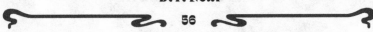
watched them with barest, long-suffering service worker for-bearance, while Austin watched Brewster bag Mushy and wrap the Grey Lady in grey paper before putting them in a black and white Grand Hotel paper bag with handles.

"What about Festival tees?" Austin asked. Brewster pointed over his shoulder, and they were there, sure enough, in cubby-hole columns and rows. The Lynchburg Fungus Festival 2019 tee. It was red ink on white, and there was Mushy, running through town, winking at them. "I'll take one in a Men's Large. And the Fun Guy tee in black. Same size. Y'all can get your own tee shirts."

Jess enthusiastically picked up her own pink ink and baby blue Festival tee in a Women's Small, liking the cropped sleeves and the V-neck, and got a Mushette tee in pink cotton with baby blue ink, while Jake got a Men's XL tank top tee in black and yellow. Mallory abstained, laughing at them mockingly.

"You guys are such tourists, oh my god," Mallory said. "No shame whatsoever. I'm embarrassed to be seen with you."

Austin stuffed his tee into his bag and sneered at Mallory.

"You're welcome, by the way, for the hat," Austin said.

"Thanks, Austin," Mallory said. "For everything."

Jake swatted Austin on the arm.

"Yeah, Moneybags," Jake said, flopping his own tee over his shoulder. "'Preciate it, Bro. Let's go see our rooms."

"Sure thing," Austin said, as they took their luggage and made their way to the elevators. Austin could see Cloris watch-ing them, her smile as unbroken as ever.

# 7

**Emily and Ash did their people-watching from the safety**
of Sylvia's. It was already filling up with the dinnertime crowd,
more tourists arriving by the hour. The Festival would have the
place intolerably crowded soon enough.

Sylvia's was nice in the way that the Grand Hotel was nice—
minimalist and unassuming, with just a hint of urban polish
that they likely thought would help sell the place as fine dining. What it had, which Emily appreciated, was shadows. It was
one of those dark wood-dressed places with red-glassed tabletop candles that threw off a conspiratorial glow, and plentiful
semicircular booths that, to Emily's eye, resembled clusters of
mushrooms.

"Do you think there was ever a Sylvia with this place?" Ash
asked, nursing a local draft lager she'd ordered from the bar.
Emily fidgeted with her own gin and tonic.

"Does it matter?" she asked.

"Kinda," Ash said. "I mean, you name a place like that, people want to know the back story."

"Sylvia Templeton," Emily said. "It's printed in the front,
near that bench."

"The Templeton name carries a lot of weight around here,"
Ash said.

"That it does," Emily said. She had done her research before coming to this place. The Templetons had carefully leveraged their money and bought up chunks of the town back when
Lynchburg was even more of a nothing than it was, now.

Not that it was a nothing—it was a pointedly quaint little
Pennsylvania town. She hardly cared how much of it was legitimate and how much of it was manufactured. It was a clean,
prosperous place that owed a tremendous amount of that success to the machinations of the Templeton Family.

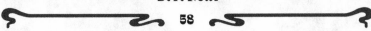
All Emily really cared about was finding out what she could about Nightcap. In that way, she felt like a spy. And Ash and Marquis offered her cover. That helped.

"Where's Marquis, anyway?" Emily asked.

"Scouting," Ash said. "All he'd tell me. The man plays it very close to the vest. I don't think he trusts us very much."

"I don't think I do, either," Emily said, and the two of them shared a laugh.

The food at Sylvia's was upscale American standard fare—steak and potatoes, unassuming vegetables, sauces that lacked ostentation, but were flavorful.

"There's money here," Ash said. "I mean, you can smell it. Taste it."

"Money is always good," Emily said. Ash laughed, a quiet thing.

"I'm just saying, they're working it," Ash said. "Lynchburg. Whoever is behind the scenes. They're mining everything they've got to draw people here. It's a tourist town in the middle of nowhere. Doesn't that seem weird?"

"People use what they have," Emily said. "I grew up in New Orleans. I get it."

"That had to be crazy," Ash said.

"Oh, it was," Emily said. "Every year. It puts a lot of people to work."

Emily looked down the end of her nose at Ash. She thought the other woman was wrestling with something but couldn't pin it down. As a mycologist, she understood that many truths lived beneath the surface. She wasn't about to excavate Ash's past to sort out her secrets, but she knew the secrets were there.

"This place seems like it's working it," Ash said.

"You make it sound sinister," Emily said.

"It is," Ash said.

"Wow," Emily said. "And what makes you think that?"

Sometimes, just a little turning over of the earth could reveal things worth finding.

Ash quietly looked Emily over, and Emily was sure she was weighing how much to trust her. She did a little more digging.

"I'm not meaning to pry," Emily said. "I'm sure you have your reasons."

"My sister," Ash said. "She disappeared here last year. I mean, she was at last year's Festival, and she just never came back."

*So there it is,* Emily thought.

"You think something happened to her here," Emily said.

"Yeah," Ash said. "I'm positive something did. Melinda was a free spirit, but, you know, she was as careful as she was carefree, if that makes sense. She came here last year, and never came back."

Emily looked around them, feeling suspicious, even paranoid. But everything looked normal—just restaurant patrons doing their thing: talking, eating, laughing, conspiring. All of those everyday things people did in restaurants. Nothing out of the ordinary.

"Did you check with the local authorities?" Emily asked.

"Yes, last year," Ash said. "The sheriff is William Leonard. He didn't have any information. No bodies, no nothing. No sign of Melinda. No body, I mean. She just vanished."

Their food arrived, and Emily picked at her mashed potatoes, making a little well for some butter, like it was a miniature volcano she dusted with flecks of pepper and salt.

"So, a missing persons case," Emily said.

"No suspicion of foul play, however," Ash said. "Couldn't get anybody official to look into it. They just assumed Melinda took off somewhere. But she wouldn't do that."

"Weird," Emily said. "And it was here?"

"Lynchburg," Ash said. "She was close to my mom and my sister Elissa. Closer than me. I'm the oldest. She'd said she was having a great time and would be home soon. Then that was it. Gone. My mom has never really recovered from it."

Emily felt sympathy for Ash, who was trying to keep it together for her sake, she assumed. She never knew what to tell people in those moments.

"How old was she?"

"Melinda was 25 when she disappeared," Ash said.

"I'm sorry," Emily said.

"I'm going to find her," Ash said. "I know she's here somewhere. I know somebody knows."

"I hope you find her," Emily said. Emily could see the determination in Ash's face and felt real sympathy for her. Ash seemed to feel better after confiding in Emily.

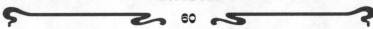
"Someone knows," Ash said, looking around them. "I did some research after Melinda vanished. People disappear around here all the time. Like during the Festival."

Emily watched some young people come into Sylvia's, a group of four, full of life and laughter in that carefree way kids sometimes had.

"What do you mean, during the Festival?" Emily asked.

"I mean during the Festival," Ash said. "Or after. Whatever. I'm saying that people go missing."

"Ah," Emily said. "What do you think? Like a serial killer or something?"

Ash glanced around them a moment, leaning in.

"I don't know," Ash said. "But over the last dozen years, at least a dozen people have gone missing after attending the Festival. It probably goes far deeper than that. I just researched the most recent records."

Emily didn't think that was very many people, but one disappearance was too many, obviously. Especially when one of the disappeared was Ash's sister.

"Not enough to draw too much attention," Emily said. "Just one or two a year."

"Yes," Ash said. "But, when you look over time, it starts to seem like a correlative trend."

Ash looked like she needed to get this out, and Emily understood the importance of being a good listener at times like these.

"2007, Justin Cartwright. 2008, Dan Silvers. 2009, Monica Smith. 2010, Sharon Finnerty. 2011, Stephen Cunningham. 2012, Helena Oxbridge. 2013, Kevin Richards. 2014, Willow Williams. 2015, Peter Ryan. 2016, Connor Bergen. 2017, Shawn Boyd. 2018, Melinda Dunn, and the Taylor Triplets—April, May, and June Taylor," Ash said. "Like I said, I bet it goes deeper, but I stopped after a point. I had enough to spot a trend."

Emily thought about the names a moment, her scientist's mind trying to find a pattern. Ash seemed to read her face and her mind.

"Seven guys, eight women," Ash said. "Ages 18 to 25. They came from all over the country. No discernible pattern."

"Have you gone to the police or FBI with this?" Emily asked.

"They blew me off," Ash said. "Since they're simply disappearances without any appearance of foul play, they just

assume they're somewhere else. But nobody's ever seen those people again. The common element I found is they all came to Lynchburg for the Festival. I started a website—*Lost in Lynchburg*—which lists all the disappeared. It's a place where family members can post anything about lost loved ones."

"I'm sure the Lynchburg Chamber of Commerce wasn't happy about that," Emily said.

"No," Ash said. "But I don't care what they think. Although I do get comments from trolls about it, like people who go after me. Or they talk about how much fun the Festival is, and why somebody like me has to go ruining it. That kind of thing."

Emily ordered coffee and a slice of apple pie when their server came back. Ash passed on dessert, getting only coffee.

"You're pretty bold to come here, then," Emily said. "Marquis and me, I get it. But you? You've got some pretty personal reasons."

"I want to find out what happened to my sister," Ash said. "Simple as that. Once I learned how intent Jerry was on meddling in Lynchburg, I thought it was a great chance for me to get him to bankroll my own search to find my sister."

"Very enterprising," Emily said.

Emily didn't know why she said it, but she felt compelled to do so. In the face of Ash's quest to find her lost sister, Emily felt like her own mission was far more mercenary in nature. It made her feel uneasy.

"I'll help you find Melinda," Emily said.

"No, you don't have to do that," Ash said.

"But I want to," Emily said. Ash smiled at Emily, patted her hand.

"That's nice of you," Ash said. "I just wouldn't want to drag you into something weird."

"Weird, I can handle. I can bring some scientific rigor to your efforts," Emily said. "Let me help you, Ash."

"Alright," Ash said. "Just don't blame me if things go sideways."

"Now that sounds promising," Emily said. "And I won't blame you, I promise."

# 8

**Logan could see more people turning up, even though**
they were still a day away from the Festival proper. The streets
were getting more crowded with more tourists and their idiotic mushroom hats—those comical, conical hats that were
cropping up like, well, mushrooms, throughout Lynchburg. In
white, brown, and red with white speckles.

They had already marked off Grand Avenue for the Festival, with local artists and artisans setting up in their assigned
pavilion tents, which were being readily assembled by diligent
workmen. The tents were red with white polka dots on them,
keeping to that particular mushroom theme. As each tent went
up, it began to look a little more otherworldly, transforming the
quiet Pennsylvania town into a festival wonderland, at least
along Grand Avenue.

The iconic Fly Agaric mushroom was always the go-to toad-
stool for people when they thought about mushrooms. Everyone knew it when they saw it, and of course they'd run with it
in Lynchburg. The bright red mushroom was all over the place,
apparent in the mascot, Mushy, who was winking at him from
posters in business windows and from banners that hung from
lampposts.

Workers had also been stringing up round paper lanterns
along both sides of Grand Avenue. The hanging lanterns gave
off a warm white-orange glow that Logan found welcoming.
They looked like puffballs or spores floating along the way, and
lent a pleasant, almost intimate vibe to the street.

From the Festival guide he'd picked up at the Grand Hotel
lobby, it said that the Fungus Festival Parade would travel the
length of Templeton Lane on Saturday, starting at the edge of
town near the wrought iron gates of Old Lynchburg and ending

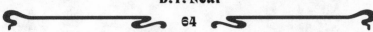
at the Temple of *La Signora,* an old Masonic lodge that had been built in 1899.

In the heart of the town, at the intersection of Grand Avenue and Templeton Lane, in the shadow of the old clock tower, was a statue of *La Signora Grigia,* the patron saint of Lynchburg, if such a word even applied, since she was not an official saint, obviously. It was like the cult of *Santa Muerte,* as he saw it, or *El Tio.* Somehow, she had taken root here in Lynchburg, and was acknowledged by the locals as a patron and protector.

The shrine to her—again, it was the only word Logan could use—was a circular park space he approached. It was the kind of place where, in other towns, a cannon or howitzer might have been placed, or perhaps a Confederate statue by some wistful, wannabe seditionists.

Instead, it was a grove of sycamore trees and some park benches, and the statue of *La Signora Grigia* in the center of it. He walked up to her, seeing her atop her pedestal, standing regally over him. Carved into the pedestal was *La Signora Grigia* in Roman lettering. The image itself was striking, as the locals had left clusters of lit candles clustered around her, a sea of waxy white luminescence.

The statue—or was it an idol—was a stern-faced woman who was classically lovely, wearing robes, with upswept hair that looked like shelf fungus styled by the ghost of Marie Antoinette's hairdresser. Her arms were upraised, with one arm holding out a hand, palm raised, and the other hand gesturing, almost as if she were offering a benediction. At her waist Logan could see some sort of blade, hanging from a belt, and a basket at her feet, containing carved mushrooms of various kinds.

He could see clustered around the sycamore tree trunks were mushrooms growing, of types he could not identify, mostly because he only knew edible mushrooms. These were brownwhite mushrooms, and they were thriving in the shadows of the park shrine.

"What do you think, Mr. Stephens?"

Logan startled, turning to see Maura Templeton looking at him, smiling around a cigarette she was smoking.

"Maura," Logan said. "Call me Logan."

"Logan," Maura said. "What do you think of our little shrine?"

"Uh, it's cool," Logan said. "Nice sculpture."

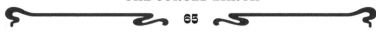
"One of my ancestors, John Templeton, made it," Maura said. "He was an enthusiastic sculptor, back in the day. He's long dead now, but his work, it endures."

She was in street clothes—a black rolled neck ribbed sweater and grey slacks and ballet flats, wore a white hairband that kept her dark hair out of her darker eyes.

"It's lovely," Logan said. "What's the story about *La Signora*, anyway?"

"Story?" Maura asked.

In the little grove, it felt private, quiet, even, despite all the activity in the town, things moving around in preparation for the Festival.

"Yeah, you know," Logan said. "What's the deal?"

"The Grey Lady provides," Maura said. "We honor Her. That's pretty much the whole 'story' as I see it. Mushroom farming is hard work. Endless work. People need something—someone— to be there for them. She fills that role."

Logan couldn't tell if he offended her. Her delivery was matter-of-fact, coolly nonchalant, and she watched him while she smoked.

"What about God?" Logan asked, and Maura smiled.

"What about God?" Maura asked. "There is no God on a mushroom farm. Only mountains of manure composting in the darkness. I should take you on a tour of Nightcap. You could see the doubles where we grow them. I mean, you want to work with me to start a chain of Shroom Rooms, the least you can do is see how we do what we do."

"Ah, so you're considering the proposal I didn't quite get around to making?" Logan asked.

"Sure," Maura said. She crushed out her cigarette in a cigarette disposal urn that was near the entrance. "But if you want to run with me on something like that, you need to get into the muck of mushrooms, just to get a proper taste—and smell—of it."

Logan was pleased that Maura was even considering it. Her work was exemplary. So was his. He wondered if maybe she'd looked him up. His work at Chevron had been very well-received in the culinary community of Philadelphia and beyond.

"Alright," Logan said. "I'm game for that."

Maura smiled at him, through him.

"Good," she said. "I don't want to hear any complaining from you while we're doing it."

"Not a problem," Logan said. "I've got a cast-iron stomach."

Maura looked him up and down, nodding.

"That'll help," Maura said. "It's going to be insane this weekend. I mean, like really crazy. But we should be able to drop in at Nightcap today. No way this weekend, however. This is like our big thing in Lynchburg. We live for this."

Her voice was like molasses, low-toned and husky, both savory and sweet. He liked the sound of her voice, wanted to talk to her more, if only to hear what she'd say.

"What happens if it rains during the Festival?" Logan asked.

"Well, then people get wet," Maura said. "We sell mushroom umbrellas."

"Of course you do," Logan said. "I should have guessed that."

"Yes, you should have," Maura said. "Come on, let's take my car."

# 9

**Miguel had followed his brother's directives and reached**
out to Eduardo *"El Morro"* and Tuco "Fleece" Martinez. The Martinez brothers were two of the most reliable enforcers among
the *Rojas*. They were like more sinister reflections of Carlos and
Miguel—with Morro being the big, bad older brother whose
stone-faced bearing filled enemies of the gang with terror.
Morro wore his hair cut very close to his hard head, and his dark
eyes were like cut onyx. He was well-built and strong.

Fleece, on the other hand, was baby-faced and earned that
name from his shoulder-length curly black locks. He had a more
affable disposition than his big brother but was in his madcap
way as much of a killer—where Morro could frown someone to
death, Fleece would laugh them into oblivion.

Miguel reached them in the garage, working on Fleece's red
Mustang.

"Carlo wants us to find out who killed Franco and Teo," Miguel said. He was more than a little intimidated by the Martinez brothers, who were lodging in one of the nearby houses in
Hidden Hollow. The *Rojas* owned a number of houses in Hidden
Hollow, and Carlos had their men scattered across a dozen of
them, which provided them a whole block in the gated community that they could call their own territory.

"Okay," Morro said. "Is that all?"

"It's a woman," Miguel said. "A woman called Carlo from
Teo's phone. She called herself *La Signora Grigia*, which means
'The Grey Lady.'"

"I know what it means," Morro said. "It's Italian. Are we
dealing with the Italians?"

Miguel found Morro's gravelly voice disarming.

"We don't know," Miguel said. "It's why we're trying to find
out. Carlo wants this 'Lady' brought in. And he wants us to

lean on the workers at the mushroom farm as part of the larger shakedown effort."

Fleece emerged from beneath Mustang, laughing as he wiped his hands with a rag he tossed aside.

"Which does he want more, Mig? The Lady or the workers?" Fleece asked.

"He wants both," Miguel said. "He was really pissed. Also, the woman has Teo's phone. So, if you call, she might answer."

Fleece got up, clapping his hands together, while Morro closed the garage door, cutting off the street. He didn't like anybody seeing them all together this way. Miguel watched the door close, feeling nervous. He didn't like the idea of sharing this space with the Martinez Brothers.

"Fleece," Morro said. "Dial her up."

Fleece fished out his phone and dialed up Matteo's number.

"Seems like that would be stupid of her to hold onto his phone, don't you think?" Fleece asked. Morro shrugged.

"Not half as stupid as killing Franco and Teo. Put it on speaker."

The Lady answered.

"Yeah?"

"Hello, Lady," Fleece said. "This is the Grey Lady, yes?"

"I am *La Signora Grigia*," the woman said. "You're one of Mendoza's goons, I take it?"

"I am," Fleece said. "We just wanted you to know that we are coming for you, *Puta*."

The Lady sounded unafraid.

"Your boss said the same thing, Fleece," she said.

Fleece gulped. Of course, Matteo would have had him logged in his phone.

"We know all about you," she said. "About all of you. Is your brother Morro there? Hello, Eduardo. We're watching everything you *Rojas* do."

"Is that right?" Fleece asked. "What am I doing right now?"

"You're in a garage at Hidden Hollow," the woman said. This made Miguel and Morro jump to their feet. They drew their pistols, Morro walking to the side door of the garage, peering out. "You think Hidden Hollow will keep you safe, but you're wrong. You're in our territory. What you *Rojas* need to do is go back to Pittsburgh and forget all about this place."

Fleece looked to his brother for guidance, unsure how to proceed. He'd never encountered something like this before.

"But we like it here," Fleece said. "So peaceful, so quiet. We look forward to crashing your Fungus Festival."

Morro walked away from the door, toward Fleece and his phone.

"Listen, *Puta*," Morro said. "You don't know what you've gotten yourself into."

"Oh, I know," the woman said. "I know everything. And I know why you're here. I have Francisco's notebook. Go back where you came from, and we can forget all about each other. Keep at it and you'll all end up in the ground, where you belong."

The Lady hung up.

Morro cursed, while Fleece stuffed his phone into a pocket. Miguel looked disturbed and uncertain, shifting his weight from one foot to another. The *Rojas* were used to all sorts of things, but disrespect was not one of them.

"What now, Morro?" Fleece asked.

"Stupid Teo had us all in his contacts lists," Morro said. "Idiot. And hadn't password-locked his phone, so she has access to it. Call records, all of that. Call her back."

Fleece took out his phone again and dialed, but it went to voicemail. Fleece hung up before leaving a message.

"Okay, first order of business," Morro said. "Fleece, call his phone provider and pretend to be Matteo's brother. Get his phone canceled and wiped. I'll do the same for Franco, just in case."

Miguel piped up.

"What about tracking the phone?" he asked. "Can we do something like that?"

"I suppose so," Morro said. "Maybe we find out where she's calling from. Then we pay her a visit."

"Maybe she's thought of that," Fleece said. "Maybe she wants that. Maybe she's provoking us with full knowledge that this is what we'd do."

"Maybe maybe maybe," Morro said. "The only certainty I want is this *puta's* death. Nobody talks to us this way. Okay, track it first. If we can't find her, then we blank it."

"Carlos wants her brought to him alive," Miguel said. "He was very clear about that, Morro."

"Fine," Morro said. "We'll bust her up but keep her breathing. Carlo can take care of the rest. He won't mind. Second order of business—we're being watched in Hidden Hollow."

Morro's phone rang, chirping in his pocket.

He pulled it out, looked at it, his face going slack.

"It's Teo," Morro said. "She's calling me, now."

"Answer it," Fleece said.

Morro did.

"Yeah?" Morro said, putting it on speaker.

"Why don't you come out of that garage so we can talk face-to-face?" the Lady asked.

Morro gestured for Fleece to check the side door. Fleece went over there, gun drawn.

"Oh, so you're out there, are you?" Morro said.

"Closer than you know," the Lady said.

"*Puta*, you've really stepped in it," Morro said.

"Have I?" the Lady said. "Step outside, let's see if you're right."

Morro muted his phone a moment. He didn't want to appear weak by calling for help, but he thought if some other *Rojas* could turn up, that might be a good move. Then again, who was he to be afraid of some crazy woman? He unmuted.

"Alright," Morro said. "I'll step out. I'm not afraid of you."

"Of course not," the Lady said. "Why would you be?"

Morro hit the garage opener and opened it, waiting for it to stop before he stepped outside. It was dark, with only the streetlights of Hidden Hollow illuminating the quiet street.

"Alright," Morro said, stepping out of the confines of the garage. Miguel and Fleece hovered nearby, guns out, looking nervous.

"Good man," the Lady said.

"So, where are you?" Morro asked.

"I didn't say we'd have our face-to-face right here, Morro," the Lady said. "I'm close. Very close. Walk around the garage, toward the back yard."

"I'm not doing any such thing," Morro said. "You come to me, not the other way around."

Fleece cried out, pointing to the side door. It was an apparition, a fleeting glimpse of someone in grey.

"Morro!" Fleece said. "I saw her!"

Fleece ran around the side of the garage onto the lawn.

"Fleece, wait!" Morro said, but it was too late. Fleece grunted as he was hit by some tranquilizer darts, dropping him in moments.

Then a half-dozen grey-robed figures appeared on either side of the garage, wearing grey masks and conical hats, bearing tranquilizer pistols. They fired shots into Miguel and Morro, both men catching several in their chests.

"Sweet dreams, Morro," the Lady said, as Morro dropped to the driveway, his eyes blurring to black even as he saw a van pull up.

# 10

**"They've got it all here,"** **Mallory said. "I know a guy** who can get us what we need."

The four of them were streetside, watching the pavilion tents get put up, seeing the vendors staking out their appointed stalls. Jess was wearing her conical hat and her Mushette tee shirt, while Jake was in a grey Fun Guy tee shirt he'd picked up at one of the shops. Austin was still in his Fungus Festival '18 tee with a black leather jacket, and Mallory was wearing some coveralls and a rainbow-colored blouse.

"You know a guy," Austin said. "Everybody 'knows a guy' Mallory."

Mallory laughed and led them down Grand Avenue, past the busy workers setting up the tents.

"It's like a dream," Jess said. "I can blur my eyes and almost see it."

They'd smoked some marijuana in their hotel rooms, once they'd decided they were okay and had set up on the balconies, taking it all in. Austin and Mallory had passed, but the Jordan Twins had gone all in.

"I see it, Sis," Jake said, waving his hands in front of his face. "Total dreamsville."

Austin laughed, and Mallory joined in. Jess and Jake did love their weed, which had made selling them on Lynchburg's Fungus Festival just about the easiest thing in the world. The prospect of scoring some great psilocybin was beyond persuasive.

"So, who's this guy?" Austin asked. "Should I be jealous?"

Mallory smiled at him as they walked down Grand Avenue past The Mush Room.

"When are you not jealous, Austin?" Mallory asked. She pointed to a narrow storefront next to the Mush Room. It said

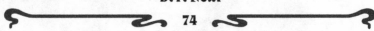
Capper's and had a sign showing a grinning mushroom sporting a baseball cap and making a finger pistol gesture. "This is the place. Happy Cappy's Hat Emporium."

"Happy Cappy?" Austin asked.

"That's right," Mallory said. "Problem?"

"Nope," Austin said, holding up his hands.

She opened the front door, a brass bell hanging from the door jangling as she entered.

"Cappy? You in here?" Mallory asked.

"Cappy?" Austin said, snorting.

Jess and Jake followed on his heels. There were all sorts of baseball caps hanging from the walls of the narrow shop. It was like a long hallway, lit overhead by a trio of glass globes that gave off a strong amber LED light.

Austin surveyed the hats, which looked to have the National League on the left wall, and the American League on the right, as well as assorted other caps. Jake picked up a Brewers cap and put it on his head backwards, making a face.

Cappy came out to see them. He was a Baby Boomer by the look of him, with a greying beard and wearing a brown flannel shirt and blue jeans. He was sporting a wiry ponytail, with round-rimmed eyeglasses on his big nose. He was wearing a grey baseball cap that had a white mushroom dancing on the front.

"Can I help you?" Cappy asked.

"It's me, Cappy," Mallory said. "Mallory Tilton? I was here last year. Mallory with two Ls."

"Ah," Cappy said, without seeming to recognize her. "Ah, Mallory Two Ls Tilton. Nice to see you again. What can I do you for?"

Mallory smiled fetchingly at Austin and the Twins, who were giggling and poking around the inventory of caps. Jess had found a Minnesota Twins cap she immediately put on, ribbing her brother, pointing to it. He shook his head, and she grimaced at him.

"I'm looking for some stuff," Mallory said. "You know, stuff."

"Ah," Cappy said. "You're out for stuffing, are you?"

"Yeah," Austin said. "And it's not even Thanksgiving, yet."

Cappy looked at Austin a moment before turning his attention back to Mallory.

"What do you have in mind, Mallory?" Cappy asked. "Maybe we should step into the back. Son, can you turn that door sign to CLOSED for me?"

Jake realized after he asked again that he was talking to him, and he cheerfully went to the boutique door and flipped the sign.

"Done deal," Jake said, giving a thumbs up.

"Great, son," Cappy said. "Now let's go in the back a moment."

Austin looked around skeptically.

"Just like that?" Austin asked.

"Just like that," Cappy said, grinning. "Like magic. You can wait up front if you want to. But nobody's going to bother us back here."

In the back of his store were orderly stacks of boxes, Cappy's hat inventory on racks and shelves, but he moved past that to a table. He turned on an overhead light and fished out some lined boxes, setting them up in a row.

"We have Wavy Caps and Liberty Caps, Flying Saucers, Blue Meanies, Jedi Mind Fuck, Luminous Lucies, Penis Envy," Cappy said.

"Austin definitely wants some Penis Envy," Mallory said, winking at him.

"Austin?" Cappy said, laughing. "You from Austin, Austin?"

"Nope," Austin said. "Austintown, Ohio."

Cappy laughed some more. "Austin from Austintown. Wow, man. Your parents did a number on you, didn't they?"

Austin forced a grin. "They sure did. It's how I ended up where I am today."

"We're from Akron," Jess said. "My brother and me. Akron, Ohio. You know it?"

"Of course I do. You seem very Akron to me," Cappy said. "You all Ohio kids or what?"

"I'm not," Mallory said. "I'm Pennsylvanian."

"Local girl?" Cappy asked.

"Not native to Lynchburg, no," Mallory said.

Cappy smiled at her, clapping the table in amusement. "Hell, I knew that, Miss Mallory Tilton. I know a Lynchburg girl when I see one. You look—and sound—like a Pittsburgh girl to me."

"Bingo," Mallory said.

Austin smacked his hands together, growing impatient.

"What say we buy some shrooms, yeah?" Austin said.

Cappy looked Austin over, taking stock of the young man.

"You a cop?" Cappy asked.

"What?"

"Just kidding," Cappy said. "You don't look like one. Not even close. Alright, are we talking grams, eighths, or pounds? How much do you want?"

Mallory counted on her fingers.

"Well, there are four of us, and we're here all weekend," Mallory said. "So, I'm thinking like maybe twelve grams."

"Thirty-five grams," Austin said. "Like a buffet. Let's have five grams of each of what you have here, Cappy."

Cappy clapped the table again, taking out a calculator, while the Twins peered over Mallory's shoulders, their eyes big and round. Jess wanted to reach out to touch the shrooms on the table, but Mallory swatted her hand away.

"Not until we buy, Jess," Mallory said.

"Five hundred dollars," Cappy said, holding up his calculator with $500 punched into it in liquid crystal.

"Five hundred bucks?" Austin said. "Are you fucking kidding me?"

"For the buffet," Cappy said, sweeping his bearlike paw over the trays of mushrooms. "Five grams of seven types. That's a feast for the Festival, young man. It's a seller's market. In another day, this place is going to be swarmed and you're not going to be able to find a one—or what you will find will be jacked even higher. Best jump on it now while you can, yeah?"

Austin grumbled, while Mallory shrugged and Jess and Jake laughed.

"You're gouging us, Cappy," Austin said. "Alright, Mallory, Jess, Jake. Pony up."

"That's like $125 apiece, Austin," Mallory said. "Who has that kind of cash?"

Austin glared at them.

"You assheads are not having me spring for this," Austin said. "I already got us the hotel and we drove here in my damned van. Come on."

He held out his palm, twitching his fingers to try to conjure up some cash.

"Can't we, like, barter for it?" Jess asked. "Like work a trade, Austin?"

"A trade?" Austin said. "Give me a break. You know what? I'm going to buy the lot, you fucking freeloaders. I'm buying it right now."

He pulled out five crisp hundred dollar bills and put them on the table. Cappy was happy with that, pocketing the money, while he took out some bags and a scale and quickly went about bagging up the shrooms.

"I like a decisive man," Cappy said. "This young man knows what he wants, and I'll be damned if he's not going to get it."

Cappy's big hands worked quickly, clearly well-practiced with such transactions. Mallory smiled at Austin, shrugging her shoulders.

"We're so glad you're here, Austin," Mallory said. "You're the best kind of friend to have."

"Yeah," Jess said. "A friend without need is the friend you need."

"No, a friend with weed is the friend you need," Jake said, cackling. Jess joined in, laughing, her shoulders shaking.

Cappy finished bagging and produced another bag, a black bag, into which he dropped the gram bags of shrooms.

"Now, don't go about telling anybody you got these from me, kids," Cappy said. "Sheriff Leonard is a good man, but he's a bit of a stickler where, you know, the law comes into it sometimes. Let's just keep this between us."

He handed over the bag to Austin, who took it and slipped it into one of the cargo pockets of the pants he was wearing.

"Your secret's safe with us, Cappy," Austin said. "Let's get out of here, how about?"

"Have a nice trip," Cappy said, shooing them out of his back room. "Flip the sign back when you go."

"I'm buying this cap," Jess said, pointing to the Twins cap she'd snagged and giving Jake a scalding side eye. Cappy smiled. "Sure thing, Babydoll."

Mallory nodded as Jess bought her cap. Mallory gave Cappy a hug.

"We will have a great trip thanks to you, Cappy," Mallory said. "Thanks for being so awesome."

"Always happy to do so," Cappy said. "Be careful out there, now."

"We will," Mallory said, hooking Austin's arm as they made their way out.

"You all owe me big time," Austin said. "Like even more than before."

"Sure, sure," Mallory said. "I'm sure we can repay you somehow, Austin. We'll find a way. We're all very resourceful."

She flipped the sign to OPEN as they left Capper's.

# 11

**Emily and Ash walked together down Templeton Lane,**
marveling at both the street decorations and the greater numbers of people milling around the streets. Tourists were arriving in droves, with only another day until the start of the Festival. There were RVs rolling through, headed to one of several RV
parks outside of town.

"What's the plan, anyway?" Emily asked. "How do you find
people who aren't here?"

"I was going to check with Sheriff Leonard," Ash said.

Emily laughed dryly.

"Oh, come on, Ash. The sheriff's always in on these sorts
of things. The last thing you want to do is tip your hand that
you're investigating something like that. I mean, Sheriff Leonard has to have been involved on some level."

"I suppose," Ash said. "I still would like to confront him."

"No, that'll just make you a target," Emily said.

Ash glanced at Emily, who looked the picture of elegant
nonchalance in her grey wool overcoat and red scarf and black
boots with jeans. Ash was wearing hiking boots and leggings
with a shearling coat, was carrying "Have You Seen Me?" flyers of her missing sister that bore her face. She'd been affixing
them to phone poles along Templeton Lane.

"What do you suggest?" Ash asked.

Emily wanted to get to the Nightcap Mushroom Farm, was
trying to figure how she might steer Ash there.

"Let's hit Nightcap. I'm betting they're giving tours."

"What will that do?" Ash asked. "How does that help me
find my sister?"

"We show it to the Nightcap people, see if anybody has seen
her," Emily said.

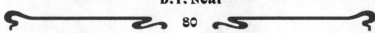
Ash found another phone pole and pinned another flyer on it. Her sister smiled at them both, and Emily found it made her sad. She'd never known someone who had a missing loved one before.

"I don't see how that's any better than talking to the sheriff," Ash said. "If they're in on it, we'll be tipping our hand either way."

Emily gestured to the flyers.

"Seems like these will have somebody calling you in short order. Unless somebody takes them down ahead of the Festival."

Ash was earnest, Emily could see that. But earnestness only counted for so much in this world.

"Here, you said you wanted to help," Ash said, giving Emily half of the flyers. "So, you canvas the other side of Templeton Lane, and I'll get this side."

"Alright," Emily said, tucking the flyers under her arm. "I'll meet up with you at the top of the street. At the Temple of the Lady."

They turned their eyes down Templeton Lane, seeing the stone lodge.

"What's with that place, anyway?" Ash asked. "There's not an actual cathedral in town. Or any other churches or synagogues or mosques."

"Nope," Emily said. "The Temple is it."

"Don't you think that's weird?" Ash asked.

"Sure," Emily said. "Maybe we can tour the Temple when we're done leafletting."

"Yeah," Ash said. "Okay."

Emily crossed the street, her boots clacking on the brick road as she made her way. Unlike Grand Avenue with its boutiques and quaint shops, Templeton Lane had different sorts of businesses, like taverns and restaurants, parking decks, and municipal buildings, including the Sheriff and the County Courthouse.

She handed out flyers at each of the businesses, asking people if they had seen Melinda Dunn, but nobody had. She paused in front of the Sheriff's Office, thinking of her own advice to Ash, but then thought maybe if she looked into it herself, she'd have more luck.

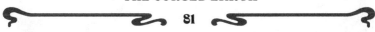
How she'd allowed herself to get roped into Ash's search was par for the course for Emily. She knew the benefit of meandering. This was a meander.

Emily meandered into the Sheriff's Office, which was a grey stone blockhouse with columns in the front of it. Inside it were deputies and office workers behind desks. On the far side, down the hall from the entrance, was a shrine to the Grey Lady, beneath three interlocking blue circles.

"Can I help you, ma'am?" one of the deputies asked. He was a young man with "Stirner" on his nametag and a grey and black uniform. He was brown-haired with blue eyes and had a mustache.

"Hello, Deputy Stirner," Emily said, holding out a flyer, which Stirner took. "Missing person."

"Missing for some time," Stirner said. "You want this for our bulletin board?"

He nodded toward a bulletin board across the hall from them.

"Yes, please," Emily said.

"I'm Max Stirner," he said, holding out a hand, which she shook.

"Emily Carver," she said, figuring it didn't make much point in using an alias.

"Nice to meet you, Ms. Carver," Stirner said, tacking the flyer onto the bulletin board with various other notices showing outlaws and other things. "Melinda Dunn. Can't say I ever saw her. But we get a lot of people in Lynchburg for the Festival."

"A lot of people missing, too," Emily said. He looked at her a moment, assessing her clearly.

"Is that a fact?" Stirner asked.

"That's a fact," Emily said. Stirner was handsome in his law enforcement sort of way—that unvarnished masculine entitlement rooted in being a uniformed lawman.

"People disappear all the time and everywhere, Ms. Carver," Stirner said. "Lynchburg is a quiet little town. Don't let the Festival fool you. Normally, it's dead quiet around here. Just us and the mushrooms."

"Are you from here, Deputy Stirner?" Emily asked.

"Nope," Stirner said. "I'm from Philadelphia, actually. I went west for something quieter."

"I'd say you found it here," Emily said.

"Who was Melinda Dunn to you, if you don't mind me asking?" Stirner asked.

"I'm actually helping a friend," Emily said. "It's her sister."

"You're a good friend to help out," Stirner said.

"I try to help," Emily said.

"Tell you what, Ms. Carver," Stirner said. "If I see anything about Melinda Dunn, I'll call that number and tell what I know. Is that your number?"

Emily smiled at the deputy, who smiled back.

"Are you really asking for my number, Deputy Stirner?" Emily asked.

"I might be," Stirner said. "Call me Max."

"Is that for 'Maximilian' or 'Maxwell'?" Emily asked.

"Just Max," Stirner said. "I'm merely a Max. It means 'greatest'."

Emily laughed. "Are you the greatest, Max?"

"I do my best," Stirner said.

"How about you give me your direct line, and I'll give you mine," Emily said.

"That's a fair trade," Stirner said, and they did. "If I find anything out about Melinda Dunn, I'll let you know. And your friend."

"Great," Emily said. "I suppose I should be going, now."

She fluffed the flyers she was carrying.

"Yeah," Stirner said. "I suppose you should. Be careful posting those. The Sheriff gets salty about people posting bills."

"I will, Deputy Stirner," Emily said. "Thanks for your help."

"Any time, Ms. Carver," Stirner said.

"You can call me Emily," Emily said. "Or Dr. Carver."

"Dr. Carver, eh?"

He looked both confused and impressed, so Emily clarified.

"I'm a mycologist," Emily said. "I study fungi."

Deputy Stirner smiled, chuckling.

"Believe it or not, I actually knew that, Dr. Carver," Stirner said. "One doesn't become a deputy in Lynchburg without learning what a mycologist does pretty quickly. We get them here all the time, and not just for the Festival."

Stirner walked her to the door of the Sheriff's Office, which he held open for her. Emily went through it, thanking him.

"Thanks for your time, Deputy Stirner," Emily said.

"You be careful out there, now, Dr. Carver. It's going to get wild here during the Festival."

"That's what I keep hearing," Emily said. "It's just a mushroom harvest festival, right? What's the big deal, anyway?"

Max laughed, shaking his head as he walked her through the entryway out onto the front steps of the office.

"Not in Lynchburg," he said. "No, it's something else entirely, here. People go *crazy* for their mushrooms here. I mean like crazy. Word of advice: if you see anybody masked up like the Grey Lady, you just leave them be, alright?"

Emily was intrigued by this cryptic bit of advice, couldn't resist probing a bit, glancing up and down Templeton Lane to see anything out of place, but only saw pedestrians making their way to shops and restaurants.

"The Grey Lady?" Emily asked.

"*La Signora Grigia,*" Stirner said, nodding at the temple down the street, which stood like a fortress at the intersection of Templeton and First Street. "There are some locals who take all of that pretty seriously. And I'm just saying if you see some Grey Ladies walking around town, just give them a wide berth."

"Certainly sounds menacing," Emily said. "I'm admittedly intrigued. What are they, terrorists? Vigilantes? Thugs?"

Deputy Stirner grimaced, half-laughing, half-scratching his forehead, glancing around to see if anyone had overheard them.

"They're local enthusiasts," Stirner said, under his breath. "All too often, that's what they are. Kooks. People get all up in their shrooms, like magic mushrooms, and they just trip out."

"Seems like public intoxication to me," Emily said. "Wouldn't you just lock them up?"

"It's complicated," Stirner said. "Sheriff Leonard has a thing about free expression of religion, particularly as it relates to *La Signora*. He doesn't want a stink around that, so he lets the Grey Ladies do their thing."

"And what is 'their thing'?" Emily asked. She was mindful of people passing them to get into the Sheriff's Office. "I mean, are they a gang or something?"

"No," Stirner said. "They're just fanatics. You ever heard of those Opus Dei people? Or like the Knights of Malta or the Freemasons? The Grey Ladies are like that. They feel like they've

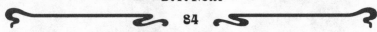
been personally tapped by *La Signora Grigia*. Like they're doing the Lady's work."

Emily had all but forgotten about the flyers she was carrying.

"How fascinatingly strange," Emily said. "It's like, what, the Junior League for fanatical followers of fungi?"

Stirner laughed.

"Yeah, alright," Stirner said. "You get the idea. Just be mindful if you see them."

"Are you trying to protect me, Deputy?" Emily asked. "Because I don't need protecting."

"I'm sure you don't, Dr. Carver," Stirner said. "Just saying that if you see them, please be careful. And, perhaps more on point—if they see you, you'd best get to running. And call me. Like any time of day or night. I'll help you out."

"Wow," Emily said. "They sound like a public menace."

"They just get carried away is all," Stirner said. "True believers, that kind of thing."

"I'll keep my eyes out for them," Emily said.

"You do that," Stirner said. "Good day, now. Enjoy the Festival, and good luck finding your friend's missing friend."

Emily just smiled and waved and went on her way with a laugh and a nod, with visions of the Grey Lady squirming in her head.

# 12

**Logan was well-impressed by the Nightcap Mushroom**
Farm. It was a sprawling complex, far larger than he'd imagined. Maura drove them up to the security gate and got them in. There were fleets of trucks and earth movers handy to deal with the mounds of compost and manure which threw off an unforgettable stench that hardly seemed to faze Maura.

She got them parked in a parking lot, and they could see the Nightcap Mushroom Farm logo on display over the building—a great big "NMF" in neon, the red light coloring everything in range of it.

"Wow, the smell," Logan said.

"You get used to it quickly," Maura said. "NMF has some advanced techniques to keep things aerated. It used to be a lot worse, trust me."

She walked them over to the business offices of the farm. The place looked jarringly modern to Logan. He hadn't known what precisely to expect, but the NMF complex would have looked at home in any industrial park. There was clearly money here.

"Not what you expected?" Maura asked. "You were thinking, what, quaintly rustic villagers happily tending to mushrooms growing on fallen trees ritually arranged in open fields?"

"Maybe," Logan said. He saw workers tending to the compost and going in and out of the doubles. The workers were Latinx, wearing grey uniforms that bore three white, interlocking circles on their backs. They seemed wary of Maura and Logan watching them, were busy going about their labors.

"My family's farm is an industrial enterprise," Maura said. "We grow mushrooms all year round. Harvests are taking place constantly. There's no season proper, not with mushrooms. Our process involves nonstop cultivation. Mushrooms are money, and if you're good to them, they'll be very good to you."

"I can see that," Logan said, as she took them into the offices, which looked very mid-century modern to him. On one wall was a great collection of prints that showed all the types of mushrooms NMF produced.

"There are nearly 70 mushroom farms in Pennsylvania," Maura said. "With an economic footprint of over $760 million. When you factor in spawn, compost, and casing, it funnels money from all around the country to the Commonwealth, supporting over 8,000 jobs worth almost $300 million in compensation and well over $320 million in direct and indirect spending for an industry that's worth over $1 billion to the economy."

"It's impressive as hell," Logan said.

"Damn right," Maura said.

The people who worked there also wore grey uniforms, and Logan could see a shrine to the Grey Lady in an alcove at the far end of the lobby. The Lady seemed to stare out at them from her spot, surrounded by lit candles, holding her stony hands out. Maura could see his eyes on the Lady and laughed.

"The Lady's been good to us," Maura said. "We honor Her."

"Yeah," Logan said.

Maura guided Logan down the main hallway, leaving the shrine behind, heading to some offices. She talked along the way.

"There are a half-dozen major steps to mushroom farming," Maura said. "There are two phases of composting, for example—we use wheat straw and horse manure for the initial composting, as well as a lot of water and gypsum and a compost turner to get everything mixed up nicely. The microorganisms in the compost generate a lot of heat and ammonia and carbon dioxide, so we place that prepared compost into concrete bunkers and use forced aeration to help deal with that."

"Okay," Logan said, looking around them as they went. There were paintings on the walls, various Templetons by the nameplates on them, and by the look of them. "Horse manure. You have horse stables or what?"

"Yeah," Maura said. "Has to be horse manure. Cow or pig manure won't work. We have access to plenty of horses. Have to

have that kind of access for it to work. We have a deal with the Hecate Horse Ranch. Rena Hecate's real close to us."

"Trippy," Logan said. "Rena Hecate. That's a name for you. What is she, a witch?"

Maura smiled at Logan, like she was humoring him.

"It's a complicated dance, to be sure," Maura said. "We have to encourage the growth of the microorganisms we want and discourage unwanted fungi and bacteria. It's a very fussy process, especially at the scale we do it here at NMF. We have compost piles on one side of the farm. Not the stuff you saw piled up on the drive in, but long tracts of it, protected. It's all water, nitrogen and gypsum supplements, and turning to keep everything aerated and to regulate the temperature."

Maura led him into a meeting room, which had a long oval table and a row of windows that looked out. On the wall were poster-sized prints of various mushroom lineages, while overhead was an oval of light that indirectly illuminated the room. Maura took a seat at the table, and gestured for Logan to sit across from her. He took his seat while she continued talking.

"Phase I composting takes around six to fourteen days," Maura said. "The ammonia smell is pretty overpowering if you're not ready for it. Phase II composting is necessary to kill pests and other unwanted impurities in the compost, including the damned ammonia, which inhibits mushroom growth. At NMF, we use bulk system tunnels to place the compost on beds where it gets the treatment."

"You know a helluva lot about it all," Logan said.

"I ought to," Maura said. "I grew up with it."

"What are we doing here, anyway?" Logan asked.

"Waiting for my father," Maura said.

Logan laughed uneasily.

"You're having me meet your dad?" Logan said. Maura nodded, eyeing him with private amusement. Logan felt uneasy under her gaze.

"All part of the business," Maura said. "I like your idea about the franchising. I think there's an opportunity there. I wanted to run it by Daddy."

Logan laughed again, even more uneasily.

"I don't want us getting too far ahead of ourselves," Logan said. "I was just suggesting that your Shroom Rooms had promise in other markets."

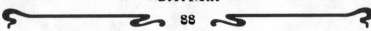
Maura nodded.

"I understand that," she said. "But why not hit the ground running?"

"I don't have the kind of financing for that," Logan said. "Investors need to be lined up."

"Meh," Maura said. "We have plenty of money here. More so if Daddy gets involved."

"Daddy," Logan said. "Would 'Daddy' mind?"

Maura all but leered at him, and Logan couldn't tell if she was making sport of him or not.

"Daddy loves seizing opportunities," Maura said. "He's a born opportunist."

"Guilty as charged, Maura," said Ned Templeton IV, a genial smiling older man who wore a blue button-down shirt with grey slacks and wore a navy blue blazer with a red and white enamel mushroom pin at his lapel. He was a tall, lean older man with silvery-white hair and sharp blue eyes and a straight nose. At least some of Maura's own strong features were apparent in the visage of her father.

"Daddy," Maura said. "This is Logan Stephens, the chef I mentioned to you. The one from Philadelphia."

"Mr. Stephens," Templeton said, holding out a big hand, which Logan took. Ned smiled at him like a jack-o'-lantern, his voice simply syrup-smooth. "Call me Ned, would you, Logan?"

"Happy to meet you, sir," Logan said.

"Maura told me you liked her cuisine at her restaurant," Ned said, taking a seat at the head of the oval table. Maura sat to his right, and Logan took his seat at his left.

"I loved it," Logan said. "She's an extraordinary chef. I think people would really dig that kind of boutique rustic cuisine in the city."

Maura smiled at Logan from across the table, looking bewitching in the light of the conference room.

"We're very proud of our mushrooms here in Lynchburg, Logan," Ned said. "We breed some of the very best. We grow all types here—specialty varieties and the more mundane types for everyday use. We're also diversifying into the beverage market, if you were wondering. I think there's a real opportunity for mushroom coffees, among other beverages."

Templeton's fatherly enthusiasm was apparent in every word.

"The Templetons have been involved in mushroom farming since the late 1800s," Ned said. "Shortly after the founding of Lynchburg, in fact. It's been nothing but good for us, and good to us. We appreciate someone like yourself coming from where you do with an open mind."

Logan could appreciate that. As a chef, he approached all foods with that kind of open-minded objectivity. Opportunities presented themselves to those who kept their options open.

"I'm surprised others haven't approached you before," Logan said.

"Who says they haven't?" Maura said. "But we're very protective of our brand."

Ned nodded, smiling at his daughter. The love between them was apparent, and Logan envied that. His own family was more fractured. His father, a welder by trade, hadn't approved of him becoming a chef. Logan had done it in spite of his father's disapproval.

"Maura's so right," Ned said. "There are so many factors to consider with those sorts of ventures. The right partner is critical. Maura told me about your Chevron restaurant in Philadelphia, showed me some of it on the Internet. Your Franco-American style would play well with Maura's mushrooms. She's got a great eye and an impeccable palate."

Logan chuckled and leaned in a bit. Part of making inroads involved knowing there the leverage was, and how to apply it.

"I am the first to admit that I'm only here myself on a kind of fact-finding mission," Logan said. "I might be able to pull some investors into the mix, although I'm mostly here as an enthusiast. I love good food, and when I learned about the Shroom Room, I had to come and try it for myself. It takes a particular bravado to run with a theme like that so completely in so remote a location."

Ned acknowledged that with an ingratiating smile.

"My Maura has that bravado," Ned said. "But mushrooms are incredibly versatile that way. Occupying a liminal space between plant and animal, they are the ultimate survivors. The world could die and fungi would somehow survive and even thrive. All Maura did was build a menu exclusive to mushrooms that would play nicely with the modern palate."

"I tell you, you don't sound like a mushroom farmer to me, Ned," Logan said. "At least not at all what I imagined."

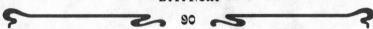
"I'm more businessman than farmer these days, Logan," Ned said. "I trust the farming to my dedicated employees. I did my share as a young man, but it's hard work. Now that I'm older, I find it more comfortable plotting out new developments than mucking around in the compost like I did decades ago. Let's hear what you have in mind."

Logan found he liked Ned Templeton—he had an easy, comfortable confidence about him, a kind of agreeable ambition that was infectious.

"Personally, I'd love to develop a Shroom Room in Philadelphia with Maura," Logan said. "But I could see it in Pittsburgh, too. Really play with the angle in those markets—the countercultural aspects of it, and for vegetarians and vegans, you know? A viable alternative to meat-based food production."

"And that it is," Ned said. "Mushrooms are incredibly nutritious, Logan. They are great low-calorie sources of protein, rich in antioxidants and vitamins and minerals. They can even be a good source of Vitamin D under the correct tending practices. Some types, like the cremini mushroom, for example, are excellent sources of zinc. They have tons of potassium, which can help lower blood pressure. And many of them have anti-inflammatory effects which can help boost the immune system. They can also contribute to weight loss when used as a meat substitute."

"Daddy, we don't have to sell him on the health pitch," Maura said. "Logan enjoyed them because they tasted good."

"Yes," Logan said. "Honestly, I'll eat anything. But I think Shroom Rooms would really play well as destination specialty restaurants in urban settings. And if there's a direct line of supply with Nightcap here in Lynchburg, so much the better."

Logan wondered why she would not have taken up franchising with others. Maybe it was just their personalities or circumstances weren't right. Anything was possible, he thought. Maybe he was just lucky. Or maybe there was something else he couldn't see.

"Speaking of Nightcap, Maura should give you the tour," Ned said. "You can see how we do what we do. We grow all types here—including our prize morel and shiitake doubles, which we have been developing for years. Historically, those are almost impossible to properly cultivate outside of the wild, but we've come up with some interesting techniques here at Night-cap."

"I'd love to go on a tour with Maura," Logan said.

"And you should," Ned said, standing up. He held out his hand again, which Logan shook. "I've got other matters to attend to, but I'd love for you and Maura to work out a prospectus for your franchising idea. I think it might be interesting to try. We all know how difficult the restaurant business is. But opening a couple of them within the state might be doable as a springboard for a larger effort."

"Yes," Logan said. "I very much look forward to future discussions on this."

"Thanks, Daddy," Maura said, hugging Ned and kissing his cheek. Ned winked at Logan from over Maura's shoulder.

"Take him on the tour, Maura," Ned said. "Show him what we've got. But be gentle with him."

# 13

**When Morro woke, he realized he was in the woods. He** could hear the creak of the trees and heard the call of birds. He also realized he was shackled to a thick wooden post and had a gag over his mouth, his hands behind his back, chained. And that he had been stripped naked. As his eyes unblurred, he saw that Miquel and Fleece were nearby as well, similarly trussed.

They were in some kind of grove, surrounded by big old trees without leaves upon them, the daylight shining down through tangled branches. Around them were moss-covered grey pavestones, and beyond them, masses of mushrooms that looked like giant white puffballs easily the size of basketballs and softballs, as well was blue-capped, white-speckled mushrooms he'd never seen before.

A mossy stone statue of what Morro assumed was *La Signora Grigia* loomed over them a slight distance away. She stood with an arm out, palm up, like an entreaty or a supplication. The other hand was upraised in a benediction, three fingers pointing skyward. Her face was serenely mournful, and her conical hat over her head was dotted with a few stray leaves.

Three candles burned at the base of the statue—one blue, one white, one black.

*What the hell happened?* Morro thought, all but gagging on the gag.

He became aware of another Grey Lady standing near him—a masked figure with a face like stone, bearing a pointed grey hat and wearing robes, looking like a mirror image of the statue, only being flesh and blood instead of stone.

Morro glared at the Lady, who walked over to him. He could see she was wearing grey boots and had a belt at her waist that carried a blade.

"Awake at last," the Lady said. She drew the blade from her belt, the curved thing, and slid it against Morro's cheek, cutting off the duct tape that had been gagging him. She reached out a grey-gloved hand and yanked the tape off his face. It stung, but the pain sharpened him.

"You are dead, *Puta,*" Morro said, spitting on the ground.

"Am I?" the Lady asked. "Because I think just maybe that you're the dead one, Infidel."

Morro wasn't going to humiliate himself by calling for help. He was certain that wherever they were, they were far from anyplace where anyone might help them. He'd done his own interrogations for the *Rojas,* he understood this game: isolate, humiliate, interrogate, torture.

"Where are our clothes?" Morro asked.

"Given to charity," the Lady said. "You won't be needing them where you're going."

Morro struggled to pry himself loose, but his bonds wouldn't give.

"Do you *Rojas* think you're the first hardcases to try to shake us down?" the Lady asked. "We get them every few years or so. Someone finds out about us and wants to muscle in. Gangsters from the cities who try to get their hands in our business. We do the Lady's work here, Infidel. We don't have time for your petty extortion rackets. We built Hidden Hollow as a kind of trap. Nobody moves or breathes there without us knowing about it."

Morro wasn't the type to be intimidated. He was an enforcer—there was a brutal discipline in being one, an understanding of the nature of the world and his place within it. However, he had not expected the Lynchburg locals to be as prepared as they were.

Miguel and Fleece were stirring as well, coming to. Bad as it was, Morro wasn't going to let them get themselves in a twist over this.

"You killed Franco and Teo, yes?" Morro asked.

"Of course we did," the Lady said. "We watched what they were watching and when the time was right, when we understood what they were up to, we killed them."

"So why didn't you just kill us?" Morro asked.

The Grey Lady walked back and forth in front of Morro, out of range even if he could reach her. She was cautious, clear-headed, alert. Dangerous. Morro had never encountered a

woman like this before. Her blank-faced, blue-lipped Grey Lady mask betrayed nothing, was as blank and dead-eyed as a doll.

"We didn't want to disrupt the quietly artificial harmony of Hidden Hollow," the Grey Lady said. "Your boss will find that out soon enough—we like our quiet harmony in Lynchburg. Even with the Festival. We like it how we like it. You thugs think you can come out our way and, what? Lean in on our business?"

"Seemed like a good plan at the time," Morro said.

"Mmmph," Miguel said.

"The question you haven't answered is why we're still alive," Morro said.

"Sacrifices to the Lady," the Lady said, running a gloved hand across her scarved neck. "Duh. Do you know what today is, Infidel? It's Friday the 13th. Your lucky day."

"Yeah?" Morro said, straining at his bonds. The post appeared to be stout wood, sunk deep in the ground. "Ironic, I think, maybe—cuffed to a post in the woods by a masked and murderous stranger, without a hope in the world."

"Yes," the Lady said. "And there's a full moon tomorrow. Right during the Festival. How perfect is that, I ask you? *La Signora* has made it possible—She makes everything possible. She wants this very badly."

"We have money," Morro said. He wasn't above at least a little negotiation. Anything, whether good or bad, was worth trying at least once.

"We have all the money we require," the Lady said. "Please, Infidel, don't embarrass yourself that way. I thought you were made of stronger stuff than that. You three are to be sacrifices to Her, and your Lady Red Death can't protect you."

Morro saw other masked Grey Ladies emerge from beyond the ring of puffballs, the statue and the tall trees. They were all dressed the same as the Lady who was talking to him, although they were different heights. The other Ladies wore grey shrouds upon their conical hats, which hung down like silvery mesh, menacingly shadowing their masked features. The shrouds had bells that hung from them, clanking as they moved with a weird, clashing sort of rhythm.

It was weird to see them like this, these lunatics with their masks and hats. Several of them carried little drums that they began to beat with small mallets, sounding a curious thrumming with each step as they fanned out and circled them in the

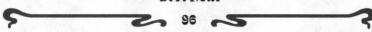
grove, the steady beat countering the jangly sound of the bells. Miguel and Fleece strained in their chains and gag-spoke their fear.

"Sacrifices?" Morro said. "To *La Signora?*"

"Yes," the Lady said. "Your blood will run into the earth itself, nourishing it. A good omen for the opening of the Festival."

Miguel and Fleece wailed behind their gags, struggling to free themselves. Three of the veiled Ladies walked up with three broad bowls—one gold, one silver, one copper. The gold bowl was placed at Morro's feet. The silver bowl was placed at Fleece's. The copper bowl was placed at Miguel's.

"I'm not afraid to die," Morro said.

"I know," the Lady said. "It's why I removed your gag. The others, not so much. Their fear flows off of them. But not you, Morro. You're the brave one. For a cowardly gangster, I mean. It's why you get the golden bowl. The strongest blood, the richest harvest of your valor."

"Cowardly? I'm not the one wearing a mask," Morro said.

The Lady laughed at that.

"We do the Lady's work," the Lady said. "We are the Lady. She is us. We wear our masks in Her honor, to manifest Her will."

The other Ladies reformed a circle in the grove, surrounding the *Rojas*. The Talking Lady stood in front of the statue, turning and bowing to it.

"Dearest Lady, Queen of Fleeting Life, Lingering Decay, and Inevitable Death, we, Your humble servants, ask that You accept this sacrifice in Your name," the Talking Lady said. "Let their blood feed the ground, providing the nourishment to keep the Wheel of Life turning. Grant us a good Festival, Dearest Lady, that we might honor You and You might bless us with abundant harvests into the next year and beyond. We ask for this in Your name, Almighty *Signora*, let it be so."

"Let it be so," the other Ladies said.

"Wait, wait, wait, wait," Morro said, while Miguel and Fleece cried out and flailed against their bonds their wrists chafing and bleeding from their straining against their bonds.

The Lady turned away from the idol and drew the long, curved knife from her belt. The blade looked sharp and well-maintained. Two other Ladies flanked her, and they walked to Miguel, who was gnashing and screaming behind his gag, whipping his head around. The two shrouded Ladies knelt

and picked up the copper bowl and held it out beneath Miguel's chin, out of reach of his twisting head.

A fourth Lady, a big and tall one, clearly a man to Morro's eye, drew a well-worn leather strap and put it around Miguel's forehead, holding him fast. The cords on Miguel's neck swelled as he was held still against his will.

"That's Miguel Mendoza, you freaks," Morro said. "Brother to Carlos Mendoza, the Underboss of *Las Muertes Rojas*. Brother of Santino Mendoza, the *Jefe*. You kill him, and you're declaring war. You do not want war with us. We will burn your farms to the ground. We will murder every last one of you. Our soldiers will come and destroy your little town."

"The Lady is with us," the Talking Lady said. She held up her long knife skyward, the waning light of the day glancing off the blade. "For the Lady."

"For the Lady," the others said, echoing her. The Talking Lady turned her masked gaze to Miguel, meeting his wild eyes with her black and empty ones.

"This is not death for you, but only the passage to another, better life," the Talking Lady said. "Your blood and your body will nourish the Cursed Earth and give new life. For all that lives must one day die."

"All that lives must one day die," the other Ladies said.

"All who live must one day die," the Talking Lady said.

"All who live must one day die," the other Ladies echoed.

"I will avenge you, Miguel," Morro said, yelling. He did not think much of Miguel, and never had, but in that horrible moment, he felt kinship with the lesser Mendoza. He felt the brotherly bond of the *Rojas* more than he ever had and cried out even as the Lady slit Miguel's throat, his blood draining into the copper bowl as Miguel thrashed and quickly stilled. The Tall Lady removed the strap from Miguel's head and his head lolled forward as his blood gushed into the bowl as his heart mindlessly pumped its last beats.

The Talking Lady walked to Fleece, who was shrieking behind his gag and using every bit of his strength to try to free himself, to no avail.

"Fleece is my baby brother," Morro said. "You monsters. Take me instead. Please, not him!"

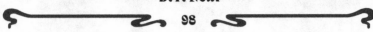
"We're taking you already, Infidel," the Talking Lady said. "You're already an offering. You have nothing more to offer us than your blood, your body, and your soul."

"Fleece!" Morro screamed. "*Hermanito!* I'm so sorry, Tuco."

The Talking Lady repeated her rituals with Fleece, while Morro burned every bit of his strength to try to free himself, but the metal bonds were too strong, only cut into his wrists, making them bleed.

The wooden posts that held them were clearly purpose-built for this bloody work. Probably by mad Quakers, Morro thought bitterly. The workmanship was superb, and their sturdiness was undeniable. In his wild-eyed desperation, Morro could see that someone had carved scenes in the wood—scenes of merry mushrooms cavorting riotously along the otherwise smooth wood.

In his terror, he saw the dancing mushrooms gleefully weaving patterns on the wood, dancing around people tied to poles, while the Lady looked on, arms out, beneath the light of the moon or the sun, he could not tell.

Fleece's eyes flicked to Morro's before he was obscured by the grey-cloaked Ladies who held the silver bowl beneath his chin. The Strapman, as Morro thought of the Tall Lady, again applied the strap, and again the Talking Lady went through her ritualistic oration, while Morro threw his pride aside and began to scream loud and long.

The other Ladies—the ones with the copper bowl—carefully and solemnly walked to the idol of *La Signora* and laid the bowl at its feet, the red of the steaming blood contrasting with the white of the puffball mushrooms and the grey-green of the mossy stone, and the blue-capped mushrooms clustered about the place, like mute witnesses.

"Go from this life into the one we have prepared for you, Little Brother," the Lady said. "Your blood and your body will nourish the Cursed Earth and give new life. For all that lives must one day die."

"All that lives must one day die," the other Ladies said, as they had before.

"All who live must one day die," the Lady said again.

"All who live must one day die," the other Ladies echoed, again.

"*¡Ustedes, los maníacos de los hongos, se arrepentirán de esto!*" Morro yelled out in Spanish instinctively, before switching back to English. "We will be avenged!"

The Talking Lady slit Fleece's throat with as steady and practiced hand as she'd slain Miguel, and Morro cried the first tears he'd shed since he was a boy, when their beloved family dog Honcho had died in their neighborhood after being hit by a car. It was an absurd sort of memory that flowed like Fleece's blood, but there it was, that well of pain hitting him as he saw his brother's blood gush into the silver bowl, saw his muffled screaming cease, saw his struggles end.

How horrible it was to be a sacrifice, Morro thought.

To be so helpless, so caught up in something greater than oneself. Seeing Fleece's head tip forward, his black curly hair soaked in his own blood, the heathens filling their silver bowl with stolen blood, the rage rose in Morro again. Somehow, he felt righteous in that moment.

"We are the Red Death," Morro snarled at the Ladies who approached him. "You will all pay for this day with your lives. I curse you all to die at the hand of *Las Muertes Rojas*. We will throw down *La Signora Grigia* and raze your town. You will all die, and you will all burn. I go to God Almighty or the Devil with a clear heart."

Morro spat at the ground as the Talking Lady approached, and the Tall Lady, the Strapman, hovering nearby, holding the smooth, well-used leather strap in his hand.

"Do you need the strap, or will you face your end like a man?" the Talking Lady asked.

"Do your worst," Morro said. He was not going to give them the satisfaction of groveling or pleading for his life. Not after what they did to his brother. He watched the shrouded Ladies walk the silver bowl to sit beside the copper one, paying their respects to their Grey Lady.

"All who live must one day die, Infidel," the Talking Lady said. He saw that she cleaned off the knife after each sacrifice, taking a white cloth and wiping it of blood. Why she even bothered was something only she knew.

"We will be avenged," Morro said. "*¡La Muerte Roja vive para la venganza—los maldigo a todos!*"

The Talking Lady cocked her head, holding out the long, curved knife in front of her, so that Morro could see his reflec-

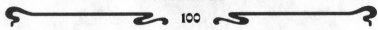
tion in it. His eyes looked animal-wild, the sweat running down his brow. Despite his courage and rage, he was deathly afraid.

Morro tore his gaze away from his reflection and stared hard at the Talking Lady, then turned his eyes to the blue sky, far overhead, to wherever God or the Devil might be, hoping they were listening. As a bad man, he had no hope for God's grace, but prayed that at least the Devil might be there for him.

His answer came in Spanish, from the Talking Lady.

*"La Señora convierte tu maldición en un beso de muerte,"* the Talking Lady said. "Be still and feed the ground with your blood, body, and soul, Infidel. With this sacrifice, our Festival will be blessed, indeed! For the Lady!"

"For the Lady!" the others said. The drummers beat their tiny drums, sounding a rhythm like a heartbeat that Morro thought was picked up by the wind that blew through the bare trees, along with the sound of the bells that dangled from their deathly shrouds.

When the cut came, it came clean, and Morro died without another word, his blood flowing into the golden bowl in a torrent. As his vision blurred to black, he could see that same everlasting sky reflected in his own blood.

# PART TWO:
# NEARLY THERE

# 1

Emily and Ash had managed to finish their canvassing without earning the ire of Sheriff Leonard, meeting up in front of the Temple of the Lady on the intersection of Templeton Lane and First Street, which, aside from being unaffiliated with any other established religion, looked as toweringly unassuming as a cathedral, mosque, or synagogue.

In front of it was a fluorescent-lit sign that said "The Lady welcomes all Festivalgoers! Lynchburg's worth the trip!" in white letters on a black felt display board.

It had started to rain, one of those soft Pennsylvania rains that often fell, and the two of them made their way up the approach to the Temple of the Lady.

The temple was well-built and classically square, looking to be three stories tall and pillared. Upon the flat roof was a columned tower and the hint of a dome. The place was the color of natural stone, and the main door to the temple looked to be heavy and made of bronze that had been emblazoned with mushroom patterns.

"Weird to think the Freemasons were out here," Ash said. "Like of all the places to set up a lodge, they came to Lynchburg."

"Yeah," Emily said. "Weird. Masons are always weird."

Ash laughed at that, nodding.

In the shadow of the columns at the entry, Emily and Ash felt small, but perhaps that was by design. Over the door was the face of the Grey Lady (Emily presumed), scowling beautifully down on them.

"Do we just go in?" Ash asked.

"Sure, why not?" Emily said. "It says it's open."

Ash smiled nervously at Emily.

"After you," she said.

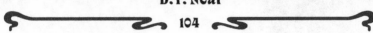
"Alright," Emily said. She would have preferred to be anywhere but the Temple of the Grey Lady. However, part of being who she was involved rolling with what was presented by circumstance. She tugged on the heavy metal door, which slid outward smoothly on its well-oiled hinges, revealing a grand tiled lobby of black and white.

A young woman in a black dress walked up, her blond hair back in a smooth ponytail. She smiled widely at Emily and Ash, hands folded in front of her. Emily could see her fingernails were painted a lacquered grey, and her wide-mouthed smile was as welcoming as her grey eyes. She had a blue and white enamel mushroom brooch pinned to her dress.

"Hello, welcome to the First Temple of the Lady," the young woman said. "I'm Clea."

"Hi, Clea," Emily said. "Are you, what, a priestess of the temple?"

Clea smiled sweetly at Emily.

"If only," Clea said. "No, I'm merely one of the tour guides."

"What religion is this place affiliated with?" Ash asked.

"Affiliated?" Clea asked, wrinkling her lovely brow a moment. "Why, we're not affiliated with anyone. The Temple of the Lady is independent of any other religious tradition."

"Ah," Ash said.

"It's a lovely building," Emily said, which put Clea on surer footing. She broke into her clearly well-rehearsed tour guide routine.

"Yes, it's very special," Clea said. "It was made by the Freemason architect, Lincoln Turner Lee, opening in 1899. He was of a mind that the world was going to end. It served ten years as a Freemason lodge, before being sold to Ned Templeton in 1909. The Templeton Family has worked to lovingly preserve the Temple in their own way, honoring *La Signora Grigia* throughout it while retaining the architectural excellence for which the Freemasons are renowned throughout the world."

Clea gestured for them to follow. The lobby was lovely beyond the black and white checked tiles. There was a vaulted ceiling overhead that was painted with a scene of the night's star-filled sky. There were flanking stairs of white stone, as well as a main concourse that led to a pair of strong-looking polished wooden doors.

Emily could see mushroom motifs throughout the place—gold-painted mushrooms flecking the blue-painted walls, carved mushrooms on the doors. Little mushroom patterns on the wainscotting. Everywhere in the little details.

"Does the Temple hold religious services?" Emily asked.

"We sure do," Clea said.

"What do those services entail?" Ash asked, following Emily's lead.

Clea led them to the far side of the lobby, where they could see pastoral paintings of the Pennsylvania forests on the walls, as well as paintings of groves and glades. *La Signora* was evident in the paintings as well, always a spectral presence in shimmering grey, robed, her cold countenance apparent, whether shrouded or not, always wearing her conical hat.

"*La Signora* teaches us the cyclical nature of life," Clea said. "The inevitability of death, and the finding of joy in being a part of the dance of decay occurring between life and death."

"That's morbid," Emily said.

"It's life," Clea said. "Entropy, yes?"

"I suppose," Emily said. Clea held onto her smile.

"Is there a priest here or what?" Ash asked. "Who's in charge?"

"The Temple of the Lady only has priestesses," Clea said.

"And is there a High Priestess around?" Ash asked.

Clea's smile didn't waver an iota.

"She's otherwise occupied," Clea said.

"Who is she?" Ash asked.

"That would be Mona Templeton," Clea said. "Short for Desdemona."

Emily glanced at Ash, who smirked at her.

"Desdemona," Emily said. "An ill-omened name."

"A real mouthful—Desdemona Templeton," Ash said, snickering.

Clea glanced at both of them and held her tongue.

"It's why she tends to go by Mona. Prefers it, even."

"So many Templetons," Ash said, as Clea opened the doors to the main temple chamber, throwing them open with vigor.

"The Templetons made Lynchburg what it is today," Clea said. "We are all very fortunate to have them. This is the Grand Hall of the Temple. It has the capacity to seat a thousand souls."

"Interestingly put," Emily said.

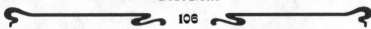
"Six hundred in the lower gallery, and four hundred in the upper," Clea said, pointing.

The Grand Hall was indeed impressive, being a great round auditorium that had two levels of seating arranged in twinned semicircles with gold-upholstered chairs and purple carpeting. In the center of the room, at the focal point, was a great statue—Emily considered it more of an idol—of *La Signora Grigia*, looking grand in the room upon a dais. She stood in robes and held her arms out, her blankly beautiful face betraying nothing, even as she gazed down on them. In here, unlike the little idols she'd seen elsewhere, *La Signora* wore no hat—instead, her hair could be seen, looking like some sort of sculpted promontory of scalloped fungi that rose upward off her neck in a regal-seeming hairstyle.

Behind her, on the wall, hung a great banner of black and gold that held a sea of gold and silver stars upon it, surrounding three interlocking golden circles.

Overhead was a beautiful dome that Emily could see allowed a look into the sky through little rectangular panes of glass. The dome resembled the underside of a mushroom cap, with the supporting silvery arches of it appearing like fungus gills.

"The Temple Dome is one of the largest and loveliest in the world, rivaling the Tiffany Dome in Chicago," Clea said. "It contains 15,000 individual glass panes and has nearly 700 square feet of mosaics representing the Lady. You can see a host of arcane, occult, and alchemical symbols at the apex of the dome. We're very proud to have it."

"Pretty. Breathtaking, even," Emily said.

Emily thought the Grand Hall was very lovely, but wondered what the locals did in this place, what kind of services were held here. It was clearly designed to comfortably accommodate a lot of people. She couldn't imagine what those assembled people might do in a place such as this.

"What does the High Priestess do?" Emily asked.

"She guides us," Clea said. "She's a vessel of the Lady—the Lady speaks through her."

"What does she say?" Ash asked. Clea seemed perplexed by that.

"She invokes the Lady," Clea said.

"Are there other faiths in Lynchburg?" Emily asked.

"Oh, I'm sure there are," Clea said. "But only the Temple in town. Like no cathedrals or other buildings, if that's what you mean. We're a pretty small town. There were troubles in the late 19th century and early 20th century between Lynchburg locals and Protestants and Catholics. But those were sorted out around World War I, to be honest. Way before my time."

Clea laughed self-consciously a moment.

"Way before ours, too," Emily said.

"Say, you should attend one of our services," Clea said. "I think you'd like them. It's easier to experience them than explain them."

"Yeah, how does that go?" Ash asked.

"Well," Clea said. "There's an invocation, and then we drink the Lady's Tears. Then we celebrate Her through dance."

"The Lady's Tears?" Ash asked, eyeing Emily. "What're those?"

Clea pointed to one of the mosaics on the walls, showing the Grey Lady weeping into a chalice held by grey-robed priestesses.

"Yeah? And?" Ash asked.

"The Lady weeps for the world," Clea said. "And in Her weeping, She heals us all. Her tears take away our pain. There's a service tonight at sunset. You should come. All are welcome."

Emily walked up to the idol, which seemed to preside over them. Ash joined her, with Clea close on her heels. She could see there was a set of blue doors behind the idol, beneath the big banner. The blue doors were carved with mushroom shapes, and had the three interlocking circles painted on them in silver.

"She looks so serious," Emily said. "What are your celebrations like?"

"Joyful," Clea said. "It's impossible to be sad in the Temple. *La Signora* soaks up our sorrow and gives us joy in return—pure, unbridled joy that is Hers and Hers alone to give."

Emily had some suspicions about what the Lady's Tears might be.

"Can we see the Lady's Tears?" Emily asked.

Clea shook her head. "Not part of the tour. But if you attend our Sunset Service, you can have some. We give some to the congregants."

"What's behind those doors?" Emily asked.

Clea looked at the blue doors and at Emily and Ash, her smile tightening across her face.

"That's the Round Room," Clea said. "Only the Priestess has access to it."

Emily glanced at Ash, who shrugged.

"It's a sacred shrine," Clea said. "Off-limits to nonbelievers, unfortunately."

"Okay, thanks," Emily said, not wanting to push the issue. "What else can we see around here?"

Clea guided them out of the Grand Hall, back into the lobby, and pointed out the stairs.

"As this was formerly a Mason lodge, as I said, there are smaller lodge rooms upstairs, each one themed. The Templetons retained some of them. They're all very lovely. There's the Gothic Lodge, the Regency Lodge, the Colonial Lodge, and the Lady's Lodge."

"Lodges within lodges," Ash said.

"Would you liked to see them?" Clea asked.

"Sure," Emily said. "You're not the only person here, I hope."

"Oh, no," Clea said. "I'm only one tour guide among several. There are plenty of people in the Temple all the time. There's always so much to do."

"Like what?" Ash asked.

"For one thing, maintaining a building of this size requires a lot of effort," Clea said. "Plus, we do a lot for the community. There are always charity events and the like we have to attend. The High Priestess is very civic-minded. We're all very proud of Lynchburg."

Emily hadn't seen another soul, wondered where they might be. The quiet of the place was calming and disquieting at the same time. Moving upstairs, the beauty of the temple continued to impress her, with ornate and well-maintained architectural mushroom motifs throughout it.

The seamless and ornate blend of stone, wood, giltwork and wainscotting was dazzling to behold, with certain colors evident throughout, always tastefully rendered—blues, whites, browns, reds, greens, purples and golds in particular. The Templetons had clearly spent a lot of money on the place.

At the top of the stairs, Emily could see a hanging chandelier that gave off a warm light, and a red carpet that went either way.

"The upper galleries are on either side," Clea said. "During the Festival, it gets very crowded. Obviously, you can do as you like, but if you want to see a more typical service, tonight would be the night to attend. Over the weekend, it'll get packed tight with tourists. We hold services several times during Festival weekend."

"That sounds exhausting," Emily said. Clea nodded, letting out an exhausted sigh.

"It really is," she said. "Three services takes about twelve hours. You can blow a whole day during them."

"Twelve hours?" Ash asked. "Jesus."

"Yes," Clea said. "They are, as I said, celebrations. They're very cathartic. But for the acolytes and deacons, they're a lot of work."

"Acolytes," Ash said. "Say, you wouldn't know of one named Melinda Dunn, would you?"

Ash thought it was worth a shot.

"Melinda?" Clea said. "You know Melinda?"

Ash glanced at Emily.

"I do," Ash said. "Is she around?"

Clea laughed.

"Somewhere, I'm sure."

"I'd love to meet up with her," Ash said.

"She'll probably be at the service tonight," Clea said. "Most of us try to make that service before the Festival."

"That'd be great," Ash said. "Does she have a phone? I'd love to call her."

"Uh, yes, I imagine, but I don't have her number handy," Clea said. "Why don't you give me your number? I can make sure she gets it."

Emily gave her phone number before Ash could give hers, exchanging a look with her to communicate that she wanted to do this, wanted Ash to hold back.

"Tell her Emily wants to say 'hi'," Emily said. "Dr. Emily Carver."

"Got it," Clea said, looking at Ash, who was simply looking on. "Will do, Dr. Carver."

"Tell you what, Clea," Ash said. "I think we can take a literal rain check on those little lodge rooms. Maybe we'll catch them over the Festival weekend. Em and I have to get a bite to eat if we're going to make the Sunset Service."

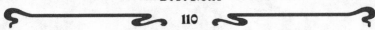
Clea took that in with a sugary smile replacing the more cautious one she had earlier.

"Of course," Clea said. "Yeah, I would definitely recommend you get something in you before you have any Lady's Tears. You never want to drink Lady's Tears on an empty stomach."

"And why is that?" Ash asked.

"It's just not good," Clea said. "So sorry you won't be taking the rest of the tour with me. It was really nice meeting you both. Emily and what did you say your name was?"

"Ashley," Ash said.

"Very nice to meet you both," Clea said. "I really hope you can make the Sunset Service. It'll impress you, I promise. The Lady never disappoints."

"I'll bet," Ash said. "C'mon, Em, let's go get some dinner."

They went to Bentley's House of Chops on Templeton Lane, a half-block away from the Temple, Ash barely able to contain herself as she ordered a pork chop and mashed potatoes and peas, while Emily ordered some cream of mushroom soup and a roasted garlic appetizer.

"She's here," Ash said. "Goddammit, Emily, she's here. Do you think that mannequin at the Temple had any clue?"

"I don't know," Emily said. "Hard to tell, to be honest. I hate to break this to you, Ash, but your sister joined a cult."

"Yeah, she did," Ash said. "For damned sure she did. I mean, what the hell? An acolyte?"

Emily didn't know what one did with cultists, like how one might go about deprogramming them. It wasn't something she signed on for. Whatever was going on with Melinda, she had severed all contact with her family and was apparently living her new life in Lynchburg somewhere.

"What are you going to do?" Emily asked.

"I'm going to confront her, that's for sure," Ash said. She'd already called her parents to tell them what she'd uncovered. They had been ecstatic and they were worried for Ash, despite her reassurances.

"What do you think happened?" Emily asked.

"Not a clue," Ash said. "I suppose I'm just really glad she's not dead."

"Not to be a dick, but I'm not doing some cult deprogramming evacuation with you," Emily said. "I mean, I'll go with you back to the Temple, but if you're planning something drastic, don't count on me for that. Marquis wants us to be discreet. "And two women conspiring to kidnap a third from a small town Pennsylvania cult? That headline practically writes itself."

Ash laughed at Emily. Marquis had been so discreet as to be all but invisible since he'd come to town. She wondered what he might be up to, but then thought maybe she didn't want to know. He would be in touch with them when he was ready.

"Don't worry," Ash said. "I wouldn't do that to you. But I have to know—why'd you give Clea your number?"

Ash thought about it a moment before answering her own question.

"To not tip off Melinda," Ash said. "Right?"

"Yeah," Emily said. "Just in case."

"Melinda's smart," Ash said. "If Clea even says my name, she's going to know it's me. But I appreciate you going on the mat for me that way, for even thinking of that."

"Least I could do," Emily said. She didn't envy what Ash might have to unpack with her sister. She was morbidly curious what might make her sister jettison whatever life she had and join the strange Temple of the Lady.

All of that was curious to Emily. She was used to small towns being pretty churchy, but always along mainstream denominations. Whatever was going on in Lynchburg was decidedly far off from the mainstream. How that had evolved was anyone's guess. She assumed the remoteness of the town likely played a part in it, but she also wondered what happened to the other faiths in the area, the troubles referred to by the otherwise innocent-seeming Clea. Towns like this still took their churching pretty seriously. That the cult had commandeered the religious life of Lynchburg was unusual.

Everything about Lynchburg was strange. The town seemed ludicrously quaint, even welcoming. But there were the unusual undercurrents in the form of the Grey Lady. The mushroom business she could understand. There were plenty of company towns throughout America, companies who were run by influential families and might have one industry.

With Lynchburg, however, despite being a farming town, there was a determined effort for it to be as accessible as possible to outsiders. That was part of the strangeness. Emily could appreciate insularity and even understand. But accessibility? Not so much. Not here. Not in a place that seemed to worship some strange pagan goddess.

"Tell me about that sheriff's deputy you were flirting with," Ash said.

"I wasn't flirting," Emily said. "Not really. Maybe a little."

"Yeah? And?" Ash asked.

"He seemed like a nice guy," Emily said. "He kinda warned me about a group called the 'Grey Ladies'—said I should be careful around them."

Ash laughed into her drink, an iced tea.

"Sounds like a sewing circle or something," Ash said.

"I don't think so," Emily said. "Not the way he put it. He just said if I ran into them, I should run away or something."

"Okay, that's cryptic," Ash said. "Do you think he's part of the cult?"

"You know, I don't think so," Emily said. She was uneasy talking about them in the open this way. Even at a bustling place like Bentley's, she felt exposed. "It's just a vibe I get. I feel like I can spot the people who've, you know, drunk the Kool-Aid."

Ash laughed at that.

"Speaking of that, what the hell with the Lady's Tears? I mean, are we really going to sit in on that Sunset Service?" Ash asked. "What if they make *us* drink the Kool-Aid?"

Emily was wondering about that herself. Part of her was curious about it, the other part, wary. She had tried hallucinogens back in college and had found them interesting and even revelatory in a way. Part of her interest in fungi revolved around her appreciation of their biochemical potency. With around 200 species of psychedelic mushroom out there, she felt there was still plenty of research ground to cover.

"I feel like if they were planning some kind of ambush, they'd not have the Temple be so, I don't know, open?" Emily said. "I brought some sample bottles we can use."

Ash leaned forward, spearing peas with her fork in a tidy sequence.

"Maybe *that's* the trap," Ash said. "Maybe the openness is part of it."

"Or maybe they're so chill because they really are harmless," Emily said. "That's not out of the realm of possibility. Nothing around here has made me think we're in actual danger."

Ash's smile faded, and she pried off the peas from her fork one at a time.

"They took my sister," Ash said. "That's not benign, no matter how you slice it."

"You know, there's also the possibility—maybe even the probability—that your sister simply joined them. That your sister is happy here," Emily said. "Just playing devil's advocate."

"Yeah," Ash said. "Maybe. Melinda was always a seeker. Maybe she found something here she couldn't get anywhere else. If she's legitimately happy, I can respect that, I guess. However, her just cutting off our family? Not cool. That's wrong. And that makes me think something's wrong about it all."

Emily still wanted to get to Nightcap. She hoped they were open over the weekend. Or, if the Festival really was such a big deal, maybe most people would be at it, and she might be able to poke around the place herself. She texted Marquis about it, cc'ing Ash.

*Have you gotten to the Nightcap?*

His reply came quickly.

*Yes. Big farm. Nothing jumped out at me, but I was only on the tour, scoping it out.*

*We're going to the Temple tonight.*

*Be careful.*

*Plan to. Are we in danger?*

*I just said be careful.*

"I don't trust anyone around here," Ash said. "I don't trust Marquis, either."

"Trust your instincts, I guess," Emily said. "What do you say we get some dessert and then trek over for the Sunset Service, see what all this is about?"

# 2

**Logan had found the day exhausting in the best sort of** way. Maura had taken him on the tour of the Nightcap Mushroom Farm and it had impressed the hell out of him. The farm was like an agricultural generator, pumping out product on a nearly industrial scale. He mulled over that as Maura drove them back into Lynchburg, which Logan was sure was starting to swell with tourists and Festival attendees.

The workers—overwhelmingly Latin to his eye—presided over long rows of white mushrooms that crowded the long rooms.

"What's your main crop of mushroom at Nightcap?" Logan asked.

"We have all types," Maura said. "The three dominant cultivars of smooth white, off-white, and brown. Buttons, creminis, portobellos, shiitakes, oysters, maitakes, beeches, enokis, pom poms. They're all here. Also we have special areas for porcinis and morels."

"It's impressive," Logan said. "Really impressive."

Maura accepted that praise with a knowing smile while keeping her eye on the lone country road flanked by massive oak trees.

"We're very proud of the work we've done here. It's taken a long time. It's hard to believe it was once a family farm a couple of generations ago."

"It's way more than a farm," Logan said. "It's, I don't know what it is. An empire."

"Empires are good," Maura said. "Fungi are hugely important in the life cycle of the world. As decomposers, they break down dead things and recycle their nutrients. Do you know what the Robigalia is?"

"Uh, no," Logan said.

"It was a Roman celebration to honor Robigus, the Roman God of Rust," Maura said. "The Romans were so terrified of wheat rust that they created Robigus to try to deal with it. The Robigalia was a festival on April 25, and they'd do animal sacrifices—dogs, specifically—to try to stave off the rust. They'd also have games and races, and would honor Mars, as well. The color red was very big with it, as a nod to the rust."

"Those Romans, I tellya," Logan said. "Always sacrificing something."

"Sacrifices are important," Maura said. "Our gifts to the gods. Letting them know we're thinking about them."

Logan glanced at Maura, who treated him to a smiling side eye as she drove.

"Do you celebrate Robigalia in Lynchburg?" Logan asked.

"Of course. This is the Rust Belt, after all," Maura said, smiling at her own quip. "Not the same rust, of course, but you know what I mean. The Robigalia's not as important as our Fungus Festival. That's the real show."

"The Lady," Logan said. "What's that all about, anyway?"

"She protects us," Maura said. "Keeps the mushrooms growing. Keeps us happy."

"What about, you know, God?" Logan asked. Maura laughed, actually glancing at him a moment.

"What about God?" Maura asked. "We have our own god, and She takes good care of us. Like for real. Not pretend."

The trees whooshed by, and Logan couldn't stop thinking about that. It had been a great day, and he knew bringing up religion was a surefire way to ruin it, but the Philadelphia boy that he was required him to at least talk about it with Maura.

"I mean, how'd that even happen? *La Signora* and all of that?" Logan asked. "This isn't some isolated European island; this is Pennsylvania."

Maura laughed a moment, gripping the wheel.

"You'd be surprised what goes on out here," Maura said. "We're in hilljack country out here, Logan. Or haven't you noticed?"

Logan was a proud city guy. The mean streets of Philadelphia made their own kind of sense to him, were a wilderness unto themselves.

"I don't know," Logan said. "I guess."

"You want me to give you a brief history of the Grey Lady, Logan?" Maura asked. "Come on, now. Haven't I talked enough for you today?"

"I'm just saying," Logan said. "You can't have your whole mushroom goddess shrines and Fungus Festivals and not expect a few questions from the curious."

Maura chuckled at that.

"Okay, that's a fair point," she said. "Mushroom farming is hard work. It's endless work. They're good crops, but it's so much work, like all farming and tending of the spawn. Workers needed something—someone to be there for them. Back in the day, early in the founding of Lynchburg, there was a heavy Italian population. Italians and Quakers. Weird blend, right? My great-great grandmother, Lucretia Bianchi, brought *La Signora* with her. Some said she was a witch. My great-great grandfather, Ned, owned a successful apothecary business. They built the mushroom farm out in the middle of nowhere, in Lynchburg. The Grey Lady helped them out. Built the first shrine out in the woods, where nobody knew. And from there, it grew."

They reached the outskirts of town, which was packed with people and cars. Everyone was wandering about, walking the streets with umbrellas in the light rain, the cars clogging the streets as people slowed down to drive more carefully.

"Can't imagine the Quakers were down with that," Logan said.

"They weren't," Maura said. "It's why they're no longer involved in the work we do at Nightcap. It's also why you can't really find Quakers around here anymore."

"That certainly sounds menacing," Logan said.

"Does it?" Maura asked. "My family made a lot of sacrifices to get where it is today. The Grey Lady helped us in those times of sacrifice."

"Okay," Logan said. He could only imagine what that actually meant, but Maura delivered it with a calm and cool demeanor. "So how did the Latinx population get way out here?"

"People go where the work is," Maura said. "For most of them, they liked the fact that mushroom farming is stable, steady work, and you don't have to travel with it. It stays right in one place. It's a lot of work, but families could put down roots here, and they did. The populations grew here in the 20th century. *La Signora* protected them and their families. They all

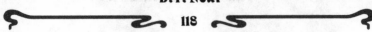

have their own little shrines to Her in their homes. They worked for us. She works for us. We work for them. It all works."

She managed to get them behind the Grand Hotel, to the parking deck on Sycamore Lane, which ran parallel to Grand Avenue.

"Thanks for an interesting day," Logan said. "You want to come with me? Maybe get, you know, a nightcap?"

He was proud of his wordplay, but Maura just smiled and shook her head.

"No, I can't," Maura said. "I've got to drop by the Shroom Room and terrorize my minions. But this was fun, Logan. How about you give me a call tomorrow and we can get together?"

"Sure," Logan said. "Absolutely."

"Great," Maura said. She leaned over and gave him a kiss on his cheek. He tipped his head and kissed her back on the lips. She smiled and looked in his eyes a moment. "You're one smooth operator, Logan."

"That's me," Logan said. A car behind them honked at them. "Alright, I'm out of here."

"See you soon," Maura said, as he got out. Logan shot a glare at the car behind them, which was just a Honda with New York license plates with some aggrieved mushroom tourists gesturing at him. Logan flipped them off and went strolling into the Grand Hotel, glancing back at Maura, who was laughing as she drove off.

## 3

**Mallory had talked them into hitting the Temple of** *La Signora Grigia* after they'd all downed doses of the *Cubensis* shrooms in the tidy cubes Cappy had provided them. It hadn't taken much persuading, despite the rain that was falling, and Cloris, the Grand Hotel concierge, had lent them blue mushroom umbrellas they could take across town.

"Just please make sure to bring them back," Cloris had said as they were leaving. "Or we'll have to charge you for them."

With the rain and clouds, the sunset was largely obscured, and they just made their way on the quickish walk down Grand Avenue and taking a right on Templeton Lane, Jess convinced that she was already tripping from the shrooms, talking about the way the neon and lights and lanterns were reflected on the rain-soaked brick road.

They had all loaded the Fungo App from a QR code displayed in the lobby that had Mushy winking at them—"Have more FUN with Fungo!" Mushy said in a dialogue balloon.

The Fungo App offered them an interactive Festival map as well as a map of downtown Lynchburg. There were also icons that offered them deals at all of the taverns, bars, restaurants, and other businesses in town in the form of Fungible tokens. Jess in particular was fixated on the Fungible tokens, kept selecting arcane formulations in order to garner the best bargains.

"It doesn't kick in that fast, Jess," Austin said, scoffing. "For all we know, Cappy Dick gave us some dried buttons or something."

"He's legit, Austin," Mallory said. "You're so mean, I swear."

"I swear I'm tripping," Jake said. "I'm seeing things, guys."

"Too soon," Austin said. "Not for another twenty minutes by my estimation."

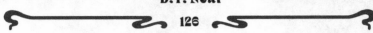
Heading down Templeton Lane, with Jess needlessly narrating as she followed the map on the Fungo App, they could see the Temple at the end of the street, like maybe three football fields away, illuminated from within.

Even from this distance, it looked beautiful, with narrow, vertical stained glass windows catching the light within and casting it outward, and the columned tower on the roof of the place illuminated by some spotlights that had come on when it had gotten dark. And there was the lustrous dome of the Temple, too, which was lovely and well-lit as well.

"I'm feeling it," Jess said. "I can see through my hand, I swear to god."

Jess held up her hand and stared at each of them through it, like her hand was a magnifying glass and she was the master sleuth.

Austin laughed, swatting at her, while Mallory hooked his arm and guided him in the direction of the Temple every time he swayed out into the street.

"You guys are going to love this," Mallory said. "I mean, it's crazy as fuck."

"That's pretty crazy," Austin said.

There were large groups of people showing up to the Temple, which didn't have a churchbell, but as they were nearing it, Austin was sure he could hear someone playing drums. Jess pointed to the roof of the Temple, and they could see there were some robed drummers standing there, banging away at some big drums.

"They're like Taiko drums," Jess said, grateful that she was wearing her conical hat, which was acting as an umbrella. "I've heard those."

The drums did sound like distant thunder, Austin thought, could see the drummers clubbing away at them.

"Why drums?" Austin asked.

"Drums are cool," Jake said, batting his shoulder with a knuckle. "That's why."

"Drums symbolize the beating heart of the world," Mallory said in a dreamy tone, which made Austin and Jake break out in giggles as they got in line. "It's true, you ingrates!"

There were brown-robed deacons ahead, using clickers to count people as they made their way in. They were young peo-

ple like they were but looked very serious in their robes and conical hats.

"Fun fact," Austin said. "The more orthodox and extreme a faith, the weirder the hats. It's a barometer for their religious extremism."

"Bullshit," Jake said.

"Any time you see crazy hats, you'll see bizarro orthodox people doing crazy shit," Austin said. "The crazier the hat, the more ludicrously orthodox the people wearing them are."

"Based on what?" Jake said.

"My empirical observations," Austin said.

"Oh, right," Jake said, rolling his eyes.

"Their hats aren't that crazy," Mallory said. "They seem practical to me."

"I hope we can get in," Jess said, looking at them solemnly from beneath the cover of her own hat.

"It's got good capacity," Mallory said. "Like a thousand people or something."

"Or something," Austin said. He glanced behind them, saw a long line of people with umbrellas behind them. "I don't know, you guys. Anybody feeling it, yet?"

"I am," Jess said, swaying. "I totally am. Everybody's covered in sparkly moonbeams."

"Lordy," Austin said. He wasn't feeling anything, yet. Just a bit queasy, which was to be expected. They reached the deacons, who clicked them in. He could see they were each wearing a blue glowstick around their necks, which made them look otherworldly and creepily underlit, which struck Austin as funny. He laughed as he saw them and couldn't stop.

"You can go," one of them said, waving them through.

"Glowsticks?" Austin said. "What the hell, man?"

"I love *anything* that glows," Jess said, waving her hand in front of her face. "Jake and I were at Burning Man one year where we saw a dude had made an entire suit out of glowsticks."

"True story," Jake said.

"Must've been heavy," Austin said.

"Oh, it was heavy, alright," Jess said, grinning goofily at Austin. "He was a moving sea of color."

Mallory grabbed Austin's arm, pulling him along.

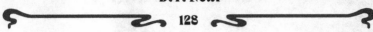

"We should try to get in the lower seating area," Mallory said. "It's better. I mean, the upper deck is nice, but lower is better."

"Upper deck?" Austin said. "What is this, a baseball game?"

"It's a spiritual grand slam, man," Jake said.

They made their way into the lobby of the Temple, which didn't smell like a church to Austin. It didn't have that old musty smell. Rather, it smelled like cloves and cinnamon and patchouli, and he could see some robed acolytes and deacons walking around with their conical hats, swinging lit censers around on golden chains, emitting puffs of sweet-smelling smoke.

Again, the acolytes looked roughly to be Austin's age, their faces beatific as they went about their business.

"Are we allowed to photograph?" Jess asked.

"Yeah, totes," Mallory said.

Jess took out her phone and took a quick selfie with Mallory, mugging for the camera, making "peace" signs and devil horns. She snapped shots of Austin and Jake, too, and then got around to taking pictures of the lovely lobby.

They were shepherded down the hallway toward the big open door that led to the Grand Hall, where people were being guided in by more acolytes and deacons.

"Wow," Jake said. "Look at that statue. It's like Lady Liberty in a bad mood."

"That's THE Lady," Mallory said. *"La Signora."*

Austin could see many of the attendees were maybe Mexican. They were talking to each other animatedly in Spanish, and he couldn't understand a word of it.

*"La Signora,"* Austin said, with added emphasis, taking pictures with his phone.

The Grand Hall looked amazing, and Mallory had been able to work past the robed ushers to get them to some of the lower seats that afforded them a great view of the idol of the Lady and everything else. Jess was transfixed by the dome overhead, and kept taking photographs of it while spinning in circles and laughing until Jake grabbed her and pulled her to her seat.

"That dome is cray," Jess said. "It's like a giant space spiderweb. I'm definitely tripping, you guys."

"Yeah, I'm starting to feel it, too," Jake said.

Austin thought he was, as well, having seen everyone haloed by rainbow colors of light, like he was staring through a prism.

"How much did we take?" Jess asked.

"Like a dose apiece," Austin said. "We have to make it last the weekend."

"Yeah," Jess said. "I love you guys."

She started crying, taking more selfies and showing them what she took with each shot.

"Yeah, that's a keeper, Jess," Austin said. "We probably shouldn't have all dosed. One of us should have stayed clean."

The Grand Hall was illuminated with indirect lighting that threw off a warm ivory glow that played nicely with the hallucinations Austin was starting to have. Each point of light was bursting with a fractal symmetry that made everything look like he was staring at it inside of a kaleidoscope.

"Cappy Dick really came through," Austin said.

"Happy Cappy," Mallory said. "Don't make me say it again, Austin."

"I'm so happy right now," Jess said. Somebody somewhere began playing a synthesizer, as music began to fill the room. Jess gasped, calling out that she could see the music notes that were being played. "They're floating on magic moonbeams, you guys. Each note pops like a soap bubble after it's played. I'm not making this up."

The music wasn't churchlike per se, but was something else, like more exuberant, less stately. There was a lilting wildness to it that made Jess squirm in her chair, and even Austin liked it more than he cared to admit.

"I don't know how they can do this stuff without, I don't know, the Bible Beaters coming down on them," Austin said. "This is positively pagan. I mean, how does that even happen in America? Where are the thoughts and prayers?"

"Please, Austin," Mallory said. "No philosophy or politics, I beg you. Just trip out with us. You'll love it once the light show starts."

"Light show?" Jake asked.

As if on cue, the lights changed from the ivory hue to an otherworldly blue that made Jess cry out, trying to grab at unseen things. Austin could feel the blue, seeing it in layered waves rolling down upon them. The walls began to cry drips of

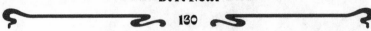
blue. He could see the drips appearing and beginning to run. The blue was luminous.

And then some drums sounded behind them, and they saw a procession of white-robed and hat-wearing acolytes make their way down the central aisle, accompanied by the censer swingers. The movement was mesmerizing, the steps timed with the beat of the drums, which weren't snare drums, but were more like toms, with a molasses-rich tone. Austin saw six drummers, and as they reached the end of the aisle, they fanned out, three to a side in the Grand Hall, each accompanied by a censer swinger.

"Oh ho ho," Jess said, taking pictures and filming. "Yessssss."

"I don't even like church," Jake said. "But this is trippy."

"This isn't church," Austin said watching the brown-robed deacons proceed after the acolytes. There were a half-dozen of them, walking in time to the beating of the drums. They were wearing brown hats and brown, netlike shrouds that concealed their faces. They filed out to both sides of the Grand Hall.

"Creepy," Jake said. "Like creepy."

The blue light went to a more reassuring amber, and a woman went down the main aisle wearing a grey robe with a red stole that was covered in curious glyphs that Austin could not comprehend.

The woman walked to the front of the room, beneath the great dome overhead, and turned her gaze onto the crowd. She was pretty in a strong-featured way, with piercing eyes and a powerful jaw and prominent nose. Her hair was black and only just touched her shoulders. She had dark eyes, and Austin thought she might be surrounded by an aura of purple light, which he blamed on the shrooms they'd already taken.

The woman turned her back to the audience and held her arms up in a Y shape, addressed the idol.

"*Signora*, we are here for You tonight," the woman said. "As the light of the day wanes, we are here for You, to honor Your divine glory with song and dance."

She turned and looked out at all of them, her eyes lit by a sort of holy zeal as she smiled.

"The Lady is with us," the woman said. "I am Mona Templeton, High Priestess of the Temple of the Grey Lady. Welcome, visitors and congregants, the faithful and the curious."

As she spoke, the lights slowly brightened, bringing her features into sharper relief. Her voice was sharp but somehow reassuring.

"The Lady tells us that our lives are brief," Mona said. "And in our short lives, before decay sets in and inevitable death comes upon us, we are to find hope and happiness. How can we find such things? How does one go about that? How does one find happiness with the burden of this knowledge?"

Austin wasn't sure if she was using a microphone, as he was into his trip, and her voice seemed to echo. The Twins were rocking in their seats, and Mallory was leaning forward, fingers steepled against her lips.

"How does one find happiness in the suffering world?" Mona asked. "The Lady understands. She cries for all of your pain. She cries for the pain of life. She cries Her Lady's Tears. And we, Her humblest, most devout servants, accept Her gift with gratitude. And we share it with you tonight."

The acolytes filed out along the rows with silver trays that carried little cups.

"Here comes the Kool-Aid," Austin said, watching them pass the trays along the row. The faithful took the little cups, while tourists alternately took them or passed them on. Austin didn't think Mona and the others cared whether or not people took them, but he couldn't be sure.

He saw the Twins each take one, saw Mallory take one, and decided he should, too. He handed the tray to the pair of women sitting next to him.

The little cup contained a clear blue liquid. He smelled it, thought it smelled nice, although he could not compare it with anything he'd smelled before, beyond a hint of citrus.

He saw the women sitting next to him palm the little cups, and then thought he was seeing things from the shrooms he'd taken—one of the women had circumspectly poured the Lady's Tears into a vial, cupping it in her hands. The other woman handed her cup to her, and again it went into the vial.

"You want my Windex, too?" Austin asked, startling the women.

"What?" one of them said. Austin wasn't sure who had said it.

Austin gestured to his little cup, which was doubling, tripling in his multiplying hands.

"No way am I drinking this."

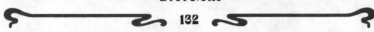
"Sure," the woman said, taking it and handing it to her friend.

"I'm Austin," he said. The woman sitting next to him looked a little older than he was, but not much. She was pretty and blond and blue-eyed, and petite. Austin liked petite women, and she looked fit. He liked that, too. Maybe it was the shrooms, but he liked this woman. Maybe he even loved her. Maybe not at first sight, but at second sight.

"Nice to meet you," the woman said. "You're tripping, aren't you?"

"Yeah," Austin said. "Tripping balls."

"Your eyes look it," she said. "Practically pinwheels."

"What's your name?" Austin asked.

"I'm Ash," she said, and when she said it, her voice echoed and Austin saw starbursts of magenta, teal, and fuchsia flowing around her. The other woman was Black, tall, and had dark brown hair and glasses, had pocketed the vial.

Another tray came by, and Austin saw that his friends had put their empty cups into it. He handed the tray to Ash, who quickly put the emptied cups into it and passed it along.

The lights in the Grand Hall began to change, and Austin wasn't sure whether it was him or them, but the lights swirled and turned colors, began looking like stars that were flowing.

"It's like a planetarium," Austin said. "You see it, Ash?"

The people who had drunk the Lady's Tears were getting out of their seats and dancing, while the drummers were playing and the keyboardist upstairs was playing a song that was driving people into a frenzy. Mona held up a grey mask that looked like the Grey Lady to Austin, and she turned and nodded to the crowd by sections, always with the mask aloft. After seemingly blessing the crowd with it, she brought the mask to her face and put it on. The grey mask was polished shiny, its thin black eyebrows looking sinister, as did the blue lips painted on the thing. With the vestments she was wearing, the mask made her look particularly frightening, and Austin could see her enveloped by a neon-like blue glow. She raised her arms again and blessed the crowd with upraised arms, like she was trying to hug everyone there.

"Austin," Mallory said, pawing at him while she swayed. "Dance with us."

Austin wasn't sure what to do, wanted to keep talking to Ash, but when he looked back for her, he saw that she was gone, like a ghost, like she'd never been there. She and the other woman were gone, and there were only technicolor starbursts where they had been.

"Wow," Austin said, getting up, letting Mallory lead him to the—what was it—dancefloor? He didn't know what else to call it, as people were dancing and crying out in ecstasy.

The floor of the Grand Hall was filling with people cavorting around, whether tourists or locals, outsiders or insiders. Everyone was dancing, and Austin could see Jess and Jake whirling around, Jess gazing up at the dome overhead. He looked up at it, too, and could see the dome spinning and flying off into outer space. He could see the sky overhead, the night's sky. Without a sound, it had flown up and outward, trailing streamers of colorful light as it flew.

High Priestess Mona stood beneath the idol of *La Signora* and watched with arms outstretched and upraised. She was speaking behind her mask, but Austin could only taste her words, not hear her amid all of the music and movement. Her words tasted like nutmeg and cloves and something else he could not define.

*La Signora*, the great idol, leaned down and reached out for Austin, taking him in Her cupped hands, holding him aloft. She moved smoothly, with statuesque grace and inevitability.

"Austin," the Lady said. "I shed My tears for you."

He could see that the idol was weeping, now, beautiful blue tears against her grey face, a young face, a goddess face, but carved from stone.

"Don't cry," Austin said. "Please, don't cry, Lady."

"I cry for you," the Lady said. "For all of you."

And Austin could see from his vantage point in her hands that her tears were falling like rain down on the dancers below, could see the floor filling with the radiant blue of her tears. He could see Mallory and Jess and Jake dancing and splashing in it, then wading, then swimming, then drowning. Everyone in the room was drowning except for him.

"Mallory! Jess! Jake! Ash!" Austin said, crying out, reaching for them.

But they were out of reach in the luminous blue, as he was still in the Lady's hands. Only he was high and dry, gazing into the brightly burning lapis eyes of the goddess.

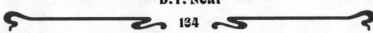

"What do I do, Lady?" Austin asked.

"You dance, you cry, you live, you die," the Lady said. Overhead, the roof blown off of the temple, there was only a lattice of pulsing light, like a ladder to the heavens that contrasted with the sea of tears at the Lady's ankles, while his friends thrashed below.

"I'm sorry," Austin said. "I'm so sorry. Did I make you cry?"

"You all did," the Lady said. "You all do. You always do. Your fleeing lives against My own immortality."

"I'm really high," Austin said.

"I know," the Lady said. "I know, My lost child. I know."

And, weeping, She let Her palms turn and Austin felt himself fall, landing with a great splash into the tears of the Lady, where everyone was still thrashing. He held his breath as he sank to the bottom, the character of the light altering with the rippling cerulean goddess water and the shadows of the bodies above him, their voices muffled in that watery way that matched the light.

Unsure what to do next, Austin swam for it, and didn't stop until he reached the squirming sapphire shore.

# 4

**Carlos Mendoza was beside himself with anger. Miguel,**
Morro, and Fleece had all vanished without a trace. He'd tried
to call them, and nobody had answered their phones. It was like
they'd fallen off the face of the world. He'd sent another of his
men, Santiago, to discreetly investigate in town.

He paced in his living room, unsure what to do. Lilli lurked
nearby.

"Something happened," Carlos said. "Something happened
to them. Just like with Franco and Teo."

"You think?" Lilli said. She was wearing a black track suit
with gold piping up the sides, had her hair up in a provocative
topknot, and wore gold bangle bracelets that danced on her fit-
ful wrists.

"Yes, I do," Carlos said. "None of them would just disappear
like that if something hadn't happened."

He went to one of the cabinets in his place and pulled out a
Glock 20, which he put in his waistband.

"I don't like this," Carlos said. "We should get out of here.
Like now."

"Babe," Lilli said. "And go where? Come on, you can't let
some mushroom farmers scare you off."

Her tone was both solicitous and challenging, and Carlos
took umbrage at it.

"Nobody's 'scaring me off' here," Carlos said. "But two of
my guys dead, three of them missing? That's a problem. Somebody's having a go at me."

He stomped over to the shuttered living room windows and
peered out. Hidden Hollow was as affluently quiet as ever. The
Fungus Festival crap didn't touch Hidden Hollow.

"Maybe we should go into town," Lilli said. "We've been cooped up here too much. Get into town and maybe get some dinner."

Carlos snorted.

"You want to go on a date?" Carlos asked. "I'm being harassed by some *loco* farmers and you want to go on a date?"

Lilli pouted at him.

"I'm only saying that you're getting a little, what, cabin fever, all cooped up in here," Lilli said. "Some fresh air and time in town might help."

"I don't see how," Carlos said. "At least here, I can see when somebody's coming for me. In town, with all the people around? Too much to keep track of."

Lilli walked over and put her arms on his shoulders, leaned her head against his back.

"I don't like seeing you this way, Carlo," Lilli said. "The Grand Hotel holds the penthouse for you. So, let's use that. Let's go to town and just chill out in the penthouse. Room service, you know? We can relax. Like a little vacation. Versus exile out here. It's too quiet out here, anyway."

Carlos pried himself free of her, looked her over. She maybe wasn't wrong, but he wasn't about to admit that she was right.

"Exile, huh?" Carlos said. "It's what it feels like. Here's the thing, though—here, there's private security. In town, there's the damned sheriff and his deputies. I go into town, and I'm vulnerable. I'm exposed."

"But you haven't done anything illegal here," Lilli said. "You're outside of the sheriff's jurisdiction. I mean what you did in Pittsburgh doesn't count here."

What he did in Pittsburgh would take a team of stenographers to document. *Las Rojas* were an active and enterprising gang. And while Carlos had been careful to keep his fingerprints off of most of what went on, RICO statutes still could bring him down if he wasn't careful. Santino had him as *Segundo* to draw the heat.

The whole point of Hidden Hollow was for him to lay low. Maybe it was ill-advised of him to try to lean on the mushroom farmers, but money was money. Every day squirreled away out here was another day when *Las Rojas* weren't taking what was theirs. Earning was everything. He always needed to be mak-

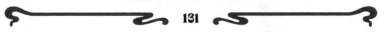
ing more money to help deal with rivals, who were already no doubt taking advantage of his absence from Pittsburgh.

The last straw for Carlos had been a drug deal that had led to the death of some DEA guys who had been trying to set him up. With them dead, the federal agents were casting about looking for him. Carlos had made it look like he'd been headed to Cleveland with a decoy group, while he'd snuck off to Hidden Hollow with three dozen *Rojas*. Maybe they thought he'd try to flee the country, were probably bird-dogging the border, but Carlos thought it was better to hide in the hinterlands. He and Santino had not been in touch, wary of what feds might have in terms of tapped lines.

"No, we should stay out of town," Carlos said. "All I need is some zealous deputy recognizing me and then I'm really in for it."

"You know, it's kind of curious that the farmers haven't done that, don't you think?" Lilli asked. "I mean, they *know* who you are. So, why haven't they turned you in?"

"It's because they don't want the law nosing into their business any more than they want us in it," Carlos said.

"Exactly, Carlo," Lilli said. "You have some leverage there. What if you sent some of your guys to burn the Nightcap farm? I mean, yeah, you wanted to shake them down, but what if you burned it down instead?"

"Yeah," Carlos said. "That'd be satisfying."

Lilli leaned into him, pressing herself against him. He could feel her breasts against his chest, could feel her warmth.

"You're a bad influence on me, Lilli," Carlos said.

"I know," she said, grinning up at him.

Someone rang the doorbell to his place, which had one of his bodyguards, Alejandro, head to the door. Alejandro looked through the peephole.

"Who is it, Alejandro?" Carlos asked.

"It's Santiago," Alejandro said.

"Let him in," Carlos said, holding onto his pistol. Alejandro unbolted the door and Santiago Espinoza entered. He was another of the midlevel *Rojas* members, a contemporary of Franco and Morro, one of the most trusted. He was sternly handsome and had a bald-shaved head and a black goatee beard that earned him the nickname *"El Diablo"* among his peers.

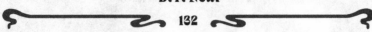
He waited in the foyer while Alejandro secured the door, and then walked up to Carlos, embracing him.

"Carlos," Santiago said. "I come from the town. No sign of Morro, Fleece, or your brother. They're just gone. Nobody's seen anything."

"Alright," Carlos said, waving for Santiago to join him in the living room. Lilli got them all some tequila, setting the glasses down on the coffee table.

"I checked with the security log, too," Santiago said. "Nobody even saw them leave Hidden Hollow."

"What?" Carlos asked.

"You said to check everything," Santiago said. "So I checked everything. The security company keeps closed circuit camera logs of who comes and goes, and they never left. At least not on their own. A van came in and took off at one point."

"A van? What van?"

"Couldn't make out the plates," Santiago said.

"What'd the security guy say?" Carlos asked.

"He said it was a cable van," Santiago said.

"Bullshit it was," Carlos said. "Did you lean on the guy?"

Santiago glanced at Lilli, who was watching, sipping her tequila. He drank his down in one shot.

"No, Carlo," Santiago said. "I didn't have to lean. We've got that guy on our payroll. He said it was a cable guy named Finn Thatcher."

"Doesn't sound like a real name to me," Lilli said.

"He's a local," Santiago said. "A cable guy."

Carlos considered that. Maybe it was a lead. Maybe it was a dead end.

"Here's the thing, Carlo," Santiago said. "I think maybe they're watching us in Hidden Hollow. I think we're under active surveillance."

That made Carlos edgy.

"What makes you think that?" Carlos asked. He took a drink of his own tequila, took no comfort in it.

"Morro, your brother, and Fleece never got out of Hidden Hollow," Santiago said. "At least not on their own. Somebody pounced on them directly. Why? Somebody knew what they were up to, who they were. Somebody was watching. They're probably watching right now."

"You're just speculating," Carlos said.

"I'm saying that the three of them met with you, and then they went to go do their thing," Santiago said. "And somebody got to them before they could leave. The only way that's possible is if your place is being watched."

"We swept the place for bugs when we moved in," Carlos said. "We checked."

"Yeah," Santiago said. "But I think there's a serious neighborhood watch going on. When you got here, somebody found out who you are. Maybe they're using some major geofencing or something like that."

"But we used burner phones," Carlos said. "We were careful. We're always careful."

Santiago poured himself another tequila and drank it down.

"Yeah, Carlo," Santiago said. "But they somehow found out who you are. Maybe when they took Franco and Teo. I mean, you said they had Teo's phone. And who knows what they may have said before they killed them. Somehow, they found out who you are, and they've been watching ever since."

Carlos didn't like that one bit. They'd picked up the properties in Hidden Hollow specifically as a hiding place. That was the whole point of it. That somebody had violated that angered him. A safehouse was supposed to be safe.

"Okay," Carlos said. "But you came and went safely enough. What's up with that, *Diablo?*"

"I don't know," Santiago said. "I'm really careful. Maybe more careful than the others."

"Maybe you're in on it," Lilli said. Santiago laughed at her.

"Lilli, come on, now," Santiago said. "I'm not in on anything. You think I want to side with some townies against Carlo, here? Insane. I'm *Rojas* to my last breath. I swore an oath, and I stick to that."

"You went into town looking for the others, and you don't think you were followed?" Carlos asked.

"I didn't see any tails," Santiago said. "And I was looking. It's busy in town with the Festival beginning. Cars and people everywhere. I mean, somebody could have tailed me and I might not have noticed."

"They let you go to town and come back," Carlos said.

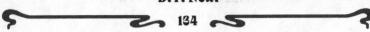
"Maybe because it was just me," Santiago said. "Versus Miguel and the Rodriguez Brothers. Or maybe the place is bugged. Have you swept since you first got in here?"

"No," Carlos said. "Alejandro, get the thing and check for bugs."

"Right, *Segundo*," Alejandro said, stepping to it.

"There's either active surveillance going on, or they just decided to jump Miguel and the others because there was a group of them," Santiago said. "Their dragnet—if you can excuse me calling it that—maybe lets one or two of us go, but if a group goes, it triggers a response."

"I suppose we could test that," Carlos said. "Lilli had the idea that maybe we should burn that mushroom farm. Just to send a message. All that ammonia there? Something ought to explode, right?"

Santiago glanced at Lilli, who smiled at him over the lip of her drinking glass.

"I thought we were going to extort the place," Santiago said. Carlos shrugged.

"That was before they went at us," Carlos said. "Arson provides a certain clarity, if you ask me. Lets them know we're not playing around."

"There's only so much I can do as one man," Santiago said.

"Oh, I know," Carlos said. "But you're *El Diablo*, Santiago. You and fire go way back. I'm only wanting to send a message. You find something at that farm that burns and you burn it. A big fire. Something to get their attention."

Carlos wondered if Santiago knew that he was using him as bait in that moment. If the place was bugged the way Santiago suspected, then whoever was watching the house would likely intercept Santiago before he went on his arson mission. As he saw it, if Santiago disappeared before going on his way, then there was proof that the place was bugged. If he managed to carry out the arson, then that was also useful information.

"Okay, *Segundo*," Santiago said. "I can do that. A big fire. Hell, it's a farm. There's always something you can find to burn on a farm."

"Yeah," Carlos said. "Just use your imagination. Send a message. Make some things burn. And come back and tell us all about it."

Santiago nodded.

"Sounds like a plan," he said.

Alejandro came back with his bug detector, looking pale.

"This place is bugged, *Segundo,*" he said.

# 5

**Emily and Ash hadn't found Melinda before things had** gotten crazy at the Temple. They had, as planned, slipped out with some of the Lady's Tears in the stoppered vial Emily had brought.

"Marquis is going to be happy about this," Emily said as they walked out of the Temple. It had, thankfully, finally stopped raining, and everything smelled pleasantly wet, the almost cinnamon-like scent of rain-soaked fallen autumn leaves.

"I didn't see Melinda," Ash said.

"You can go back there, if you want," Emily said. "But I'm going to deliver this to Marquis."

"Yeah," Ash said. "Alright, although I'm kind of skeeved out to go in there by myself. Didn't realize their services were going to turn into a rave."

"I don't know if people still call them 'raves' these days, Ash," Emily said, laughing.

"You know what I mean," Ash said. "That thing in there. Whatever the hell that was."

"I think you'll be fine to go in there," Emily said. "They're likely all tripping out right now, and you can probably hunt for Melinda without anybody doing more than group-hugging you or thinking you're a pixie or something."

"Hah," Ash said, glancing back at the Temple. From here, the music could be heard, albeit muted, and the lights danced upon the stained glass windows. "Okay, I guess. I'll go back and see if I can find Melinda. What'll you do after you meet up with Marquis?"

"I'd really like to get out to Nightcap and see it for myself," Emily said. "But I'll probably just rest up and wait until morning."

Templeton Lane was buzzing with people heading out to dinner and otherwise walking around. Ash steeled herself to head back to the Temple.

"They do services like this every night? I mean, people trip out in there daily?" Ash asked.

"Seems that way," Emily said. "Or else this is a special show for the tourists. Not sure."

"Weird," Ash said. "Just seems like, I don't know, a lot of work."

Emily smiled at her, shaking her head.

"I don't know," Emily said. "They brew up their Lady's Tears, they play a little music, dose up the congregation, and everybody has a big party. Beats sermons, I guess, if that's your thing. Growing up back home in New Orleans, church was a big old party."

Ash waved a finger at Emily.

"If you join that cult, consider our friendship ended, Em," Ash said.

"Don't worry about me," Emily said. "I'm the kooky mycologist, don't forget. I'm immune to cult indoctrination because of my line of work. We're trippy enough already."

"Jeez," Ash said. "Well, good luck with Marquis. Give him my regards."

"Will do. And you, too," Emily said. "We need all the luck we can get. It's Friday the 13th, after all."

The two hugged and parted, Emily racing off to the Grand Hotel, while Ash was heading back to the Temple.

As Ash walked closer, she could see there were a pair of acolytes at the doors of the Temple watching her approach. They were a young man and a young woman, and they smiled nervously as Ash came up to them.

"Hey," Ash said. "I was just in there. Can I get back in?"

"Of course you can," the young man said, holding open the door for her. The music within surged out, and Ash nodded, making her way back into the Temple.

She wondered why the Temple even had those acolytes posted if they were just simply letting people back in. Or maybe they were spotters or something. She didn't know, and didn't care. She just had to find Melinda.

The music had shifted from the drums and synthesizer music before to something wilder, more potent and powerful,

like throbbing bass and pounding rhythm. People's exclamations and exhortations were floating out while people were cavorting within.

Ash decided it might be better to try the upper galleries, so she could get a look over everything taking place down below.

She made her way up the stairs and passed some more acolytes, young people again, neither of them Melinda. On a whim, she spoke to them, acting like she was tripping.

"Have any of you seen Melinda?" Ash asked.

"We're *all* Melinda here. Even you," one of them, a girl, said, and they shared a laugh.

"Thanks," Ash said, trotting up the stairs to vent her irritation.

The upstairs was as before, except for the music and the noise. She went to the gallery door nearest to her and opened it, awash in the phantasmagoria taking place below. There was a mirror ball sending sparkling motes of light spinning throughout the Grand Hall, and somewhere there were black lights offering the glowing luminosity on the various colors people were wearing.

The upper gallery people were all tripping on the Lady's Tears, laughing and dancing, swaying and catching themselves repeatedly on the railing. Ash could see there were acolytes and deacons tending to them, as well, ensuring nobody hurled themselves over the side. But as she made her way, looking at them in turn, none of them were Melinda.

"Little sister," a tall, white-haired man said, holding his arms out to her. "Dance with me?"

"You *are* the dance," Ash said, an answer which seemed to satisfy the man, as he began laughing and declaring he was the dance to anyone who would listen.

Down below was a throng of people, grooving to the music. Some folks were taking off their clothes, and the acolytes and deacons weren't stopping them. Ash wondered how the authorities handled this, or maybe they were simply part of it.

Mona Templeton was still presiding over it, cutting the air with chops of her hands like she was a conductor. She'd taken off her mask, which hung from her sash, dancing its own odd rhythm as she moved. Mona's grin was infectious, a U-shaped rictus of triumph in the black light, her teeth seeming to glow. Then Ash saw her turn from her perch beneath the idol and head toward that forbidden door, the one the tour guide wouldn't let them access, and she unlocked it and went in.

Ash could only get a glimpse as the door opened, seeing a splash of blue light and then Mona was gone.

"Feed the trees," a young woman said to Ash, tugging at her arm. "We've got to feed the trees. They kiss the sky, but who feeds them? The soil? The stones? Who'll feed the trees?"

"The sun," Ash said, prying herself free from the girl's grasp. "The sun and the sky, the rain."

"The rain. You're right," the girl said, her eyes wide. "You're right as rain."

She hugged Ash, who squirmed her way loose and trotted to the back of the gallery. Melinda had to be here. She could feel it. Her sister was here somewhere.

People were making out in the back, ignoring Ash, groping each other. Ash exited the gallery and went back into the corridor, where she could see the signs over the various Mason rooms Clea the tour guide had mentioned.

On a whim, Ash walked over to the Gothic Lodge and tried the door, but it was locked.

"We keep those lodges locked during services," Clea said, startling Ash. She'd seemingly appeared out of nowhere. "Are you enjoying our service?"

"Yeah," Ash said, pretending to be tripping. "I'm flying like a kite."

Clea smiled, reaching out to guide her.

"We can't get you stuck in a tree, Little Kite," Clea said. "Let's let the wind guide you back to the open field, where you belong."

Clea gently led Ash back toward the gallery, where she didn't want to go. Ash had a thought, noting that Clea was in heels, versus her own sneakers. Ash slipped free of Clea's grasp and took off jogging down the hallway, laughing as she ran.

"The kite's flying free!" Ash said. "This kite's as free as a tree!"

"Oh, no," Clea said, clacking after Ash. "Come back, Little Kite!"

Ash poured on some speed while zig-zagging with her arms out to her sides.

"Free to be me," Ash said. "I'm a kite flying high in the syrupy sky!"

She could hear Clea saying something on a walkie talkie, and Ash knew there'd be some more acolytes or deacons or bouncers or someone else coming for her.

It was easy to get lost in the Temple, but Ash had a good sense of direction, and assumed one of the closed doors to her left led to where the keyboardist was playing. She went to it and tried the door, but it was locked.

She knocked on the door, pounding it with her fist.

"Open sesame!" Ash said, seeing Clea emerge from the hallway, having taking off her heels so she could come after her more effectively. Ash could see some acolytes and deacons making their way up the stairs, eyes on Ash.

"Little Kite, come this way," Clea said, holding out her hands, which held her heels. Ash pointed and laughed.

"You've got hands on your feet," Ash said. "Neat! Neat! Neat!"

"I do," Clea said. "Come now, Little Kite. You're stuck on some branches."

Ash hammered the door again with her hand, and, to her surprise, the door opened. And out popped her sister Melinda's head, wearing a wine-red robe and looking irritated.

"Melinda," Ash said, shocked.

"Ash?" Melinda replied, stunned.

**The Grand Hotel was jam-packed, now, and Emily had**
a tough time getting past the throngs of people on the street.
But she made her way in, mindful of the various people wearing their mushroom cone hats and playing with glowsticks and whatever other junk they'd picked up along the way.

Cloris was holding court at the front desk, all smiles. Emily thought she'd noted her arrival with a nod that Emily smilingly returned as she got to the elevator, which she had to share with four other tourists who were young people she did not recognize.

"Dude, the fried mushroom eating contest is tomorrow, Sean," one of them, a young man, said. "Are you registered?"

"Totes," Sean said. "I used the Fungo App."

"Cool cool," the young man said. "That's gonna be sick!"

"Just so long as Sean doesn't get sick," another of them said. She was a young woman in pigtails, her face covered in freckles. "Ten bucks says he does. Ten bucks says you do, Sean."

"Alright," Sean said. "Ten bucks."

"I'm in," the others said, one by one.

"Easy money," Sean said. "You all owe me like thirty bucks."

"Right, right," the girl in pigtails said.

Emily's floor was reached and she excused herself while the kids laughed, their laughter cut off as the elevator doors closed.

Grateful for the quiet, Emily worked her way down the hall to their suite, where she keyed in, shutting the door behind her.

She dialed up Marquis.

"Yeah, Em?" Marquis said, picking up on the first ring.

"I got a sample," Emily said. "From the Temple."

"Excellent," Marquis said. "Where are you?"

"Hotel," Emily said. "Where are you?"

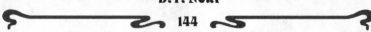
"Sylvia's," Marquis said. "Getting some dinner. You care to join me?"

"Well, hell," Emily said. "Honestly, going back down there? It's nice and quiet up here."

"Come on," Marquis said. "It'll be fun."

"Alright," Emily said. She steeled herself to head back down, opting to take the stairs instead of the elevator, which felt somehow more healthy. She just couldn't bear to share another elevator trip with some zany mushroom tourists.

She made her way back down to the lobby, popping out into the noise and the line of people queued up to get their rooms, and walked across the lobby to Sylvia's, noting that Cloris was watching her yet again, returning her smile with another nod.

"Damn, Cloris," Emily muttered to herself before donning a smile for the hostess, who beamed back radiantly at her. "I'm looking for Marquis Allen's table."

"Right this way," the hostess said. Her nametag said her name was Lisa. Sylvia's was packed, the dark booths full of restaurant patrons. Marquis was in a booth by himself, nursing a steak. Marquis was as handsome as ever—he was wearing a black ribbed turtleneck and grey slacks, wore an Omega watch on his left wrist.

Emily thanked Lisa and took her seat. Marquis looked Emily over, then over her shoulder.

"Where's Ash?" he asked.

"She's still at the Temple," Emily said.

Marquis paused with a forkful of steak at the ready.

"She's not, you know...?"

"No," Emily said. "We poured our samples into the vial I'm carrying. We're not tripping, hello?"

Marquis chomped on the piece of steak, nodding.

"Good," Marquis said. "Can't lose your head in a place like this."

"Nope," Emily said, nosing through the menu. When their server came by, a young woman pleasantly surprised to find another patron there, Emily ordered the grilled salmon salad and a lager beer. "And where've you been all day?"

"Scouting," Marquis said. "I wanted to check everything out before they started blocking off the roads."

"And what'd you see?" Emily asked.

"Nightcap is huge," Marquis said. "Even on the guided tour, it was almost too much to take in. They are running a hell of an operation out there."

"I'll bet," Emily said, although she thought the Mycopharmix facilities were particularly impressive, thought it would take a lot to impress him.

Emily pulled the blue vial from her pocket and handed it to Marquis under the table, in the shadows of the booth. He took it and pocketed it.

"Nice job, Dr. Carver," Marquis said. "Lady's Tears?"

Emily nodded.

"Can't wait to have somebody spectrograph the sample," Marquis said. "Jerry's gonna love this."

"I'm sure he will," Emily said. "What about Nightcap? Like for me?"

Marquis shook his head.

"Too hot," Marquis said. "There's something going on. Security's way up. I don't know what's happening, but it's too risky. These Tears make it all worth it."

Emily's beer arrived and she took a sip, processing what Marquis had said.

"What do you mean it's too hot?"

"Like I said, I don't really know," Marquis said. "Only I know heightened security when I see it. Something's going on."

"I really want to see their operation," Emily said. "They have to be giving tours all weekend."

"Sure they are," Marquis said. "But that's all you can do."

"It's enough," Emily said. "I'd like to take a look tomorrow if I can."

"Fine," Marquis said. "We're all out of here EOD Sunday at the latest, though."

"Of course," Emily said. "I'm surprised you'd linger. Jerry's going to be hot to trot to get that sample. By the way, I think they might grow the source on-site at the Temple."

Marquis poked around the mashed potatoes on his plate, trying to appear casual.

"You think?"

Emily nodded as her salmon salad arrived.

"There's a room," Emily said. "The tour guide wouldn't let us check it out. But I think it's their grow room. I would love to get in there. See just what they're growing."

Marquis laughed at her, sipping his Manhattan.

"What does it matter? We've got the sample," Marquis said.

"But I want to see what made it," Emily said. "If I could get some spores or some fruiting bodies."

"We can produce it synthetically," Marquis said. "Once we get it analyzed."

"Maybe," Emily said. "But I want the source. I'm kind of a completist."

Marquis sneered, giving his drink a swirl with his wrist.

"That's on you," Marquis said. "As I see it, you've done right by Jerry with this. Everything else you do is extra credit."

"I understand that," Emily said.

"And these people play for keeps," Marquis said. "Like for real."

"I gather that," Emily said. Emily never imagined herself as this kind of field operative, but she found corporate espionage was kind of to her liking. There was a thrill she found in it that was only analogous to the thrill she'd find out in the woods hunting out mushrooms. It sounded absurd, but she couldn't deny it.

Plus, if she could actually identify the source of the Lady's Tears on her own, that might give her still more leverage. Or maybe she could cultivate her own. Leave Mycopharmix with their synthetic Lady's Tears. She could have the real deal.

"Whatever you do, we're gone at sunset Sunday," Marquis said. "Like hell and gone for Pittsburgh. Then on a flight to California the next day."

"I got it," Emily said. "You know, if you're caught with those Lady's Tears, they'll bust you for it. There's got to be a ton of psilocybin in it."

Marquis smiled at her like she'd made a joke.

"I've got it covered," Marquis said. "Smuggler's gonna smuggle, you know what I mean? Nobody looks twice at what they're looking at."

"Whatever that even means," Emily said.

"People see what they expect to see," Marquis said. "How nice for me that this stuff looks like mouthwash or aftershave, right?"

Emily laughed into her beer.

"I see your point," Emily said.

"Yeah, you do," Marquis said. "I am what you'd call the Voice of Reason."

He smiled at her while she dug into her salad. Emily wondered if she shouldn't have stayed with Ash at the Temple but had to discipline herself to understand that she was here for a specific purpose that didn't necessarily play nicely with Ash's own plans to find her sister. For Ash it was personal, for Emily, it was purely professional.

"Alright, Voice of Reason," Emily said. "I know what I'm doing tomorrow. What about you?"

"What about me?" Marquis asked, ordering another drink when their server turned up. "I need to know what you do. You don't need to know what I do. That's how this works. I'm *your* handler."

"Ooh," Emily said. "Is that what you're doing? Handling me?"

"Totally," Marquis said. "I mean, look at me. I'm a Black man doing corporate tradecraft in central Pennsylvania. I can handle myself."

"And I'm a Black woman mycologist attending a family-friendly fungus festival in central Pennsylvania," Emily said. "I'm a damned unicorn, Marquis."

Marquis smiled at that, conceding the point.

Emily watched the other patrons happily eating their meals.

"Okay," Emily said. "But what if I get in a jam at Nightcap?"

Marquis waved that off as another Manhattan arrived.

"Don't do anything that gets you in a jam," Marquis said. "You get in trouble, you're on your own."

"As my handler, you should be there for me," Emily said.

"That's me being there for you, Em—like telling you not to do anything that gets you into trouble," Marquis said. "Because if these nutcases get their hands on you, then POOF. You're gone."

Emily chewed on that as she noshed on her salmon salad.

"About that," Emily said. "Ash shared out all those disappearances. People disappear here every year."

"Yeah? People disappear all over the place," Marquis said.

"But every year," Emily said. "Like gone."

Marquis shrugged as he dug back into his steak.

"Not my problem," he said.

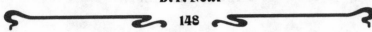
"But don't you wonder?" Emily asked. Whatever Marquis had been in his life, he struck her as a very Operations sort of guy—a man rooted in the here-and-now, untroubled by more abstract considerations. That dedication to the present and the practical likely made him excellent at these types of jobs.

"Jerry paid me to get some samples from this place," Marquis said. "That's what I'm doing. Let the Sheriff's office deal with the missing persons."

"Yeah," Emily said. "I don't think they're worried about it too much, to be honest."

Marquis speared some steak and smothered it in mashed potatoes.

"There you have it," Marquis said. "I'm not going anywhere near that. Hell, they'd try to pin that on me if they could."

"Who's 'they' in this equation?" Emily asked, drinking some of her beer. It was an adequate lager, if not an ostentatious one.

"'They' are who they are," Marquis said. "They know exactly who they are, and so do I. They do their thing, I do mine."

"Well, alright," Emily said. She liked Marquis. There was something blithely self-assured about him that brought her solace. His serene insouciance moved her in some way she couldn't entirely define. She thought maybe he had been a soldier in an earlier part of his life and was confident that she was not wrong. She could imagine him on a battlefield, coming out without so much as a scratch.

"When you say these people are dangerous, what do you really mean by that?" Emily asked. "What do you know?"

Marquis glanced around them, like this way and that in the comfortable confines of the booth, like he was a Father Confessor sharing some deep secret. Emily liked that he seemed to trust her enough with those confidences.

"Cults are cults," Marquis said. "They do cult stuff. I mean, think about it, Em—Lionel Templeton is the mayor. You have Mona Templeton heading the Temple. Maura Templeton runs the Shroom Room. And above them all is Big Daddy, Ned Templeton IV, CEO of Nightcap. It's a family business. Daddy is running the farm, while his kids are running the town."

Emily hadn't seen much of Lionel Templeton, but wondered why he wasn't Ned V. It only made sense to her. The Templetons had been pretty diehard about that.

"Why isn't Lionel Ned V?" Emily asked.

"The daughters really run the show," Marquis said. "Like this generation. They call the tune. I don't know why, but there you have it. Maura and Mona are the show. Lionel's, I don't know, a figurehead. He's the resident gladhander. He handles the political apparatus, while his sisters run the family business."

Emily thought it was weird that there had been so many Ned Templetons over the span of time.

"Technically, yeah, Lionel's Ned V," Marquis said. "He's Lionel Edward Templeton. But instead of being Ned V, he went with his first name. No idea why."

Emily could only wonder what was going on in the heads of the Templetons. Maybe it was the half-assed lager she was drinking, but her mind was wandering.

"Mind, body, spirit," Emily said. "The three circles. I saw that motif at the Temple—the tour guide Clea talked about it. The three connected circles: mind, body, spirit."

"Yeah," Marquis said. "Lionel is the Body. Maura is the Mind. And Mona is the Spirit."

"Okay," Emily said. "That's kind of weird. Are you getting metaphysical on me, Marquis?"

Marquis finished his steak, putting his fork and steak knife on his plate in a "V" shape and pushing the plate away.

"I call them as I see them," Marquis said. "As a Handler, I have to."

The server came and got his plate, and Marquis begged off dessert, only wanted coffee. Emily kept going with her salad, feeling like she had to keep up.

"I saw Mona at the Temple," Emily said. "She's impressive. She could command the room. Charismatic. Haven't met Maura or Lionel, yet."

"Right," Marquis said. "Lionel's a bookkeeper, as I see it. A stenographer. His job is to keep everything running smoothly. Maura, can't say I know what to make of her. Nor Ned, either. He's there and not-there at the same time. Busy running the farm. The Templetons own Lynchburg, though. Not bad for some upstarts who slummed it this way from Pittsburgh over a century ago. It's taken a few generations, but they've got it all buttoned up."

Emily liked hearing Marquis talk through his thoughts. She enjoyed working with him, even though she doubted she'd ever understand him.

"What do they have sewn up?" Emily asked.

"All of it," Marquis said. "You have the legit trade—the buttons, the produce, the other varieties. They export those to the cities. Brisk trade. And there's the specialty mushrooms, the cultivars they've worked out. Heh—putting the 'cult' in 'cultivar' when you think about it. And there's the drug trade. I'm convinced they're running psilocybin trade as well."

"Yeah?"

"Yeah," Marquis said, as the coffee arrived. He finished his Manhattan before delving into the coffee. "They're covering all the lanes. Legit and illicit. I can see the Temple bullshit being, I don't know, like an open-ended focus group where they test out their product on people by wrapping it up in some bogus holy ritual."

Emily laughed at his relentless cynicism. She didn't think she'd ever met a more cynical man than Marquis, and she kind of loved him for it.

"I think maybe it is a holy ritual for them," Emily said. "I mean, Ash and I were in there, and I don't think they were going through the motions in the Temple."

Marquis sipped his coffee, nodding. No cream or sugar for him. He took it black, unadulterated.

"Sure," Marquis said. "I believe that. I don't doubt that Mona's all-in on that stuff. But somebody like Ned IV, I don't know. I can't see him being who he is, doing what he does, and being in on the hocus pocus. I think he knows exactly what he's doing."

She wanted to see everything they did at Nightcap, wanted to take it for her own use. Wanted to see their techniques and, ideally, see the spawn they were working with. She didn't bear Mycopharmix any malice, but part of her wanted to strip-mine what she could from Nightcap and set herself up in her own business elsewhere. She knew how to do it, what needed to be done. Knowledge was the power supply. The spores merely made it all possible. They were the delivery system.

"And what is he doing?" Emily asked. She found that asking Marquis questions got him talking. Talking was good.

"He's conjuring up himself a cartel," Marquis said. "Lynchburg is the, I don't know, breeding ground. The Festival's the

front. He's got bigger plans. Broader plans. Here in Pennsylvania, that's all well and good. Plenty of mushroom farmers here. But I think Ned Templeton's got his sights on bigger things. The man's ambitious. I can't fault him for that."

"Alright," Emily said. Her phone pinged, and it was Ash.

*I found her.*

That's all it said. Emily felt a sense of happiness and trepidation for Ash. It was good to find what you were looking for, even as it was fraught with the concerns of what you did when you found it. Like a dog chasing a car—what did the dog do when it caught the car it was chasing after?

*Now what?* She texted back.

*Stay tuned,* Ash replied.

Marquis noticed, of course.

"What's up?" he asked.

"Ash found her sister," Emily said. She knew that Marquis didn't care about that. How could he? Ash's own familial issues were a world away from his assignment.

"Great," Marquis said.

*She's the keyboardist,* Ash said. *Isn't that ridiculous?*

*Certainly,* Emily keyed back. *Are you okay?*

*Fine,* Ash said. *Stay tuned.*

"Is she okay?" Marquis asked. Emily knew he didn't care, beyond how her status affected his own work.

"Seemingly," Emily said. She had no idea. When she pinged Ash again, she got no response. She hoped she was okay.

"Cryptic," Marquis said.

"You can handle that, Handler?" Emily asked.

"Handlers can handle anything," Marquis said. "That's nice that she found her sister, but it has fuck-all to do with what we're doing here."

"Why'd Jerry bring her in, then?" Emily asked.

"Only Jerry knows What and Why," Marquis said. "I'm more of a How guy, myself."

"Right," Emily said. She agreed with him, even as she was planning to drop by the Temple again, if only to help out her friend.

# 7

**Austin felt left out. Watching Mallory, Jess, and Jake**
dance themselves into a tizzy in the Grand Hall, he felt maybe
like a chode for not having drunk the Lady's Tears like the others had. They looked like they were having fun, dancing around
like a group of dervishes, whereas he was merely tripping.

Something had gone askew, and he was feeling it in his trip.
This didn't come about as proper awareness, as the dose they'd
taken was sufficient for him to be flying as high as he might
wish to go, but in the flash and burn of the kaleidoscopic vista
he was witnessing in the Grand Hall, Austin understood that he
was, somehow, missing out.

His technicolors had gone toward more somber, muted
shades and tones, the geometry of the fractal splinters that
flowed into his eyes like unshed tears. He saw Mallory as a distant apparition, spinning and dancing to the ever-present beat
that thundered down from the dome overhead, which had apparently landed again, which no longer looked like a spiderweb
to him, but seemed increasingly like an unblinking eye from
above.

Having swum the churning sapphire sea and reached the
crystalline shores, Austin struggled to find his footing when he
saw Ash again, this time on the upper deck, hovering like an
angel. She was there, he could see. Her face was unmistakable,
the set of her jaw and the sharpness of her gaze. She was surrounded by a pulsing nimbus of radiance.

"Ash," Austin said, looking up at her, reaching for her, his
arms as far away as islands on distant shores, even as he gazed
at her and saw her, like really saw her. Who she was, who she
would and could be.

Austin pushed off the dance floor, away from his gyrating friends, making his way up the towering ramp that led him away from the pulsing sound and light of the Grand Hall.

"Ash," Austin said, knowing that he loved her without properly comprehending the implications of the word and the ideas behind it, but knowing that it was, in fact, correct.

In the hallway, which swelled and receded like it was breathing, Austin went to the stairs, and tried to climb them, taking care not to lose his footing, watching tangled grasses weave themselves with every step he took.

It seemed to take forever, but he persevered and reached the top, where he saw Ash surrounded by white snowglobe people who were themselves enrobed in color and shapes like snowflakes.

"Ash?" Austin said. But she'd already gone, whisked away by a woman robed in flowing red wine (blood?) who vanished into the wall with her. The other glowing acolytes turned and looked at Austin, while a lovely hall nymph who called herself "Clea" spoke to Austin in a soothing tone, her snowy blond hair curled into beckoning wisps.

"This way, Friend," Clea said, guiding him, taking him farther away from wherever Ash had gone to.

"Ash," Austin said.

"Clea," Clea said. "Nice to meet you, Ash."

"No, I'm not Ash," Austin said. "I'm Austin."

"Austin," Clea said, her voice lilting as she guided him down the waterfall stairs, the ones he'd scaled before. "Let's get you back to where you ought to be."

"What about Ash?" Austin asked.

"There's no ash around here," Clea said.

"No, Ash," Austin said, pointing up. "She's the lady in the wall."

"The Lady is everywhere," Clea said, not seeming to mind that she was walking through a waterfall with him. Austin was scooping some of the water up with each step and splashing it on his face. The sparkles of it were enchanting and musical.

The music everywhere kept throbbing, and Austin could see the walls were bleeding color with each beat, running rivulets of rhythm.

"Come down, now," Clea said. "With me, Little Lost Lamb."

She guided him, her voice echoing in the spirit wilderness, her eyes upon him, her smile captivatingly catlike. She opened a door in the bleeding wall and the light from within danced upon the noise of the music and the cries of the revelers and while Austin knew it was not where he wanted to go, he went along, anyway.

Sometimes that was all you could really do on a trip—you went on the journey wherever it took you. Clea walked him to the glittering shores of the Grand Hall, where the people danced, where the great idol of the Lady even danced, her luminous blue eyes fixating on him again as he entered, like twin blue stars, her steps making waves in the wondrous water.

"She sees you, Little Lamb," Clea said. "The Lady sees you. She sees all."

She guided him into the throng, where Mallory and Jess and Jake saw him and smilingly encircled him, the three of them laughing, spinning around him, creating a vortex of light and color and shape as they went. It went high in the sky, to the unblinking eye of the overhead dome.

"But what about Ash?" Austin asked. "What about Ash?"

"Ashes, Ashes, we all fall down," Jess said, giggling, joined by the others.

"Ring around the nosy," Mallory said. "Thought he'd go for a mosey. Ash is, Ash is, gone to town!"

And they fell down, dragging, Austin back into the sapphire water, which had become something else, now—it was a turquoise crystalline causeway that led to the Lady.

"Come on, Austin," Mallory said, her hand enfolding his and coiling against him like a cluster of tree roots. He followed, although he was aware of the great dome overhead, now blinking at him with its one great eye, watching every step he took.

"Ash," Austin said, glancing back, but she was long gone.

# 8

**Logan poured himself a tiny bottle whiskey and nosed**
through the Fungus Festival guide, walked himself through it
on his Fungo App. He was pleased that the Grand Hotel had balconies, and had gone out on his, watching the festivities below.

From his floor, he could look out across town, could see the
Temple in the distance, flashing lights even visible from where
he sat. He could see the Shroom Room across the street, its
neon lights glowing enticingly. It looked busy. Everything here
looked busy. He wondered if the locals planned this event all
year. They had to.

Friday night, there was an Evening Invocation led by Mona
Templeton at 9:00, whatever that was, held on Grand Avenue.

Saturday, there was an address by the mayor, Lionel Templeton, at the opening ceremony. And the growers' exhibits
would be open. There was a mushroom cook-off, a fried mushroom-eating competition, Miss Mushroom's Magic Show, as
well as the Parade down Templeton Lane at noon. Some musi-
cians were performing at different times of the day, including
the Toadstools, Country Bob & the Wayseeds, as well as Eclectic Electric Groove Ensemble. There was also the Nightcap Pub
Crawl that involved a half-dozen local taverns and ended at the
All-Nightclub.

Sunday morning had the Lady's Procession, whatever that
was, and the Lynchburg Fungus Run 5K that ended at the Temple of the Lady. There was also Fun Gus the Laughing Clown
for the kids, as well as music by the Alkaline Quartet and the
folk music stylings of the Sundersons. More growers' exhibits,
of course, and some educational workshops about the health
benefits of mushrooms sponsored by the Nightcap Mushroom
Farm. There was a Closing Ceremony at 6 p.m.

Logan texted Maura, amusing himself.

*I'm going over the Festival Guide. I'm thinking I'll check out all of it.*

There was a delay, and Logan sipped at his whiskey while he waited. He was sure Maura was swamped at the Shroom Room, judging from the crowds out and about streetside.

*Good plan.*

Logan smiled, glad she replied. He knew how busy it got back in the kitchen, could only imagine what she was dealing with. Still, he couldn't help himself.

*What's 'the Lady's Procession' about?*

Another pause, and Logan could hear laughter wafting up streetside. From up here, the pavilion tents created an endless chain of red and white speckled mushrooms, while the hanging lanterns hovered and gave off their softly mesmerizing light.

*You should go.*

*I will.*

Logan bit his lip and took the plunge.

*I'd like to see you again.*

A long pause, long enough to make Logan feel like an idiot for having even sent the text to begin with. His mind wandered as he wondered what she might be doing and thinking.

*That could be fun.*

Okay, it wasn't an outright rejection. He could live with that. But, of course, he pushed it.

*Is that a yes?*

A shorter pause.

*Sure.*

Logan laughed, finished his drink, leaned on his elbows, peered down at the street below. He imagined Maura in the back of the Shroom Room, surrounded by her team, busy cooking the hell out of all of those mushrooms.

"Sure" was good enough for him, and he left it at that. They could sort out the details tomorrow.

Logan could see the fly agaric water tower lurking in the distance to the south, lit by various spotlights, with the only difference being that this one was blue. He laughed to himself, figuring some enterprising Lynchburger—what else could he call them—had opted for that blue agaric because it was a water tower, after all. Logan could almost imagine them high-fiving one another over the cleverness of their design.

Just thinking about someone being up their and painting that thing made him nervous. Logan could deal with just about anything but heights. He hated heights. Peering over the balcony was about as far as it went for him, and even then, he gripped the railing tight.

Looking down streetside, he could see the tourists piling in, mostly hitting the restaurants, bars, and taverns.

Lynchburg had to clean up with this festival. According to what he'd researched, they had somewhere around 100,000 people visit the little town during the Festival, including people from all around—including Ohio, West Virginia, New Jersey, Delaware, Maryland, New York, and even farther away.

Those were good numbers for a place like this. It meant a lot of money changing hands, all of those precious tourist dollars. He had to hand it to the people of Lynchburg to even make something as mundane and, yeah, maybe even silly, as mushrooms and turn it into a profitable thing.

His phone chimed, and it was Maura.

*I'm off at 11. I'll drop by the Grand if you're around.*

That made Logan happy, and he debated how long to wait until replying. He counted to thirty, taking his time. It was a digital eternity.

*Sure, I'll be around.*

Logan thought his evening prospects might have just picked up. He poured himself another whiskey and took everything in.

# 9

**Melinda was Ash's baby sister, but you wouldn't have** guessed it by the way she scolded Ash from the close confines of her cubby as the organist of the Temple of the Lady. She glared at Ash, her blond hair tied back in a ponytail, her eyes flashing.

"What the hell are you doing here, Ash?" Melinda said. "I'm working, goddammit."

Ash wasn't about to let Melinda put her on the defensive, all but shoved her robed sister.

"What am I doing here? What are *you* doing here?" Ash said. "We all thought you were dead, Melinda. I mean, Christ."

Melinda rolled her eyes.

"I'm not dead," Melinda said. "I'm living my best life."

Ash scoffed, looking at her extensive synthesizer rig, all the lights and buttons. Melinda had always been a great piano player when they'd been kids, had a real knack for it. The plan had been for her to go to Juilliard.

"Here?" Ash said. "Being an organist for a cult?"

Melinda scoffed right back at her.

"It's not a cult, Ash," Melinda said. "Give me a break. This is meaningful work I'm doing here. They pay me well to do the music for their services."

Ash couldn't even believe it, watched her sister hover over at her synthesizer, keeping the music flowing.

"Mom and Dad are going to shit, Melinda," Ash said.

"Let them," Melinda said, over her shoulder. "You shouldn't be here."

"What did you think I was going to do?" Ash said.

Melinda programmed the next songs on the playlist, while below, oblivious people continued dancing and tripping.

"This is ridiculous," Ash said. Melinda turned on her, leaning into her. Ash was shorter than Melinda, something her younger sister always delighted in since the year she passed her, when she was 17 years old.

"Would you rather I was dead?" Melinda asked. "I mean, fuck, Sis. At least you know I'm alive."

"Why didn't you tell us?" Ash said. Melinda laughed bitterly at her.

"You think any of you would listen if I told you I was going to take a job in Lynchburg, Pennsylvania? Give me a break. It's my life, my choice."

"It's a cult, Melinda," Ash said. "They're a motherfucking cult."

"You don't understand," Melinda said. "You have no idea what you're even talking about."

The idol of *La Signora* stood over them from across the Grand Hall, seeming to watch the Dunn Sisters. Ash hated the Grey Lady even more, now.

"Come home with me," Ash said. "Please, Melinda. You don't belong here."

"I do," Melinda said. "You'd know if you drank some of the Lady's Tears."

"Oh, is that so?" Ash said, her journalistic instincts bubbling up past her anger. Melinda was always the impetuous one, running off and doing things. This wasn't much different from her other adventures in her past.

"Yes," Melinda said. "Look how happy those people are down there. The Lady's Tears, Ash. She cries so we don't have to—unless we *want* to."

Ash could tell her sister wasn't tripping, doubted she'd be able to work all of the synthesizer equipment if she had been.

"What the hell are you even talking about, Melinda?" Ash said. "You drank that junk and, what, had a vision?"

"Yeah," Melinda said. "It's not junk. It's the Lady's Tears. It's like a vision quest. I knew this was the place for me. I mean, you have no idea the peace it brings you. This place, everyone here. They understand it. They feel it. You'd feel it, too, if you weren't so busy being you."

"I'm not having my little sister be the keyboardist for some creepy cult," Ash said. "I swear to God, that's not happening."

Melinda laughed at her, poking her in the chest with her finger.

"It's happening. You don't have a say in what I do, Ash," Melinda said. "Not anymore. I'm an adult. I decide what I do. This is what I'm doing. Do I look, what, mind-controlled to you? Do I look insane to you? I'm still Melinda."

Ash couldn't figure out how to reach Melinda. She was always so stubborn.

"I didn't change my name to Moonlight or something," Melinda said. "I'm still Melinda. And this is what I want. All this place does is bring joy. What kind of job can you hope to have where you're just making people happy? Seeing people reach a level of themselves they didn't even know was possible. It's beautiful. I make beauty."

Ash wondered how she'd even break this to their parents. They'd send some cult deprogrammers or something to try to sort Melinda out. Melinda just looked her hard in the eye.

"I belong here," Melinda said. "This is where I belong. This place. My talent. Mona saw it right away. She understood. She understood me. More than you ever did. You're a, what, investigative journalist? Does that make you happy, Ash? No. It just pisses you off. You're *always* pissed off. And everybody hates you. I've found my place, and it's here."

Ash tried to cool off, to not let her temper continue to drive the discussion. The key was to try to be as objective and dispassionate as she could be.

"Okay, Melinda," Ash said. "You have actual talent. Like you remember when we were little, all the piano recitals, all of that? People loved to hear you play. You loved to play. And you're good at it. This place, they're just using you. They're feeding off of your talent."

"Everyone uses everybody," Melinda said. "At least here, I know I'm appreciated."

It made Ash's head hurt.

"But Juilliard," Ash said.

"That was Mom and Dad's dream for me," Melinda said. "That wasn't my dream."

Ash waved around them, pointed at Melinda in her red robes with a golden stole that had the three interlocking circles in red printed upon them in mindless repetition.

"This is your dream, Melinda? Is that what I'm supposed to believe? This fucking place?" Ash asked. "Out in the middle of nowhere?"

"Yes," Melinda said. "You're looking at it."

"I don't believe you," Ash said. "I literally don't believe you."

"Seeing is believing, Ash," Melinda said. "I'm here. I'm the Temple organist. Get used to it."

Ash wanted to scream, she wanted to stomp her feet. She remembered when she used to fight with her sisters, when they were kids.

"You should have told me, at the very least," Ash said. "You should have said something."

"You'd have told Mom and Dad," Melinda said. "This is mine. Respect it, Ash. Even if you don't understand it."

Ash massaged her temples with her fingers, closed her eyes.

"I have to work," Melinda said. "Mona likes me to mix up the playlist night after night. I'm never playing the same thing twice. It's not boring."

"Melinda," Ash said. "You're meant for bigger things than this. Better things. Symphonies. Concert halls. Fame and fortune."

"I don't need those things," Melinda said. "I have everything I need here. *La Signora* provides for us all. You'd know that if you spent some time here. Mona would help you understand."

"Is that right?" Ash said, scoffing. Melinda nodded, slipping back into her chair, pushing some buttons and adjusting her mix.

"That's right," Melinda said.

"How about you set up something where I can interview Mona?" Ash asked. Melinda laughed.

"I'd die of embarrassment," Melinda said. "You'll embarrass me. I'm in Mona's good graces. Why would I want to risk that so you could say or do something stupid and annoying and ruin all of that?"

Ash had calmed herself down. There had to be some way of extricating Melinda from this place.

"You think I could ruin it for you?" Ash asked.

Melinda sighed.

"I think you'd die trying to," Melinda said.

"Melinda, I love you," Ash said. "I'm here for *you*. Not for any other reason. I came to this crazy little town for you. To find you."

"And you've found me," Melinda said. "You see I'm alive and healthy. I'm not dead, I'm not a prisoner. I mean, seriously. I could leave the Temple any time I liked. I could leave Lynchburg behind. Mona wouldn't stop me. I'm here because I want to be. How long are you in town?"

"For the Festival," Ash said. "I leave on Sunday."

Melinda glanced over her shoulder at her sister.

"Well, there you have it," Melinda said. "Enjoy the Festival. Maybe we can have lunch or something over the weekend, before you go."

Ash walked to her sister and she hugged her. As furious as she was, as frustrated, she was still so happy Melinda was alive.

"Okay," Ash said. "I'll hold you to that. Don't stand me up."

"I won't, Ash," Melinda said. "Jeez. Now get out of here. I have the service to attend to."

# 10

**Emily found Ash leaving the Temple as she got there,** cursing and wiping tears from her eyes. The acolytes watched them wordlessly, and Emily walked up warily.

"Ash, are you okay?" Emily asked.

"No," Ash said. "I found Melinda. She's their goddamned church organist."

Emily guided Ash away from the Temple, toward Templeton Lane, and the cold comfort of the crowds.

"What are you talking about?" Emily asked.

"You heard me," Ash said. "She's joined their cult. She was the one playing the music in there."

Emily held back her reaction, didn't want Ash to feel any worse, so she tried to offer her some comfort. Sometimes it was enough.

"At least she's alive," Emily said. "That's something."

Ash glared back at the Temple as they walked away from it. The music could still be heard, the lights dancing upon the stained glass. Her sister's music.

"Only barely," Ash said. "I want to destroy that place for brainwashing my sister. Melinda's always been a free spirit, but I never would have imagined her landing here."

They passed some tourists wearing the conical mushroom hats and were playing with some glow necklaces which gave their faces a haunting underlit quality that made them look like ghosts.

"I hate this place," Ash said. "Everything about it. I mean, I really hate it. That creepy Clea was chasing me around, and that's when I had this idea that maybe it was Melinda playing the music. She was always a prodigy at the piano. She was supposed to go to Juilliard."

"Wow," Emily said. "That's impressive."

"I mean, you know how hard it is to get into there? She was slated to start last year and she just vanishes. Joins a cult. I mean, what the hell am I going to tell our parents?"

"Tell them the truth," Emily said. "You're the journalist. Isn't that your thing?"

Ash laughed as bitterly as she was able to.

"Yeah," Ash said. "I have to get Melinda out of here by Sunday. Somehow."

Emily could only imagine how that would go. She wasn't going to let it interfere with what she was here to do, although capturing the Lady's Tears was at least enough of an accomplishment that Jerry would be thrilled with that. For Emily, it was a personal quest to try to find the actual source of the Lady's Tears. Clearly some sort of fungi, but what type? She could only imagine.

"Melinda claims she's happy here, that she doesn't want to go," Ash said. "I refuse to believe that. She's too young to settle in a place like this. In Lynchburg? Give me a break."

"Maybe it's a phase," Emily said.

"It's not a phase," Ash said. They passed a bunch of boutiques and shops, saw the clock tower at the intersection of Grand and Templeton indicating that it was almost eight o'clock. "Mona Templeton brainwashed her somehow. Something with the Lady's Tears."

Emily glanced around them, not wanting Ash to speak too freely, for she couldn't be sure who might be listening. Everyone looked tourist-innocuous, but you never knew.

"Let's get back to the Grand and we can strategize," Emily said.

"Strategize?" Ash asked. "What, how we're going to spring my sister?"

"Just brainstorm," Emily said. "You know. Ideation. That sort of thing."

"Ideation," Ash said. "You're a nut, you know that?"

"Oh, I know it," Emily said. "I'm a trip all by myself."

Ash laughed despite herself, and they headed back to the Grand. The Grand Hotel looked lovely by night, its name illuminated by warm white lights and they went in, and Emily could see Cloris noting her entry, smiling at her. Emily sort of hated Cloris, even though the young woman had done her no wrong. Her officious and affable alertness just bothered her.

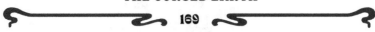
"Let's figure out options for you," Emily said, as they reached the elevators. "You know, battle plans. I mean, it's clear you're not going to leave without your sister."

"Damn right I'm not," Ash said.

"Well, Marquis and I are here until Sunday," Emily said. "No way will Marquis help you out, but I'll try to lend a hand if I can."

Ash softened a little, patted Emily on the arm.

"You're sweet," Ash said, as they got to their floor. "It's my problem, though. I have to deal with it."

Emily keyed them into their place, savoring the quiet of the corridor as they went in. She locked the door and raided the mini fridge for some overpriced little bottles of white wine, which she unscrewed. Ash went to the balcony and took a seat.

Emily joined her. From up where they were, on the sixth floor, they could hear the streetside revelry without it being too obtrusive.

"Okay, so what's your plan?" Emily asked.

"I don't have one," Ash said. "She claimed she joined of her own free will, that she wasn't coerced. She spoke fondly of Mona Templeton, the High Priestess we saw. She said Mona had selected her for the role. I don't know what to make of that."

"We can't kidnap your sister," Emily said. "I wouldn't even know the first thing about that. Marquis might have some ideas, but, like I said, no way would he want in on this."

Emily felt wary talking about it, but the chill of the white wine loosened her tongue a little.

"No," Ash said. "She doesn't want to go. She says she's free to go anytime she wants. But I don't know. All I know is I couldn't persuade her. She's always been impossible to move if she didn't want to."

"Right," Emily said.

"I'll have to tell our parents," Ash said. "They'll have some ideas, I'm sure. In fact, I should tell them now. Give me a second."

Ash got up and slid the door and went back into the hotel room, shutting the door. Emily didn't envy what Ash had to deal with. Emily had an older brother, Martin, but they'd always gotten along. He worked as a mechanical engineer, had a family in Virginia, lived an ordinary-good sort of life.

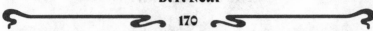
Emily had been the wanderer and weirdo of her family. Her love of mushrooms had started early, from her discovery of a fairy ring in their backyard when she was a girl. It had looked so magical, and her father's admonishments about the dangers of mushrooms had entranced her.

Mycology had been the most logical step for her. She'd been happy doing fieldwork and research and was good at it. How Jerry had gotten wind of her was something she never quite knew, but Mycopharmix was one of those up-and-coming companies that Emily was sure was going places. Jerry's vision was impressive—the efficacy of adaptogenic mushrooms, the use of psilocybin in psychiatric treatment, and other areas of research. His company was going places, and he was generous toward his employees. Emily didn't like to think of herself as being bought, but Jerry had been there for her, and she reciprocated with trying to do right by him, within reason.

While dealing in corporate espionage wasn't her cup of mushroom tea, Emily did find herself intrigued by what was going on in Lynchburg. Nightcap was doing some extraordinary things out here, things most people wouldn't even understand. Emily could hardly wait for the next day, made a note to herself to make sure she got enough sleep.

She wondered about the blue elixir that was the Lady's Tears. It was clearly a kind of tea that had been made to facilitate delivery of the psychedelic compound in the Tears. Which meant that they were brewing it somewhere within the Temple, since she doubted they were trucking it in.

The source of the Tears had to be in the Temple somewhere. Emily wanted to see it, to know what was going on in there. She just didn't know how she could go about doing it.

Marquis appeared at the sliding glass door, which made Emily stand up. She always felt more formal when he was around. Not like he was her employer, but she felt like he had a closer pipeline to Jerry than she did.

"Marquis," Emily said, glancing in at Ash, who was pacing around the room, talking to her parents. "What's wrong?"

"Nothing," Marquis said. "I just wanted to stop by and see how you both were doing. Ash let me in."

"Alright," Emily said. "Well, have a seat. Do you want a drink?"

"No, I'm fine," Marquis said. "I wanted to see if you were going to the Evening Invocation."

"What the hell is that?" Emily asked. Marquis held up his Fungo App, having clicked on the Fungus Festival Flyer.

"I don't know," Marquis said. "Something involving their crazy goddess, I'm guessing. I was going to say that if you were inclined to maybe drop by the Temple again, it might be a good time to do it."

"Marquis, I'm exhausted," Emily said. "It's been an exhausting day."

Marquis judged her silently with his eyes, and Emily wanted to squirm. His face was unreadable. In other circumstances, it might have been impressive.

"Doing this kind of work means taking advantage of opportunities," Marquis said. "It means taking initiative. Mona Templeton's the High Priestess of this cult. She's doing some mumbo-jumbo event on Grand Avenue. Cults being cults, I'm betting most of their people are going to be in attendance. Maybe it gives us a chance to snoop around the Temple and see what's behind that secret door you saw at the feet of the idol."

Emily felt annoyed at the suggestion.

"Maybe you can go check it out, Marquis," Emily said. "That seems like your kind of thing."

"Sure," Marquis said. "You're right about that. However, I'm not the fungus expert. I wouldn't know what to look for. Whereas you would know just what to look for."

The last thing Emily wanted to do was go back to that Temple again. As lovely as it was, it made her uneasy.

"What if we get caught?" Emily asked.

"I'll take care of that," Marquis said. "Look, you're the expert. I'm the Operations guy. I'll get us in and out of there before anybody knows something's up."

"Jesus," Emily said.

"Don't blaspheme, now," Marquis said.

"You could've told me about this over dinner," Emily said.

"No, I couldn't," Marquis said. "You never knew who might be listening at that place."

"They could be listening to us now," Emily said.

"I already checked for bugs," Marquis said. "It's clean."

"You've thought of everything," Emily said.

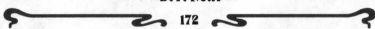
"I always do," Marquis said. "As I see it, we take advantage of the Evening Invocation. We sneak over to the Temple, we break in—assuming we even need to—lord knows how these cultists operate in terms of security. And we do some proper snooping. We get what we're looking for, assuming it's even there, and we slip the hell out. No harm, no foul."

"Sounds like such a bad idea, I wouldn't even know where to begin," Emily said.

"I brought us ski masks," Marquis said. "They won't see our faces."

Emily didn't want to miss the chance to find the source of the Lady's Tears, although it was so much speculation on her part. They hadn't even done any lab analysis on the samples they'd acquired. But it was, perhaps, an opportunity as Marquis said. A chance for them to find whatever fungi might be getting cultivated in that Temple.

"I was really hoping to just have an early night," Emily said.

Marquis smiled thinly at her.

"Jerry wanted me to remind you," Marquis said. "There's a stake in any cultivars you're able to isolate here. It's a gamble, of course. Maybe it's useless spores and spawn you'll find. But if you find something that Mycopharmix can develop, well, then you get a share in that. And let's say you find a half-dozen strains here—that's five one percent shares in those strains. You know how Jerry's got that Midas Touch, right? The man sniffs out opportunities and he turns them into money. You can be part of that."

"You're the Devil, Marquis," Emily said. "You know that?"

Marquis smiled at her again, more broadly this time.

"I've been called worse," Marquis said. "You're good at math. You could be a multimillionaire if any strains get developed. And all for just one night out in an unfamiliar town filled with crazy-ass cultists during their high holy days, or whatever this really is."

"When you put it that way, how can I say no? Although I expect Jerry will find some way to screw me over when he gets the chance," Emily said. Ash reappeared, looking stressed. Her eyes darted between Marquis and Emily.

"What are you two scheming about?" Ash asked.

"Nothing," Marquis said. "We were talking about there being an Evening Invocation tonight at Grand Avenue. Something the cultists are throwing. Nine o'clock tonight."

Ash took a seat between them.

"I told my parents about Melinda," Ash said. "They freaked out, of course."

"What about Melinda?" Marquis asked.

"She's not dead," Ash said. "She's part of the cult. It's a long story."

"Maybe she'll be at the Evening Invocation," Marquis said.

"She might be," Ash said. "Although I don't see me being able to make a dent in her newfound piety."

Emily could see what Marquis was doing. He was very smooth. She didn't interrupt, because part of her did want to see what fungi might be available in the Temple. The share incentive was just that—it was a chance she was willing to take. If anyone could grow from samples obtained in Lynchburg, it was Emily.

"You should show up," Marquis said. "Even if you were just standing there, I bet that would make a dent."

"I don't know," Ash said. "I don't know if I could face Melinda again. We had sharp words."

"There's a story there," Marquis said. "Attending that invocation might be a good scoop for you, a chance to witness firsthand some of the strange stuff going on in this town. That seems like a story that could be pitched to any number of publications."

"Yeah," Ash said. "I suppose. I'm just not in a good place, mindwise."

"Just a thought," Marquis said. Emily was amazed to see him work. Marquis was a masterful manipulator. "Em, I was hoping to process some of the sample you picked up. Can you come back to my room?"

"Uh, sure," Emily said. Ash hardly noticed, was all up in her head. "Ash, are you going to be okay?"

"I don't know," Ash said. "Yeah? Maybe?"

Emily didn't want to leave Ash behind, felt like she needed someone to talk to, but Marquis was leaving, and Emily wanted to leave with him to see what he was up to.

"I'll be back later," Emily said.

"Okay," Ash said, leaning forward, cradling her face in her hands. "I'll be fine."

Emily followed Marquis out, and he closed the sliding glass door, leaving Ash to her own thoughts.

"Get good running shoes and bring your coat," Marquis said.

"That's not reassuring," Emily said.

"Just in case," Marquis said, waiting for her to put on her sneakers and grab her coat.

"You're really the Devil," Emily said. "She needs someone there for her."

Marquis shook his head.

"She needs some alone time to process it all," Marquis said. "As I told you before, her thing is her thing. Our thing is our thing. This is *our* thing."

"Jerry knew her sister had joined, yeah?" Emily asked.

Marquis nodded. "He knew."

"Is Ash intended to be a distraction or something?" Emily asked.

"He wanted somebody he could count on to be motivated to stick it to Lynchburg," Marquis said. "More than simply money-motivated."

"Like you," Emily said.

"Like me," Marquis said. He led her out of their room and walked down the hall with her. He keyed into his hotel room, which was down the hall from theirs. He dug into one of his bags and produced the black ski masks, one of which he gave to Emily. He also produced two pairs of black gloves, one of which he handed to her.

"You came prepared," Emily said.

"There's more," Marquis said, producing a black turtleneck shirt and some black leggings.

"What, you sized me up?" Emily asked.

"The moment I met you," Marquis said.

Emily looked at the clothes, laughing.

"We're going to look like cat burglars," Emily said. "I'd be suspicious if I saw me dressed like this."

"Nobody will think twice," Marquis said. "Just get dressed in the bathroom. Your coat will break up the silhouette."

Emily quickly put on the outfit, admittedly feeling a thrill at doing something so espionage-like. She looked at herself in

the mirror, marveling at how sleek she looked in the all-black ensemble. She wasn't as fireplug-fit as Ash was, but she did a lot of hiking, and prided herself on taking care of herself and eating well. She put on her coat and stuffed the ski mask and gloves in one of its cargo pockets.

She emerged, and Marquis was at the other end of the room, wearing his own outfit. He looked naturally badass.

"You've done this kind of work before," Emily said. It wasn't a question.

"There's good money in corporate espionage," Marquis said. "If you know what you're doing and are choosy about your clients."

He handed a satchel to Emily, what looked like a black leather messenger bag.

"What's this?" Emily asked.

"Open it and see," Marquis said. Emily did so, and saw that inside the bag was another container, which she took out. Opening that, she saw that it contained a half-dozen black six by six-inch wax envelopes that were protected from one another by partitions.

"Sample collections," Emily said.

"Yep," Marquis said. "Aerobic envelopes. Adequate?"

"Yeah, I think so," Emily said. "At least for the short run. No way this'll get past airline inspectors, Marquis."

"You're the researcher," Marquis said. "Scientific samples. You'll be able to talk your way past the TSA."

"There won't be time to dry the samples and properly stow them," Emily said. "We'll have to mail them. Or else drive them to Mycopharmix."

"Hah," Marquis said. "Well, maybe we drive them to Pittsburgh, then you can mail them to Mycopharmix. Then we fly out."

"That would work," Emily said.

Marquis looked her over that scrutinizing way he always did, making Emily self-conscious.

"You ready?" Marquis asked.

"Not really, but sure," Emily said.

"Alright, then," Marquis said. "Let's go check out the Evening Invocation."

# 11

**When Alejandro had detected the bugs, Carlos didn't**
waste a minute. Without a word, he signaled to Lilli and Santiago that they had to get out of there.

"Interesting, Alejandro," Carlos said. "Can you find them?"

"I can try, *Segundo*," Alejandro said.

Carlos mimed for them to get to the garage, to his car. It was a black Mercedes CLS, and they all got in. Carlos gestured for Alejandro to follow him, which he did.

Carlos got in the driver's seat, while Alejandro and Lilli sat in back, with Santiago sitting beside him. Carlos opened the garage door and fired up the car, whipping it out of the driveway and taking off down the quiet street.

At least out here, if anyone was following them, he'd be able to see them coming.

"Everybody have guns?" Carlos asked. Everybody did. Pistols. "There are HKs in the trunk. Three of them, I think. And cash."

He kept his eyes ahead of them and in the rearview mirror, just to see if anybody was pursuing. Nobody appeared to be.

"I wonder when they re-bugged my place," Carlos said, gripping the steering wheel with anger. He had to resist the urge to shoot the security guy in his little booth at the entrance to Hidden Hollow as he pulled up, using his smartphone to open the gate.

He glared at the security man in his booth, who smiled uneasily at him. A nothing man, a middle-aged man with a brown mustache.

"Can I help you, Sir?" the man asked.

"You tell your bosses that I'm coming for them," Carlos said.

"Excuse me, Sir?" the man said.

"You heard me," Carlos said. "You know who I am?"

"I do," the man said. His nametag said he was Dan Humboldt. Carlos made a note of that.

"Then you know who I am," Carlos said. "And what that means for people I don't like."

The gate was open and Carlos shot out of there.

"Santiago, call the others," Carlos said. "Tell them where we're going."

"Alright," Santiago said.

Outside the confines of Hidden Hollow, the roads were country-dark and hilly, with masses of hulking trees on either side.

"Be careful of deer, Carlo," Lilli said in the back. "They're all over the place out here. Especially at night."

Having cleared the gated community, Carlos let his nerves ease a bit, drove less quickly. Since nobody appeared to be after them, he thought he could be more careful.

"Humboldt the security man is probably calling them right now," Carlos said. "I should have shot him."

"Always time for that later, *Segundo,*" Santiago said, busy dialing numbers. Lilli was unhappy in the back, and Alejandro was nervous.

"We should have packed," Lilli said. "Where are we even going, Carlo?"

"Lynchburg," Carlos said. "Your idea. The penthouse at the Grand. That's where we're going, Baby. If those *Cultistas Locas* want to come for us, let them come for us there."

"I don't want to be stuck in the same clothes, Carlo," Lilli said.

"We can buy some in town," Carlos said. That did nothing to placate her. Carlos glanced at Santiago, who was looking concerned.

"What is it, *Diablo?*" Carlos asked.

"Nobody's picking up, *Segundo,*" Santiago said.

"Nobody?"

Santiago shook his head.

"What the fuck," Carlos said. What kind of deathtrap had he unintentionally walked into at Hidden Hollow? Who were these people who could so easily dispatch his men? He'd arrived at Hidden Hollow with three dozen *Rojas* men. Now it was just the four of them? It wasn't possible.

"Nobody's picking up," Santiago said. "I'm going through the numbers."

All of the men he'd brought along were professionals. They knew how to handle themselves. That was the whole point of it. He'd planned it out so carefully. Six men per house flanking his own in the Hollow. Six houses. Those maniacs had managed to snuff out all of his men? Maybe at the same time? How could that even be?

His men had regular check-ins, they had procedures for all of that. Whatever had happened had happened quickly, or somebody would have been alerted.

"Nobody," Santiago said. "I went through the whole list."

Carlos hard his phone ring, keeping his attention on the road as he pulled it out. It was Teo's phone yet again.

"Everybody keep quiet," Carlos said, answering it.

"Carlos," the Lady said. "Going for a little road trip, I hope?"

"You bitch," Carlos said. "You think I wouldn't find out you'd bugged my place?"

"It's all bugged, Carlos," the Lady said. "We knew what you were doing before you did."

"I'm going to kill you when I see you," Carlos said.

"If you see me, you're going to be dead," the Lady said. "Unless you leave town. Are you leaving town, Carlos?"

"Yeah, I am," Carlos said. "I'm getting out of here. You think I care about your stinking mushrooms? I've got bigger things."

"Of course you do," the Lady said. "And you should go do those things. Leave Lynchburg far behind. Just a happy memory."

"Where are my men?" Carlos asked.

"The ones we killed?" the Lady said. "In the Cursed Earth, where they belong."

"The Cursed Earth," Carlos said. "What does that even mean?"

"They're in the ground, Carlos," the Lady said. "We whisked them away and buried them. Such strong men, too. Good food for the soil. Good nourishment for the land, that strength. Good for the Goddess."

"How did you even catch them?" Carlos asked. He really wanted to know, couldn't imagine how all of those men had been caught off-guard.

"It's not that hard," the Lady said. "Hidden Hollow is a quiet place. A peaceful place. Men let down their guard in a place like that. We know how to cull, Carlos. This was just another cull."

"A cull?" Carlos said. "What the hell are you even talking about?"

"It's like a harvest," the Lady said. "I know you're a city boy, and don't know these sorts of things. We culled your men, Carlos."

"But not me?"

"Not you, not yet," the Lady said. "We're saving the best—or worst—for last. Unless, of course, you leave us far behind and never come back here. Forget you were ever here."

"I'm going to send an army to your little town," Carlos said. "I'm going to burn it down. Every inch of the place."

"No, you're not," the Lady said. "You're marked, Carlos. If we see another Red Death in our town, we'll come for you wherever you go, wherever you are. You'll never be safe."

Carlos was fuming as he drove, and the others were watching him, gauging his reaction. Nobody talked to him this way, never. He hadn't carved out his place as *Segundo* by putting up with things like this.

"Think so?"

"I know so," the Lady said.

"I'm going to kill every one of you," Carlos said. He saw some vehicles heading his way from the direction of the town. Two sets of headlights, shining in his face.

"We don't think you are, Carlos," the Lady said.

He passed the vehicles. Two grey vans.

Carlos muted the phone, stabbed a finger at Santiago, who was watching intently.

"Those vans," Carlos said, glancing in the rearview mirror. Sure enough, the vans whipped around and turned around.

Carlos floored it and the Mercedes growled and picked up speed.

"Carlos, are you there?" the Lady asked. He turned off the mute.

"I'm here, *Signora*," Carlos said.

Carlos saw it before he could react—a spike strip on the dark road leading into Lynchburg, which was still far away. He could see the light from it in the distance, illuminating the sky, even as the spike strip shredded his car's tires in four quick ex-

plosions. Carlos cursed, trying to keep his car from spinning out of control as he swerved onto the shoulder and brought the car to a stop, even as Lilli and Alejandro were crying out. Santiago was silent, was already drawing his pistol. He knew what was expected of him.

"The trunk, *Segundo*," Santiago said, as the vans were fast approaching. Carlos popped the trunk and Santiago called for Alejandro to join him.

"Something the matter, Carlos?" the Lady asked. "Car trouble?"

Carlos got out of the car as Lilli was cursing. Santiago and Alejandro had both grabbed HK MP5s, jamming clips into them and drawing their bolts.

"Nothing I can't handle," Carlos said. "I'll see you soon."

Carlos pocketed the phone and went to the trunk and fished out an HK 433, his personal favorite. The assault rifle was reassuring, even as the vans were rolling up. He saw the spike strip slither off the road but couldn't see who was pulling it.

"Hey," Carlos said, firing some blind shots into the darkness of the woods, in the direction of the vanishing spike strip. The report of the assault rifle made Lilli cry out, but no fire was returned. "Shoot the vans when they're in range."

The vans slammed on the brakes when Carlos had fired, and he turned the 433 on them, squinting into the light. He began firing shots at them, above the lights, where the windshield would be.

He was gratified to see the doors fly open and saw robed figures fleeing the driver and passenger seats.

"Shoot them," Carlos yelled, and Santiago and Alejandro raised their submachine guns, firing off shots at the fleeing cultists. Carlos laughed, turning his 433 on the front tires of the vans, bursting the tires. "You want to play with me now, *Cultistas?*"

Alejandro and Santiago jogged toward the vans with their MP5s at the ready, even as they could hear the scuffling of the cultists as they'd fled the back of the van. The combination of the blinding headlights and the darkness around them made it difficult to find a target. Alejandro fired off some blind bursts, hoping to hit someone, while Santiago quickly scanned the emptied vans.

"Cowards," Carlos yelled, his assault rifle on his hip. "That's right, run away."

He laughed, even as he marveled at how they appeared to have vanished into the surrounding woods.

"I'll burn your trees, too," Carlos yelled, waving his rifle around. "All of this."

Santiago called for Alejandro to help him take the spare tires off the vans.

"What are you doing, *Diablo?*" Carlos said.

"You shot the front tires on the vans," Santiago said. "So, we'll swap them out with the spares on one of the vans and drive it in. I don't want to walk into town, do you, *Segundo?*"

Carlos laughed again, louder, so the cultists could hear him.

"You hear that? We're taking your van," Carlos said.

The crossbow bolt that struck him caught him in the shoulder, knocking Carlos off his feet. He hit the pavement with a squawk, while Santiago and Alejandro sprayed fire from their MP5s, the submachine guns flashing as they did so. As it had been fired silently, they had no idea where it had come from, beyond the rough direction of where it had hit him.

Cursing, Carlos fought to get to his feet, wanting to pull the blue-feathered bolt from his shoulder, but afraid to when he felt the pain from moving. He'd been perhaps too cocky. He should not have underestimated them, but his pride was as wounded as he was, and pride drove men to do reckless things.

Lilli emerged from the Mercedes, ducking low. Her dark eyes were on him, her face was full of fear.

"Carlo, what are you doing?" Lilli asked. "They shot you."

"I'm fine," Carlos said, although he knew that he wasn't fine. He'd have to get to the hospital, or whatever passed for it in this little town.

There was the sound of sirens coming from Lynchburg, and Carlos cursed. His phone rang, and Carlos struggled to slip it from his pocket, his vision blurring.

"You should have left town, Carlos," the Lady said. "I warned you."

# 12

**The Evening Invocation was weirdly spellbinding, with**
Mona Templeton onstage at the head of Grand Avenue, surrounded by whirling acolytes in white, while some masked,
brown-clad deacons hovered nearby on the fringes, looking
menacing. Some of the acolytes were playing drums as Mona
went to the microphone, holding out her arms.

"*Signora*, we humbly ask You to bless this Festival we hold
in Your name," Mona said. "Guide us in Your wisdom, let everyone here sample Your generosity, Your plenitude, Your unfailing
grace. Guide us, Your humble servants, that we might make our
time upon the Cursed Earth a pleasant one for ourselves and
our guests."

Emily and Marquis watched the invocation from the edge of
the crowd, seeing the acolytes and deacons raising their hands
and holding up white streamers which they then took out into
the crowd, holding their arms up high, the white streamers un-
furling as they made their way, to the puzzled delight of the
onlookers. The streamers all flowed outward from Mona, in a
growing wedge that stretched deeper into the crowd.

"The mycelium binds us all," Mona said. "We are all on this
journey together, bound up in the Web of Life."

"She does like her showmanship," Marquis said. "Come on,
Em. Let's go."

"Right," Emily said, following Marquis even as she wanted to see how the Invocation played out. Mona Templeton
had a commanding speaking voice and presence. There was
something magisterial about her. Emily had never met a High
Priestess before.

Heading down Templeton Lane, Emily was nervous. She felt
like everyone was watching them, even though nobody actually was. People were just making their way and not paying them

any attention. Marquis moved smoothly through the crowd like a shark—he knew where he was going, what he was doing. Emily envied that presence of mind, that coolness.

The Temple was still playing its music, was still flashing light. Emily knew that most mushroom trips took anywhere from four to six hours, which meant that some of them were likely coming down, but others might still be in the throes of the hallucinogen.

"How are we going to even slip in there with all those people still around, Marquis?" Emily asked in a whisper.

"They're all high as kites," Marquis said. "All those people will be keeping the staff busy. We just slip in unobtrusively and nobody will notice us."

"That's crap," Emily said. "I think somebody will think some people wearing ski masks might be a bit weird."

Marquis laughed at her.

"Only the staff," Marquis said. "If any of the trippers see us, we can just pretend we're part of their hallucination. Seriously, this is the way to go. Get them while they're busy minding the congregation, or whatever you want to call it."

They were halfway to the Temple when Emily heard someone call her name, and she startled. It was Deputy Stirner, standing by his patrol car.

"Dr. Carver," Stirner said, smiling at her, glancing at Marquis. "Going to the Temple?"

"Hey, Deputy Stirner," Emily said. "Yeah."

"You look like you've seen a ghost," Stirner said. "Who's your friend?"

"Oh, this is Mark," Emily said.

"Hello, Deputy Stirner," Marquis said, holding out a hand, which Stirner shook.

"You missed the Evening Service," Stirner said. "It was at six o'clock."

"We caught some of the Invocation, though," Emily said. "That's something."

Stirner glanced back at Grand Avenue. From here, Emily couldn't see it, just the people going back and forth to the blocked-off street.

"Yeah," Stirner said. "Mona Templeton really goes gangbusters with that stuff. Everybody does."

Stirner eyed Marquis and Emily both, just looked them over. Emily didn't know how not to look suspicious, but Marquis played it cool.

"Are there, you know, normal churches around here?" Marquis asked.

The deputy shrugged. "Not really. Not anymore. Not for a long time, honestly. *La Signora,* She's what you'd call a jealous goddess, I suppose. She doesn't like to share."

Stirner's radio squawked, and his attention turned from them a moment. Marquis glanced at Emily, who was trying her best to not throw up. She was sure her guilt for what she'd not even done was written all over her face.

"Copy that," Stirner said, turning back to them. "Nice seeing you again, Dr. Carver. I've got to go tend to something outside of town. Maybe I'll see you again. Nice meeting you, Mark."

"You, too, Deputy," Marquis said, watching Stirner hop into his patrol car and turn on the siren and roll out.

"We are so busted," Emily said.

"We haven't done anything yet, Em," Marquis said. "You didn't tell me you were BFFs with one of the deputies."

"I'm not," Emily said, watching Stirner race off. She wondered what had sent him on his way, but was grateful for whatever it was, since it cleared the way for them to make the Temple. She saw the Sheriff's Office light up as several other cruisers shot out of there.

"Something's going on," Marquis said. "Let's take advantage of that, too. Come on."

He guided them across the street, Emily composing herself again. This wasn't the kind of fieldwork she was used to doing. She saw the pair of acolytes by the front doors. They weren't the same ones she'd seen earlier.

Marquis walked them around the block, to the back of the Temple, where there was a fire escape and a freight entrance. It was shadowy here, with just a couple of lights offering some illumination.

"Put on your mask," Marquis said, slipping on his ski mask. Emily followed suit, feeling particularly uncomfortable and exposed, even though they were not making noise in the shadows.

"Take off your coat," Marquis said, having already doffed his. He stuffed them in a duffle bag, which he set behind a bush

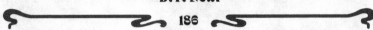
in a corner of the Temple. He put on his gloves, and Emily did as well. "Now, we keep really quiet. Follow my lead."

The thumping music of the Temple kept going, muted by the windows. Marquis went to the back entrance, a heavy steel service door with the interlocking triple circle of the Temple painted on it in white. He tried the door. It was locked, and he took out some lockpicks and began to work on the door.

"Keep an eye out," Marquis said.

Emily didn't relish being busted for breaking and entering, but when Marquis successfully picked the lock and opened the door, she eagerly went inside with him. Somehow it felt less illegal if she was indoors, versus in the doorway.

Inside the Temple, behind the scenes, it looked like any other place—boxes stacked, filing cabinets. Orderly, but otherwise unassuming. Emily didn't know what she expected, but it could have been anywhere. Even cults had everyday business to attend to, she assumed.

The music was muffled but could be heard pumping through the building. Marquis moved smoothly through this part of the place, which had storerooms and doors.

"There has to be a kitchen somewhere," Emily whispered. "To brew the Lady's Tears. Assuming they even make it here."

"Right," Marquis said. "You put your phone on mute, right?"

"Whoops," Emily said. She quickly muted her phone, put on her "Do Not Disturb" message. She felt like an idiot for even forgetting that.

There wasn't anybody back here; all the action was in the Grand Hall, by the sound of things. Past the storerooms were some offices, which looked ordinary with desks and computers and filing cabinets.

The first weird thing Emily saw was one hallway where there were a lot of hooks on the wall, and some grey robes hanging from them, with grey masks hanging on hooks above them. There were a half-dozen of them, and at least two dozen empty hooks.

Emily pointed to them. Opposite them were hanging some conical hats, also grey, as well as some grey scarves and shrouds.

"Ritual attire," Marquis said.

"Maybe we should put that on?" Emily asked. "So we can blend in better?"

Marquis considered it a moment, then nodded.

"Not a bad idea," he said. "Grab one and suit up. I'll cover while you do that."

Emily looked around them for cameras, didn't see any, prayed there weren't any around and quickly snatched a grey robe and put it on. Then she put the grey mask on her face, over her ski mask, then reconsidered and pulled her ski mask up into a stocking cap and then put the mask on. She grabbed one of the conical hats and slipped it on, noting that it had a strap that kept it in place. She took the grey scarf and slipped it on as well and grabbed a shroud.

"How do I look?" Emily asked, mindful of the sound of her voice behind the mask.

"Fucked up," Marquis said. He did the same thing, slipping on his own.

Emily heard Deputy Stirner's voice in her head, warning her about messing with the Grey Ladies. This was most certainly messing with them. Marquis suited up quicker than she had and looked twice as menacing. There was a full-length mirror on one side, and the two of them looked at each other's reflections in it.

"Good call," Marquis said. "Now we can poke around and look less obvious."

"I wonder where the other Greys are," Emily said.

"Not here," Marquis said. "That's all that matters. Let's go."

Emily wondered why no effort would have been made to conceal the vestments, but she assumed that perhaps the Grey Ladies were something of an open secret within the Temple. The arrangement was not unlike what she'd seen in firehouses, where equipment was set up for ease of access. She inferred that the Greys functioned in that sort of capacity at the Temple. Like soldier ants or bees, maybe, ready to scramble at a moment's notice.

Marquis walked them down the hallway, which led to a couple of doors, one that opened out into the Grand Hall, they discovered the moment they opened it a crack. There were people coming down from their trips, being tended to by the acolytes, while the music played and the lights flashed.

Closing that door, they went to the other door, which led to the kitchen space that Emily had suspected was there. There were sinks and silvery cup trays and there was a big stainless

steel cauldron that contained the blue tea and various pitchers and ewers.

"What a pain in the ass to pour all those little cups," Emily said.

"Cultists gonna cult," Marquis said. "See any samples?"

Emily went to several stainless steel worktables that were in three rows near the cauldron, next to a butcher's block. She could see there were mushroom remnants on the countertops, a chopped up blend of white and indigo. There were strainers and cleavers.

"What type of mushrooms?" Marquis asked.

"I don't recognize the type," Emily said, genuinely intrigued by what she was seeing. This looked to be a hitherto unknown species of mushroom, but it was difficult to tell from the chopped bits she was seeing. She took out an envelope from her messenger bag and snapped some photos of the samples from various angles, before sweeping them into one of the black envelopes, which she carefully stowed.

"No?" Marquis said. Emily shook her head.

"They've got a double boiler system here," Emily said, pointing to another cauldron at the other end, and then another. "No, a triple. They start here. They decoct from here. Then they transfer to the second cauldron and repeat the process. And then they strain and put in the third cauldron."

"How can you be sure they're not just using three cauldrons to boil?" Marquis asked.

"There's a sequence, here," Emily said, pointing to some laminated instructions tacked on the wall showing a three-cauldron flow with arrows.

Marquis was taking pictures with his phone while she talked.

"The fact that they need to triple boil these means that they're highly toxic," Emily said. "The boiling reduces the toxicity. That the Lady's Tears are still so potent even after this means they have to be very strong. All the blue stain means there's ample psilocin and psilocybin in these mushrooms, but the triple boiling points to something else, as well. Likely ibotenic acid and muscimol—both neurotoxins. We'll know after analysis on them."

Emily took out some stoppered vials from her bag and she marked them quickly: Cauldron 1, Cauldron 2, Cauldron 3 and

took samples from each of the cauldrons, filling the vials and sealing them tightly. It would be useful to see the chemical composition of each cauldron.

An acolyte came into the kitchen, a young woman with brown eyes and glasses with buckwheat brown hair in pigtails. She looked to be in her 20s.

"Oh, I'm sorry, Exemplars," she said. "I was going to get some water for the congregants, Brethren. They're leaving the Lady's Grace."

"Go about it, then," Marquis said, and the acolyte quickly went to the sink and filled a pitcher, grabbing a stack of paper cups.

"Is something the matter?" the acolyte asked. "Are we in danger?"

"No," Marquis said. "The Lady protects us all."

"Yes," the acolyte said, smiling nervously, even as she side-eyed Marquis and Emily. "I had thought all of the Exemplars had gone afield in search of the Red Deaths."

"Clearly, you were mistaken, Acolyte," Emily said. "Tend to the flock."

"At once," the acolyte said, topping off the pitcher. She scuttled out of there, glancing back at them a moment before disappearing down the hallway.

"We need to keep moving," Marquis said.

"Yeah, we do," Emily said.

Exemplars. Okay, that made some sense, then, she thought. Within the cult's hierarchy, the grey-clad Exemplars were a higher echelon than the acolytes or the deacons.

"The mushrooms have to be somewhere relatively close," Emily said. She could see there were wicker baskets on the third worktable. She made mental map of where they were, remembered where Mona Templeton had absconded to during the ceremony.

Emily walked over to the far side of the kitchen, picturing the Grand Hall to her right, where the music and the light was coming from.

She saw a utility door ahead of her that was painted with the three interlocking circles that had been on the rear entrance.

Emily tried the door, but it was locked. She called Marquis over and he went to work on it while she kept watch.

"It has to be this room," Emily said. "Although with the volume they're producing, I don't know. It would have to be cavernous. Or else they get a lot of mileage out of that tea they're brewing."

She walked over to one of several stainless steel refrigerators that were on one side of the kitchen and she opened them. Inside were many rows of the Lady's Tears. They'd been labeled as such:

"Grove 6: Batch 11, Grove 9: Batch 15, Grove 7: Batch 27," Emily said, noting the dates. "They brew constantly. From multiple groves. Groves. Hmm. That makes me think these might be wild-harvested mushrooms that are brought in. Maybe out in the forests."

Emily went from fridge to fridge, seeing that there were scores of bottles brewed.

"Of course, if they had bottles handy, why bother fresh-brewing their tea at all?" Emily asked aloud, although the question was for herself.

"What do you mean?" Marquis asked.

"Well, they could just heat up a batch from the fridge," Emily said. "Versus making something fresh."

"Maybe it's because it's Festival weekend or something," Marquis said. "You know, like cult ritual stuff."

"That could be," Emily said. "Or maybe they're making it for export or something. I don't know."

Marquis grunted with satisfaction, stowing his lockpicks.

"I got it," he said, and Emily went over as he opened the door. She was not prepared for what she saw next. The door opened into a circular room.

"The Round Room," Emily said, recalling what Clea had called it.

In the Round Room, which was illuminated with black lights and grow lights, was a kind of artificially constructed fairyland—Emily didn't know what else to consider it. The room was like a little garden of sorts with a path running around it in a ring. The path led to a door at the far side, but what was of particular interest to Emily was what was in the center of that pavestone path. There were *Amanita* mushrooms of the most otherworldly blue she'd ever seen, growing within a grove of bizarre and gnarly clusters of sweet cherry trees. Within the grove, shadowed by the winding arms of the trees, was an idol

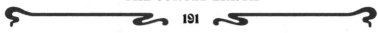
of *La Signora,* surrounded by the blue mushrooms at its base, as well as an empty golden throne inscribed with arcane glyphs.

"Blue *Amanitas,*" Emily said, in wonder. "I've never seen anything like these before."

They grew profligately on the inside of the path, among the twisted roots of the sweet cherry trees. She took out her phone and began photographing the mushrooms from every angle, wanting to capture them in all of their surreal glory. They looked like Fly Agarics, with the same shape, except instead of red and white speckled caps, they were an almost royal blue with white speckles, and the speckles glowed in the black light.

"As I suspected, they've got to be brimming with muscimol and ibotenic acid, as well as, bizarrely, psilocin and psilocybin. I don't know if this is a cultivated strain or something they found in the wild and bred. *Amanita dominaelacrimae.*"

"What the hell did you just say?" Marquis said.

"Lady's Tears *Amanita,*" Emily said. "Most likely *Amanita.*"

Painted on the walls of the garden, around the ring of the path, were frescoes depicting the Grey Lady, holding out the blue mushrooms to Her faithful. The story showed this, showed them settling in Lynchburg, surrounded by trees, depicted them planting mushroom crops, showed them sacrificing people to the Grey Lady, who received the sacrifices with Her characteristically stony-faced visage. Some of the people were black-clad Puritan-looking types lashed to wooden posts, while followers carried bowls of blood to sacrificial altars. Dead sacrifices were buried under the ground, and blue mushrooms grew atop them. The Temple was depicted as well as a kind of great stone monolith. Marquis and Emily both recorded it with their phones.

"Get some samples, and let's get the hell out of here," Marquis said.

"Right," Emily said. She copiously photographed the mushrooms before carefully picking a dozen of them, which she painstakingly put in the envelopes of the messenger bag. She wanted to get these mushrooms on one of the tables, so she could cross-section them while they were still fresh. "This is amazing. But no way are they using this to source what they were producing in the kitchen."

"What do you mean?" Marquis asked.

"The volume is too great for what they are growing here," Emily said. "There must be some other room somewhere. A bigger room. Maybe in the basement. And the other groves, wherever they are."

"Do you think these are the Lady's Tears?" Marquis asked.

"I think they could be," Emily said. "But we'd have to analyze everything. We've got samples of the Tears, and we've got these mushrooms. We need a lab, need to just study it all."

"Do you have enough?" Marquis asked.

Emily wanted to stay and study these in detail, despite their situation, but she knew she only had so much time. She took another of the stoppered vials and hastily took a soil sample with it, securing it.

"Okay," Emily said. "I think that's enough for now."

"For now," Marquis said, scoffing. "Like we're ever coming back here."

He went back out the way they'd come in, avoiding the door on the far side that led to the Grand Hall.

"Why the black lights?" Marquis asked.

"Not sure," Emily said. "Maybe ultraviolet light plays a role for them. Maybe it's weirdly ceremonial. Not entirely sure."

She snapped some photographs of the garden and the grove before they stepped back into the normal light, Marquis shutting the door, retriggering the lock.

Emily blinked away the black light, her mind swimming with the possibilities.

The pigtailed acolyte had returned with two other acolytes, a pair of strong-looking young men—one black-haired, the other blond. They were accompanied by Clea. Emily recognized her from earlier in the evening. She looked at them with genuine confusion.

"Exemplars," Clea said. "We didn't expect you to be here. Is there a problem? Where are the others?"

"We'd heard the Red Deaths were making a play for the Temple," Marquis said. "We're doing a search to make sure that they don't. Have you seen any sign of them?"

"It's not possible, Exemplars," Clea said. "We took care of them in the Hollow."

"Not likely all of them," Marquis said. "There are more."

Clea took out her phone, dialing someone.

"Eminence," Clea said. "There are some Exemplars here. They say the Red Deaths are trying something."

Clea looked genuinely upset, afraid, even. She held out the phone to Marquis.

"She wants to talk to you, Exemplar," Clea said. Emily watched the other acolytes, who were wary and unsure of what to do, either.

"Alright," Marquis said, taking the phone. "Eminence, there are Red Deaths making a move on the Temple."

"Who is this? Is this Regis?" the woman asked.

"Yes," Marquis said.

"I thought you were moving to intercept them in the Hollow," the woman said.

"We were," Marquis said. "There was trouble."

"The Sheriff was dispatched," the woman said. "I received the report. Stay there, Regis. I'm heading back to Temple."

"We don't want to interrupt the Invocation, Eminence," Marquis said.

"It's already happened," the woman said. "Hold fast until I return. Put Clea back on."

Emily was more grateful than ever that she was wearing a mask, as she was terrified. She couldn't believe how good Marquis was at brazening his way through this.

Clea spoke quickly to the Eminence.

"Yes, Eminence," Clea said. "I understand. They're coming out from under the Lady's Grace. Yes. Probably another hour. Okay, see you then."

Clea hung up.

"The Eminence instructed me to tell you that we need to get the congregants out of the Temple," Clea said. "Acolytes, get them out of the Grand Hall. Be gentle with them but lead them out. Services must conclude at once. Exemplars, you are to continue your searching and are to call her if there's anything amiss. She'll be here momentarily."

The acolytes sprang into action, heading back into the Grand Hall, while Clea watched the two of them a moment.

"The Red Deaths are nearly finished here," Clea said. "The other Exemplars have seen to it. How you two managed to get here is nothing short of miraculous."

"The Lady works in mysterious ways," Marquis said. "Go tend to the congregants. We'll keep patrolling."

"Yes, Exemplar," Clea said. "As you command."

She clacked away, and Marquis and Emily hastened to get out of the Temple, Emily finding her hands were shaking.

"You're really good at that," Emily said.

"It's not that hard," Marquis said. "You just, you know, bluff a little."

"Just a little," Emily said. "Do you think they suspect us?"

"Maybe," Marquis said. "That's the thing about cults—everybody's suspecting everyone else on some level. But you play with their expectations, and their own cult hierarchical logic kind of eats its own tail. You see an Exemplar, you slip into the role that's expected of an Exemplar. The Exemplars are their middle management, so the rank-and-file listen to them. It falls into place."

"Who was the Eminence?" Emily asked, as they made their way to the loading entrance.

"I don't know," Marquis said. "I'm assuming it was Mona Templeton."

He reached the back door and opened it, the two of them slipping out.

"Okay, so we're keeping these damned robes," Marquis said as they worked their way back to the spot where they had stashed their coats. "We'll change out here and stash this in the bag."

They quickly changed, slipping everything into his gym bag, and they made their way through the shadows to a spot where they could doff their ski masks. As they did so, Emily could see a procession of a half-dozen Grey Ladies making their way to the Temple with Mona Templeton at the head of them.

"Look," Emily said.

"I see them," Marquis said. "Let's just take the scenic route back to the Grand."

They went down First Street, which intersected with Broad Street, which took them to the other side of Grand, which got them back into the Festival District, which was cordoned off.

Emily still felt terrified, coming down off of that rush she'd experienced.

"I can't believe we pulled that off," Emily said. "I mean, you did. I'm so glad you were there."

"It's all good," Marquis said. "We just have to play it cool, now. Just relax, okay? Don't look so nervous, Em. If they have

that place wired up with cameras, they might figure out what we did. Otherwise, they won't have a clue. They're busy looking for those Red Deaths, not us."

The Festival District was still humming around the taverns and bars, as Emily could see the clock tower showing that it was ten o'clock.

"Yeah, what was that all about?" Emily asked.

"No idea," Marquis said.

They reached the Grand Hotel without incident, and Emily was relieved that Cloris was apparently finally off duty. She didn't know if she could bear having the young concierge watching her from the front desk yet again.

It was somewhat quieter in the lobby than it had been earlier in the evening, and they got to the elevator without incident.

"I want to study these samples," Emily said. "While they're fresh."

"A hotel room's hardly laboratory conditions," Marquis said.

"Right, but they're fresh, like I said," Emily said. "Worth a look."

"We can use my room," Marquis said.

"We should check on Ash, see how she is," Emily said, when they got to their floor.

"Later," Marquis said. "First things first."

Emily ignored him and keyed into their room. Ash had been laying on the bed, hopped up when the door opened.

"Emily," Ash said. "Christ, where'd you guys go?"

Marquis glanced at Emily, who was irritated that she'd made this stop.

"Out," Emily said. "Field trip. Just checking on you, seeing if you're okay."

"Thanks," Ash said, looking weary. "I'm fine."

"See? She's fine," Marquis said. "Can we go, now?"

Ash looked searchingly at them both.

"What were you two up to?" Ash asked, eyeing the bag Emily was carrying.

"Nothing you need to worry about," Marquis said. "Come on, Em."

"Wait, you guys can't just ditch me again," Ash said.

Marquis was not thrilled at the prospect of having the investigative journalist coming along with them.

Emily set the bag down on the table and opened it, despite Marquis protesting.

"Em, what are you doing?" Marquis asked. "I said we should use my room."

"Nah," Emily said. "This is better. Ash needs to see this, too."

"I don't see why that matters," Marquis said.

"She's part of it, too," Emily said.

Emily fished out the envelopes and carefully opened them, revealing the blue-capped mushrooms. Ash whistled.

"What the heck are those?" Ash asked.

"Lady's Tears, is my guess," Emily said. "Remember that back room in the Temple? The Round Room? The one behind the idol? It was filled with these, among other things."

Ash glowered at Marquis and Emily.

"You guys went to the Temple again without me?" Ash said. "Dammit, you guys."

"You had a lot on your mind," Marquis said. "We handled it. You know, two's company, three's a crowd."

"The hell with that," Ash said. "You should have told me."

Emily took one of the mushrooms and looked it over carefully, turning it in her hand. She snapped photos of it, and Ash followed suit, only to have Marquis intervene.

"These are for Mycopharmix," Marquis said. "Not some news article you're writing."

"Oh, sure," Ash said. "Proprietary. People need to know about these."

"Not yet," Marquis said. "Don't you dare write or post anything about it yet. Remember our deal."

Ash sulked, while Emily worked. She took out her mushroom knife and sliced one of the blue mushrooms in half, carefully arranging the cross-sectioned mushroom and taking more photographs of it.

"Definitely looks like some *Amanita* variant," Emily said. "Although I've never seen a Fly Agaric that was blue before."

She snapped her own photographs of it, capturing every angle.

"You think that's what they're brewing for the Lady's Tears," Ash said.

"Yeah," Emily said. "They have a whole brewing operation in the back of that Temple. Although the volume of Lady's Tears they were producing makes me think there had to be a larger

area someplace where they were growing them. Maybe some tunnels in the basement or something like that. And we saw bottles indicating other groves."

"I could have found this out," Ash said, giving Marquis another hard look.

"There wasn't time," Marquis said. "Alright, are you done with Show & Tell, now, Em? We need to get these packed away. Frankly, I'm inclined to slip out of town tonight with them."

Ash and Emily both turned to look at Marquis, who sighed.

"What? This changes things a bit as far as I'm concerned," Marquis said. "Right now, those freaks don't know what we just did. If I get out of here directly, I can get these samples to Pittsburgh and get them shipped to Jerry straightaway."

"Come on, Marquis," Emily said. "We don't know for sure if there are other species we need to gather."

"This is enough," Marquis said. "It sure as hell is something. Jerry'll be happy with that. Pack them up, and I'll leave."

"What about Ash and me?" Emily asked.

"You do what you want," Marquis said. "I'll make sure you're compensated. Enjoy the Festival. Deal with Ash's sister. Whatever you need to do."

Emily couldn't entirely dispute his logic, but she was annoyed by it all the same. She took some comfort in Marquis being with them.

"You're abandoning us," Emily said. "I thought you were our handler."

"It's a festival," Marquis said. "The town's going to be really jumping tomorrow. I'd rather get out ahead of it than get stuck here during high tide. Look, if I can get these shipped out, it works out best for you. You'll both get paid."

As tired as she was, Emily didn't want to part with the mushrooms. But she understood the man's logic.

"You're the team leader," Emily said. "It's your call to make."

"That's right," Marquis said. "And I'm making that call. Pack it up."

Emily reluctantly put everything back in the messenger bag. She understood that the tabletop was hardly an ideal place to study the fungus, but she wanted to examine it all the same. Marquis watched her closely as she put everything back, clearly wanting to make sure Jerry got all of his samples. Since this was a Mycopharmix operation, since she'd agreed to it, Emily went along with it.

"Not cool, Marquis," Ash said. "First you ditch me, now you're ditching us."

Marquis took the messenger bag, shrugging.

"Enjoy the festival, ladies," Marquis said. "Be seeing you. Oh, and you can have this."

He dropped the gym bag, the one that contained the robes.

"Wait, what?" Emily asked.

"Don't need those," Marquis said. "You can have them."

"Are you setting us up, Marquis?" Emily asked.

"Nope," Marquis said. "I'm just traveling light. And that right there is baggage I don't need."

Ash looked at Emily and Marquis in confusion, before bending and opening the gym bag.

"What the hell?" Ash asked. "Masks and robes? Are these official?"

"Yeah," Emily said. "From the Temple."

"Maybe we could use these to get Melinda," Ash said.

"Or not," Emily said, while Ash toyed with one of the grey masks, turning it over in her hands. They looked like they were papier-mâché, carefully constructed and both painted and lacquered for durability. On the inside of the mask, she saw the three interlocking circles painted upon them on the forehead in blue.

Marquis grinned at Emily, shrugging shamefacedly as he left them in the hotel room. Emily ran to the door and locked the deadbolt, but also the chain.

"He's setting us up to take the fall," Emily said. "I just know it."

Ash had taken the hats and robes out and set them on the bed, studying them.

"You two posed as cultists and then stole the samples?" Ash asked. "That's some real spy shit right there."

"Yeah," Emily said. "You should have seen that, I don't know what you'd call it—shrine? Wait, I took pictures. I'll send them."

She sent the various pictures to Ash, who was transfixed by them as she clicked through the images.

"Freaky," Ash said. "It is a shrine. What's with the weird lighting?"

"They had black lights in there," Emily said. "Not sure why. It made the white speckles on the mushrooms glow."

"Trippy," Ash said.

Emily was trying to think of what they should do. Marquis was taking advantage of her own burgeoning friendship with Ash to keep her here while he slipped out of town. If and when the cultists became aware of the theft, they'd be scouring the town for the culprits. It likely served her own interests to leave town as well, but Emily still wanted to tour the Nightcap farm and see what else she might uncover.

The classic *Amanita muscaria* was ectomycorrhizal, which meant that it formed symbiotic relationships with trees. The Fly Agaric did this with all sorts of trees. Emily went back to her photographs and looked at the shrine, at the sweet cherry trees.

"We know they like to grow with the sweet cherry trees," Emily said. "Although if they're like other *Amanita* species, they can form partnerships with all sorts of trees."

Ash studied the photographs, making comments as she did so.

"It's weird," Ash said. "Those twisted trees in there. Why would they do that?"

Emily shrugged.

"I'm not a psychologist," Emily said. "No idea why they'd have that little grove in there. It must be for some ritualistic reason."

"Creepy," Ash said. "Can't believe you guys went without me. I'm hurt."

"Sorry," Emily said. "You were dealing with your sister, your parents, all of that stuff."

"Still, I am a professional," Ash said, clicking through the pictures. "This is some weird shit."

Emily wondered where those blue *Amanitas* might be found in the wild. They had to have come from the mysterious groves indicated on the bottles in the Temple fridges. Everything about their presence here in Lynchburg pointed to it. Maybe someone had discovered them out here, likely old Ned Templeton and his wife. They'd built something around their discovery, once they'd realized what they had.

The triple cauldrons were interesting. It played with the three circle motif of the cult's symbology as well. Three circles, three cauldrons. She wasn't an anthropologist or sociolo-

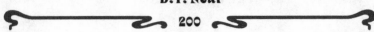
gist, but there had to be some significance to that. How they'd discovered that they needed to do three boilings was curious. People must have died back then. Any *Amanita* was dangerous if improperly handled. The Lady's Tears had to be particularly potent, and, therefore, dangerous.

Emily's mind wandered to what it must have been like in Lynchburg in the 19th century, with the Quakers and Native Americans and fur trappers and others, surrounded by the thick forests, worshipping their strange Grey Lady in secret.

Given how openly the cultists were operating here, the secrecy of it overall was curious to Emily. It had been a well-kept secret. The remoteness of Lynchburg was certainly a factor. Back in the day, it would have been something of a jaunt to get way out here. That would have helped. But she thought that the locals must have done other things to ensure word didn't get out too quickly about what they were up to.

"What are we going to do about your sister?" Emily asked. Ash shook her head, paced around the room.

"I don't have a good answer to that one," Ash said. "My folks are looking up some experts on cults, are going to keep me posted on that."

"Okay," Emily said. "I imagine that'll take some time. Are you going to stay here?"

"Yeah," Ash said. "No way am I just leaving Melinda here. I'll just try to set up regular meet-ups or something. Stay in her mix."

Emily didn't envy Ash having to do that. She was torn between wanting to help out her friend and chase after Marquis and not give him the satisfaction of showing off "his" discoveries to Jerry. She thought she'd give Jerry a call and tell him what they'd found.

# 13

**Austin came to his senses roughly between Templeton** and Main, with Mallory and the Twins close by. It was weird because they had found themselves on a street tinged with colors and shapes, guided by the acolytes—who still looked like gleaming ghosts to him. But it was just the aftermath of the trip, because the street slowly started to look like itself again.

He'd been coming down since being inside the Temple, but the others, having drunk the Lady's Tears, were still floating around in whatever headspace they'd found themselves in. By virtue of having been the only one to not drink the proverbial Kool-Aid, Austin became chaperone by default.

"Come on, you guys," Austin said.

"Austin," Mallory said, clawing for his hand. "My best friend in the whole universe."

"Mine, too," Jess said, taking his other hand.

"And mine," Jake said, taking his sister's hand.

They walked like that down Main Street, Austin trying to keep them from wandering into traffic.

"Just follow my lead," Austin said.

"It's all too beautiful," Jess said, and she began to cry. Mallory squeezed Austin's hand.

"You're beautiful, Austin," Mallory said. "You're so there, you know? Did you know that you can't be 'there' without being 'here' as well? Think about it."

"Yeah," Austin said. He was trying to process the evening, which was a pile of sensations. He'd fallen in love, he knew that. Then the roof had blown off the Temple, before settling back onto the building and becoming an eyeball. Dancing and a sea of shapes and colors. He'd seen all of that. And the Goddess had spoken to him. He'd seen that, too. Like She'd held him in Her hands. She'd told him something.

They were actually walking down Ambrose Alley, which ran between Templeton and Main, leading to Grand. He could see the pavilion tents at the end of it, and the lantern lights.

"I'm tired," Jess said. "My feet are roller skates, but I'm so tired. Tired of just skating along."

She promptly sat on the ground, and Austin and the others had to help her up, but she whined and complained with every jostle.

"You don't understand," Jess said. "You don't understand. You don't understand me. You don't understand this. You don't understand Her."

"Why don't you tell us, Jess?" Austin said, counting on her getting occupied enough with that to quit fighting them in the alley. True to form, she kept talking while he and the others moved on.

"It's the Web," Jess said. "The Lady is at the center of the Web. I saw the Web in the Temple. Right over our heads."

"You mean the Internet?" Austin asked. He knew it was the wrong answer, but he also knew that it would keep Jess rolling as she sought to explain it.

"No," Jess said. "Not the Net. The Web. I'm saying the Web, not the Net. The Net will catch you, but the Web will keep you."

Mallory laughed, shaking out her hair.

"I'm still so high," Mallory said. "I can literally see through my own hand."

She held up her free hand for Austin to look at, laughing.

"I can't even play Peek-a-Boo," Mallory said. "You can't play Peek-a-Boo with X-ray vision, Austin. Peek-a-Boo! Peek-a-Boo!"

Mallory kept holding her free hand over her eyes and saying "Peek-a-Boo" while remarking about how she could see through her hand.

"Can you see through me?" Austin asked.

"I can see right through you, Austin," Mallory said, leering at him.

"Guys," Jess said. "I'm telling you about the Web. Jeezus."

Austin hated being the only almost-sober one, the designated driver. The responsibility was just too great. He was charged with getting everybody to the hotel safely. Not that he didn't think he could do it, but it was three on one. Jake's trip was a quieter, more introspective one, while Jess was the jab-

berjaw and Mallory was busy alternately flirting with him and teasing him.

"The Web entangles us all," Jess said. "I mean, I see it. Like strands of it, silver strands. Maybe white. Maybe both. Quantum entanglement. It's right there. And the Lady's watching us. She's out there. Up there."

Jess nodded at the night's sky, which looked beautiful despite the light pollution of Lynchburg. The moon would be full tomorrow. It already looked lovely.

"She spins Her webs, and we're caught in them," Jess said. "Cosmic cobwebs."

That made her laugh, and Mallory joined in. Jake was just staring at his shoes. Austin could only wonder what he was seeing.

The clock tower heralded midnight, and the tolling of the bell amused the hell out of his friends, who kept saying "Bong!" with each tolling of the bell.

"It's officially tomorrow," Jake said. "Dudes, it's, like tomorrow today. Right now."

"Clocks are contrivances," Mallory said. "Arbitrary and meaningless."

"The Web has no clocks," Jess said. "We're on Her time."

They cleared the alley and were on Grand Avenue, which was quieter, now. The lantern lights still burned, but most of the people were gone, aside from the bars and taverns.

"Tomorrow's the big day," Mallory said. "And by 'tomorrow' I mean 'today' of course."

They saw the clown on Grand, near the hotel.

Austin actually had to blink a moment to be sure he was seeing what he was seeing. It was a big clown in a red suit with white polka dots. He had big red clown shoes and had a white neck ruffle and ruffled cuffs and bone-white gloves. His face was painted white with a big-ass grin and big red nose and had black slashes above and below his eyes. He wore a royal blue wig and wore a red conical hat that made it look like someone had dropped an ice cream cone on his head. He was carrying three red balloons in one hand and was taunting tourists that were making their way into the Grand.

"Are you fucking kidding me?" Austin said. "You're all seeing that, right?"

"Wait, is that Pennywise?" Jake said, squinting.

"No, you idiot! It's Fun Gus," Mallory said, freeing her hands and clapping them. She ran up.

"Fun Gus," Austin said. "Oh, ha, I get it."

Fun Gus beamed at them, honking a bike horn.

"Hey, Kids," Fun Gus said. He had a gravelly voice that sounded like it had endured one too many whiskeys over the years. "Having a Grand time of it, are we?"

"We are, Fun Gus," Mallory said. "I remember you from last year. You're Fun Gus the Laughing Clown."

"That's me," Fun Gus said, clutching his belly and mock-laughing, shaking his shoulders. "And I've got three red balloons left. One for each of you."

"But there's four of us," Austin said.

Fun Gus guffawed.

"Math never was my strong suit, Boyo Toyo," Fun Gus said. "Let's see, Ladies first, am I right?"

Fun Gus took one red balloon and tied it to Mallory's wrist with a flourish. She loved it, batting her arm around, making the helium balloon dance. Austin could see Mushy was printed on the balloon, winking at them.

"Me next," Jess said, elbowing her way past Mallory, holding out her left wrist. Fun Gus took her wrist in his white-gloved hand and tied the balloon to it, making another flourish as he did so.

"Voila!" Fun Gus said. "You are hereby protected by the wicked wit and bewitching whimsy of Fun Gus, my darlings."

He honked his bike horn two times—honk-honk, honk-honk, and Mallory and Jess laughed, high-fiving each other. Austin wanted only to go into the hotel, but the others were captivated by Fun Gus.

Fun Gus was taller than both Austin and Jake, was a genuinely big man, and his garrulous laugh was powerful. Austin could see he had a top hat on the ground that had coins and bills in it. Fun Gus saw him looking, winked at him.

"Just clowning around, Son," Fun Gus said. "No law against that. Not yet, anyway. So, one balloon left, and two boys to give it to. Whatever am I to do? Ladies, how about you decide the fate of these young men. You decide."

"I don't want a fucking balloon," Jake said. "What am I, three?"

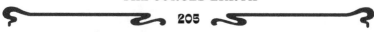
"You're Number Three," Fun Gus said. "If you're lucky, you see. You decide, Ladies. Who gets the last balloon from Uncle Fun Gus?"

Austin hated clowns. Everyone in their right mind hated clowns. A clown at the end of a long night was about the worst thing he could have imagined, but he was glad he wasn't still tripping. Lord knows what he would have seen.

"Austin," Mallory said.

"Jake," Jess said.

"My, oh, my, we have a tie," Fun Gus said. "Austin, Texas, or Jake the Snake. My, oh, my. I could just die. Or you could. It's anybody's ballgame, Kids. Should I do the Eenie Meenie? Or the Hokey Pokey? Or Ring Around the Rosey?"

"Ashes, Ashes," Jess said, laughing uproariously.

*Ash,* Austin thought, remembering her again, in her radiant glory. Ash.

"And the winner is," Fun Gus said. "Less than Jake."

"Aren't you onstage tonight?" Jake said.

"A clown's work is never done," Fun Gus said. "And, no, not tonight. Sunday, Sunday, Sunday! Fun Gus has all day today to sleep it off. But I'll be out tonight, you can be sure of it. Where there are tourists to be had, there's money to be made, am I right? Rent doesn't pay the bills. Now, gimme your wrist, Kid. Don't worry, I'm not gonna slash it."

Jake glared at Fun Gus, but Jess and Mallory persuaded him to hold out his arm, and Fun Gus gamely tied the balloon to his wrist. Fun Gus honked his horn three times.

"There, was that so bad?" Fun Gus said. "Poor Austintatious. Odd man out."

The clown made mock tear-mopping with his hand, pretend pouting.

"Alright, can we go, now?" Austin asked.

"No balloons left to give," Fun Gus said. "You know what that means."

"What does it mean?" Austin asked.

Fun Gus laughed in his face.

"Oh, you'll see, you'll see," Fun Gus said. He honked his horn once at Austin—honk-honk. Then, with a deft sleight-of-hand, produced three tickets with his free hand. They were white cardstock with "Fun Gus the Laughing Clown" on them printed in red, showing the grinning clown clutching three balloons,

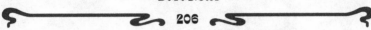
performing before a rapt audience of little mushrooms. On the back of the card was "Admit One" printed in red ink.

"See? I'm a fun guy" Fun Gus said. "You can be a fungi, too, Fun Guy."

"Double-sided," Austin said. "Nice."

He reached for the tickets, but Fun Gus pulled them just out of reach.

"Don't you dare be late, Austin Martin," Fun Gus said, pressing the tickets into his hand. Austin wanted to recoil from his touch. "You have to decide. Savvy? You decide."

Then he broke off into a raspy cackle, honking his horn.

"All out of balloons," Fun Gus said. "It's never over until the Grey Lady sings, and She sings my tune at midnight. I'm afraid I've got to go."

"Aww," Jess said. "Don't leave us, Fun Gus."

"I have to, my dear," Fun Gus said. "Or else I turn into a pumpkin. Or was it a glass slipper? Who can tell?"

He bent down and picked up his top hat, held it out to them expectantly.

"Help a clown in need?" Fun Gus said. Everybody looked at Austin, of course. "The Bank of Austin. I like it."

He gave the top hat a shake, the coins inside jingling a bit, his greasepainted face leering, his blue eyes boring into him, suggestively glancing back at the mouth of the hat, his eyebrows flicking up and down.

"Come on, Austin Villa," Fun Gus said. "I mean, I gave you three tickets, and gave your friends each a balloon. Isn't that worth something?"

Austin produced a crisp twenty-dollar bill, and the clown's eyes lit up.

"Now you're talking," Fun Gus said. "Feed me, Sunshine."

Austin tossed the twenty into the hat, and the clown honked his horn again.

"Sold American!" Fun Gus said. "See you soon, Kiddies!"

He then walked down the street, heading into one of the open bars, in this case, Staley's Tavern, up the street.

"I can't believe I just got shaken down by a clown," Austin said.

"Not just an ordinary clown," Mallory said. "Fun Gus is a local celebrity."

"Whatever," Austin said.

"I can believe it," Jake said.

*You decide,* Austin heard in his head, the clown's grizzled face grinning over him as he and the others went into the brightly-lit lobby of the Grand Hotel. He didn't know what the hell that even meant.

*You decide.*

# PART THREE:
# DURING

# 1

**Logan woke up feeling good and tired, his head still**
buzzing. In bed with him was Maura, who was sleeping on her
stomach, her dark hair splayed on the pillow. He glanced at the
digital clock on the nightstand, indicating that it was almost
six o'clock in the morning. Logan was always an early riser.

The Shroom Room food she'd brought after shift was piled
up on the table, and there was a spent champagne bottle in a
bucket near some overturned plastic cups.

Getting up carefully so as not to disturb her, he glanced
back, realizing that she was looking at him with one eye, her
face against the pillow.

"Sorry, did I wake you?" Logan asked.

"Only just," Maura said. "You ready for Festival Day?"

She perched her head on her elbow, and Logan could see she
wore a silver three-circle pendant. He half-remembered that
during the night, the way it danced against her chest as she
rode him. Or the way it tumbled when he rode her. She'd been
enthusiastic during the night, despite her no doubt exhausting
workday.

"I think we started the festivities early," Logan said.

"Can't argue with that," Maura said.

Maura had been insatiable, and Logan had both welcomed
and feared it. He'd had his fair share of lovers in his busy life,
but Maura had been something spectacular.

"So, now what?" Logan asked. She laughed—at him, with
him—he didn't care.

"Daddy agrees to the franchising opportunity on one condition," Maura said. She made one of her hands into a little figure
walking pertly along the pillowtops, like a pixie. She watched it
walk a moment before flicking her eyes to him.

"Oh?" Logan asked.

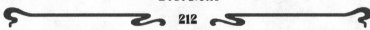
"Yeah," Maura said. "He wants you to join our faith."

Logan's Catholic boy childhood squirmed inside him. Not that he was anything but lapsed these days, but the roots were still there within him.

"Your faith," Logan said. *"La Signora?"*

"Yep," Maura said.

"What does that entail?" Logan asked. As a chef, he was used to breaking things down to their component parts.

Maura laughed again, rolled onto her back, putting her hands behind her head, propping herself. Logan's eyes went to her pendant that slipped between her breasts as he heard the tongue stud she had clicking against her teeth while she pondered.

"Problem, Logan?" Maura asked.

"Nope," Logan said. "Only I don't know if I'm ready to do something like that."

Maura sighed, staring off into the middle distance, like she was recalling a distant memory, which she probably was.

"We have a ritual for it," Maura said. "An initiation. I've grown up in the faith all my life. I did it when I turned 13 years old. So did my sister and brother. Everybody does. It's not like we don't let in adults. Of course we do. But I suppose it's different when you're older."

Logan sat on the edge of the bed.

"I'm not that old," he said.

"Don't I know it," Maura said. "I'm just saying that it's perhaps a little different for everyone. And different for adults than for children. You have to unencumber yourself of your baggage when you walk with the Lady."

"Baggage?"

Maura nodded, grinning at him.

"Do I seem encumbered to you?"

"Positively burdened," Logan said. They laughed, both knew it was untrue. Maura seemed unfathomably free.

"The Lady is there for us," Maura said. "I can't put it into words you would understand."

"Try me," Logan said. They could hear the clock tower bell tolling six o'clock, forlorn and haunting, and Logan felt the urge to walk to the window and open the blinds. He gave in to that urge while Maura spoke. As he did so, he let in grey light, as a fog had rolled in during the night, obscuring the town—the

rooftops were like tips of mountains swimming in a swirling sea.

"You need to go into the forest with us," Maura said. "And you need to drink the Lady's Tears. Not a tourist dose like they do in Mona's Temple, mind you. But a heroic dose."

"A heroic dose?" Logan said, laughing. "That sounds, well, heroic."

"It is," Maura said. "We all do it. It's something special."

Logan had done his share of drugs in his youth and wasn't particularly afraid of them. He wasn't a fan of hallucinogens, however. He didn't like unmooring his conscious mind from the everyday world. He lived professionally in a kind of constant here and now as well as fretting about the future.

"Okay, so a heroic dose of Lady's Tears, whatever that is," Logan said. "What else?"

Maura's voice was soothing, lower-toned and measured.

"That's between you and the Lady," Maura said. "I mean, a trip is a personal thing. It's different for everyone. Then there's whether or not the Lady accepts you into Her embrace. If She does, then you'll be able to join our family—not the Templetons, of course—but I mean the family of the Faith."

"And if She rejects me?" Logan asked.

"Then you become part of the Cursed Earth," Maura said. "As must we all, eventually. Some go sooner than later."

"What the hell does that even mean?" Logan asked. "What, I die?"

"Ego death is at the heart of a heroic trip," Maura said. "You lose yourself. The you that you are dies a psychic death. The rest is just a formality."

"What does 'the Cursed Earth' even mean? Why's it cursed?" Logan asked.

"The Earth is cursed to bear the pain and suffering of life itself," Maura said. "The Earth as we know it, the ground upon which we stand, the thin crust of life upon it, is rooted in death and decay. Without decay, there could be no life. Without life, there would be no decay. They dance together, life and death, the blessing and the curse together, interchangeable, switching roles as the moment requires it. Life itself is a blessing and a curse, a gift and a torment, depending on the moment. So it is with death, as well: it is both a blessed and a cursed thing. Life is the beginning, death is the ending, and the Cursed Earth

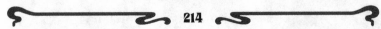
bears the everlasting memory of that sacred dance between them. Beauty blossoms, beauty fades. Love flowers, love fades. All that is shiny and new one day rots and ruins. Decay is the handmaiden of both life and death. Decay is the curse of life and the promise of death. It sits between them in the sacred trilogy. The Lady guides us along that path."

"Um, that sounds intense," Logan said.

"It simply is," Maura said. "I accept it."

"Seems, I don't know, grim," Logan said. "Like there's no hope in that."

Logan turned away from the fog and saw that Maura was slipping on her clothes.

"The Lady's Kiss is what you are looking for," Maura said. "Contact with the divine. She bestows Her Kiss upon you and you'll be transported and transformed. We all went through it."

"She kissed you?"

Maura nodded. "She kisses Her chosen people."

"What's that like?"

"Beautiful," Maura said.

Logan watched her get dressed, felt self-conscious standing there naked, grabbed his boxers and slipped them on. He didn't want it to be awkward between them.

"Okay, so then what?" Logan asked.

"If you receive the Lady's Kiss and She accepts you, then you become one of us," Maura said. "You get your restaurants in Pittsburgh and Philadelphia. We become partners, you and I."

"Partners? What, are we talking marriage, now?"

Maura laughed.

"Business partners, Stupid," Maura said. "You gain access to Nightcap's produce for your own Shroom Rooms. You work with me, we set up the rest of it. You become rich."

"I'm already rich," Logan said. It was only the hint of a brag, like a pinch of seasoning. He made good money with Chevron. Not stratospheric cash, but enough to be way more than comfortable.

"You become richer, then," Maura said. "So much richer—in body, mind, and spirit. Those are the roots of our three circles, you know: Body, Mind, and Spirit, just as much as Life, Decay, and Death."

"Circles," Logan said.

Her hand went to her silver pendant, tracing the circles with an outstretched index finger.

"The Lady tends to them all," Maura said.

Logan didn't want her to go, tried to keep her there with more questions.

"What does being part of your faith entail, though?" Logan asked. "Are we talking weekly services or what?"

"We have sacred rituals," Maura said. "As an acolyte, you'd be at the start of your journey. There's a lot of ground to cover. You lose your way, you find your way, you make your way. The Lady is there with every step once you join Her. It's a great comfort, having Her with you."

Logan watched her button up her blouse, her deft hands making short work of it. With Maura, no motion was wasted.

"There are deeper mysteries to our faith," Maura said. "Discoveries to be made along the way. But we're there for you, with you. You're never truly alone again."

Maura stood up, having slipped on her pants and buttoned them. She was tall, Logan was reminded. She had a coltish beauty he found alluring and comforting in the same breath.

"Maybe I like being alone," Logan said. "Or going my own way."

"Sure, sure, I get that," Maura said. "Lone Wolf Logan."

"Yeah," Logan said.

"That's the price of the franchising," Maura said. "That's *my* price. I like you, Logan. But if you want to partner with me, that's my price. Just so we have that understanding."

"You want me to join your cult," Logan said.

"Call us what you want," Maura said. "It's what we are. It's who we are. It's who and what I am. She slipped on her pumps, grabbed her coat.

Logan walked over to help her with it, which she accepted with a smirk.

"How long do I have to decide?" Logan asked.

"You can take as long as you like," Maura said. "But it IS Festival weekend. And there's a full moon tonight. From the perspective of the Lady—not that I would presume to speak for Her—today is a portentous day. A spirit walk with the Lady under the light of the full moon is a blessed event. You would be blessed in Her eyes. Any other day is another day. You can find the good in anything if you squint your eyes hard enough.

Tonight, however, would give you great standing among the faithful."

"But only if She accepts me," Logan said.

"Exactly," Maura said. "It's a risk, I suppose. People take risks all the time. The question is whether the risk is worth the reward. Only you can answer that."

Logan laughed, and Maura's eyes danced about the room, making sure she hadn't forgotten anything. She hadn't.

"I've never been recruited by a cult before," Logan said, and Maura reached out and caressed his cheek with a cool hand.

"Christianity's a cult," she said. "It always was, and always will be. It just mushroomed into something big. But we all know how it began. This isn't any different, except that *La Signora* isn't Jesus. I'm giving you the chance to belong to something greater than yourself, Logan. And to be rich in body, mind, and spirit. Don't blow it."

She leaned into him and gave him a long kiss. He embraced her and held her there a moment while they kissed, and she held his arms in hers, giving him a squeeze on his elbows with her hands. They parted, and she smiled at him.

"I won't," Logan said. "It's a big decision, is all."

"You ping me with your decision," Maura said. "I'll take care of the rest."

She left him in the hotel room, awash in the grey light of the fog and endless possibilities.

# 2

**Carlos did not know when he had passed out, only when** he woke up. He was bandaged in a prison cell, with Alejandro and Santiago in the cell with him. Carlos felt his arm throbbing, sat up.

"What the hell happened?" Carlos asked, in Spanish.

"We surrendered when you passed out, *Segundo*," Santiago said. "The Sheriff had turned up with a bunch of deputies. We figured if the choice was between them and those freaky cultists in the woods, we went with the lesser of two evils."

"Fuck," Carlos said. "This is crap. We are so dead. Santino is going to kill me. I was supposed to iron everything out. This has been a disaster."

Santino was not a forgiving man. He had entrusted Carlos as his Underboss with the understanding that he'd blaze whatever trails needed to be blazed. His failure with the cultists would not go without consequence.

Carlos looked around.

"Where's Lilli?" he asked.

"They took her to another part of the jail," Santiago said. "She didn't go quietly."

"I'll bet," Carlos said.

"Well, well, well," came a voice. A big man walked over, dressed in his uniform, bearing the eight-pointed star badge. "Morning, *Hombres*. I'm Sheriff Bill Leonard. You want to tell me why you were popping off automatic weapons at god-fearing Lynchburg townsfolk?"

"I want a lawyer," Carlos said, in English.

Sheriff Leonard had dusty blond hair and cornflower blue eyes and a craggy sort of face that played amiably with his ample white sideburns. He looked like a werewolf by way of a 1970s action hero.

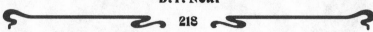
"I'll bet you do," Leonard said. "We have you for multiple weapons violations and a bunch of other things if I'm feeling creative. What are you doing here in Lynchburg, Mr. Mendoza?"

"Vacationing," Carlos said. "But we had a run-in with some crazy locals."

"Here's the thing," Leonard said. "The Fungus Festival is a family event. Family-friendly. Families come here. It's really good for tourist dollars. You know what's not good for that? People firing assault rifles and submachine guns at each other on Route 219."

Carlos glared up at Leonard, unsure how complicit he might be in everything that went on. Sheriff Leonard looked perfectly at ease, his low voice smooth.

"They killed my men," Carlos said.

"Who did?" Leonard asked.

"Masked weirdos," Carlos said. "Wearing grey robes."

Leonard laughed.

"It's Festival season," Leonard said. "Lots of people sporting robes and masks. Lotsa weirdos and hippies, too. What you don't do is shoot them down."

"Are you sure? They slashed our tires," Carlos said. "The car. Doesn't take a detective to spot that. And somebody shot me with a crossbow. I was the one who was shot. I'm the one who lost men at Hidden Hollow."

Leonard pulled up a chair, taking a seat.

"You thought you'd squirrel away in the Hollow," Leonard said. "You think you're the first fellas to do that? Not by a longshot. As for your missing men, what can I say to that? There's no trace of them."

"The Hollow," Carlos said.

"I sent deputies to the Hollow," Leonard said. "They said it was just you there."

"They're lying," Carlos said. "I had three dozen...associates there with me. They're all gone."

"Poof," Leonard said, making a little explosion in the air with his hand. "Gone, like they never existed."

Carlos couldn't tell if the Sheriff was incompetent or complicit. There was a fine line between cluelessness, collusion, corruption, and conspiracy.

"Yeah, like that," Carlos said. "The *cultistas* took their bodies and, I don't know, disappeared them. Probably buried them in the woods somewhere."

"That's quite a claim, Mr. Mendoza. But no bodies, no murder," Leonard said. "Missing is all you get out of that. I'm sure you know all about that. If you want to identify these missing men for me, I can see what I can do. We did some looking into you and your *Las Rojas*. You're some bad *hombres* in Pittsburgh, aren't you? Racketeering, drug trade, extortion, money laundering. All that kind of stuff. But you're not cartel guys, are you? Just local. I suppose that's good for you."

"How so?"

Leonard exhaled like the weariness of the world was leaving his lungs.

"Let's say there really was a bunch of masked cultists after you," Leonard said. "Let's just say that was for real. And I'm not saying it's real. If I'd been part of that, wouldn't I have just given you over to them on Route 219? Wouldn't that have been what I'd done?"

"I don't know," Carlos said. "They're *loco*. Maybe you're *loco*, too."

"What's an unarmed gangster?" Leonard said.

"Is this a joke?"

"I only wish it were," Leonard said. "An unarmed gangster is just a man. Just a fella. We confiscated your weapons. You're nothing but flesh and fists, no more bullets and bravado. I'm willing to let you walk, can you believe that? You get the hell out of my town, and you never come back. You set so much as a foot in Lynchburg again, and you lose that foot. That's not even a threat; it's a promise, and I'm a man of my word."

Carlos was convinced the Sheriff was in on it. It's why he wanted them gone. He didn't want federal agents in town. He wanted to sweep this under the rug. But why? Why had his other men been killed off and he still lived?

"Are you kidding me?" Carlos said, glancing at Santiago and Alejandro.

"Do I look like I'm joking?" Leonard said. "I'm giving you a literal Get Out of Jail Free card, Mr. Mendoza. On the condition that you never come to Lynchburg again. It's a rare thing in this world to be given a second chance. This is that second chance."

"Why?" Carlos said.

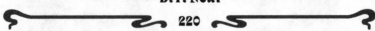
"What do you mean, 'why'? Haven't you ever heard of the proverbial gift horse? Don't look it in the mouth, son. Don't let pride nip at you. You haven't killed anybody in my town. You just fired off some guns at what you thought was, I don't know, self-defense. Let's let bygones be bygones, and you go back to Pittsburgh. You forget Lynchburg even exists."

Pride did well up in him. Carlos was furious at having been tuned up by these gringos. Absolutely everything he'd intended upon arrival had been turned on its head.

"Hey, Max," Leonard said. "Get a load of this one. This one's a hater."

One of the deputies appeared, a fit-looking younger man with brown hair and a mustache and piercing blue eyes.

"Yeah, you can see it, Sheriff," Max said. "He's bristling."

"How many second chances do you need to get, Mr. Mendoza?" Leonard asked. "Pack up, walk out, and never come back. From where I'm standing, that's a damned good deal. You can go get killed in Pittsburgh, where you belong."

"My men," Carlos said. "Do I really have to name them all? Three dozen of my men."

"Ghosts," Leonard said. "Nobody's seen them. That's neither here nor there. What I'm saying is that *you're* alive. Keep it that way, make the most of it. Get out of town. I promise you this is the best deal you're going to get."

Angry as he was, Carlos knew a good deal when he heard one. He couldn't understand why the Sheriff was making that deal with him at all. Then it occurred to him.

"You don't want us disrupting your festival," Carlos said. "That's it, isn't it?"

The Sheriff smiled at him, a wolfish sort of smile.

"That's right, Mr. Mendoza," Leonard said. "This is a family-friendly Festival, like I said. We're about family here. We want families to have a good time. What we don't want is some gang war breaking out on our streets, some crazy *Roja* bangers shooting up the place, stirring people up. That'd be bad press. Now, I could keep you locked up all weekend. Hell, I could keep you locked up and get you in court for the weapons violations. We could send you to Munroe Penitentiary to make some new friends. I could get on the phone and contact the feds, and then your problems would just blossom from there. Or, you could hear when I'm saying and get the hell out of Lynchburg. You can

go back to Pittsburgh and live your best gangster life far away from here."

"No honest lawman would give me that kind of deal," Carlos said. "I don't know what you're up to, exactly, but, yeah, I'll take your deal. My men and I will leave town. Only your people trashed our car. You're gonna give us a car, too?"

"No, we impounded that car. But there's an SUV parked outside that'll take you where you need to go," Leonard said. "Lynchburg's a quiet little town. We enjoy our forests and our festivals. We live a peaceful life out here. We like it that way. Do your part to help the town, Mr. Mendoza."

"Fine," Carlos said. "Fine, fine. Sure, whatever. What about Lilli?"

"Lilli stays," Leonard said.

"Excuse me?" Carlos said.

"Call her collateral if you want," Leonard said. "She's our guest until we have assurances that you're actually gone from town. Then she can rejoin you in Pittsburgh."

"That's ridiculous," Carlos said. "You're holding her hostage?"

"Believe me, that's the least of her worries," Leonard said. "Don't you worry, now. She'll be right as rain. So long as you are on your best behavior. But you do something—anything—we don't like, and, gosh, I don't even want to think about what might happen."

Deputy Stirner winced, walking away. Sheriff Leonard watched him go.

"That's not going to happen, though, now is it?" Leonard said. "You're going to be a good boy and take that SUV we picked up from the Hollow and you're going to get out of here. And your lovely Lilli will be returned to you."

Carlos could barely contain his rage at this smug sheriff. He could only imagine how Lilli would handle that. She was a fighter. She'd give them hell.

"I have to ask you, man to man," Carlos said. "Why not simply kill me and my men? Your people have already killed all my other men."

"They're not my people," Leonard said. "And is that what you want? You want us to just kill you? Take you out into the woods and kill you dead? Bury your bodies in the Cursed Earth and let your rot bring new life to the things around you?"

Alejandro looked pale, while Santiago just brooded, knowing better than to cross an angry Carlos.

"I'm only asking," Carlos said. "Three dozen of my men are dead. What's three or four more of us added to that pile? What makes us so special?"

"You're not special, Mr. Mendoza," Leonard said. "Not in the cosmic scheme of things. Hell, we're all equal in the Lady's eyes. We understand that you're part of a larger thing, just as we are. Your men? The ghosts? They're like your fingers, prying into our business. You tried to put your fingers into our pies. A man can live without his fingers. Maybe not as comfortably as he'd like, but he can live. You're right, of course. We could snuff you out and that would be that."

The Sheriff patted the pistol at his side, and for a moment, Carlos feared that he might draw it. But he only chuckled.

"The Lady's taken Her cut," Leonard said. "There's a balance, you know, between Life and Death. And She's had Her share of the Red Death. You've fed Her well, Mr. Mendoza. A feast of evil. You want to be dessert for the Lady? You come right back to Lynchburg once I spring you. Waste the gift of life I've given you. Your choice. Or, you take the opportunity to reflect upon the blessing you've been given, and you take that and build something out of it somewhere else."

"Let us go," Carlos said. "We'll take your deal. Only I want our phones."

"No phones," Leonard said. "You drive out of here as you are and that's that. Or I have my deputies fetch some shovels from Biff's Hardware on Main and we settle our accounts that way."

"Fine," Carlos said. He would torture this sheriff a long time before he killed him. They'd had $300K in the trunk of his car, too. He knew better than to even ask about that, where it had gone.

"That's great to hear," Leonard said. "Max, Phil, Dan, Shannon. You get those shotguns at the ready. We're going to escort the prisoners to their vehicle."

Carlos saw the deputies cock their slide-action pump shotguns, resting them on their hips, watching him and his men stand up. The Sheriff took out some keys and unlocked the jail cell, swinging it open. The well-oiled door didn't let out even so much as a squeak.

"That's right," Leonard said, his voice almost fatherly. "Out you go, boys. *Uno, dos, tres.* On your way. You'll be happy to know that we covered your medical expenses, Mr. Mendoza. Getting that ol' crossbow bolt out—you've got no *quarrel* with us, yeah?"

Sheriff Leonard laughed to himself like he'd said something funny, but Carlos was too angry to dwell on it. Even if he'd wanted to do something, Carlos knew he was in no condition to do it. And the deputies were watching them like hawks. Carlos memorized their faces. They'd all pay for the indignity he'd suffered here. The humiliation of the clemency itself was more than he could stomach.

His wounded pride hurt him more than the bolt he'd taken. The only salve he had was the consolation that he would have his revenge when the time was right. This was simply not the right time for it, was what he told himself.

They marched them outside, the deputies flanking while the Sheriff brought up the rear. Outside, in the foggy morning light, the streetlights glowed with halos of light around them, and the town was unconscionably quiet. The black SUV was parked streetside, and he recognized it as definitely one of their own.

"What about our other vehicles at the Hollow?" Carlos asked over his shoulder.

"Seizure and forfeiture," Leonard said. "They're in the impound lot, I'm afraid. As are all the weapons and anything else we found. Quite a haul, Mr. Mendoza. You boys came to do some business, alright."

"All of those vehicles, from people you're pretending didn't exist," Carlos said, glaring at the Sheriff, who just smiled back at him.

"Ghost cars," Leonard said. "The damnedest thing. Parking violations. We have vagrancy laws in Lynchburg, especially in Hidden Hollow. What are you going to do about it, Mr. Mendoza? You're a criminal. You going to file a complaint?"

They reached the SUV and one of the deputies opened the doors while the others covered.

"I'm taking the back," Carlos said to his men. "Santiago, you drive. Alejandro, shotgun."

His men followed, while Carlos turned to look back at the Sheriff, who was smiling down at him from where he stood atop the trio of steps on the path that led to the police station.

"You take care, now, Mr. Mendoza," Leonard said. "Thank you for coming to see us."

Carlos shut the SUV door with his good arm.

"*Diablo,* let's get the hell out of here," Carlos said.

## ℬ

**The Mayor of Lynchburg, Lionel Templeton, looked to** Emily much like his sister, Mona. Tall, handsome in a retrograde sort of way—dark-haired, bearded, with the barest hints of white at his temples. He had a strong nose and piercing eyes, wore a black suit and a blue necktie with a gold three-circle symbol pinned to his lapel.

"Good Morning, Friends," Lionel said, with Mona standing nearby on the stage in her grey robes complete with blue chasuble with the symbol of the Lady brocaded upon it in green thread. "Welcome to 50th Annual Fungus Festival. We are so glad to have you here with us this weekend."

The assembled crowd of mushroom enthusiasts, epicureans, tourists, and party people thronged the stage, many of them wearing their conical (and, to Emily's eyes, comical) red mushroom hats with white polka dots upon them. She was terrible at estimating crowd numbers, but a lot of people had turned out for it. Many hundreds, at the very least.

Lionel smiled out at the crowd, his eyes raking over everyone present.

"It's hard to believe that it's been 50 years," Lionel said. "My sisters and I were just kids. We've lived in Lynchburg all our lives. We love this town. We love everyone here. We *know* everyone here. This festival is something near and dear to our hearts. It's a chance for us to show the world what we're made of. Thanks to our sponsors, to the Nightcap Mushroom Farm most especially, for making this possible. We've got a lot of great stuff here for you. Be sure to hit the growers' tents—we've got three of them this year, which is new. And we've got a great slate of performers that'll be on this stage or the south stage. Can't miss it. Have fun, most of all. That's what we believe here in Lynchburg. We believe in putting the 'fun' in 'fungus.'"

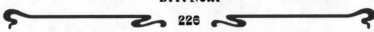
People alternately groaned and applauded. Emily couldn't believe how corny Lionel Templeton was, versus the more magisterial Mona. He looked like he was her little brother. She could only imagine what it was like growing up in Mona's shadow.

"I want everyone to have a great time this weekend," Lionel said. "We want that, right, Sis?"

Mona nodded slowly, smiling, her hands folded in front of her.

"We'd like to open this festival with a prayer," Lionel said. "Led by my sister, Desdemona."

Mona sidled past her brother and took the microphone with a smile. Lionel stepped back, nodding to his sister.

"Thank you, Your Honor," Mona said, her rich voice captivating the crowd. "Thank you everyone who has made the long trek to Lynchburg. It's a scenic ride, isn't it? But what's Pennsylvania without lots of trees?"

The audience laughed, and Mona held out her arms to either side, like she was preparing to embrace the crowd, turning her head skyward.

"Please bow your heads," Mona said. "And let us honor the Lady in our way."

Emily noted that there were clearly members of the Temple in the crowd, for they threw their fists in the air, their heads bowed.

"*Signora,* we ask that You bless this Festival," Mona said. "Our most holy ritual we carry out in Your name. Let us honor Your generosity in the way that You feed us, nourish us, enlighten us, enrich us, protect us. We ask that You turn Your all-seeing eyes upon us, and You show us Your mercy. We ask these things in Your name, *Signora.* Enjoy these days, for all that lives must one day die."

"For all that lives must one day die," said various voices from the crowd, a chorus of people amid the raised fists and bowed heads, like a murmur.

"But today and tomorrow, let us live well in Your name," Mona said, smiling at the crowd. "The Lady's blessing be upon you."

"And upon you," the congregants in the crowd said. Ash glanced at Emily, looking nervous.

"This creeps me out," Ash said.

"Yeah," Emily said.

"I feel like they're going to get out sickles and cut our throats at any moment," Ash said under her breath.

"Nice imagery, Ash, Jesus," Emily said.

"Just saying," Ash said.

The clock tower tolled nine o'clock, and Mona raised her hands again.

"The Festival has begun!" Mona said. "Blessings to you all."

She handed the microphone back to her brother, who accepted it as she strode offstage in a skirring of her robes.

"You heard her," Lionel said. "Everybody have a great time. Special thanks to the Nightcap Mushroom Farm, The Templeton Family Foundation, the Grower's Guild of Lynchburg, the Lynchburg Chamber of Commerce, Lynchburg Community Hospital, Happy Cappy's Cap Emporium, The Shroom Room, the Grand Hotel, Rena Hecate's Horse Farm, Ezekiel Crane's Mushroom Powdered Beverage Cooperative, the Triple Six Tavern, and, of course The Temple of the Lady, for your generous support."

He waited for the applause, which came most effusively from the Temple faithful, joined by the tourists, who followed suit.

"And on this very stage, at ten o'clock, we have none other than Country Bob & the Wayseeds bring their alt-folk music here," Lionel said. "Can't miss it! And don't forget to use your Fungus Festival Fungo App to keep abreast of everything. Fungible tokens are same as cash where applicable!"

He nodded to the QR codes at some of the tents, prominently displayed.

"Just scan the QR codes or download it in the app store," Lionel said. A Mushy the Mushroom mascot walked across the stage, and Lionel laughed. "Uh, oh, Mushy's coming for me! That's my signal to go!"

He put the microphone on its stand while Mushy silently mock-laughed and waved out to the crowd, his winking visage seeming to look out at the crowd. Mushy carried a basket in one of his hands, and playfully tossed out handfuls of confetti at the crowd, which streamed like spores, to the delight of some of the children present, who giggled and ran around in the falling confetti.

"I hate Mushy," Ash said. "Glad it's fairly cool this morning. I imagine the person in there is cooking."

"Maybe it's your sister," Emily said.

"God, I hope not," Ash said. Although her sister had been a mascot at their high school, so she couldn't put that past her.

"Have you seen her?' Emily asked.

"No," Ash said. "I called her this morning, but it went to voicemail. She's always been terrible about calling back."

Emily had called Jerry the night before. She'd brought him up to speed on what they'd found, what Marquis was bringing him. Jerry had been very pleased with the news, which Marquis had apparently already shared.

"You've done a great job, Dr. Carver," Jerry had said.

"Thanks, Jerry," Emily said. "Keep in mind that I'm not entirely sure it's the source of the Lady's Tears. Also, I'm a bit irritated that Marquis left so abruptly."

"I had told him if he got some samples that he should get out of there as soon as possible," Jerry said. "People disappear there, Dr. Carver. This way, I'd like to think maybe we got ahead of it. Ahead of them, anyway."

"You knowingly put us in danger," Emily said.

"Risk and reward, Dr. Carver," Jerry said. "You know how that goes. All I'm saying is that people seem to vanish in Lynchburg. So, just don't vanish."

"If I find any other strains, I want my share of the profits," Emily said.

"Of course," Jerry said. "As we agreed. I'm good for it, Dr. Carver."

"Alright," Emily said. "I'm going to Nightcap tomorrow."

"I would be very careful if I were you," Jerry said. "They watch their stocks very closely."

"I will be careful," Emily said. "Count on it."

"You're a risk-taker, Dr. Carver," Jerry said. "I respect that."

Mushy the Mushroom took Emily out of her reverie, as the mascot had tossed confetti at them. It was a dusting that caught in Emily's hair and on her clothes. Ash was sputtering from it, irritated.

"Oh, great," Ash said. Mushy again mock-laughed, clutching its sides.

"Thanks, Mushy," Emily said. "Hey, are you Melinda Dunn?"

Mushy shook his head after pretending to think about it a moment. Ash glowered at the mascot.

"It better not be you, Melinda," Ash said. Mushy shrugged his shoulders, capered off to toss confetti at other festivalgoers.

"Great," Emily said. "I've got confetti all over me, now."

"You look festive," Ash said, laughing at her. "I'm not seeing Melinda here, but she's got to be around. All I know is we need to get away from this stage before Country Bob turns up. I don't think I could take that."

Emily laughed at her, looking around, trying to shake off the confetti.

"Let's hit the growers' tents," Emily said, hooking Ash's arm in her own, guiding her to one of the tents as she consulted the Fungo App. "They broke them up between basic grocery mushrooms, specialty ones, and adaptogenics, looks like. This one's the grocery tent."

Ash could see the rows of white and brown button mushrooms arranged in racks and other containers, an otherworldly sea of white, as well as fat portobellos and chubby cremini mushrooms. Emily was in heaven.

"*Agaricus bisporus*," Emily said. "That's what these all are. It's just a matter of aging. The white buttons are the youngest. The cremini mushrooms are the, I don't know, teenagers. And the portobellos are the oldest of the lot."

"Wow," Ash said. "Never knew that. Thought they were different types."

"Nope," Emily said. "Same species. Just differently aged and marketed."

Ash saw her sister wearing a Volunteer polo—grey with a red Mushy logo stitched over her heart. She was animatedly talking to some tourists about the button mushrooms around them.

"Melinda," Ash said, watching her sister's eye. Melinda sighed at the sight of her sister, as the chubby tourist couple worked their way down the rows of white mushrooms.

"Oh, come on, Ash," Melinda said. "I don't want to have to deal with your bullshit today."

Melinda's eyes went to Emily, who felt self-conscious under the younger woman's hard gaze. Both Dunn sisters had that hard gaze, and Emily could only wonder where it had come from, whether it was Mama Dunn's or Papa Dunn's.

"Bullshit?" Ash said. "Okay, yeah, don't worry, I'm not going to ruin your cult festival crap. I'm just, you know, looking around."

"Who's this?" Melinda asked.

"Dr. Emily Carver," Emily said, extending her hand, which Melinda shook.

"So sorry my sister dragged you here, Dr. Carver," Melinda said.

"Are you kidding? I'm a mycologist," Emily said. "I love all of this."

Normally, Emily had to explain what a mycologist was, but Melinda brightened at that, knew just what that was. She even warmed to her, contrasting her umbrage at her sister.

"Oh, yeah," Melinda said. "This place is paradise. They have everything here."

Ash was piqued that Melinda clicked with Emily, but Emily figured that was maybe something they could work to their advantage.

"I'm planning on going to the Nightcap Farm today," Emily said. "They do tours, right?"

"Totes," Melinda said. "Are you looking to work there or something?"

"Oh, no," Emily said. "I'm no farmer. Just a researcher."

"Ah," Melinda said. It wounded Ash that Melinda could so readily warm up to Emily, while she only got attitude from her.

"We're here together," Ash said. "I thought I'd bring Emily along."

Melinda looked down the end of her nose at her sister.

"Right, so you'd have someone here who knew what they were talking about," Melinda said. "I hope my sister didn't rope you into working on one of her stories. Make sure you get a byline, is all I'm saying."

Emily laughed, catching Ash's withering glance, while Melinda smiled.

"The Lady provides abundantly," Melinda said. "All of this you see here. That's from Her. Bountiful harvests, over and over again, without fail."

"Yeah," Emily said. "If well-tended, they definitely can, that's for sure."

"Yes," Melinda said, exuberantly. "You get it. Thank you. Have you been to the Temple?"

"We were there last night," Emily said.

"I play organ at the Temple," Melinda said, frowning at Ash, who returned the frown. "My sister thinks I'm slumming it here, but isn't the Temple beautiful?"

"It's very lovely," Emily said. "Almost, I don't know, Classical."

"Yeah, Classical," Melinda said. "Did you, you know, have any of the Lady's Tears?"

"No," Emily said. "Afraid not."

Melinda seemed shocked, touched her arm.

"Oh, you should do them," Melinda said. "The Lady's Tears help you see. I mean, you see things. More than just what's around you. You see through things. Into things. Into yourself. It's incredible."

Emily had no doubt that the distillates of the *Amanita* variant made people see things. She could only imagine what people taking them saw.

"How often do you take them?" Emily asked. Psychedelics were non-addictive, but she was clinically curious about usage patterns among regular users.

"Weekly," Melinda said. "Sometimes you can see more than you want. I try to dose once a week."

"Pretty regular, then," Emily said. "And how much of a dose?"

Ash was watching them both, but Melinda was riveted on Emily, didn't notice. Emily saw it as a kind of interview, a chance to get a sense of the local experience with them.

"It doesn't take much," Melinda said. "The Lady's Tears are strong. Like you saw the little cups we serve it in at the Temple. That's a light dose, but it still hits hard. You do a heroic dose and you're in outer space, I swear. Like another dimension. Just you and the Lady out there, drifting along in infinity."

"Right," Emily said. "Potent."

"You should totally dose with me," Melinda said. "I promise you won't regret it. It's safest to dose with somebody else chaperoning, honestly."

"Maybe another time," Emily said. "Thanks."

"You're missing out," Melinda said. "That's all I'm saying."

"Thanks, Melinda," Ash said. "I told Mom and Dad you were here."

"Of course you did," Melinda said, her voice going cold. "Have they called in the Army, yet?"

Emily could see Mushy gamboling around, still tossing confetti here and there. Mushy was attended by two Temple acolytes who were ensuring that Mushy's basket of confetti never ran dry. They carried bags of confetti they'd periodically feed to the basket.

"Not yet," Ash said. "But they will."

"I'm an adult, Ash," Melinda said. "I don't need rescuing. Do I look unhappy? Do I look scared?"

Admittedly, she didn't. Ash thought Melinda looked more at peace than she'd ever been. From her perspective, however, that was part of the problem. Melinda had never been the type to be contented. She was always a firebrand.

"You're not in your right mind," Ash said.

"Come on," Melinda said. "Give me a break. See what I have to deal with, Emily? Rampant disrespect—of me, my faith, my life choices."

Emily smiled awkwardly, not wanting to get enmeshed in the sisterly dispute. She knew there was nothing in this Growers' Tent that she needed to study. She doubted there'd be anything in the Festival proper that would prove revelatory, but she would likely wander some of the other Growers' Tents and see what they had available.

She could see Mona Templeton making her way through the crowd, benevolently shaking hands with people as she went. She also wondered if Mona and her Exemplars had realized that there'd been a theft at the Temple. It all depended on the level of surveillance they had in place. The woman carried herself with both a power and grace that Emily found disarming. She was charismatic in that cult leader way that was both repellant and in some sinister way, attractive.

Mona walked with a trio of disciples who flanked her, their eyes on the crowd. Mushy saw Mona and mock-bowed, holding out his almost mitten-like paw hands as he did so. Mona received the homage of Mushy with amusement, reaching out to lay a hand on the back of the mascot's speckled cap.

"Bless you, Mushy," Mona said, prompting laughter from the onlookers. "I think the kids at the face-painting and mask-making tent might appreciate a visit from you."

Mushy rose and clasped his hands together, feigning a shuddering swoon, to the delight of the onlookers, as he headed off to the Kids' Tent, where Emily could see children getting mushrooms painted on their faces and some of them crafting makeshift Grey Lady papier-mâché masks under the guidance of Festival volunteers. So many smiling, laughing faces. It almost passed for normal to Emily's eyes until she thought about what they were doing.

"Ohmigod," Melinda said, pointing. "Mona! Mona!"

Mona joined them, glancing at Ash and Emily, the wrinkles at the corners of her eyes remaining as she smiled at them both.

"Melinda," Mona said. "And this must be your sister, Ashley. I've heard so much about you, Ashley."

"Just Ash," Ash said, shaking Mona's extended hand.

"Ash it is, then. And who's this?" Mona said, turning her lighthouse eyes to Emily. There was an unfathomable radiance to her that was jarring up close. It was like the charismatic equivalent of stage makeup—what played well onstage was almost overpowering up close.

"This is Emily," Melinda said. "She's a mycologist, Eminence."

"A mycologist? How enchanting," Mona said, holding out her hand for Emily to shake. Emily could see she had a big green ring on her finger, what looked like cut jade in the form of a braided vine. "We get a lot of mycologists visiting the Festival. They just can't resist us."

Emily shook her offered hand.

"I'm hoping to tour the Nightcap Farm today," Emily said.

"Ah, Daddy will be so pleased," Mona said. "He just loves having guests drop by the farm. Have you been to the Temple?"

"Last night," Emily said.

"They were at the Sunset Service, Eminence," Melinda said. Ash was glaring at Mona, hating the reverence with which Melinda held the High Priestess. Her entire demeanor changed from one of defiance that Ash inevitably encountered to fawning deference to Mona, even adoration.

"I hope it was illuminating for you," Mona said. Her voice was rich like honey and spiced wine, warm and intoxicating in the way that those accustomed to public speaking could modulate their tone in pleasing ways.

"Very," Emily said. "It's a lovely temple."

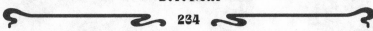
"We're very proud of it," Mona said.

Some part of her, the risk-taker, perhaps, couldn't resist poking the serene eminence of Mona Templeton.

"I heard rumors that the Red Death were in town," Emily said.

Mona cocked an eyebrow at the mention.

"You know about them?" Mona asked. "Dreadful gang. Nasty people. Drug dealers and gun runners. Not at all appropriate for an event such as this. But from what I heard, Sheriff Leonard and his deputies have ensured that we won't have any trouble with them here."

"That's a relief," Emily said. "I wouldn't want some gangsters crashing the party."

Mona nodded, and Melinda piped up.

"I was trying to get Emily to try the Lady's Tears," Melinda said. "But she didn't want to."

"You mean you went to our Sunset Service and you didn't partake? How very tragic. You really should. It's unlike anything you ever experienced."

Emily glanced at Ash, who was fuming.

"We were looking for my sister," Ash said.

"I'd say you've found her," Mona said, smirking at her, giving Melinda a measured glance that Emily thought was one part amusement, one part bemusement.

"Is that how you bring people into your cult?" Ash asked. "You drug them?"

Mona slow-turned her gaze to Ash, who held her ground before the taller woman. Mona was nearly as tall as Emily was, which made Ash look positively diminutive by comparison.

"The Lady doesn't require tricks to draw the Faithful to Her," Mona said. "She simply is. Her tears, the tears She sheds for us and our plight, they are Her blessings. We drink them down in hopes of attaining a measure of Her godly grace and fortitude in the face of adversity."

"Where do the Lady's Tears come from?" Emily asked. She thought she'd do a little probing, see how candid Her Eminence was prepared to be.

"From the Goddess, of course," Mona said. "Her tears rain down from the heavens themselves to bathe us in Her everlasting favor."

Emily smiled politely at Mona but found her condescension vexing.

Ash scoffed, clearly dissatisfied with that answer.

"Right," Ash said. "I'm thinking more like mushrooms. You know, like magic mushrooms."

"Magic is such a convoluted word," Mona said. "We don't divulge our Temple secrets to the nonbeliever. Transcendental experiences are inherent in most religious traditions. Ours is no different."

"Trade secrets, Em," Ash said, laughing. "She won't spill the magic beans."

"You're both welcome to attend a private service with me," Mona said. "I'm happy to pencil you in, although I admit that this is a very crowded weekend for us. We're having a moonlight service tonight, in fact. It's going to be a full moon. Not to be missed. Not only for the Faithful—but for some of our special guests."

Mona produced a pair of royal blue cards that had silvery-white lettering upon them. On one side were the three interlocking circles, on the other, the invitation:

### ADMIT ONE to the Sacred Grove

*Midnight Moonlight Ministry*
*of the Temple of the Lady*

Follow your phone to the Sacred Grove
using the Fungo App

Melinda's eyes went big, and she grinned at Emily.

"Dr. Carver, you're so blessed," Melinda said. "Her Eminence doesn't just give those invitations out to anybody. I'm playing music there. It's going to be insane!"

Emily turned the card over in her hand a couple of times, watching Mona watching her.

"What's the Sacred Grove?" Emily asked.

"We don't do everything at the Temple," Mona said. "Some things are best done under the open sky, in the forest shadows. In fact, before we acquired the Temple, our services were held in the forests. We still carry out services in the forests. Special services."

"Special how? Is this a human sacrifice sort of thing?" Ash asked. Mona chuckled at her.

"Is it?" Mona said. "We all make sacrifices for what—and who—we love. For what matters to us."

"Didn't answer my question," Ash said.

"Do you think I'd bring an investigative journalist and a mycologist to a human sacrifice?" Mona asked. "Please, Ms. Dunn. Don't be absurd."

"Still didn't answer," Ash said.

"Dr. Carver," Mona said, ignoring Ash. "I think you'd find our sacred grove fascinating. It's where the Lady's Tears first fell. I would think you'd find that very interesting, indeed. Transformative, even."

"I would," Emily said. "I'll be there."

"I wouldn't miss it for the world," Ash said, staring hard at Mona, who merely retained her smile.

"Splendid," Mona said. "Now, if you'll excuse me, I have to make my way through the rest of the Festival grounds. A pleasure meeting you both in person. I hope to see you again tonight, Dr. Carver."

And then she glided away, pursued by a dazzled Melinda, leaving an angry Ash and a bewildered Emily in her wake.

"Later, Eminence," Ash called after her. "Boy, she liked you, Emily."

"What can I say?" Emily said. "I am pretty charming."

They shared an unsteady laugh between them, ending only when they saw some black-suited men walking toward Mona. There were a half-dozen of them, all in black suits, their faces full of scorn and rage. All of them had severe haircuts—mop tops that looked like the same barber had shorn their hair close around their ears. All of them carried well-worn bibles in their hands. Their leader was an older man with a craggy face and nut-brown hair.

"Heathen priestess!" the Leader said, calling out. Mona turned and looked at the assembled men in turn, smiling at them.

"Yes?" Mona said.

"Your idolatrous festival may have these good people fooled, but we know you and your kind for what they are," the Leader said. The men formed a Christian crescent around Mona, as if they were afraid to get too close. "We pray for the souls of everyone here."

"Very thoughtful of you," Mona said. "But this is our time of celebration. It is not a time for recrimination."

"There is no god but Almighty God," the Leader said, his wild eyes flicking back and forth at the passing tourists, who looked on with dismay as he held aloft his bible.

Mona was unfazed by the threatening presence of the men, Emily noticed. Her confidence was impressive.

"Brothers, you have it all wrong," Mona said, her voice soothing. "And, in the spirit of the Lady's eternal grace, I will forgive you for this impertinent outburst. Join me in this."

She held out her arms, palms upraised.

"Succubus! Harlot!" the Leader said. "We are not like the others who have fallen before you and your devil's tongue."

"But you are," Mona said. "You are all so very similar to me. You are always the same."

Onlookers were gathering around them, curious at the confrontation. Ash and Emily were among them. Ash had out her phone and was recording it, while Emily was concentrating on what was being said.

"Repent, and there is still hope for you," the Leader said. "Cast your Grey Goddess into the fire and ask Almighty God for forgiveness."

"I have a better idea," Mona said. "Why don't you drop to your knees and beg for *my* forgiveness, instead?"

The Leader and his men looked at one another in confusion, gasping as, one by one, they dropped to their knees, like a cluster of dominoes falling.

"What sorcery is this?" the Leader said. "What witchcraft?"

"Down, Brothers," Mona said, turning her hands so her palms faced earthward, and she made patting motions with her hands, and the assembled men cried out as they found themselves captive to her words. "Toss those holy books to the ground in front of you."

Crying out, the men did as they were told, the bibles thumping as they struck the ground, forming a little pile.

"Witch," the Leader said, all but choking out the word.

"Shhhh," Mona said, bringing a finger to her lips. "Not another word from you, now."

The Leader's eyes bulged as he strained. Mona noted everyone watching and addressed the crowd with her velvety voice.

"The Lady's Grace is all-encompassing," Mona said. Her eyes went back to the fundamentalists. "Clasp your hands together, Brothers."

The black-suited men did, knitting their hands together. Mona motioned to some of the nearby acolytes, who grabbed up the bibles, putting them in a wicker basket.

"Now, rise, Brothers," Mona said. "And follow me."

The men got to their feet as Mona had told them, lining up. Emily thought the Leader's head was going to burst as he strained against the ineffable control Mona seemed to have over him with only her voice.

"And everyone else," Mona said. "All of you onlookers. Forget this ugly interlude and enjoy the Festival as if nothing had happened at all."

And, incredibly, Emily and Ash, along with everyone else gathered around, felt something strange come over them. What had been a bizarre moment had lost all context and clarity, and it was just Mona standing there with a line of black-suited men who looked unfamiliar to Emily, but not worth her time and attention.

Ash laughed, seeing her phone in her hand, like she wasn't sure why she'd been filming such a stupid thing.

"I don't know what I'm even doing," Ash said, laughing. She turned off her camera and pocketed her phone. "Reflex, I guess."

"I guess," Emily said, watching everybody moving about their business without concern, while Mona led the column of black-suited men away. "Who are those guys?"

"No idea," Ash said. "Hey, you want to get some fried mushrooms?"

"Sure," Emily said, unable to shake the feeling that something significant had just happened, but not finding the words to properly express it.

# 4

**Austin was in better shape than the others. Not literally,**
but because they'd all swigged the magic blue juice at the
Temple, they were wiped.. He'd gotten up before the rest, even
though he'd slept in as well. The music outside got his attention, and Austin went out onto the balcony, peering down on
the festivities below.

It was an overcast day, the grey-white sky packed solid
with unassuming clouds. Down below, crowds were shuffling
around the bright red speckled tents, while some folksy yokels
were strumming banjos and mandolins on the north stage.
Austin fished out his phone and checked his Fungo App.

"Country Bob & the Wayseeds," Austin said, snorting.
"Should've been the Hayseeds. What the hell's a 'Wayseed' anyway?"

"It's nothing," Mallory said, appearing at the sliding door,
looking bleary-eyed, her red hair a shaggy mess. She wore a
very faded Suck Junkies tee shirt and baby blue pajama pants
with little pink mushrooms upon them. Her tattooed sleeves
were apparent with the short-sleeved shirt—images of trees,
unicorns, octopi, and succubi cavorted on her forearms in a
panoply of colored inks. On her upper arms were vistas of otherworldly places, mushrooms cavorting, and an image of a
ghostly robed woman, swirling around in a sea of blue, with
stars around her.

Austin studied her a moment and shook his head, laughing.

"I made coffee," Austin said.

"I could smell it," Mallory said, sitting next to him. Down
below, throngs of people were noodling about, heedless of them
on the balcony above.

"Nobody ever looks up," Austin said. "Maybe one in dozens
might glance up."

"We're not celebrities," Mallory said. "Nothing to see here, Austin."

"How are you feeling?" Austin asked.

"Fine," Mallory said. "That music's not helping, though."

Austin took his phone and zoomed in on Country Bob & the Wayseeds. They were an older-looking man and a half-dozen young towheaded men in mullets and playing their various instruments. Country Bob had the mandolin and was yodeling something about the Devil taking all his grain.

"This is Austin Adams reporting live from the Lynchburg Fungus Festival," Austin said. "I'm here with my friend Mallory."

"Don't you dare film me, Austin," Mallory said, holding up her hands in front of her face.

"We're living our best lives here," Austin said, grinning into the camera. "That's Country Bob & the Wayseeds."

He posted it to his Instagram and hashtagged it appropriately, was amused as the likes started popping in shortly thereafter.

"What's on the menu for today, I wonder?" Austin asked. "I mean once you and the Twins sober up?"

"I'm sober," Mallory said. "We should get down there and check it out, obviously. There's jewelry makers and stuff."

"I see Crappy Cappy's got a tent down there," Austin said, holding up his phone so she could see.

"Happy Cappy," Mallory said. "You're such a dick, Austin."

"I know, I know," Austin said. "Slap Happy Cappy sold us some primo shrooms, I'd say."

"Yeah," Mallory said. "You should be grateful."

"I'm nothing but grateful," Austin said. "I'm a bottomless well of gratitude."

"More like attitude," Mallory said.

*You decide.*

It was like an intruder in his head, just hopping out of the bushes of his midbrain.

"That fucking clown was weird," Austin said.

"Fun Gus is great," Mallory said. "He's so funny."

"I don't see it," Austin said. "He was totes not-funny. Did you lose your balloon?"

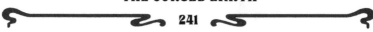
"What balloon?" Mallory asked.

"The one he creepily tied to your wrist," Austin said.

"No," Mallory said. "It's in the room. Dancing on the ceiling or whatever."

*You decide.*

What the hell did that even mean? What kind of trippy shit was that to lay on somebody, anyway? It was just rude. But Austin doubted consideration came into it with clowns. Austin hated to think that Fun Gus was going to be lurking around down there. The last thing in the world he wanted was to run into that big-ass clown. Even a little clown was scary. But a big, tall, middle-aged one? Worse still.

Mallory sparked up a joint she'd conjured out of seeming nowhere, like she was a street magician, she just palmed it and lit up.

"Really?" Austin asked. "A wake and bake, Mallory?"

"What?" Mallory said, holding it out to him. Austin shook his head, holding up his coffee. "We had a big night. And today's going to be a big day. I need to fortify myself."

"I think they have continental breakfast in the lobby," Austin said. Mallory laughed at him, puffing smoke in his direction.

*You decide.*

"There's no way we're going to be dicking around on Grand all day, are we?" Austin asked. "I can only take so much Family Friendly Fun in one day."

"Yeah, okay," Mallory said, puffing away. "There's other stuff. I mean, that's what you're talking about, yeah? Off-campus, if you know what I mean."

Austin nodded, laughing. He could see Mushy the Mushroom walking around streetside, tossing confetti into people's faces like an asshole.

"Let me guess, you know a guy," Austin said.

"Oh, I know a bunch of guys," Mallory said, fluffing her hair with her free hand. "There's a place in the forest. It's like the after-party for the Festival. For the people who know."

"Yeah?"

Mallory nodded. Another magic trick, like sleight-of-hand she was somehow doing with literally no sleeves. She produced a royal blue card.

"Sacred Grove," Mallory said.

"Where'd you get that?" Austin said, as she slapped it on the table, slid it toward him.

It was a cardstock ticket, basically, with the three-circle symbol on one side, and the invitation on the other.

"It says 'Admit One'," Austin said.

"I've got four tickets," Mallory said.

"Where'd you score those?" Austin asked.

"They were giving them out at the Temple, Dumbass," Mallory said. "You must have missed it while you were swimming across the floor."

"I must have," Austin said. He had no recollection of it. But he knew that he'd been distracted in the Temple.

"Anyway," Mallory said. "If you thought the Temple thing was fun, that's like the bunny slope, Austin. Sacred Grove is like, I don't know, the real deal. It's the fucking Vail of Neverwhere, man. Steep as fuck."

Mallory was already high as a kite, and Austin wanted to laugh. When she tied one on, she tied one on. She got sweary when she was high.

*You decide.*

"Neverwhere, huh?" Austin said.

"Yeah," Mallory said, her head in a cloud of her own making. "I was there last year. In-fucking-tense. We can't have come all this way and not go to motherfucking Neverwhere."

Austin wasn't sure he'd actually do any more shrooms this weekend. Not like he had a problem with it, but he didn't like the idea of tripping out in the forest with a bunch of strangers. Plus, somebody had to keep it together, or who knew what might happen. They'd probably end up robbed and naked, with dicks drawn on their faces with magic markers by the locals.

"Alright," Austin said. "Sounds like a plan."

"Yeah," Mallory said. "Speaking of the best-laid plans, do you want to, you know, bang?"

Austin was about to answer when he saw, for a moment, plain as day, Ash on the street. He almost had a flashback to the

night before, the sight of her there, frowning with that woman she'd been with. He could see her, and then she turned and she was gone.

"Holy shit," Austin said, hopping up.

"Um, what?" Mallory said.

"Gotta go," Austin said. He slipped on some loafers and grabbed a coat and shot out of there, making a mental note of where Ash would have been.

*You decide.*

He thought just maybe that he had.

# 5

**Logan was ogling the specialty mushrooms growing in** the Growers' Exhibit tent, marveling at the chanterelles somebody had brought in. They were gorgeous. He wanted to get his hands on them and start making something delicious.

"They have Brunette and Smooth Chanterelles as well as the basic ones," a young Black woman said to him, over his shoulder. Logan turned, surprised, as she was tall, bespectacled and dark-haired. She had confetti in her hair.

"Are you a chef?" Logan asked.

"No, I'm a mycologist," she said. "Dr. Emily Carver."

She shot a hand out to him, which he shook.

"Logan Stephens," he said. "Yeah, they're beauties. I'd love to cook them right here."

"I think there's a cook-off at eleven o'clock," she said. "Right before the parade."

"Heh," Logan said. "Wouldn't be fair. I mean, I'm a professional."

"You could probably save the mushrooms from being abused," Emily said. "That's important. People butcher them."

She said it so earnestly, he found it amusing. Emily smiled at him. She was joined by a scowling petite blonde woman who looked him over once. She looked sporty to Logan, one of those fitness freaks who jogged with a grim determination to get to where she was going.

"This is Ash Dunn," Emily said. "Ash, this is Logan Stephens. He's a chef."

"Nice to meet you," Ash said, looking very distracted.

"There's a fried mushroom-eating competition this morning, too," Emily said.

"For sure not doing that," Logan said. He hated eating competitions. Food was a joy, meant to be savored, not shoveled headlong into one's mouth under a time limit. Logan was pretty sure if there was a Hell, competitive eating had to be part of it.

"When are you going, Em?" Ash asked.

"Probably after the parade," Emily said. "No way do I want to deal with the traffic detours. I'll get lost for sure."

"Alright," Ash said. "Makes sense. I'm going to go bother Melinda some more. I'll ping you."

Ash stomped off for the first Growers' Tent, and Emily could only imagine how that would go for her, the Dunn Sisters having another round of arguing.

"I'm going to tour the Nightcap Mushroom Farm," Emily said to Logan.

"Been there, done that," Logan said, which made Emily brighten up.

"Really? What's it like?"

Logan laughed.

"It's huge, for one thing," he said. "It's a big-ass mushroom farm they have there. Massive on a level I didn't expect out here in the middle of nowhere. 'Farm' isn't quite the right way to describe it. It's too industrial to be rustic."

"I can't wait to see it," Emily said.

Logan checked out some neighboring mushrooms on display, Emily tagging along on his heels. He saw a cluster of white mushrooms that looked like a tangled, almost brainlike braid that made Logan think of cauliflower, if cauliflower had come from outer space. They smelled vaguely like bread to him, with a hint of cucumber.

"*Entoloma abortivum,*" Emily said. "Aborted *Entoloma* parasitized by *Armillaria*. Shrimp-of-the-Woods. You get the hyphae of two different species coming together and they create something else entirely, a carpophoroid, technically speaking. Yummy."

He saw the hand-drawn sign indicating they were, in fact, Shrimp-of-the-Woods.

"You're a handy one to have around," Logan said, taking a toothpicked sample of one of them and tasting it while the grower looked on. It had a mild taste and a good mouth feel that did call to mind lobster or shrimp in texture.

"You can make a dandy Shrimp-of-the-Woods Scampi with these," the grower said. He was a middle-aged balding man with hefty black sideburns.

"I'll bet," Emily said.

Logan recognized shiitakes at the next table.

"Now these, I know," Logan said.

"*Lentinula edodes*," Emily said.

Logan laughed again.

"You have all those Latin names memorized?" Logan asked.

"Sorry," Emily said. "Drilled into my head at Berkeley, I suppose."

"You're a long way from California," Logan said.

"Certainly," Emily said. "But for mushrooms in America, you have to come to Pennsylvania. The farming here is out of control."

Logan definitely agreed with that. Nightcap had created an empire out here in the hinterlands.

"Have you been to the Shroom Room?" Logan asked, nodding in the direction of Maura's restaurant, which wasn't open, yet. He figured Maura was in there getting ready for lunchtime service. He doubted even Maura could sell breakfast mushrooms beyond, say, scrambled eggs and omelets.

Emily followed his eyes to the restaurant.

"I haven't," Emily said. "Should I?"

"You should," Logan said. "How about lunch? My treat?"

Emily sized him up with a smile.

"Lunch with a chef?" Emily asked. "Sounds delicious."

"I've never dined with a mycologist," Logan said. "Seems on-message for the Fungus Festival."

Logan lived in the moment, and when living in the moment, there had to be a recognition that opportunities were meant to be seized. Emily the Mycologist seemed like an amusing person to hang out with. She had a hint of an accent he couldn't place. Something Southern, maybe, just a whisper of it, well-concealed.

They moved to another table, where there were some unfamiliar, almost frothy white-looking mushrooms on display. They looked like tangled clusters of bone-white coral. The sign said "Comb Tooth Fungus" in a calligraphic script.

"*Hericium coralloides*," Emily said, blushing. "These are lovely. They grow on hardwood trees or fallen hardwoods. But you have to get them when they're young, like these are, if you want the best flavor. They get intolerable when they get older."

Logan glanced at the grower, a brown-haired young man in a green flannel shirt and jeans who looked on with amusement at Emily.

"A problem we all share," Logan said. "I'm way less tolerable than I was when I was younger."

The grower put out a sample of it, which had been cooked on a nearby skillet and put on a saucer with toothpicks. Logan tried some, nodding. It had a nutty, even steak-like sort of taste which was very pleasing. Emily tried some, too, while the kid looked on unsmilingly.

"Also called the Coral Hedgehog," Emily said. "Just saying."

"Coral Hedgehog," Logan said, laughing. "Love it. Such goofy names. No offense."

"None taken," Emily said.

"They grow on tree branches," the kid said. "We got bunches of them out on our farm. Way out in the woods."

Logan saw there were business cards on display. This was the Whitebranch Mushroom Cooperative. He picked up a card and nodded to the kid.

"Good stuff," Logan said. He figured he'd collected a dozen cards at the Festival already, was intent on locking down some suppliers for future use. He loved these sorts of field trips, since you never knew what you might find.

"Are you from Pittsburgh?" Emily asked.

"Philadelphia," Logan said, as they moved to another table. There were tons of people around, now, queueing their way through.

"You're quite far from home, yourself," Emily said.

"Not really," Logan said. "Philadelphia's only maybe a four-hour drive from here."

"Ah," Emily said. "The state seems huge. I mean, not California-huge, but the forests just seem to go on forever."

"Are you from California?" Logan asked.

"Not really," Emily said. "I'm from New Orleans."

"Ah, there it is," Logan said. "Southern."

"I went to Berkeley on a scholarship," Emily said. "And stayed out there."

"Smart," Logan said. "I mean, the scholarship, not staying out there, I mean."

Emily smiled at that, half to herself.

"I knew what you meant," she said. "There were good opportunities out there. Startups, that kind of thing."

"They need mycologists out West?" Logan asked. Emily nodded.

"For sure," Emily said. "You'd be amazed at what you can do with fungi."

"I'll bet," Logan said. "You mean like drugs and such?"

"Among other things," Emily said. "They're very versatile."

The next table led them to a display of mushrooms called Sweet Tooth, which were big orange-tan mushrooms with dangling little spikes beneath them.

"Those are the teeth. Spines, really," Emily said, gesturing. *"Hydnum repandum.* Also called the Wood Hedgehog."

"Lotta hedgehogs in the mushroom trade," Logan said, half to Emily, half to the grower, and older woman with a long face and white hair. She looked like a witch to him, with her black dress and grey-and-white tartan shawl.

"Hedgehogs live close to the ground," the woman said. "Where they belong."

Logan tried a sample from the toothpick plate, savored the sweet nutty taste.

"They are sometimes favored over chantarelles because there are no poisonous lookalikes to these," Emily said, noting the old woman glaring at her.

Logan made a mental note of it and took the woman's card from the table—Lilith Holbrook's Mushroom Farm. Lilith Holbrook. He laughed inwardly.

"Are you Lilith Holbrook?" Logan asked.

"I am," the woman said. "Been here all my life. Lynchburg born."

"Nice to meet you, Lilith," Logan said. "I'm Logan Stephens. I'm a chef."

"Lucky you," Lilith said. "I got the best Wood Hedgehogs you'll see anywhere hereabouts. Not like that Templeton trash."

Emily sampled some, evaluating it.

"You don't like the Templetons?" Emily asked.

"They do what they do, I do what I do," Lilith said. "You want factory-farmed fungi, you go Templeton. You want forest-farmed? That's me. I don't deal in volume. I deal in quality."

"Alright," Logan said. "Good to know."

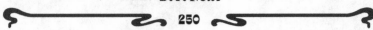
They moved on, sharing a chuckle about the feisty Lilith Holbrook, who was already turning her sour gaze on the next gawkers who came along.

"I had no idea the fungus farmers had rivalries," Logan said. "I'm friends with Maura Templeton. The way she frames it, they're the whole show. When you see Nightcap, you'll see what I mean."

"I support small farmers," Emily said. "The nice thing about fungi is they grow absolutely everywhere. You can actually have small niche farmers who can get something growing and live by what they sell. I respect that."

Emily could see Temple people wandering around amid the festivalgoers, mostly the acolytes and deacons. She didn't see anyone in grey robes. Somehow, she thought the Exemplars weren't the mingling type. All the same, she wondered if any of them were around, lurking among the innocent tourists.

Logan went to another table, which had some shaggy-capped mushrooms that were a dusky grey-white in coloration. The grower was a young woman with straight red hair tied in pigtails. She wore a rainbow-striped ribbed turtleneck and rust-colored corduroy pants. The mushroom card said "Shaggy Mane Mushroom."

Emily whistled.

"*Coprinus comatus,*" Emily said. "Lawyer's Wig, the Shaggy Inkcap, or Maned Agaric. Surprised you've got this one out here, honestly."

"Why's that?" the girl said.

"Well, they have such a narrow window of edibility," Emily said. "Only when they're immature, when the gills are white. Once the gills turn black, they're not good. Plus, they can be confused with Ink Caps, which are poisonous."

Logan laughed, glancing nervously at the young woman, who looked irritated at Emily.

"What are you, like the Mushroom Police?" the young woman said.

"Not me," Emily said. "I'm just saying those are tricky. You have to use them almost immediately after picking. And only when they're young."

"They're real good with soups and risottos," the young woman said, almost defensively.

Logan took the card from her table to be polite. Forest Friendly Farmers it said but didn't think the young woman looked very friendly.

"I make a mean risotto," Logan said, sampling the fungus.

"These'll make it even better. Use it instead of chicken stock," the young woman said, her brown eyes boring into Emily, who hastened to the next table, where a young couple were showing off their big clumps of Hen-of-the-Wood. Logan followed along, laughing.

"Wow, she hated you," Logan said.

"I'm used to it. I'm just calling them as I see them," Emily said. "They're fine but you have to put them to use right away, that's all. Just funny to see such a finnicky fungus here."

"Hen-of-the-Wood," Logan said, reading the sign, glancing at Emily for her to lob some more Latin at him, like it was a party trick. Emily sighed and put a hand on her hip.

"*Grifola frondosa*," Emily said. "I swear this is the last one I'm doing. Also known as Ram's Head, Sheep's Head, and *Signorina*. In addition to Hen-of-the-Wood."

"She's a mycologist," Logan said to the couple, who looked warily amused. They were a handsome couple, maybe in their 30s. The chisel-cheeked man had a well-tended cinnamon-colored beard and black-rimmed glasses and wore a tan button-down shirt and black jeans with red suspenders, while the cleft-chinned young woman had brown hair pixie-cut short and wore grey overalls and a blue long-sleeved, white-striped tee. Their sage green business card was Mac & Brie's Mushroom Farm.

The Hen-of-the-Wood looked like another one of those coral-like fungi to him, with a grey-brown color and curved lips to them. They had a lot on display.

"We grow a ton of them," the young woman said.

"You're Brie, I take it?" Logan said.

"Yep," she said. "And that's Mac. We're from Cleveland. Settled in Lynchburg a few years ago."

"Ah," Logan said, sampling the Hen-of-the-Wood they had. It had a savory, almost peppery taste that was very good. "This is good stuff."

Emily tried some, although she knew what it tasted like.

"It's also called *Maitake*," Mac said. "Very big in Asian markets. Not to be confused with Chicken of the Woods."

"Of course, we wouldn't want that," Logan said, glancing at Emily, who grinned.

"They're completely different," Emily said.

"Does it taste like chicken?" Logan asked.

"It does," Mac said.

"You prepare it like chicken, too," Brie said. "But that's not what we have here."

"This has all been very informative," Logan said, making a point to pocket their business card. "Shall we go, Emily?"

"Sure thing," Emily said, walking with him.

Logan could see Mushy making his rounds on the other side of the street, accompanied by his ever-present white-robed attendants.

"Mushy got you," Logan said, nodding to Emily's hair.

"Yeah," Emily said. "I think they're symbolizing spores."

Logan laughed, watching Mushy fling away at anybody in reach, sending puffs of confetti at them.

"That's kind of how mushrooms work," Emily said. "Some of them, anyway. They're profligate. I respect their fecundity."

"Ha," Logan said. "Fecundity. Did you just make that word up?"

"I did not," Emily said, and they laughed. "It means fertility."

"Nice," Logan said. "I can respect fertility."

Logan walked out of the Growers' Tent and took in the overcast sky, while Emily walked alongside him. She had that relaxed Southern and SoCal way about her, just going along with things as they happened. It made him feel particularly East Coast-pushy by comparison.

"It's all overwhelming," Logan said. "I feel like there are tons of things I could develop with any of these species. Dishes, I mean."

"Yeah, they're great," Emily said.

"I wonder, do they have a magic mushroom tent?" Logan asked, taking out his phone and consulting his Fungo App. "Doesn't look like it."

"I doubt they'd advertise if they did," Emily said. "Have you been to the Temple?"

"Not yet," Logan said. With all the *Signora*-talk Maura had with him, he was almost afraid to drop by the Temple. He hadn't

made up his mind yet about taking Maura up on her offer. Joining a cult was a major ask.

"It's kinda trippy," Emily said. "One part church, one part rave."

"Rave," Logan said, laughing. He could see people in their mushroom hats walking around, laughing and talking. Face-painted little kids chasing after Mushy, hoping for attention from the mascot. "It's really a cult, right? I mean, that's what I've gathered."

"Yep," Emily said. "Big-time. Weird to think that we're probably surrounded by them here, but aside from those young people in white robes, you wouldn't guess it. That, and the circle symbol I keep seeing everywhere."

Logan couldn't resist parading the knowledge he'd gained from Maura.

"The three circles symbolize the interaction between Mind, Body, and Spirit," Logan said. Emily laughed, raising an eyebrow.

"You don't say?" Emily said.

"Just something I picked up along the way," Logan said, smiling.

She held up that blue Sacred Grove invitation card that had the symbol on it and pointed to a jeweler's tent down the way where pendants and pins bearing the symbol were on display in gold and silver.

"What's that?" Logan asked.

"Invitation to some midnight event at the Sacred Grove," Emily said. "Mona Templeton was handing them out. Didn't you get one?"

Logan shook his head, feeling miffed that Maura hadn't mentioned it. He made a mental note to bring it up to her. Maybe if she appeared during lunch at the Shroom Room.

"What's it supposed to be?" Logan asked.

"No idea," Emily said. "I guess since it's the 50th anniversary of the Fungus Festival and a full moon, they're pretty stoked."

"Stoked," Logan said. "I haven't heard anybody use that in a long time. That's funny."

Emily slipped her invitation card into her pocket.

"All I know is that I got an invitation, and you didn't," Emily said. "Who's laughing now?"

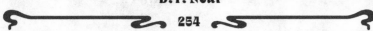
"Fair point," Logan laughed, sauntering over to the jeweler's tent. Some young women were in there, one minding the merchandise, another behind her, working on a jeweler's anvil.

The one near the counter had curly blond hair and wore a white blouse with a forest green bodice dress, while the one working in the back had her black hair beneath a bandana and wore blue jeans and a red blouse, was carefully hammering away at a length of silver wire. Both young women looked to be in their 20s.

On display were pendants, necklaces, rings, earrings, lapel pins, cufflinks, enamel pins, and brooches—all of them bearing many iterations and incarnations of the three-circle motif.

"See?" Emily said. "It's their big thing around here. Their own Holy Trinity."

"Yeah," Logan said. "They also symbolize the interplay between Life, Decay, and Death."

He was pleased to see that Emily didn't apparently know that.

"Ah," Emily said. "I guess that makes sense."

"I suppose," Logan said. "I grew up Catholic. I'm used to Holy Trinities. Even though I get kinda skeeved out by this stuff."

He looked at the endless three-circle jewelry pieces, found it weird to think that these young artisans would devote so much time and energy to one design that way. Not that their work wasn't good. There were plenty of lovely pieces. But the theme was always the same—the three circles, over and over again.

Logan thought about the pendant Maura wore, it thumping against her chest. He saw a silver lapel pin with the circles upon it, was tempted to pick one up as a lark. But he didn't want Maura to think he was making sport at her expense, or that he'd decided to join her damned cult.

"Understandable," Emily said. "The Temple was weird."

"The Temple is sacred," the young woman said behind the counter. "You should feel blessed you attended a service. Did you drink the Lady's Tears?"

"I did not," Emily said. The young woman scoffed, her scorn dancing on her freckled face.

"Then you don't know," she said. "You have no idea. The Lady cries for all of us. Her Tears heal us and make us whole."

Emily held her tongue, not wanting to tell the young woman that her religion was rooted in a highly toxic, hallucinogenic mushroom.

"How often do you drink Her Tears?" Emily asked.

"Weekly," the young woman said. "I see things."

"I'll bet you do," Emily said. "Are you going to the Midnight Service at the Sacred Grove?"

At the mention of that, the young woman's eyes narrowed.

"How do you know about that?" she asked.

Emily held up her invitation card triumphantly, savoring the young woman's unspoken umbrage.

"You shouldn't have one of those if you're not part of the Faith," she said.

"Your Eminence gave it to me herself," Emily said, seeing the young woman was even more baffled by that. The young woman hammering behind her even stopped working at her little anvil to glance at Emily and Logan.

"The Eminence must have had her reasons," the jeweler's anvil woman said.

"The Lady works in mysterious ways, I guess," Logan said. "Say, what's that stick pin run?"

"That one? 75 dollars," the young woman at the counter said.

"Wow," Emily said. "Is it antique?"

"Nope," the young woman said. Emily whistled, while Logan asked to see it and looked it over. He liked the heft of it, found it amusing. What did he care? He had money.

"I'll take it," Logan said, and the young woman deftly boxed and wrapped it, slipping it into a little grey bag with "Lynchburg Ladysilver" printed on it in an elegant script.

"Mr. Fancy," Emily said. "It'll look smashing on your lapel."

"You can wear them anywhere," the young woman at the counter said, giving Logan back his credit card. "Not just lapels."

"Naturally," Emily said. "Are you going to be at the Midnight Service?"

She figured asking again might get her the answer she didn't get before.

"Count on it," the young woman at the counter said.

Logan laughed uneasily, sensing the tension between Emily and the young woman. He toyed with the bag playfully.

"I think I'm the only one not invited to this thing," Logan said. "I'm beginning to take it personally."

"Don't," the young woman at the counter said. "Some people belong there. Some don't."

Emily thought maybe she'd found herself an Exemplar. She knew she shouldn't push, but damned if she didn't want to push, just the same.

"You seem like an Exemplar to me," Emily said, and she was pleased to see the young woman be surprised by this. Her anvil-working peer also stopped working again, looking at her with pale blue eyes, an evaluative gaze.

"What did you just call me?" the young woman at the counter said.

"I said you're an Exemplar," Emily said.

"I don't even know what that means," the young woman said.

"Me, neither," Logan said, looking between Emily and the young woman. "Why do I feel like maybe I'm missing out on something yet again?"

"Oh, I think you know exactly what I mean," Emily said. "Grey Lady."

"What's your deal?" the young woman asked.

Logan didn't understand why things were weirdly escalating and chimed in again.

"Don't mind her," Logan said. "She's a mycologist. She studies fungi."

"That I do," Emily said.

"We'll look for you at the Grove," the young woman said, glancing at her friend, who was simply watching them silently. Emily had no doubt that she would. She made a mental note to be ready.

**To say that Santino Mendoza was furious was an exercise** in understatement. Carlos and the others had managed to meet up with them outside of the village of St. Sophia, having gotten themselves a phone along the way after waylaying an unfortunate Festival-bound hitchhiker and called Santino, telling him they were holed up in St. Sophia as cryptically as he could (he texted that they were seeking solace with St. Sophia as penitents, and, thankfully, Santino ultimately understood).

At about 65 miles from Lynchburg, St. Sophia was far enough from Lynchburg to feel somewhat safer. Its primary employer was a brewery—the Augustine Brewery—which produced the well-regarded Saintly Ale.

The embarrassment Carlos felt on that call was pronounced. His failure felt absolute, but Santino told him to wait for him there, so they did, feeling like beggars.

Santino was the opposite of his younger brother. He was squat and unattractive, bulging and bald where Carlos was fey and handsome. Santino had a walrus-like mustache he dyed jet black. Santino was strong as an ox and prone to fits of violent reprisal whenever it suited him.

The *Rojas* convened in St. Sophia—Carlos with his remaining men, and Santino with a full complement of fifty *Rojas* enforcers. They had met in a warehouse, a location that Santino had acquired years before when they'd had thoughts about using St. Sophia as one of their hideaways before fatefully deciding Lynchburg had more promise. They had a dozen black SUVs, and when Carlos had turned up, Santino was already waiting for him.

"What is this, Carlo?" Santino asked. "You were supposed to secure a place for us out here in Nowheresville. And you, what? Come crawling back? Just you, Alejandro and Santiago?"

Carlos felt the sting of his big brother's reproach even more than the crossbow wound he'd taken. Santino could sink anyone with his disapproval.

"They surprised us, Santino," Carlos said. As Underboss of *Las Rojas,* he was acutely aware of the judgment of his peers. It was a title he took close to heart, and one he'd earned not just as the brother of Santino Mendoza, but one he'd won through being a capable and competent member of the organization who got things done.

"Those *gringo* bastards," Santino said, gesturing to his men who lurked around them like an army of statues. Nobody wanted to get on Santino's bad side. "They ran you out of town like, what, a clown? Is that what it is, Carlo?"

"They have Hidden Hollow," Carlos said. "I don't know how, but they do. It's not safe there. They caught all of my men. They're all gone. Damned if I know how."

Santino rubbed his forehead with a pinch of his stubby index finger and chubby thumb. Carlos knew that gesture well enough growing up. It meant that Santino was thinking and was angry. The two things flowed together.

"Tell me," Santino said.

"They just vanished," Carlos said. "I lost thirty-six men there, Santino. Gone like they never existed."

"Alright," Santino said. "So they're sneaky."

"Very," Carlos said. "We only saw them once. Grey-robed bastards. They own the sheriff, I know that much."

"Fuck the sheriff," Santino said. "And fuck Lynchburg. We are *Las Muertes Rojas.* We don't give a step to our enemies. Who are these Grey Ladies? I'm insulted even saying their name."

"They wear masks," Carlos said. "We couldn't identify them."

"Okay," Santino said. "So there's that. And they bugged the Hollow. Yeah? How do we deal with them, then?"

It wasn't a trick question. Santino was wanting an answer. Carlos felt compelled to offer something up. As the current *Segundo* who still wanted to hold onto his role, he had to say something.

"We go right at them," Carlos said. "I was going to have *El Diablo* burn down their Nightcap farm. This was before everything happened."

"Right," Santino said. "Okay. What else?"

"The Templetons," Carlos said, knowing nobody else would risk saying a word to his brother. "They run the town."

"Alright," Santino said. "Okay, we bag ourselves some Templetons. Which ones?"

"There's the father," Carlos said. "Ned Templeton. And the son, the Mayor of Lynchburg, Lionel Templeton. You have Mona Templeton—she heads their insane Temple. And there's Maura Templeton, a chef."

"A fucking chef?" Santino asked. "Yeah, that's the target. The chef. We nab the fucking cook."

"She's at the Shroom Room," Carlos said. "A restaurant in town."

Santino liked that, clapped his hands together.

"Forget the Mayor and the old man," Santino said. "And the cult leader? She's probably got an army around her. But the cook? Yeah, she's the one."

Carlos knew Santino's instinct for human weakness was infallible. He always knew which targets to go for. Carlos wanted to try to go for the top, but Santino understood the value of easier targets.

"Okay, so what do we do, Santino?" Carlos asked.

"We nab the cook," Santino said. "We take her here and we extort these Templeton *gringos* until they squeal. Then we squeeze them even harder. This is a holy war, *Rojas*. These heathen *gringos* think they can stop us? They think they can kill our men without consequence? They think they can threaten my own brother? Kill my baby brother? No way."

The assembled men cheered, some of them toting pistols which they thankfully didn't fire. The last thing they need was St. Sophia's own sheriff to come for them.

Carlos understood that this weekend was a celebration of Mexican independence, so it was even more significant. That Monday was Independence Day, and he knew that Santino would make the most of it.

"We are going to crash their little party," Santino said. "These idiotic mushroom farmers think they can stop us? We will show them."

The *Rojas* present cheered, and Carlos was heartened by it, despite what he'd encountered. With Santino, everything seemed possible. That was why he was the Boss of their organization. He made the impossible possible. There was a world of

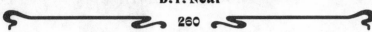
difference between Underboss and Boss, Carlos understood in that moment. His failure had been because he wasn't Santino. Where he had failed, Santino would not.

"Forget sneaking," Santino said. "I want two teams for the cook. One to go in the front, one to go in the back. The front team, you shake things up, you distract. The back team, you get this Maura Templeton and you get her out of there. We'll be gone before their damned sheriff even knows what happened."

To hear Santino say it, it sounded doable. And Carlos wasn't about to interrupt his big brother. But his memory of smug Sheriff Leonard still stung. The man was terrifying in his own homespun way. And there was the very real consequence of the threat inherent in it. That they had best not go back to Lynchburg or there would be consequences. Carlos didn't know what had happened to his men, but they had paid with their lives. However they had paid wasn't clear to him, but pay they had.

He didn't know if he could bring that up to Santino without being branded a coward. That was a fate worse than death in the *Rojas*.

"Then we take our hostage and we lean on old Farmer Templeton," Santino said. "It's easy. If he doesn't work with us, we send back pieces of his daughter until he surrenders."

The men laughed at this, grateful that Santino's ire was aimed elsewhere. That's how it always was with Santino. You always laughed with him to avoid being laughed at, or worse.

"And when he surrenders," Santino said. "We *still* kill him. There's a debt to be paid, here. He owes us. We string him up somewhere everybody can see."

Carlos enjoyed hearing the feisty rage of his brother but knew there was a world between them in St. Sophia versus Lynchburg, and a lot of miles between them. He wasn't going to say that while Santino was winding everybody up, however.

"We're going to hang them from lampposts by their heels," Santino said. "Every one of them. They call us the Red Death. We call ourselves that, for God's sake. We'll earn that name this weekend, Brothers."

The warning of the cultists still gave Carlos pause. That, and the irrevocable fact that they had made dozens of his men simply vanish as if they had never been. But he could say nothing, would say nothing. There was pride, after all. If word got out that the *Rojas* had been thumped by some half-assed coun-

try bumpkins, they'd never be able to stand up straight again in Pittsburgh.

"Brookline! Beechview!" the *Rojas* said, pumping their fists. Carlos joined in. They came from those neighborhoods, had grown up in them. They knew firsthand that there had been resistance to them even being there. It only stiffened their resolve, not just to survive, but to thrive.

"Mushroom farmers," Santino said, spitting on the ground. "That's what I think of them and their *Signora*. Give me a break. We will burn down their Temple. Right to the ground. We have two teams hitting their Shroom Room. A third team will light up their Temple. And a fourth team will burn down their Nightcap Mushroom Farm. And I mean teams. There are fifty of us here, brothers. Ten men per team. Fifth team stays with me. Let's see them deal with that."

The *Rojas* liked the sound of that, and Carlos was reassured by it, by their enthusiasm. It was like what Carlos wanted to do with Santiago, only on a far larger scale.

Carlos knew that with his own lost contingent and what Santino had brought to St. Sophia, there were several hundred *Rojas* left back home, mostly lower echelon, hiding out in various places. With Mig gone, it was Carlos and Santino heading their family. Should anything happen to them, the gang would split into various factions. Carlos forced that out of his mind. He didn't want to think of anything happening to either of them.

And yet he did. It gnawed at him, and he hated it.

Having finished his speech, Santino swaggered over to Carlos, clapping him on his unwounded shoulder.

"See, Carlo? That's how you do it," Santino said, drawing a match and lighting up a cigar, one of the Cubans he was always bragging about having. He puffed away a moment, watching the *Rojas* prepare.

"I don't know, Tino," Carlos said. "These farmers, these cultists, they are highly organized."

"So are we," Santino said. "And we have better guns."

Carlos wasn't going to mention that the cultists had taken all of the guns his men had brought with them, lest he be reminded yet again of his failure.

"We grab the cook," Santino said. "The rest will take care of itself. They'll never see us coming."

"We should wait until after the festival," Carlos said. "It'll be easier, then. Fewer people around."

Santino frowned at him around his cigar.

"This is *our* weekend, Carlo," Santino said. "Not theirs. What should have happened was you should have been able to extort them the way we wanted, and we would be counting money instead of planning a raid."

"I underestimated them," Carlos said.

"You think?" Santino said. "I don't care about their cult. I don't care about their masked ladies running around in the woods, howling at the moon. I care about their money. That's what I want."

"The whole town is in their pocket," Carlos said. "And the Hollow."

The loss of the Hollow particularly stung, as Carlos had sunk a lot of money into securing the properties to begin with. They had been turning some of them into grow houses, where they could cultivate and propagate marijuana right beneath everyone's noses.

"Not a problem," Santino said. "In fact, I'm counting on that. You're going to be the bait, Carlo."

"Wait, what?"

Santino sent a puff of smoke his way.

"You said they leaned on you about not going back to town," Santino said.

"Yeah," Carlos said.

"So, you're going to defy that," Santino said. "I'm going to send you with five guys. You're going to go back into town."

Carlos didn't like that one bit.

"They said they'd kill me," Carlos said.

"You're Red Death, Brother," Santino said. "We're already dead, remember? That's why we're Red Death. We're not afraid of dying. The point is that they'll go right after you. While they're doing that, we make our move. All you have to do is not be caught by them as easily as you were caught before. You make like a rabbit and you run. You lead them on a merry chase. Can you do that for me?"

"I don't like it," Carlos said.

"It's the only way you're still useful to me," Santino said. Carlos thought about their childhood in Brookline, the way Santino would lord it over him and Mig. As the middle sibling,

Carlos was invariably the fulcrum of Santino's power plays. "I mean, with your wound, you're no good to me in a fight, if you ever were. I know you're more a lover than a fighter, Carlo."

"That's not true," Carlos said.

"Of course it's true," Santino said. "Mig was the dog, you are the fox, and I am the wolf. It's always been that way. Maybe that's what I'll call you when this is all over—*El Zorro*."

Santino laughed at that, puffing away.

"Do I at least get to pick my five men?" Carlos asked.

"No," Santino said. "I've picked them for you: Tiago, Emiliano, Felipe, Lucas, and Diego."

Carlos wasn't happy to hear that. They were lower-rung guys, expendables all. It was insulting, because it meant that Santino considered Carlos expendable, too. Santino read the grimace on his face.

"I can't spare my best for you, Carlo," Santino said. "They're needed for those other things. You just have to use your wits is all. You're good at that. Be witty."

With Santino, even a compliment felt like an insult, and he looked sidelong at his brother as the *Rojas* loaded their SUVs and prepared.

"You said that one Grey Lady had Teo's phone, yeah?" Santino said. "So, you call her from a burner."

Santino snapped a finger and somebody lobbed a burner phone at Carlos, which he barely caught, prompting a chuckle from Santino.

"You tell her," Santino said. "Tell her off. Use that smart mouth of yours. Tell her you're coming back, and she'd better watch her step. Something like that."

"We're better off surprising them," Carlos said. "Catching them off-guard."

"Tell her that you're coming tomorrow," Santino said. "That you're coming for her tomorrow."

"Even though we're raiding tonight?" Carlos said.

"Yes, Carlo, yes," Santino said. "That's how it works when you are the bait. Use your words. Sell it."

Carlos dialed up Teo's number, and, of course, the Lady answered.

"Who's this?" the Lady asked.

"You know who it is," Carlos said, hushing the others.

"Carlos," the Lady said. "How are you feeling? Does the wound still sting?"

"I wanted you to know that I'm coming for you," Carlos said.

"Ooh, that sounds like trouble," the Lady said. "Are you bringing more of your men to fertilize our forests?"

"You'll find out tomorrow," Carlos said.

"That's so courteous of you to call," the Lady said.

"We're going to crucify you," Carlos said.

"That sounds like a biblical amount of vengeance you're looking to inflict on us," the Lady said. "We know how to deal beat bible people, Carlos."

"Laugh all you like," Carlos said. "I'm going to have my revenge."

"You don't even know how to find us," the Lady said. She didn't sound afraid. She never did. Carlos could only imagine who she was.

"Don't worry about that," Carlos said. "It's a small town. Doesn't take much to burn it all down."

"Aw, you rhymed, Carlos," the Lady said. "We'll be ready for you, whatever you and your Red Deaths are planning. Years ago, a biker gang tried to muscle in on us. They're living in the forest, now. Every year, Christian missionaries come to save us— they end up in the Cursed Earth, too. Where we all belong."

"We're not a biker gang. We're not missionaries," Carlos said. "You'll find us harder to deal with."

"We'll see," the Lady said. "When can we expect you? High noon?"

"Tomorrow," Carlos said. "That's all you get."

"Be seeing you, Carlos," the Lady said. "I honestly can't wait."

"I'll bet," Carlos said.

"Oh, and Carlos?" the Lady said. "To the Cursed Earth you will go. Where we all belong. I'll put you there myself."

Carlos hung up on her, stuffing the phone in his pocket, while Santino and some of the others looked on. They'd only heard his part of the conversation, had seen his reactions.

"Well?" Santino asked.

"It's done," Carlos said.

"Forget *El Zorro*," Santino said. "I've got an even better name for you."

Santino relit his cigar and puffed on it triumphantly a moment.

"Carlos the *Conejito,*" Santino said, clapping his hands. He led the men in a rousing cheer: *"Conejito! Conejito! Conejito!"*

Although he bore up as much as his pride would allow him to, Carlos felt like he was already dead.

# 7

**Austin had gotten streetside but hadn't been able to** find Ash. His scintillating memory of her from the night before, the image he'd had of her had framed his perception, but in the crowds of tourists and mushroomheads, he hadn't been able to spot her.

It was frustrating because Grand Avenue wasn't really that massive. It was maybe the equivalent of three city blocks. But when you stuffed those three blocks with tents and wandering pedestrians, it became labyrinthine.

Worse, Mallory and the Twins had suitably roused themselves and were pinging him, which distracted him as well. Mallory was particularly bothersome, texting him while high.

*I'm so glad we're frenz, Austinn. I'm like just glad were fiends. I'm sad you ran out because I wanted to show you how friends we are. That's how I am. You know? Like I'm friendly. That's what makes a frind. Being friendly. I'm always friendly. You're my friend. And I feel like we can be really good friend. Like today. Tonight. Tomorrow. Whatever. Whenever. You and me, Astin. Austin. Friends. Be my friend? You're my friend, right?*

*Yes, of course.*

*Cuz you should come back here. Like up here. In here with me. Real close friends. Real close. That's cool. You had to get ice, am I right? But you left the ice bucket. Come up here.*

Austin sighed.

*You're high.*

*Not that high, Friendo.*

*Right.*

*Seriously. Come up here. I want to kiss and make up.*

*I'm going to the Parade.*

*I'm a parade, my Friend.*

*Yeah, you are.*

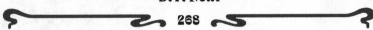
Every time he tried to disengage, his phone kept chirping with additional pings from Mallory. And when the Twins woke up, it got even more out of control, so he turned off his ringer, left his phone buzzing in his pocket while he looked for Ash.

"Ho ho ho, Sunshine," came the gravelly voice of Fun Gus, who was standing right there in front of him, his chest puffed out. Even in the light of the overcast day, the clown was a horrible vision, big and broad as ever, with scores of balloons in his white-gloved hands, and kids dancing around him, begging for balloons, which he'd give out one at a time, his bright eyes on Austin the whole time.

"Oh, fuck," Austin said.

"Have you decided?" Fun Gus asked, tying a balloon to a little girl's wrist, winking at her mom, who looked on nervously.

"I, uh, haven't," Austin said.

"Too bad, too bad," Fun Gus said. He mimed checking a wristwatch that wasn't there, grimacing as he held the phantom watch to his ear. "Time's running out for you, Sport."

"What the hell does that even mean?" Austin asked.

Fun Gus laughed, clutching his polka-dotted belly.

"Time will tell. I'll tell you tomorrow," Fun Gus said. Mushy was walking up, miming laughing like Fun Gus was, and seeing the mascot nearby, the clown laughed even harder, playfully poking the mushroom mascot in the ribs, like the two of them were in on the biggest, best joke in the whole wide world.

Austin really hated Fun Gus, wanted to punch him in the dick. Mushy held up his wicker basket and dug into it, flinging confetti at Austin, which landed in his hair and stuck to his forehead. Fun Gus guffawed and slapped his thigh.

"There's *spore* where that came from, Sunshine," Fun Gus said. "Oh, man. Good one, Mushy. Good one."

The mascot and the clown gave each other five, their gloved hands smacking as they connected.

Austin knew better than to get into an argument with a clown at a festival. The last thing he needed were the parents to think he was some kind of clown-kicking asshole in front of their balloon-addicted kids.

Meanwhile, his phone buzzed in his pocket, and worse still, the clown noticed, cocking an eyebrow at him.

"Is that a phone in your pocket or are you just happy to see me?" Fun Gus asked. Mushy tossed another handful of confetti

at him, which Austin tried to dodge, getting some in his mouth, which he spat out in aggravation. This just amused Mushy even more, with Fun Gus laughing uproariously as he handed out balloons by the handful to the happy kids. "You'd better answer, Bucky. Could be important."

"I'm fine," Austin said.

"Your decision," Fun Gus said, "You're the Decider, after all. You decide."

He fished out his bike horn from his pocket and gave it a couple of honking toots—*honk-honk, honk-honk.* The kids around giggled and Fun Gus strode away, capering with Mushy like the two of them were bound for the Emerald City, leaving a trail of children racing in their wake, braying for balloons.

Austin yanked his phone from his pocket and was treated to a pile of high-texting/sexting from Mallory as well as plaintive inquiries from Jess and Jake about where everybody should meet up for breakfast.

*That fucking clown is out here.*

*Aww, that's FUN! We'll be down in a bit.*

Austin grimaced, turned his attention back to trying to find the elusive Ash, but she was nowhere to be seen. Part of him was wondering if she had been a hallucination.

*You decide.*

What the holy hell did that even mean? Austin couldn't handle cryptic clowns. Of all the things he was prepared for on the trip to Lynchburg, that would have been dead last in his mind. And why was Fun Gus zeroing in on him? What was that even about?

His phone pinged again. It was Mallory.

She'd sent a picture of herself naked in the hotel bed, the white blankets coyly drawn up, only her bare, tattooed shoulders evident, grinning up at him.

*Friendship matters, Austin. Our friendship. Ours. Yours. Mine. Get up here. Fuck the clown. No, scratch that. Fuck ME. Be my friend. Oh, the Twins are knocking. Hold on.*

Austin stuffed his phone back into his pocket and angrily tried to shake off the confetti that was on him. Mushy pissed him off almost as much as the clown. Only someone insanely desperate or desperately insane would take a gig like that.

They were, thankfully, nowhere to be seen, so he headed the opposite direction where they'd last been heading, which appeared to be the south stage, where there was a mushroom cook-off going on. He figured Fun Gus would be shaking down people for spare change. This took him toward the clock tower to the north, toward the demarcated Templeton Lane, where the parade was setting up. He was aghast to see a dozen people on the north stage with piles of fried mushrooms they were shoveling into their mouths while a red-vested, straw-hatted emcee was narrating and a timer was going. There was a Mushy standing there, miming horror at the consumption of his people, clutching his stomach as if in agony, and touching the sides of his face as if in terror.

Were there multiple Mushy mascots walking around? Austin got pissed off even having to think about that.

The contestants each had bowls of fried mushrooms in front of them and white bibs with a red-printed Mushy winking on them.

They were ten guys and two women, most of them chunkers, a couple of skinnies, and their faces were smeared with grease as they shoveled down the mushrooms.

"Mushrooms are good food," the emcee said. "Packed with nutrition, a great source of protein that's low in fat. Of course, we solve all of that by deep-frying them, but you know, what can you do?"

*You decide.*

There were fried mushroom vendors serving up little red and white paper cones of fried mushrooms. The smell of them reminded Austin of many a carnival he'd been to growing up in Austintown. He decided to buy a cone, which satisfied the vendor, a young woman wearing a white paper garrison hat with the three-circle symbol on it in red.

"There's three types of dipping sauce at the kiosk," the young woman said. "See the bottles? Just squeeze some on one side of the cone, and dip away."

Austin saw the bottles were marked MILD, HOT, and WILD—white, yellow, and pink. He opted for the Mild, poured some as she'd advised him, and grabbed some napkins.

Meanwhile, the mushroom-gobblers were working away at their bowls, while Mushy fretted, pacing back and forth and silently taunting (or encouraging?) the contestants.

Austin dipped one of the mushrooms and took a bite, realizing at once how hungry he was, and carefully eating it, as it was hot. His phone kept buzzing, but with his hands greasy and full, he wasn't about to pick up.

"I thought there was only Mushy," Austin said. The young woman he'd bought the mushrooms from, who had "Myndi" on her nametag, enlightened him.

"That's Mrs. Mushy," Myndi said. "Mushette. She always attends the eating competition."

Mushette was clearly beside herself at the eat-off, and Austin could see upon more careful examination that she did appear female, with basically big eyelashes and blue eyeshadow and red lips indicating that she was apparently female.

Austin couldn't rightly eat his own mushrooms while watching the contestants wolfing theirs down, so he pushed his way past the north stage toward Templeton Lane, where the sawhorses had been laid out and some mounted deputies were using their horses to make their way.

The fried mushrooms were actually good, being well-seasoned and flavorful, but the way he saw it, anything deep-fried could pass for good for someone coming off a big night out.

The food got him thinking again about the portentous message from the damned clown. What did he even have to decide? It made no sense.

"The Decider, my ass," Austin said aloud while chewing.

His phone kept buzzing, and he finally dug it out and saw that it was Jess calling. He debated answering but decided he would.

"What is it, Jess?"

"Where are you, Dude?" Jess asked.

"I'm finding a spot to watch the parade," Austin said. "Past the north stage."

"On it," Jess said. "Jake and I are starving. We smell food cooking absolutely everywhere."

"The fried mushrooms are pretty good."

"Barf City," Jess said.

"Hey, where's Mallory?" Austin asked.

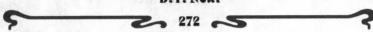
"She went back to sleep," Jess said. "Or she's showering. Maybe both. Stay put. We'll come to you."

Austin noshed on the mushrooms while scanning the crowd. It was mostly parents and their kids, old people, one or two scenesters maybe his age. No sign of Ash. But he thought maybe that she wasn't the kind of woman who'd stand around gawking at a parade. Still, you never knew.

He felt better having gotten something in his stomach, even something like the fried mushrooms. He could see the parade floats being queued up in the distance, way up Templeton Lane. Austin had to hand it to the little town. They definitely didn't skimp when rolling out the festivities.

The Temple stood to the east, as squat and square as it had been the night before, but by daylight somehow possessing a different character, an altogether cryptlike bearing that old natural stone buildings sometimes had about them. Few places seemed more forlorn than the municipal buildings in small towns. It was the Brutalist blend of utilitarian architecture coupled with the relative lack of traffic. It created a liminality that was somehow disarming.

*You decide.*

Austin laughed to himself at getting creeped out by the urban architecture of Lynchburg, but it was sort of creepy. Even the big clock tower was kind of weird. Like why did a little town like this even need that big clock tower? It was a big rectangular structure with a pointed roof, the face of the clock appearing to be Art Deco by design.

He took out his phone and snapped some photos of it on a whim.

"Hey," Jess said, tapping his elbow. She was grinning at him while eating some red ice cream with white sprinkles on it that matched her conical mushroom hat she was wearing. She had on a Mushette tee and a denim jacket with matching blue jeans, while Jake was wearing a Steelers sweatshirt and blue jeans.

"Jesus, what are you even eating, Jess?" Austin asked. "Ice cream for breakfast?"

"Sure," Jess said. Her teeth and lips were red. "Strawberry Smash ice cream with white chocolate sprinkles. It's from Acre's Ice Cream down the way."

Jake was eating a blue cone that had similar sprinkles.

"Raspberry Crash," Jake said. "Waffle cone."

"You two are too much," Austin said. Jess took out her phone and posed with her cone with her brother, the two of them grinning.

"I got 10% off using one of my Fungo Fungible tokens," Jess said. "Are we really standing here waiting for the parade?"

"I am," Austin said. He wasn't about to tell them he was hoping to find Ash.

A horn sounded that heralded that somebody had won the eating competition, and Austin felt his stomach turn even at the notion of it. He didn't care who won, but people were applauding.

"I wanted to do that," Jake said.

"You slept in, Stupid," Jess said.

"Still, I so would have won that," Jake said.

"Maybe, maybe," Jess said.

"Whenever someone wins an eating competition, everybody loses," Austin said. "We all die a little bit inside."

Jess laughed, while Jake growled into his cone. The Twins had the companionably adversarial bond that close siblings so often had. They loved each other dearly, and they also loved getting on each other's nerves.

A boat horn sounded as the clock tower tolled noon, and Austin could see the parade was beginning.

"We took some Blue Meanies before we came downstairs," Jess said, leering red-teethed at Austin.

"Oh, come on, now," Austin said.

"Guilty," Jake said, holding up an arm. "Scout's honor, Bro."

"We raided your stash," Jess said. "When we went to check on Mallory. Hope you don't mind. You should hide them better. I found them in like two minutes."

"I am Pan Cyan," Jake said. "As of like twenty minutes ago, Bro."

"You idiots," Austin said. "Those are strong. How much did you take?"

Jess shrugged. "Enough. Plenty."

Austin wasn't about to babysit the Twins. They were probably already starting to trip.

"Seriously, you two are on your own," Austin said. "If you think I'm going to handhold you while you're tripping, you're crazy."

Jess just devoured her ice cream wordlessly, while Jake laughed.

"We're going to babysit YOU, Austin," Jess said.

There was a PA system somewhere, and a reviewing stand for the parade that Austin noticed was situated on the other side of the north stage. There were some local newspeople there with microphones, emceeing the parade.

The Grand Marshal of the parade was rolling up in a black Cadillac convertible, and Austin could see it was silver-haired Ned Templeton IV, which was announced on some banners that were being carried by marching majorettes. He carried a silver scepter in his white-gloved hand that was topped with a statuette of *La Signora* by the look of things. He bore a silver sash across his chest and was wearing a black suit and had the three-circle symbol at his lapel in silver. He even had on a top hat.

Sitting beside him was his son, Mayor Lionel Templeton, who was waving to the fervent applause of the crowd. Austin thought he looked a lot like his dad, but maybe softer in bearing. He had on a top hat, too, and white gloves.

Behind them marched local members of the Armed Forces, bearing flags, and behind them was the Lynchburg High School Marching Band, who were striking out an authoritative marching beat. The kids wore blue and white uniforms, with big white hats. The high school banner identified them as the Lynchburg Cappers, with yet another mushroom mascot printed on the banner, a feisty-looking mushroom looking very determined in its sporty snarl.

"Oh, wow," Jess said, clutching her head. "I think my head just opened. Austin, is my head open?"

"Yeah, you've got an open mind," Austin said, which made Jess gasp and laugh.

"Jake, I've got an open mind," Jess said. "And there's music flying out of it. And butterflies."

Jess was running after unseen things, trying to grab them, gripping her ice cream in her other hand, while Jake was just laughing at her.

"She's such a lightweight," Jake said. "Totes."

He took out his phone and snapped pictures of his sister whirling around, her eyes as big as pie plates.

"Classic," Jake said, showing Austin. "Am I right?"

"Right as rain," Austin said, which struck Jake as incredibly funny, although Austin knew it wasn't.

The first parade float was rolling by, which featured Mushy (or a Mushy? Austin couldn't be sure if maybe there was an army of them) and the rest of the Mushy Family dancing around on a glittery green-tasseled float with a fake forest of trees around them like a little grove. Mushy and Mushette waved, while their mushroom kids tossed candies to the onlookers, to squeals of delight from kids.

Behind it came some blue-tartaned bagpipers, a smallish kiltie band that appeared to be tied to the Hecate Horse Farm. A half-dozen pipers played, accompanied by three drummers. Austin noted the three-circle symbol in blue upon the white face of the drums.

"Pipes in my head," Jess said. "I hear them, Austin. Jake. No, I see them. The notes. Flying like birds. A flock of notes, all singing and swirling around."

"Murmuration," Austin murmured.

Jake laughed, watching Jess try to catch the musical notes, laughing so hard he dropped what was left of his ice cream. Austin shrugged, declining to even bother filming Jess, keeping his eyes on the parade.

Behind the pipers came a legit weird sight—there were scores of grey-robed, masked and conical hat-wearing figures walking, bearing netlike shrouds over their hats that hung down like spiderwebs, with bells hanging from the ends of them. The bells clanked as they walked, and a dozen of them were playing these peculiar drums that were like toms by the sound of them but were longer and looked handmade. Everything looked handmade to him, with a strange, ramshackle quality to them that was bizarrely off-putting to Austin.

The figures walked without introduction, no banner, nothing. They looked like a strange, ragtag army, moving like a bunch of ghosts. Austin took out his phone and snapped shots of them, as well as some video of them as they made their jangling way, their bells ringing as the drummers carried the beat. He tagged and posted them on his feed.

"What the hell are those?" Jake asked.

"The Grey Ladies," Austin said, having heard it announced by the reporters on the viewing stand.

"Fuck," Jake said. "There are thousands of them."

There weren't actually thousands of them, Austin noted. Jake was just feeling the dose kick in properly, and it was messing with his perception. There were, however, many hundreds of them, and they moved not like they were marching, but spun to the beat of the drums, which struck a steady cadence, a plodding sort of beat. He saw a smaller one run from the audience to join their peers, beginning the strange, whirling dance they were all doing.

As the beat was struck, the apparitions moved and whirled about in their robes, their shrouds spinning with them as they moved. It was a strange and mesmerizing sort of folk dance, and Jess was spinning where she stood, filming and giggling as she went.

"I see them," Jess said. "I see them all. A rainbow of grey, Jake. There's blue and grey and white and ivory and more blue. Beautiful blue."

Austin watched them pass, grateful that they weren't looking at him, or didn't appear to be. He didn't know what they were supposed to be exactly, but he didn't like them. They looked wrong to him.

After the Grey Ladies came Mona Templeton on her own float, which bore an effigy of the Grey Lady, tended to by acolytes and deacons. Mona was wearing a blue cassock with a red stole that was inset with the three-circle glyph in silver. She was tossing out blue hard candies that were being eagerly scooped up or caught by kids.

"*I'm* the High Priestess," Jess said, having to be held back by her brother before she ran out into the street. They fell to the ground, laughing, Jake rolling around and Jess still chasing down what music notes she could find.

There came a trio of historical floats, one showing the founding of Lynchburg, Austin gathered from listening to the emcees. It showed some Pilgrim-looking people surrounded by chickenwire and papier-mâché trees. Someone was dressed as *La Signora* in the heart of this float, a lovely woman in grey, with grey makeup on her face. Austin tried to tune in to what the announcers were saying.

"Here we see Ned Templeton, his wife, Lucretia Bianchi, settling Lynchburg with Phineas Lynch, all three seeing the Grey Lady in the forest," the announcer said. "She showed them where to go, where to build. From Fort Pitt they came and founded Fort Lynch."

There were trappers and mountain men who interacted with the Pilgrim/Quaker types. Austin couldn't be sure as he watched them roll on by. He thought the chronology of it was probably screwy but wasn't going to raise a stink about it.

The next float showed a mockup of Lynchburg covered in snow, where people were huddling. They looked like frontier people, now.

"The winters were harsh, and crops were hard to grow," the announcer said. "But the Lady provided mushrooms to Her chosen people, who were able to feed and prosper. Easy to grow and maintain, they became the staple crop in Lynchburg after the 1880s."

Austin could see there were mushroom caps growing in the fake snow. Some of the frontier people in the town held baskets of mushrooms and were waving, bowing before a mocked-up statue of *La Signora*, flanked by three stout-looking wooden posts.

Jess was momentarily quiet, taking it all in, as was Jake, who was thunderstruck by the passage of the floats.

"What're the posts for?" Austin asked.

"What posts?" Jess asked. "I only see dancing trees and a shimmering sky."

"Posts," Jake said, laughing at the word. "Posts."

The third float showed a more modern-looking Lynchburg, surrounded by mushrooms, with happy children waving, carrying mushroom baskets from which they lobbed more candy.

"Thanks to the hard work of our ancestors, Lynchburg contributes to the prodigious output of mushrooms in the state of Pennsylvania. We are all doing our part, each and every day," the announcer said.

"Very educational," Austin said more to himself than anyone else, since the Twins were on the on-ramp for what would likely be one big trip.

Austin sighed and looked around the crowd, which was fuller, now. There were white and brown robes among the onlookers, although most of them were tourists. Jess was crawling

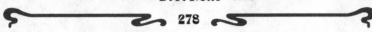
on her hands and knees, moaning and laughing, like she was trying to catch herself or hold onto the world.

"I'm flying, Jake," Jess said. "I'm looking down on everything."

There was still no sign of Ash. He thought about ditching the Twins at the parade, but felt a sense of responsibility for them, since he'd been the one to get the drugs to begin with.

After the historical floats came a red El Camino with Fun Gus riding on the back, laughing as the car zigzagged. He hung on to some roll bars on the back.

"And there's everyone's favorite clown, Lynchburg's own Fun Gus the Laughing Clown," the announcer said, as the crowd cheered. Jess even perked up from her crawling to hoot and holler, calling out the clown's name.

Fun Gus honked his bike horn playfully, leering at the crowd as he did so: *honk-honk, honk-honk*. There were helium balloons tied to the roll bars of the El Camino that fluttered as the car rolled along Templeton Lane.

"Everyone please give Fun Gus a big, big hand," the announcer said, and people cheered. Austin took some more pictures as the El Camino approached, as Fun Gus produced a giant white hand from the back of the El Camino, waving to the crowd with it.

"Already got one," Fun Gus said, cackling.

"Prop comedy," Austin said, sighing. "Fuck."

Austin wanted to shrink away from the crowd, but even as he wished this, he saw Fun Gus notice him, the clown laughing and pointing right at him. Fun Gus made a white-gloved finger pistol and shot three times at Austin, winking at him.

With his other hand, he pretended to check his invisible watch again, putting it up to his ear, nodding gleefully at Austin when he could see that he saw him. He pointed to the clock tower, then he ran a thumb across his throat, while the El Camino honked its own horn and passed them, heading down Templeton Lane.

# 8

**Everything was getting on Ash's nerves at this point,**
but that's how it so often went with Melinda, who could be terribly frustrating on her best days. Mona Templeton's eminent smugness was enraging. Emily flirting with the chef was just another thing that set her off.

What she needed was to get away from this place, but part of her was wanting to write the story that would blow the lid off of Lynchburg, and that meant working everybody she could. She waded through Grand Avenue like a hunter.

The story was that there was a cult running Lynchburg, but what Ash needed was someone willing to say that, because she wasn't going to write a story exposing her sister to all of the negative press she'd encounter by being part of that cult. She figured Jerry would be okay with it if it made Nightcap look bad.

"Part of the cult," Ash said aloud.

She then had an idea while the parade was beginning and went back to the Grand Hotel. She'd snooped around while Emily had been out and had found the gym bag that had contained the grey robes, hats and masks that Emily and Marquis had used to sneak their way through the Temple.

Working quickly, Ash put one of them on. Being shorter than either Emily or Marquis, the robe felt voluminous, but she'd have to make do with that. She slipped on the mask and the hat, which she secured so it wouldn't come off. She looked at herself in the mirror and gave herself the creeps. There was only one shroud, a netlike web that had a hole in the center that allowed her to put it on the point of her hat. Some slight adjustment and it hung down like some malevolent bridal veil, turning her visage into a silhouette. She put on her running shoes, tied them tight.

She took her digital recorder and spoke into it.

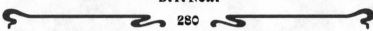
"Ash Dunn, masquerading as a Temple fanatic," Ash said. "Saturday, September 14, at the Lynchburg, Pennsylvania Fungus Festival."

Then she secured her recorder, slipped a notepad and pen in her back pocket, as well as her phone in another pocket.

She stepped out of their hotel room and and walked through the hotel corridor. Dressed this way, she felt surreally out of touch with everything around her, like one step removed. She could taste the wariness from others as she cleared the elevator and went into the lobby.

"Exemplar," said Cloris from her concierge station. Ash glanced at her without breaking her stride, seeing Cloris bow her head. The young man at the souvenir station also called her "Exemplar" and bowed his head as well as she passed.

The respect and fear that followed in her wake said a lot.

She fanned out into the street, pleased with the reaction she caused with every step. There was power and deference given to anyone in a grey robe and mask, and Ash made a mental note of it. She'd record it later. The acolytes and deacons genuflected as she passed, and as Ash made her way to the parade route, she could see people glancing at her.

Ash saw the other grey-robed Exemplars marching along the parade route, wearing belled, netlike shrouds that clanked as they traveled, and felt unfortunately exposed, since she had no clanking bells on her own shroud. Maybe nobody would notice. She didn't know how detail-oriented these cultists might be.

However, as the Exemplars whirled and danced their way along the route, Ash slipped past the parade barrier and joined in with them, capering and spinning to try to blend in. No one appeared to notice. For all she knew, they were all tripping on Lady's Tears.

Ash kept up a steady pace, following along the parade route, looking out at the tourist onlookers who were watching and taking photos with their phones. The drumbeat the Exemplars followed and the chorus of bells made her think of the marathons she'd run in the past, the infernal cowbells people loved to swing around.

The bells the other Exemplars had dangling from their shrouds were different from that, however. They were smaller

than cowbells, and their noise was more like the sound bamboo made when struck together—more clonk than clank.

Nobody talked among the Exemplars, which itself was bizarre, being in this sea of grey-robed figures moving without a word, with only their bells and the drums making a sound. Ash also realized that she was markedly shorter than the other Exemplars, which hadn't been something she'd entirely reckoned with.

Whatever the entrance requirements were for the Exemplars, there seemed to be a preference for height. Bitterly, Ash thought of carnival rides, which were a childhood bane for her as a short person—YOU MUST BE THIS TALL TO GO ON THIS RIDE—she wondered if anyone noticed or cared that she was smaller than the other Exemplars.

The parade route took them to the Temple, and then pivoted rightward down First Street, where more onlookers cheered them on. Others just watched, transfixed by the spectacle unfolding before them. The parade route ended in Templeton Park, which was a half-block from the Temple, being south and east of the Temple.

Templeton Park was a 100-acre recreational park that surrounded the Lynchburg Reservoir, and had a variety of areas in it, including a baseball and soccer field, a children's playground, a frisbee golf course, a dog park, tennis, volleyball, and basketball courts, fishing grounds, as well as a community gardens area. There were several designated forest groves in the park, including Oak, Maple, Beech, Ash, and Sycamore, with marked trails that wound throughout them.

With the parade route terminating there, people were gathered in a crowd, both the parade participants and the onlookers who happened to be watching.

Ash stayed at the edge of the Exemplars, instinctively not wanting to get stuck in the middle of them, where she'd not be able to see anything. She was grateful that she did this, as she otherwise would not have seen what she'd seen.

It happened very quickly, as she saw two black SUVs bear down on the Exemplars on First Street, swerving in front of them. Men in red ski masks were driving the SUVs, and one of them had his window down, shouting as they drove their SUVs into, over, and through the Exemplars.

"*¡La Muerte Roja ha venido para ustedes, Cultistas!*" one of the red-masked men cried, as their vehicles ran down Exemplars. The SUVs just smashed into the Exemplars, riding over them without pausing.

Onlookers were screaming at the horrible sight, and the SUVs tore through the ranks of the Exemplars. Grey-robed bodies were strewn on First Street as the SUVs punched through the throng of Exemplars and raced down Templeton Lane, honking all the while, causing parade participants to scatter to avoid them.

It all happened so fast, Ash almost couldn't believe it, took out her phone to film it and capture it with pictures.

The fallen Exemplars numbered about thirty or forty, in various states of agony and anguish, some of them bleeding out on the street, others motionless, still more crying out in pain. Masks were cracked and broken in some instances, and Ash prayed that her sister wasn't among them. The bloodied faces she saw weren't ones she recognized, inasmuch as she could make out faces amid the carnage.

The other Exemplars went to help their fallen comrades, and Ash became aware of herself standing out, filming it. She pocketed her phone even as it pinged and she didn't risk a look.

She was unsure what she should do, but figured it was best to blend in, so she ran up.

"Someone call an ambulance," one of the Exemplars said.

Several of them took out phones and dialed them up, while some of the mounted deputies rode up on their horses. The absurdity of the shrouded Exemplars on their cellphones, calling for assistance, was not lost on Ash.

"Infidels," Mona Templeton said, striding up, looking stricken as she surveyed her fallen flock. Her face was full of rage, and Ash dug out her phone again to take a shot, seeing the ping had been from Emily.

*OMG! They came! Red Deaths!*

Another black SUV shot out of Ambrose Alley, skidding as it slid and turned, racing off south on First Street. Somewhere, the howl of ambulance sirens could be heard, as well as police sirens.

A deputy had ridden up, hopping off. He was a handsome, towheaded young man with "Reeve" on his nameplate Ash saw in a blur as he paused to speak to the Exemplars.

"Nobody move anybody," Reeve said. "Did anybody see the assailants?"

"I did," Ash said, unable to help herself. "They had on red ski masks."

"*Las Muertes Rojas,*" Mona said. "The Red Deaths."

Reeve went to his radio and talked to his peers, reporting what he'd witnessed.

"Did anybody see any license plates?" Reeve asked. Nobody had. It had all occurred too quickly. They'd smashed through the Exemplars and driven off.

Exemplars were taking the masks and broken hats off of their wounded peers, setting them on the bloody road beside them, while Mona had urged the other Exemplars to form a protective ring around the fallen in the form of interlocking hands. Ash found herself holding hands with two of the cultists, one on either side, while they prayed to the Lady.

"Deliver them to the Cursed Earth, where we all belong," they said, a chorus of muttered voices, plaintive with pain. "Where we all belong."

Her mind was already forming the headline: Murder on Main Street—Blood Runs Fast and Furious at Lynchburg Festival.

"*Signora Grigia,*" Mona said. "Our loving Lady and protector, eternally gracious are You in life and death. We ask for Your help on this dark day, for our wounded and dying, our dying and our dead, murdered by the despicable cowardice of these infidel gangsters. Grant us the strength to continue, that we might continue to honor Your name, and to bring justice to the unjust. Guide our fallen to the Cursed Earth, where we all belong."

"Where we all belong," the others said, joining in.

Three ambulances pulled up, and paramedics came out to tend to the fallen Exemplars, triaging quickly as they sorted out the wounded from the dying and the dead. By Ash's count, taking what photos she could, there were at least 15 dead and around 25 wounded, most of them seriously injured. The unmasked were a mix of men and women, all races—maybe half white, one third Latin, some Black and Asian.

The Exemplars let go of each other's hands, and Ash could hear angry muttering among them, a desire for vengeance. Deputy Reeve and some of the other deputies were quickly try-

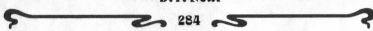
ing to cordon off the area and were doing crowd control to keep people from disrupting the crime scene.

Ash's phone pinged again, and she could see it was Emily again.

*They took Maura Templeton.*

Unable to contain her desire to share a scoop, Ash spoke up, against her best instincts. She should have just kept her mouth shut, but some part of her wanted to wound the High Priestess, the one who'd taken her own sister from her. It was petty, but from Ash's perspective, there were worse things to be.

"Eminence," Ash said. "They took your sister."

Mona turned her gaze to Ash, her wounded eyes flashing.

"What are you talking about?" Mona said.

"The Red Deaths kidnapped Maura," Ash said.

"How do you know this?" Mona asked, walking up to her. Mona was such a tall woman, and in her robes, an intimidating presence.

"I got a text," Ash said. "A friend told me."

Mona took out her phone and dialed up her sister, while the other Exemplars circled protectively around her as the harried paramedics tended to the wounded.

"Maura?" Mona said. From her face, it was clear that she did not like what she was hearing. "Put Maura on. I want to hear her. Maura. Have they hurt you?"

Ash wanted to film with her phone but didn't want to call more attention to herself.

"You must not harm my sister," Mona said. "You will regret this day, Infidel. Wherever you go, we will find you. I don't care. No. You cannot hide from us. No."

They must have hung up because Mona went about texting on her phone.

"They indeed do have my sister," Mona said to those around her. "I talked with one of their men. You were correct, Exemplar. Who are you, Little Sister, to know such things? Why do you not bear the Lady's Bells upon your holy shroud? Are you one of the defilers who snuck into our Temple last night? Could that be you, Little Mouse?"

She knew better than to delay.

Ash took off running, hiking up the robes so that she could more effectively run.

"After her!" Mona yelled, and a dozen Exemplars took off racing after Ash, out for blood or answers, whichever came first.

# 9

**The Shroom Room had been packed for lunch, but Logan** had used the Fungo App and spent some Fungible tokens to secure a booth for them both. Emily was amused by the festive décor of the place, an unironic, phantasmagoric blend of psychedelic interior design with fine dining, somehow.

"A trip, right?" Logan said, noticing her noting it.

"It's a culinary carnival," Emily said.

"Hey, I like that," Logan said. "Mind if I steal that?"

"Steal away," Emily said.

They had received their menus and Emily was peering through hers while Logan talked. His voice was confident and had a bit of East Coast braggadocio about it which Emily found appealing in some way. He was a man who knew what he wanted, and clearly was used to getting it. Emily liked that about him.

"I'm thinking of starting some Shroom Room franchises in Philadelphia and Pittsburgh," Logan said. "I think the concept of rowdy fine cuisine has something to it. Mushrooms are perfect for it—they're both silly and savory, fabulous and freaky. It'll draw an eclectic sort of patron. Just the sort I need."

"Sounds good," Emily said. "It's weird to think they've got a menu entirely made up of mushroom dishes."

"Yep," Logan said. "It's a nice gimmick. I think people would go for it. I'm banking on it. Thick heads, empty stomachs, fat wallets."

Emily could never imagine running a restaurant. It seemed so fraught and exhausting, like a trapeze act that never ended. But Logan seemed sure it was a good idea.

"Seems risky," Emily said.

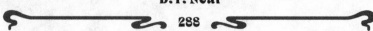
"Everything is," Logan said. "That's why I'd like to start small—just a couple of restaurants in urban settings. See how it goes."

"You think they're ready for it in those cities?" Emily asked.

"Specialization is the future," Logan said. "Niche is chic. Forget the generalists. I'm talking boutique dining experiences. Shroom Rooms popping up here and there, serving discriminating palates in an easygoing, agreeable sort of way. I tell you, I see it."

"He's a visionary, this one is," said Maura Templeton, surprising Emily and Logan both, although Logan hid his behind a well-practiced grin.

"Maura Templeton, this is Dr. Emily Carver," Logan said. "Mycologist."

Maura feigned being impressed by that as they shook hands. Her hands were cool to the touch.

"We get so many mycologists at the Festival, year after year," Maura said. "They just can't resist us."

"I'm impressed by the Growers' Tents," Emily said. "Amazing varieties."

Maura smiled beatifically.

"We attract all sorts here," Maura said.

"Lilith Holbrook didn't seem impressed," Emily said. Maura laughed.

"Old Lilith," Maura said. "She's such a dour little witch, isn't she? She's got her patch of Cursed Earth and tends to it jealously. That's really what feeds her—envy and jealousy. She covets our position in town. The Holbrooks always have. It's not our fault that the Templetons were more ambitious and thorough in our vision. We always have been."

Logan laughed, glancing between Maura and Emily, his eyes bouncing like ping pong balls on a well-worn table.

"Emily likes my idea of spreading more Shroom Rooms around," Logan said.

"I said it was risky," Emily said. "But I'd go there. This place is fun."

Maura's face was unreadable behind her smile.

"Oh, we're far more than fun," Maura said. "We offer a complete dining experience for all sorts of patrons."

It was then that the red-masked men stormed into the Shroom Room, startling the patrons. They were carrying automatic weapons and bore down on Maura in a tight group.

"You. Chef," one of the men said. He was in a brown leather jacket with a black turtleneck and black pants, his eyes bright behind the red ski mask.

Logan got up, but the man leveled his gun on him.

"Don't be a hero, *Ese,*" the man said. More men approached, and Emily was frozen in her seat with terror as the men grabbed Maura.

"What the hell is going on?" Maura asked. "Don't you know who I am?"

"Maura Templeton," the man said. "We know exactly who you are."

One of them put a black bag over Maura's head as they whisked her out of the Shroom Room before the frightened on-lookers, while Logan hopped out of his booth.

"What is this all about?" Logan asked.

"We're *Las Muertes Rojas,*" the man said. "We've come to collect a debt that is owed to us. Anyone follows us or tries to play the hero, and Maura Templeton's dead. Understand?"

The half-dozen men then hauled Maura into the kitchen, leaving all the restaurant patrons shocked. Emily pinged Ash with frenzied fingers.

*OMG! They came! Red Deaths!*

Logan was on his phone, having dialed 911. He wasn't the only one, as others had been dialing as well.

"I wanted to report a kidnapping," Logan said. "Maura Templeton. The Shroom Room. Guys in red ski masks. *Las Muertes Rojas* they called themselves. Yeah. *Las Muertes Rojas.*"

Emily got to her feet, unsure what to do or say. She'd never seen anything like that before. She thought about herself and Marquis the night before, the cultists talking about the Red Deaths. The frightening men had to have been them.

Logan pocketed his phone.

"I can't believe that," Logan said. "Who just kidnaps some-body like that? In a crowded restaurant?"

"What should we do?" Emily asked.

"There's nothing we can do," Logan said. "Fuck."

Emily texted Ash again.

*They took Maura Templeton.*

"We need to get out of here," Emily said.

"No way," Logan said. "I'm waiting for the Sheriff or somebody to turn up. We're witnesses."

Why would they even take Maura? What were they up to?

She texted Marquis and Jerry.

*A gang just kidnapped Maura Templeton. Like right in front of me.* Las Muertes Rojas.

Marquis texted her back.

*Are you okay?*

*What do you care?*

*I care.*

*I'm fine. Just rattled. They had red ski masks on. They put a bag on her head and took her.*

*Wow. You should get back to the Grand.*

*Where are you?*

*Pittsburgh. I'm flying back to California today.*

Logan was fit to be tied, and Emily was torn between laying into Marquis and commiserating with Logan. There were sirens sounding somewhere outside, like ambulances and police cars, Emily thought.

"I'm used to this kind of crap in Philly," Logan said. "But out here? Come on."

Some deputies appeared, and Emily was relieved to see Max Stirner among them as he made his way to them.

"Dr. Carver," Max said.

"Deputy Stirner," Emily said.

"She was taken right here," Logan said. "Right where you're standing. Those Red Death guys. They had guns. They just took her."

"How many?" Max asked.

"At least six," Emily said. "All heavily armed. They self-identified as *Las Muertes Rojas*."

"Yeah," Logan said. "They announced that."

Deputy Stirner took that down, nodding.

"And then they left out back?" Stirner asked.

"Through the kitchen," Logan said.

Emily's phone pinged. It was Marquis texting some more.

*Maybe you need to get out of there.*

*Not yet. I have to see.*

*See what?*

*I need to see their Sacred Grove.*

*WTF?*

*I have an invitation. Midnight.*

*What about the Nightcap Farm?*

*Forget that. You were already there. I'm going to this grove. I have to see what they're growing there.*

Emily thought it was good for Marquis to stew over that. It would bother him to think that she might find something on her own that he'd have no part of, no stake in. Jerry was competitive that way, liked to have people at each other's throats. If Emily managed to secure some strains or spores of some other exotics, they would be hers alone.

*That seems like a bad idea.*

*Does it?*

She didn't think anybody had suspected her from the night before. Not yet, anyway. She'd make that work for her at the Sacred Grove.

Deputy Stirner excused himself and interviewed some more eyewitnesses, while Logan paced around.

"I can't believe that even happened," Logan said. "All of these people. They just showed up. What's that all about?"

Emily wasn't going to share with him what she'd heard at the Temple, not exactly.

"I think they're rivals," Emily said. "The Red Deaths and the Lynchburg locals."

She didn't want to say "cultists" out loud, in case there were any around.

"Sorry lunch didn't quite pan out," Logan said. "Can I make it up to you?"

"Not necessary," Emily said. Her phone pinged again, and it was Marquis again.

*Don't go, Em. Get out of town while you can.*

*Give me a break.*

Logan watched her a moment.

"We should go, I guess," Logan said. "I don't really know what to say to all of this. I've never actually witnessed a kidnapping before. The Templetons have money. Hell, Maura has money. I can only imagine what the ransom will be. Assuming there's even a ransom. I mean, there'd have to be a ransom, wouldn't there?"

Emily shrugged. "I don't understand gang psychology. This is my first kidnapping."

"Let's get out of here," Logan said. "You're staying at the Grand?"

"Yes," Emily said. "You?"

"Same," Logan said, and they walked out of the Shroom Room still hungry.

Down Grand Avenue, a few blocks from where they were, they saw a knot of grey-robed Exemplars walking through the crowd as if they were searching for somebody.

"Wow, those are creepy," Logan said.

"They're called 'Exemplars' I think," Emily said, acting like she didn't know as much as she did.

"Exemplars," Logan said. "Weird."

"I think they're midlevels at the Temple," Emily said. The Exemplars were definitely searching the crowd. There were three on one side of the street and three on the other, moving slowly through the crowd, searching. "Like enforcers or security. Bodyguards, maybe."

The Exemplars neared them, and had their shrouds pulled back from their hats, so their grey-masked faces were in full evidence, even as tourists snapped photos of them.

They reached Emily and Logan, who looked on nervously, before passing them without a word.

"I pity any Red Deaths they find," Logan said. He dialed up Maura, and, to his surprise, someone answered.

"Yeah?" came a man's voice. "What do you want, Mr. Logan Stephens?"

Of course Maura would have had his name among her contacts. Logan immediately regretted calling.

"You sons of bitches better let Maura go," Logan said. He wasn't a fighter by nature, but he was angry.

"You know Ms. Templeton?" the man asked.

"I do," Logan said.

"Were going to hang her," the man said. "She's a witch. That's what she deserves."

"No," Logan said. "What about, you know, ransom?"

Emily listened to him negotiate with interest, even as the Exemplars continued toward the north stage.

"You willing to ransom her, Mr. Stephens?" the man asked.

"I don't want her harmed," Logan said.

"You sweet on her?" the man asked.

"She's a friend," Logan said.

"What's she worth to you, Mr. Stephens?" the man asked.

Logan hadn't planned to deal with these gangsters; he only wanted Maura back. He didn't want to put a price on her head, or even to put himself in the mix. He had been impulsive to call.

"I can't put a price tag on her value," Logan said. "It's not right."

"We'll see if her family does," the man said, hanging up. Logan cursed. He shouldn't even have called the number. Now they knew who he was, and who knew what would come of that.

There was a commotion at the other end of Grand as people realized what had happened on First Street. Emily was listening to people nervously talking.

"The Red Deaths drove through paradegoers," Emily said. "They ran people down. A bunch of Exemplars."

"Wow," Logan said. "Must be why people are losing it."

There were more Exemplars taking to the streets, Emily saw, and they were this haunting presence in the chaotic crowding of the festival. While others were running about in excitement or fear, the Exemplars merely strode calmly, methodically. They were hunting for someone.

She got her phone and texted Ash.

*Something happened. They're saying the Red Deaths ran people down in the parade.*

Emily waited for a response. It came quickly.

*I know. I was there. I saw everything. They're looking for me.*

*You? Why?*

*I took one of your robes and snuck into their ranks.*

Emily suddenly felt very vulnerable and exposed on the street, with the Exemplars searching for Ash.

*You took one of the robes?*

*Yeah. I wanted to see what I could see. But then the Rojas ran a bunch of the fanatics down and I blew my cover.*

*Where are you?*

*Hiding. I'm a better runner than they are. I ran like hell.*

*Did they see you?*

Emily was worried about Ash, but she was also thinking about her own situation. Logan was pacing about.

"I don't know what to do," Logan said.

"This is for the Sheriff to deal with," Emily said. "Not you."

"But I can help," Logan said. "Maybe if I paid their ransom."

"I don't think they'd deal in good faith," Emily said. "Call it a hunch."

She turned her eyes back to her phone.

*No, they didn't see me. I got ahead of them and was able to ditch my robes and mask.*

*Okay, so that's good, then. You could be anyone. Just another festivalgoer. Let's meet back up, we can figure out what to do next.*

*We need to get the hell out of here.*

"I've just never dealt with kidnappers before," Logan said. Emily felt like needed to get control of the situation, both with Logan and Ash. "I don't know what you say to them."

"You should go back to the hotel and lay down," Emily said. "Don't psyche yourself out. Which room are you staying in?"

"530," Logan said.

"Okay," Emily said. "We're at 416. Go on up and I'll check in on you later."

"What are you going to do?" Logan asked.

"I need to find my friend, Ash," Emily said.

"Fine," Logan said. "Sorry today was such a mess."

"Not your fault," Emily said. "It was...memorable."

Logan laughed grimly, running a hand through his hair. He was frustrated and afraid, nervous and stressed. As a chef, he was used to dealing with chaos, but kitchen chaos wasn't the same as kidnapper chaos, and he didn't feel like he had the tools to handle it. He gave Emily a quick hug and headed to the Grand. Emily watched him go, then turned her eyes back to the Exemplars, who were fanning out. Tourists gave them a wide berth.

She texted Ash back.

*I have to attend that midnight service.*

*Why on earth would you do that?*

*We have tickets. I want to see it.*

*I doubt they'll hold that with all this going on.*

*I'm going. I have to see.*

*Jesus, Em. You're crazy.*

*But I need to see.*

*That's all you.*

*That's fine. I can handle it. Where are you?*

*Cappy's.*

Emily used her Fungo App to locate Cappy's and saw it was up the street from the Grand. She saw the mushroom man

hanging from the sign, winking and making a finger pistol while wearing a ballcap.

She saw Ash emerge from the front door, wearing an Oakland A's cap in yellow and green. Ash had it jammed low on her head. She was trying to look as nonchalant as possible, giving a wary eye to the Exemplars, who kept searching, without knowing who they were actually looking for.

Emily walked up to Ash and gave her a hug. Ash forced her face to remain composed.

"It was awful," Ash said. "The *Rojas* just drove right through the crowd of Exemplars. I don't know if Melinda was among them. She's not picking up when I tried calling her."

One of the Exemplars walked up to some of the others, brandishing the robe, mask, hat and shroud that Ash had discarded. The Exemplars talked quickly, the one pointing back where they'd come from. They followed quickly, one of them taking out a phone and calling someone.

"You're lucky they didn't catch you," Emily said.

"I've never been more grateful to be a runner," Ash said.

"Ash!" came a man's voice, and both Emily and Ash turned to see a young man gaping at her. He was black-haired and had a goatee beard and wire-rimmed glasses, was wearing a black tee with Fun Guy written in white across it, with Mushy the Mushroom between the two words, giving two thumbs up and grinning.

"Do I know you?" Ash asked, then she remembered as soon as she said it. He was the kid at the Temple, the one who'd given her his cup of Lady's Tears. "Oh, wait, you're the kid, aren't you?"

"That's me," the young man said. "I'm the Kid. I mean, I'm Austin Adams. I've been looking for you the whole time since last night."

"That long?" Emily asked.

"My friends are tripping, but I'm sober," Austin said.

"This is not a good time, Austin," Ash said.

He followed her eyes, her gaze at the Exemplars who were surrounding Grindo's Rock Shop, near where Ash had tossed her disguise.

"Are they after you?" Austin said.

"Shhh," Ash said. "Jesus, Austin."

"Sorry," Austin said. "We should go somewhere."

Ash forced a smile, patted Austin on the forearm.

"This isn't a holiday hookup, Austin," Ash said. "You go have fun with your friends. My friend and I have stuff to do."

Austin shook his head.

"I'm sticking with you," Austin said. "At least give me your number."

"Umm, no," Ash said.

"No means no, Austin," Emily said. The Exemplars were fanning out from Grindo's.

"There's a clown after me," Austin said. "He told me I had to decide. I don't even know what that means."

Ash laughed sharply, like a lone firecracker going off.

"What are you talking about?"

"Fun Gus said it," Austin said.

"I hate clowns," Emily said.

"Everybody does," Ash said.

"He said I have to decide," Austin said. "He said I'm the Decider."

"While you were high?" Emily asked.

"Barely," Austin said. "I was coming down. But he saw me this morning, I mean he saw me. And he said it again."

Emily didn't know what to tell the young man, who was clearly distraught.

"I wouldn't put much faith in the prophetic mutterings of clowns," Emily said.

"Yeah, forget about it," Ash said.

"I can't," Austin said. "I just can't. Hey, what about going to the Pub Crawl tonight, Ash? Would you be cool with that?"

Ash laughed again, another firecracker going off. Emily watched the Exemplars going door-to-door looking for Ash. Their methodical searching was disarming. If anybody went snooping in their hotel room and found the other Exemplar robes she had, they'd be in a world of trouble.

"I don't think drinking's really on the menu for me tonight," Ash said.

"You should go," Emily said. "I mean, since I'm going to the Grove."

"Yeah, at midnight," Ash said, annoyed that Emily would even suggest she hang with this kid.

"We're going to the Grove, too," Austin said. "We've got tickets!"

He produced his own ticket, holding it up.

"So, you're, what? Going to the Pub Crawl and then hitting the Grove?" Ash asked.

"That's the plan," Austin said. "My friends and I are making the most of the weekend."

"Sounds like it," Ash said. "I'm flattered you'd want to include me, but you and your friends should just do your thing. They'll protect you from the scary clown."

Emily hid a laugh at Ash's almost sisterly condescension. Whatever Austin clearly seemed to feel for Ash, she just saw him as a baby.

"He said I have to decide," Austin said. "But he didn't tell me what I had to decide."

"I think that's for you to decide," Emily said. "You know how prophecies are, right? Open-ended. Open for interpretation."

Austin was clearly rattled by whatever Fun Gus had told him. He looked afraid.

"I don't *want* to decide," Austin said. "He gave them all balloons but me. I was the only one without a balloon. What does that even mean?"

"It means you were high," Ash said. "Bad trips happen."

"I wasn't *that* high," Austin said. "Not like I was when I saw you, Ash. You were like a shining star."

Emily decided to rescue Ash.

"Ash can't make your Pub Crawl," Emily said. "She's with me."

Austin blinked that away.

"You mean, like, with-with?" Austin asked.

"Totally," Emily said, putting an arm around Ash.

"Sorry, Austin," Ash said. "You've been barking up the wrong tree. Go have fun and steer clear of clowns."

The two of them left a bereft Austin curbside as they made their way back into the Grand Hotel.

# 10

**Santino's plan had gone better than expected. The SUVs** had run down some of the crazy cultists before racing down Templeton Lane and heading to the Nightcap Mushroom Farm, where they'd tossed a bunch of Molotov cocktails to get that place burning.

Daylight arson was a quicker matter than a proper night setup, which would have been far more thorough. But they'd at least gotten the place symbolically aflame before fleeing the scene. What mattered was that it was burning, and the Lynchburg Fire Department would have to arrive to put out the fires they'd set.

They had taken the winding country roads to put as much space between them and Lynchburg as possible before they stashed the SUVs, torching them before switching to three red SUVs that had been secreted along the route.

While they were doing that, the other teams had successfully snagged Maura Templeton, who was taken to their hideout in the warehouse at St. Sophia.

Carlos was watching it on a television somebody had brought to the warehouse, along with a sofa from who knew where. He'd watched it unfold, had seen the local news stations covering it.

He got to bear witness to everybody's jubilation when the triumphant *Rojas* rolled in with their prize. It was mid-afternoon. When they got a hooded Maura Templeton out of the SUV, Santino was ecstatic.

"You see?" Santino said, snapping off the hood to reveal the disheveled Maura, who looked tall, lovely, and enraged. "This is how you do things, Brothers. No pussyfooting around. Today is a good day for us."

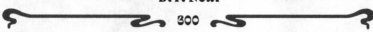
They had Maura zip-tied and gagged, and she glared at them all, although Carlos thought she looked more angry than afraid.

"You see, *Conejito?*" Santino said. "We settled the accounts our way."

He knew better than to gainsay Santino, but Carlos hated that his brother was calling him that. Credibility was precious in the *Rojas,* and nicknames stuck like superglue. He knew he'd have to live with that one for the rest of his days. It's how he'd be known forevermore. Carlos *"Conejito"* Mendoza. He'd just have to make that name mean something on his own terms.

"Okay," Carlos said. "Now what, though? Kidnapping, Tino? This is all over the news. The FBI is going to be speeding to Lynchburg soon, if they aren't already. And everyone will know it was us who did it."

Santino was unfazed.

"I wanted them to know it was us," Santino said. Somebody brought a chair and they sat Maura down on it, taping her to the chair with duct tape.

"The whole point of us coming out here was to lay low," Carlos said. "Now you've gone and literally blown everything up."

Santino walked up to his brother and softly slapped his cheek, in a brotherly gesture of mockery and reproach.

"You worry too much, *Conejito,*" Santino said. "We already had an idiot call to try to ransom Maura, according to Juan. What was his name?"

"Logan Stephens," Juan said. Carlos could see Maura's eyes tracking every word they were saying.

"He's another cook," Santino said. "We looked him up when the idiot called. He owns a restaurant in Philly."

Carlos figured they'd signed Lilli's death warrant with today's events, along with his own. They'd come for him.

"Why the long face, Carlo?" Santino said. Somebody had gotten a few bottles of tequila they were passing around. Everyone was in high spirits but him.

"Vehicular homicide, kidnapping, arson," Carlos said. "They're going to come down hard on us, Tino."

"We are *already* outlaws, Carlo. What's a little more crime among brothers?" Santino said, swigging some tequila and holding the bottle out to him. Carlos knew better than not to

take it and downed some. He could see Maura watching him, her eyes like chips of flint in the light of the warehouse.

"What about her?" Carlos asked.

"No tequila for her, *Conejito*," Santino said. He took the gag off of her, letting it sit on her neck, like a scarf. "You behave, now, Ms. Templeton. You might yet come out of this alive."

"I don't see how," Maura said. "I've seen all of you."

"You don't understand," Santino said, snapping his fingers and having someone bring him a chair. He sat across from her, the back of the chair facing her, which he leaned on while preparing a cigar. "I want people to know it was us, like I said. My brother Carlo, he likes to play it quiet. Me, I'm loud."

He said that last part loudly, to the delight of the other *Rojas,* who cheered while he drew a match and lit his cigar, blowing smoke rings at Maura.

"So I hear," Maura said. Santino guffawed.

"Tell me about your family," Santino said. "Your family's rich, yes?"

"Very," Maura said.

"For farmers," Santino said.

"For anybody," Maura said.

"That's good," Santino said. "I can work with that. What say we get your *Papi* on the phone?"

At the mention of that, one of Santino's men walked over a burner phone, held it out for Santino, who didn't take it. He nodded to Maura.

"Give us his direct line," Santino said. Maura gave him the number, which the man dialed, handing the phone to Santino, who put it on speaker. It went to voicemail:

"Hi, this is Ned. I can't come to the phone right now. Please leave your name and number and what you're calling about and I'll get back with you as soon as I can."

Santino hushed his men while he left his message:

*"Papi,* this is Carlos Mendoza," Santino said, which startled Carlos, who made a step toward his brother, but Santino stopped him with an upraised hand, the cigar pointing at him like a magic wand. "I've got your daughter Maura here. Say something, Maura."

"Daddy," Maura said. "I'm fine. Don't worry. The Lady is with me."

Santino had one of his men gag Maura again.

"You heard that, yes? She's fine, *Papi*. The Lady is with her, just like she said. But unless you pay me three million dollars, she won't be fine for long. You have until sundown tomorrow to pay it. You call me back, we'll talk more."

Santino hung up, and the men laughed and cheered.

"Tino, what the hell?" Carlos said. "You used my name?"

"Yes, *Conejito*," Santino said. "I told you, you're the bait."

"You're setting me up to take the fall," Carlos said. The punishment for aggravated kidnapping was twenty years to life in prison. He couldn't imagine why his brother would set him up like this. "They're going to think I did all of this."

Santino smoked and laughed.

"Nobody'll catch you, Carlo," Santino said. "We're going to set up a meetup and you're going to be what lures them there. But we're going to gun them all down. Then we'll get the hell out of here. Fuck these people and their magic mushrooms. Nobody messes with *Las Muertes Rojas*."

Carlos didn't like it one bit, and he could see Maura could see that as well. Their eyes locked a moment, while Santino was laughing uproariously.

"We can't camp out in this warehouse all night, Tino," Carlos said.

"Sure we can. We'll make a day of it," Santino said. "We can camp out in our cars. It'll be like when we were kids."

"What about her?" Carlos asked. "We can't just keep her tied to a chair all night."

"My gentle *Conejito*," Santino said. "We'll lay her out in one of the trucks tonight, don't worry, Carlo."

"I'm not soft," Carlos said.

The burner phone rang, and Santino hushed everyone, put it on speaker.

"Who's this?" Santino answered.

"This is Ned Templeton," said the voice on the phone. "You have my daughter. Is this Carlos?"

"Ah, yes," Santino said. "It is, and I do. I doubt they've managed to set up wiretaps so quickly, old man. But I'm going to be brief just the same—tomorrow night, around nine o'clock, at the Bianchi Gardens. I want you there with your three million dollars. Alone. Nobody else. None of your cultists. I see so much as a mask and I'll kill your daughter straightaway. You bring the money, you get sweet Maura back. Clear?"

"I want to know she's alive," Templeton said. "I want to hear her."

Santino sighed, yanking off her gag.

"I'm here, Daddy," Maura said. "I'm alive. The Lady is with me."

"You see, *Papi?*" Santino said. "She's alive."

"It'll take time to get that kind of money," Templeton said.

"Then you'd better get going on it," Santino said, hanging up. "Your *Papi* better come through for us, or you're dead."

"He will," Maura said. "He always does."

"The Lady is with you, huh? Where is your goddess now? Where's *La Signora?*" Santino asked, blowing clouds of cigar smoke at Maura.

"She's here," Maura said. "She's always here. She's right here with me."

Santino looked around, laughing. His men joined in, while Carlos studied her. She seemed entirely unafraid, which made him nervous.

"Alejandro, Santiago," Carlos said. "Take a walk around. Keep an eye out for anything unusual."

"I don't see your Lady anywhere," Santino said. "You're all alone. Well, with us, anyway."

He looked around. The other *Rojas* were hovering around them, watching with leering amusement. Santino laughed harder still. He tugged at the gag around her neck, moving to put it back in place, but Maura spoke first.

"You don't want to do that," Maura said, and Santino laughed yet again, pausing.

"You are so jumpy, *Conejito,*" Santino said, releasing the gag with a toss of his hand. "What have these cultists done to you, Carlo?"

"Look at her," Carlos said. "She's unafraid."

"And you are," Santino said, looking between them. "Why is my brother so scared of you?"

Maura looked evenly at him, without expression or any emotion other than distaste.

"I wouldn't know," Maura said. "He's a cautious man, clearly."

"Not cautious enough," Santino said. "He lost a lot of good men to your *Cultistas.* What's that all about, anyway? Why do you renounce God?"

Carlos and the others crossed themselves at the invocation of God. They were gangsters and criminals, but they were still Catholics. Carlos hadn't been to Mass since he was a boy, but he still considered himself a Catholic. He was merely banking all the things he would unburden himself of at confession in the future—when the time was right.

"He doesn't speak to me," Maura said. "*La Signora* does. She tells me things."

"Yeah, okay," Santino said. He tossed his cigar and drew a pistol—a black Beretta. He held it to Maura's forehead. "Would your goddess save you from a bullet to the head?"

Carlos was impressed how fearless she was. It was jarring to see it—she just looked up at him, her big eyes burning into Santino.

"Let's find out," Maura said. Something about her voice struck Carlos. It was familiar. He had heard it before.

Santino pressed the Beretta harder against her head, waiting for her nerve to break. But she just stared at him. Carlos thought her dark eyes were full of light, somehow.

"Don't do it," Maura said.

Santino smirked at her, and went to pull the trigger, but found, to his growing dismay, that he couldn't. Like with the gag, only worse.

Stronger.

Stranger.

Carlos watched, mesmerized, as did the other *Rojas*. Santino grunted and gripped the Beretta in both hands, sweating as he struggled to pull the trigger.

"She is with me still," Maura said. "See? Do you need more proof? Shoot your men. But not Carlos."

Santino's dark eyes went big as he raised his Beretta and began shooting the other *Rojas*.

"Shoot each other," Maura said. "Kill one another. But not Carlos or Santino."

"*Bruja*," Carlos said, compelled to draw his own pistol, a Glock 20. He began pumping bullets into the others—one shot per man, catching them in the head. They were all shooting each other, everyone within earshot of Maura Templeton. Everyone shooting each other, except for Carlos and Santino.

Just like she'd commanded.

Blood sprayed as the *Rojas* who had only moments before been watching Santino torment Maura were firing at each other.

The other *Rojas* were looking around bewildered at the outbreak of carnage in the warehouse. Carlos walked to them while reloading, killing them with shots to the face. He dropped another dozen of his *Rojas* brothers before fishing another clip from his pocket. The warehouse rang with gunfire and the frightened curses of *Rojas* as they blasted at each other.

"*Brujeria! Maleficio!*" Santino yelled, struggling to make his way to Maura, who smiled at him.

"Stop where you are, Santino Mendoza," Maura said, shouting so he'd hear over the ringing of his own ears. Santino struggled to move, but could not, his neck sticking out as he tried and failed to resist her.

Carlos emptied his last clip into his remaining brothers, the warehouse now growing silent except for the gasps and wheezes of dying men who littered the floor. It was a scene of dread and slaughter, the scent of gunpowder filling the room, and the coppery smell of spilled blood.

"Carlos, come here," Maura said, and Carlos could feel his feet moving of their own accord, like he was a puppet. The voice, her voice, he remembered it, now.

Alejandro and Santiago came running in from the far side of the warehouse, their guns drawn, not comprehending what they were seeing. Carlos gave them away, his head turning as he strained to free himself.

"What's going on, Carlo?" Santiago asked.

"You two," Maura said. "Shoot each other."

Alejandro and Santiago raised their weapons at one another and fired, blowing each other's heads off at the same time, spraying blood everywhere as they fell.

"*Bruja*," Carlos said again, between clenched teeth.

"*Strega*," Maura said. "I am a Bianchi by blood. Like my great-great grandmother, Lucretia. We all are. My whole family. We are rich, and we are witches. Rich witches."

She laughed, then, as humorless as it was hearty.

Santino and Carlos were the only two left standing, and somewhere in St. Sophia, there were police sirens.

"Carlos, cut me loose," Maura said. "Free me."

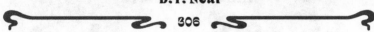
It was more than mere suggestion; it was a terrifying compulsion that drove him, again turned him into a marionette. He drew a knife from his pocket and flicked out the blade, cutting Maura loose.

"Good, Carlos," Maura said. She walked, yanking from their bloodied necks whatever gold crucifixes or St. Christopher's medals they had on them. Maura went methodically from body to body, taking them, until she had a bunch of them clutched in her fist, dangling gold and silver, blood dripping on her hand, on the floor.

Carlos and Santino looked on in horror, while Maura turned her eyes on them challengingly as she held the necklaces and pendants.

"Now, I want you and your brother to load all of these Red Deaths into those three red SUVs. Just pile them up inside them."

"Why?" Carlos asked, even as he and Santino were carefully stacking the dead into the SUVs.

"Nothing wasted," Maura said. "These are gifts for the Lady. For tonight. As are you both."

Carlos fought to free himself from the spell she'd somehow placed upon him, but he felt like he was caught in a cage, like he was held fast by unseen hands. It was impossible. How could it be happening to him? He and Santino were quickly covered in the blood of their gang brothers as they filled the SUVs, while Maura watched.

"I warned you things would go bad for you if you came back, Carlos," Maura said, finding some cigarettes from the pocket of one of the dead men. She lit one and blew smoke at him as he worked. "Didn't I warn you?"

It finally, fully hit Carlos—the terrible realization that the woman who'd called him from Teo's phone all those times, it had been Maura Templeton. She smiled at him, seeing the epiphany on his face.

"Yes, it's me," Maura said. "I was the Lady who talked to you. We know each other so well, now, Carlos, don't we?"

He could not comprehend how this woman could have such power and content herself with merely being a chef.

"Oh, I enjoy being a chef," Maura said, as if she'd read his mind. "I honor the Lady with my cooking. She appreciates it.

She is always hungry, Carlos. We honor Her by feeding Her. Now, keep filling up the backs of those SUVs."

It took Carlos and Santino nearly two hours to put all the bodies in the three SUVs. All that was left on the floor was spilled blood, bullet casings, and various firearms.

"Now we drive back home," Maura said. "Follow me."

Carlos could not believe this had transpired, even as he went to one of the loaded SUVs and got into the driver's seat. He waited for Maura to start her own and then he followed, while Santino followed after them both.

Carlos thought as he drove. Had she allowed herself to be kidnapped so she could do this to them? It was a risky move. He thought about her gagged and blindfolded. Would she have been able to cast her spell that way? Carlos did not know. He'd never faced a true witch before.

There had been rumors growing up about *Brujas*. Everyone had stories. But they were just that—stories. This was something painfully, dreadfully real.

They drove north out of St. Sophia, heading up Route 219 toward Lynchburg. Carlos gripped the steering wheel as he made his way. This was not how the day was supposed to have gone. He cursed himself for thinking about the well-being of this woman. He had wanted to be merciful. Santino had been right—he was the *Conejito*.

It took them an hour to get to the outskirts of Lynchburg when Maura took a left turn on Mill Creek Road, which led them into the surrounding forests. The sun was low in the sky, now.

She was one woman, and they'd been fifty men. Hardened killers. And now only he and Santino remained. Carlos felt tears run down his cheeks as he fought to free himself from the infernal control she had over him with just her lovely voice. It must have been how she'd so handily dispatched his other men back in Hidden Hollow. She could have told them anything and they would have gone along with it. Just like that. It was black magic.

Maura took them off Mill Creek Road onto a narrow gravel road that was blocked by a gate. She got out and moved the gate, opening the road. Then she went back into her SUV and drove down the road, which was cocooned by tree branches that waved at them like specters in the waning daylight. The sun was sinking fast, casting unfamiliar shadows.

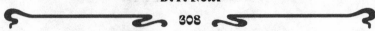
The *Bruja* parked her SUV when they reached the end of the road. She motioned for them to park as well, and Carlos and Santino obliged her, while she lit up a cigarette. There was a small wooden shed at the end of the road, painted with three blue interlocking circles.

Maura opened the door and produced a pair of shovels, which she handed to Carlos and Santino. She also fished out an electric lantern, which she turned on, bathing them in cold fluorescent light for a moment, before turning it off.

"For later," Maura said. "It'll get dark here before you know it."

She gestured for them to come, and they did, sweating in the autumnal air as they fought to free themselves from her control.

"Alright," Maura said. "The easy part's done. Come along."

She walked them a short distance into the forest, carrying the lantern. Maura guided them to a clearing that was surrounded by towering trees. The shadows were deep, here, the sun a fading memory that kissed the day goodbye in a splash of amber light in the clouds far to the west. In the center of the clearing were three dark, mossy, wooden posts, hammered deep into the ground.

"You two need to start digging," Maura said, pointing. "You're going to be digging graves."

"Graves?" Santino asked.

"Yes, Santino," Maura said, holding the lantern up in his face. "For your dead. They have a date with the Cursed Earth. And be quick about it. We have to make the Sacred Grove before midnight. Give me your phone, Carlos."

Carlos gave her his burner phone, and he and his brother began digging, while Maura finished her cigarette.

"It's not fair," Carlos said, his teeth gritted as he dug. The soil was soft at least and yielding to the shovel. It was rich and dark earth, fertile.

"What's not fair?" Maura asked.

"This," Carlos said. "Black magic."

"Oh, please," Maura said. "You're the ones who kidnapped me. You should be grateful it was me you got, and not Mona. She'd have torched you all. Even my sweet brother Lionel would have done something terrible to you. And Daddy? Don't get me

started on what he'd have done. Now be quiet and dig. I have to make a few calls."

Carlos and Santino dug in the dark while the moon began its rise, just a hint, but as the moon was full, it looked massive on the horizon.

Maura called her father.

"Daddy? Maura," she said. "Yes, I took care of them. Almost. Yeah. We're in Grove 11. Yep. 50. Well, forty-eight. Yes. I know, right? Of course I will. Yes. The Lady is with us."

She hung up.

"Daddy says 'hi'," Maura said. She dialed up Mona.

"Mona, it's me," Maura said. "Yeah, I'm fine. Right? Totally. I already called Daddy. Yes. Do you still have Lilli? Ah. He does? Well, okay, then. For the Grove. Yes. I'm at Grove 11. You won't believe it: 50. Sorry, forty-eight. Same difference. Yeah. We'll be there. The Lady is with us."

She hung up and lit another cigarette, while Carlos and Santino worked.

"Not a deep grave," Maura said. "A mass grave. It can be shallow. Just enough to cover the bodies. You guys are going to have to work quickly if we're to make the Midnight Service. So, keep at it."

Carlos sped up, as did his brother. Thankfully, the rich soil remained fairly easy to turn, although he could not imagine hauling all of the bodies to this mass grave. He wondered how many such graves the cultists had. Grove 11? At least that many. Probably many more.

"I'm tired, *Conejito*," Santino said. It was probably harder than Santino had worked his entire life. The blood that was on both of their shirts had dried and was now dusted with dirt. They looked like hell.

Between them, over the span of two hours, they had managed to dig a single lengthy ditch that was roughly two feet deep by twenty feet. Carlos looked at his blistered and bleeding hands.

Maura stopped them, surveying the grave with her lantern, which she needed now, as it was properly dark.

"That's going to have to do," Maura said. "Come on."

She had them wait by the shed while she backed one of the SUVs up to the trench.

"Carlos, fetch the bag of lime from the shed," Maura said.

Carlos wondered how many mass graves Maura had dug in her life. Or how many she'd had others dig for her. She seemed to know what she was doing.

"Stack the bodies head-to-toe in the trench," Maura said. "Get to it. Teamwork makes the dream work, guys."

Santino and Carlos unloaded the first SUV, then the second, then the third. The bodies of their peers filled up the shallow grave. Carlos could see that Santiago's headless body still had his sidearm. He fought to reach for it, pulled it from its holster. He fought with every ounce of will he had to point the gun at Maura, who only laughed.

"Throw that thing over here, *Conejito*," Maura said, and Carlos wanted to weep as he did just as she'd told him. "You have more will than I would have imagined."

She picked up the pistol and slipped it into her waistband, against her flat stomach.

"Now the lime," Maura said. "Just cover them with it, like you're dusting them with flour."

They worked to shovel white clumps of lime on the bloody bodies, the lime looking almost blue in the growing light of the full moon that was commandeering the sky.

"A perfect night for it," Maura said.

"Can't you have used magic to make the grave?" Carlos asked. Maura laughed, flicking her cigarette butt at him.

"Not my flavor of magic," Maura said. "I'm all about mindful magic. Cover the bodies with the dirt."

"A cop would have to be blind not to see this," Santino said.

"The police are in our pockets," Maura said. "Carlos knows. He met Sheriff Leonard."

Carlos bitterly recalled all of that while shoveling dirt atop the bodies.

"Why bother with this at all?" Carlos said. "Why not stage a wreck like you did with Franco and Teo?"

"That was a special case," Maura said. "I didn't have time. But tonight is very special. The Lady is with us."

"What the hell does that even mean?" Carlos asked.

"She is everywhere," Maura said. "But She is here with us. She is watching. This is a very, very special night."

Carlos could see nothing in the dark beyond the glow of Maura's lantern. Whatever Maura saw was beyond his ability to detect. But she was a *Bruja,* and no doubt saw more than he

could. The breadth and depth of his understanding of what she was, the implications of it, made him want to scream. Witches weren't supposed to exist. They weren't supposed to be real. Witches were meant to be burned, or, at the very least, hanged. They weren't meant to tangle with gangsters.

Maura chuckled, and he knew that she could read what was left of his mind.

"Witches go where we will," Maura said. "Our coven is strong. And Lynchburg has thrived because of it. Our little town. Everyone is happy here, Carlos. You could be happy here, pretty *Conejito*. I could make you happy if I wanted to."

"Your cult," Carlos said.

"Yes," Maura said. "Our cult. Our town."

It took them another hour to cover the mass grave they'd dug, and the two of them propped themselves with their shovels, Santino looking all but spent. Carlos, being younger, fared better. Santino was strong, but he was older.

"Put the shovels and the bag of lime back in shed," Maura said. She took a breath and dialed up Logan, who was overjoyed to hear from her, once he realized it was her.

"Maura," Logan said. "Are you okay?"

"I'm fine," Maura said. "I escaped those *Rojas*."

"What?" Logan said. "How?"

"Long story," Maura said.

"Where are you?" Logan asked. "Can I help?"

"I'm fine," Maura said. "I'm out and about, but I should be home soon. Are you in your hotel room?"

"Yeah," Logan said. "I'm so glad you're alright. You are alright, aren't you?"

Maura grinned at Carlos and Santino by lantern light, the two men glaring at her, but unable to move. They were right where she wanted them.

"I'm just right," Maura said. "You stay put, and I'll come to you, okay? It'll be late."

"I'm just glad you're safe," Logan said. "I was worried."

"You're sweet," Maura said. "Sorry I made you worry. I'll see you soon. Just stay put for me, can you do that?"

"Alright," Logan said. "I'll stay put. I was thinking about our deal. I'll join your faith. I can be at the Midnight Service, if you'd tell me where it is being held."

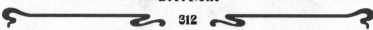

Maura chewed her lip a bit. She liked the idea of him committing to her that way, but with everything else going on, she didn't want to be distracted. Distraction was the death of magic.

"That's sweet, Babe," Maura said. "But I think we should have our own private ceremony. Just you, me, the Tears, and the trees. Okay?"

"Okay," Logan said.

"I'll make it up to you, I promise," Maura said.

She hung up, put the phone in her pocket.

"Another of your meat puppets?" Carlos asked. Maura shook her head, smiling to herself.

"Logan loves me," Maura said. "He already does, whether he knows it or not. Love is its own kind of witchcraft, isn't it? I don't have to cast a spell on my Logan."

Carlos knew better than to argue with a *Bruja*, but he couldn't help but pipe up.

"Why bother with the grave?" Carlos asked.

"We must feed the Cursed Earth," Maura said. *"La Signora* feeds well tonight. Right now, this doesn't look like much. Grove 11 and all. But soon, the Lady's Tears will fall on this place and there'll be Her blessing, and it'll become yet another Sacred Grove."

"How many do you have?" Carlos asked. Talking somehow made it tolerable.

"Many," Maura said. "But when a grove fills up, we have to make new ones. We are the Lady's careful caretakers."

Carlos could only imagine where his other men had ended up.

"Grove 13," Maura said, reading his mind again. "We put them in Grove 13."

"Someone will find out," Carlos said.

"Not likely," Maura said. "Now, hush. Take a seat. Take a rest. It's going to be a long night for both of you."

Their strings cut, Carlos and Santino dropped to the ground, Carlos laying on his back and staring up at the night sky, the star-studded firmament somewhat spoiled by the bright light of the moon. Maura was praying to *La Signora,* clutching a pendant she had around her neck. Carlos imagined strangling her with it.

"My Lady," Maura said. "I give You the gift of forty-eight souls, more Red Death heathens that have been plaguing our town. I thank You for blessing me with Your words and whispers, and humbly pray You find these sacrifices to Your liking. I give them to You with the understanding that the night is young and the Cursed Earth has not yet had Her fill. Blessed be, *Signora,* and know that as above, so below, where we all belong."

She turned her eyes to Carlos and Santino, her face shrouded in shadow.

"Say it with me," Maura said. "Where we all belong."

"Where we all belong," Carlos and Santino said.

"Now, let's get to the Sacred Grove," Maura said, turning off the lantern and putting it back in the shed, which she locked with a flip of her wrist. Carlos and Santino followed like lost lambs in the care of a mad shepherd.

# 11

**The Lynchburg Pub Crawl took place as originally planned** now that the town had some time to recover from the earlier events of the day. Mallory had emerged from her hibernation at the Grand Hotel, for which Austin was bleakly grateful, having tired of babysitting the tripping Twins hours ago.

Even coming down, the two of them were almost intolerably high, finding joy in literally everything they encountered, and exclaiming with delight at what new everyday object was no doubt bursting with color and shape and significance.

Mallory was wearing a white poet's blouse with blue jeans and some hiking boots. She looked refreshed and sprightly, as perkily pretty as she ever was. For some reason Austin couldn't fathom, she'd come down wearing blue lipstick and had painted her fingernails blue, too.

"What's with the lipstick?" Austin asked.

"Brutal Blue," Mallory said. "You like it?"

It looked good on her, of course. Everything looked good on her, really.

"Sure," Austin said. Mallory half-laughed.

"Sure? Oh, man," Mallory said.

Austin's mood was bad. Getting blown off by Ash had been almost too painful to bear. Sure, he'd only been aware of her the night before, but the combination of tripping and his vision of her in the Temple had been potent.

For her to rebuff him so completely had been wounding. He accepted it, but he was still rocked by it.

The Twins had been useless, still coming out from under their Blue Meanies trip. They were happy to find Mallory among them. Jess had managed to pick up a Cat in the Hat hat—one of those towering red-and-white striped top hats, which she had jammed down on her head.

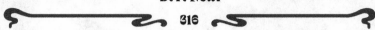
"Fungo says we start at Staley's," Mallory said. "Then the Golden Goblin Grille. Then William B. Tankard's Alehouse. The Five Corners. Then the Triple Six Tavern. Then we wrap at the All-Nightclub. If we clock in at the taverns, we win a Nightcap Pub Crawl tee shirt and a mushroom mug."

"Who even names a place 'the Triple Six Tavern'?" Austin asked. "I mean, what the hell?"

Mallory laughed at him, shrugging her shoulders.

"Don't let it get your goat, Austin."

The Twins had wandered into conversational range, their eyes alight. Jake had managed to score another tee shirt somewhere which had Mushy the Mushroom on it in red, making dual finger pistols and winking while standing on a "Lynchburg Fungus Festival 2019" pedestal.

"Cool," Jake said.

"For real," Jess said. "Mallory. You are glowing."

Mallory smiled, winking at Austin, who just rolled his eyes.

"See what I've had to deal with all day?" Austin said.

"You haven't seen anything yet," Mallory said, going back to her phone while Jess and Jake wandered around them, still reaching for unseen things.

"What about the Sacred Grove?" Austin asked. Mallory didn't look up from her phone.

"That's midnight, Austin," Mallory said. "We have hours. Don't get ahead of yourself."

"Okay," Austin said. "I just didn't want to miss out. If that fucking clown is at the Sacred Grove, I'm going to freak out."

Jake and Jess laughed like he'd said something funny.

"There's nothing funny about a clown in the moonlight," Austin said.

"Who said that?" Mallory asked, eyeing Staley's.

"Lon Chaney," Austin said. He looked over the Pub Crawl participant logos, clicking through them on his own Fungo. Five Corners had a star. The Triple Six had this weird circle with three prongs emanating from it in a swirl. The Golden Goblin Grille had this grinning golden goblin holding a sloshing goblet of beer. Staley's had a beer served on a platter, while William B. Tankard's had some stuffy looking barkeep with a jaunty derby hat, brandishing beers in each hand. The All-Nightclub had a trippy All-Seeing Eye staring down at a bottle of booze.

Word had spread about what had happened on the parade route earlier that day, and people were on edge. But they were also drowning their sorrows in spirits, and the Mayor of Lynchburg had come back out and urged people to continue to enjoy the Festival despite the impact of the assailants. People had been all too eager to do that.

"We should all get tattoos," Mallory said, nodding to The Inkpot down the street. Its logo was an inkpot rendered on skin by a very sharp-looking quill.

Austin shook his head.

"That's a crap idea," Austin said. "We're drinking, not having somebody ink us."

"I did it last year," Mallory said.

"Is that where you got that sleeve?" Austin asked. "The mushroom lady, that stuff?"

"Yeah," Mallory said. "Among other things."

"Like what?" Austin asked. Mallory played it coy.

"You'd have seen if you hadn't run off this morning. Your loss, Fun Guy," Mallory said, finger-quoting that last part. "Come on, let's go get wasted."

Staley's was pretty full, with the obligatory televisions on showing various sporting events, although it wasn't truly a sports bar. Lynchburg seemed to divide its loyalty between the Steelers and the Eagles, even though it was geographically closer to Pittsburgh.

They scored a darkwood booth, Mallory and Austin on one side, the Twins on the other. They ordered Boilermakers, which Austin thought was a step too far.

"We need to pace ourselves," Austin said. Mallory wrinkled her nose at him, gave him a flick with her finger.

"What, are you worried about bloating, Austin?" Mallory said, smiling as the drinks arrived. She and the Twins plunked their shots into their beers, holding theirs up, clanking glasses as they downed them. They laughed at Austin, who primly drank his shot first and then sipped at his beer.

"Oh, my," Mallory said, after finishing her beer in what looked like one big swig. "You are such a tidy gentleman, Austin."

Austin laughed, while Jess and Jake were racing for second place in the drinkfest.

"Seriously, what's your other tattoo?" Austin asked.

"You may see it if you're really lucky, Austin," Mallory said. "It's very, you know, personal."

"Right," Austin said. Jake came in second, while Jess came back up for air, holding a finger up as she took another dive into her beer.

"The beer is glowing," Jake said. "Like bright gold. Liquid gold."

Austin watched Jake staring at his sister drinking her beer, while Mallory was giving him a sidelong look. "What'd they take?"

"Blue Meanies," Austin said.

"Like when?"

"This morning," Austin said.

"Damn, how much did they take?" Mallory asked.

"That I do not know," Austin said. "They stole from my stash."

"They'll be coming down just in time for the Midnight Service," Mallory said. "Oh, man, that is going to be cray."

She snort-laughed, slapping the table with her hand. Austin could see she wore a trio of rings on her fingers, but her hand moved before he could see what they were.

"What's that going to be like?" Austin asked.

Mallory rested her left hand on his forearm, which only had one ring on it, which was a golden lion. Jess plonked her empty beer mug on the table and belched with laudable gusto that almost dislodged her tall hat. She took out her phone and logged it in her Fungo App.

"Mark Staley's, you guys," Jess said, and everybody else did. Nothing motivated quite like a free tee shirt and a mug prize.

"Slow your roll, Jess," Austin said. "We're not hitting all the bars in an hour."

"Yeah, well," Jess said. "That's just you talking."

She was looking nearly through him, and he ignored that while keeping after Mallory.

"What's it like, this Sacred Grove?" Austin asked.

"It's beautiful," Mallory said. "I mean, it's otherworldly. And not just because you get a big cup of Lady's Tears to drink, either."

"Is it mandatory?" Austin asked.

"You mean the Tears?" Mallory said. "There, it basically is. It's sort of the price of admission. It's not like the Temple. I

mean at the Temple, they don't want to scare people off. But in the Grove, they don't fucking care, man. If a Boilermaker makes you squeamish, a cup of Tears will freak you the hell out, Austin."

Austin rolled with Mallory's ribbing as he always did. It was part of their dance.

"A cup of tears," Austin said, making a single tear down his cheek. "So, so sad."

"It's the most beautiful thing I ever experienced," Mallory said. "I'm talking full transference. You go someplace else. Most intense trip I've ever experienced."

"Boom," Jake said, clapping his palm on the table, startling his sister. "That's what I'm talking about. Transformative transference. Fuck Staley's. What's the next one?"

"William B. Tankard's," Jess said, holding out her phone with wonder in her eyes. "A half-block north, across the street."

"Isn't one of them in Ambrose Alley?" Austin asked.

"That's the Triple Six," Mallory said. "Not yet, Austin."

"It's a pub crawl," Austin said, settling their tab before dealing with the inevitable negotiation that would come if they split it. "We can do them in any order."

"No," Jess said. "It has to make sense. Maximum bar, minimum legwork."

She shushed everybody and showed them her Fungo Pub Crawl map, the arrows.

"This is the optimal order from the Grand," Jess said. "Staley's. Then William B. Tankard's. Then Five Corners. Then the Golden Goblin. Then the Triple Six. Then the All-Nightclub."

Mallory took issue with that.

"We should hit the Goblin before Five Corners," Mallory said. But Jess wasn't having any of that.

"Nope," Jess said. "No way. Your way is madness, Mallory. You'd have us zigzagging and backtracking. My way, we're doing it in an elegant backwards 'C' shape."

Mallory consulted her own phone, and Austin even took a look, while Jake fidgeted in his seat.

"My way is better," Jess said. "No backtracking, no back alleys, right down the main drag."

"There's nothing elegant about a backwards C," Mallory said, sulking. "Alright, Jess. You get to be navigator."

"Let's navigate, then," Jack said, hopping up. "William B. Tankard's, here we come!"

Streetside, Austin could see those grey-robed, masked Festival creepers walking around, like they were earlier in the day. They just walked along, their masked faces impassive, the dark eyeholes on their masks looking particularly threatening.

"What are those guys all about?" Austin asked. "Will they be at the Grove?"

"Those are Exemplars," Mallory said. "You do not want to mess with them."

"Because they're just so badass?" Austin asked.

"Hardcore, yeah," Mallory said. "They're like holy warriors for *La Signora*. Like crusaders."

"That's weird," Austin said.

"They're fearless," Mallory said. "Literally unafraid to die."

"How do you know that?" Austin asked, watching the Exemplars pass them wordlessly.

"It's what I've heard," Mallory said. "Like for followers of the Faith, they actually welcome death in the service of *La Signora*."

"So, like a death cult," Austin said.

Mallory swatted him.

"You make that sound like a bad thing, Goofus," Mallory said. "Their willingness to kill and die for the Lady is what makes them Exemplars."

Austin scoffed, grateful for heading under the bright lights of William B. Tankard's, which was particularly pub-like in construction, with black paint and gold trim. Inside, the staff and the bartender were all wearing green derby hats at jaunty angles.

Jake and Jess scored them a spot at a standing table near the long bar, and there was a good crowd in there, mostly tourists by the look of them, judging from their Festival attire.

"Why isn't there a Mexican bar included on the Pub Crawl?" Jess asked.

"Locals only," Mallory said. "The Pub Crawl is strictly for tourists. In, like, the Historic District."

"The Latinos who live in Lynchburg are part of that history," Jess said. "They should be represented on the Pub Crawl."

Austin laughed as Jake ordered them a round of shots from their red-haired server, a young woman in a ponytail and a striped shirt, wearing black suspenders.

"Maybe they don't want a bunch of inebriated *gringos* clogging up their *taquerias*," Austin said.

"Just saying," Jess said. "Seems like an oversight. I'd be pissed if were them."

Austin wondered how that played out as their server brought them four blue shots, which she set down in front of them.

"Wait," Austin said. "What the hell are these?"

"We call them 'The Lady's Cheers'," the server said. Her name badge said she was Wendy.

"The Lady's Cheers," Austin said. "Not mushroom-based, I hope. Like are we going to trip on these?"

Wendy shook her head.

"Just booze," she said. "Nothing, you know, extra."

"Is it Blue Curaçao or what?" Austin asked.

"Bingo," Wendy said. Jake took up his shot, and the others joined in, clinking their glasses together while Wendy went off to another table.

"Cheers," Jake said, and they all did their shots. The orange flavor was welcome and refreshing, although Austin felt like he needed to get some bar food to settle his stomach before they got too far in.

Jess grimaced at the shot, but dutifully clanked down her glass and whipped out her phone again to log it.

"I hope they don't run out of prizes," Jess said, jamming her tall hat down hard on her head.

"Pretty sure we're hitting this one at a pretty good clip," Mallory said.

"The Lady's Cheers," Austin said, snorting. "Isn't that, like, sacrilege or blasphemy or something?"

"There is no blasphemy or sacrilege with the Faith," Mallory said. "The Lady accepts everyone."

"Ha," Austin said. "Seems like it should have another name. Like Signorans or Grigians or something like that. Grigianity?"

Mallory laughed at Austin, her teeth momentarily blued by the drink.

"That's funny," Mallory said. "Grigianity. You should tell that to the High Priestess. I'm sure they'd really appreciate you naming it for them."

"Nomenclature matters," Austin said. "Names stick."

Austin ordered them some scotch eggs, which made Jake laugh and grossed Jess out. Mallory seemed fine with it.

Tankard's had a mix of patrons, like what looked like maybe locals and tourists rubbing elbows. Austin found the noise and light comforting. He liked how busy Lynchburg was. Having lived most of his life in the city, he got weirded out when it was too quiet.

"Somebody already completed the Crawl," Jess said. "Jesus Fuck!"

Austin and the others laughed about that, but Austin was grateful the scotch eggs came pretty quickly, since he didn't want to hear Jess whining about them falling behind. She took pictures of them and of them eating them, making faces with each bite.

"Those are the most horrifying things I've seen here," Jess said.

"Just wait," Mallory said. "The night is young."

The scotch eggs were good and filling, and he and Mallory and Jake split the fourth one.

"This has been nagging at me," Austin said. "Fun Gus said I was the Decider. What does that even mean, Mallory?"

Mallory shrugged. "I think he just maybe wanted you to not feel bad because you didn't get a balloon. Like he wanted you to feel special, even though you weren't. And aren't."

"Oh, wow," Austin said, miming getting stabbed in the heart. Jake patted his shoulder, while Jess was elbowing Jake to pay the tab.

"Stop," Jake said.

"We gotta hit Five Corners next, dammit, Jake," Jess said. "You're harshing my buzz."

"Wasn't Five Corners in New York City?" Austin asked.

"That's Five POINTS, Austin," Mallory said. "Completely different."

Austin held up his wrists to Mallory in mock-guilt.

"Slap the cuffs on me," Austin said.

"Later," Mallory said, poking Austin while Jake charged the bill.

They slipped out of Tankard's and hustled to Five Corners, the big star hanging from the shingle. Jess went to the alley and barfed, holding up a finger for them to wait for her, while Jake

laughed and took her picture. Her finger changed to a middle finger as she flipped off her brother.

"Where do the Latinos all live?" Austin asked.

"Southville," Mallory said. "South Street, near the water tower, south of Bianchi Gardens. They drive in to work at the mushroom farms. Not just Nightcap, but all the ones in town."

Jess had recovered and wiped her mouth with the back of her hand.

"You know way too much about Lynchburg, Mallomar," Jess said.

"I drink and I know things," Mallory said, shrugging her shoulders. They went into Five Corners, which was a rowdy place with a lot of locals and some pool tables in the back, as well as darts.

"Still, it's weird," Jess said. She ordered them four Lady Fingers, which she explained were gin, cherry brandy, and *kirschwasser* cocktails served in classic cocktail glasses.

"Gross," Mallory said. "I hate gin."

"I love it," Austin said. Jake was noncommittal, while Jess was just happy to have picked up where her brother left off.

"You sure you're up to it, Jess?" Jake asked.

"What, because I hurled? Whatever," Jess said.

Austin was feeling the drinks, couldn't imagine dragging his ass out into the woods or whatever for the Midnight Service.

"Regarding that Sacred Grove, how's that going to work, anyway?" Austin asked, when the Lady Fingers arrived. Jake derided them as girl drinks before Mallory and Jess shut him down, and they all raised their glasses and clinked them together. "I mean, we're supposed to what, exactly?"

"We register with our invites," Mallory said. "And we get a guide to the Sacred Grove. Like a direction finder. The Sacred Grove changes every year."

"Does it?" Austin asked, sipping his drink.

"It does," Mallory said. "They change it annually."

"Okay," Austin said. "So, there are really sacred *groves*, then, not just one. Cuz when the invite says 'The Sacred Grove' it implies a specific destination."

Austin held up his own invitation like it was an exhibit in court, and the Twins snickered, while Mallory heaved a sigh.

"I think the Midnight Service sanctifies the damned grove, Austin," Mallory said. "It's *the* Sacred Grove, as in the grove they're making sacred that night. There's only one per Festival. And this one's special because of the full moon tonight. And it's the 50th anniversary. So, like double special."

"Right," Austin said. "Double special."

"Aw, man," Jess said. "Three other groups have wrapped up the Crawl. Goddammit, but we're moving too slowly. Everybody chug their Lady Fingers. Come on, now. Chug! Chug! Chug!"

"It's just wrong to chug gin," Austin said, but he did it, anyway. He knew better than to get between Jess and any free prize.

"Gin is wrong," Mallory said, wincing with her own efforts. "It's like drinking Pine-Sol."

"Now, *that* is blasphemous," Austin said. "Besides, I've never drunk Pine-Sol, so I wouldn't know what that tastes like."

They'd spent a half-hour at Staley's, then about forty-five minutes at Tankard's. Five Corners ended up another hour *in toto,* since Mallory and Jake got caught up in some pool-playing with some locals before Jess and Austin were able to pry them away and steer them toward the Golden Goblin, after Jess made everybody update their Fungo Pub Crawl entries.

"None of you are going to fuck up my winnings," Jess said. Austin was getting pretty trashed already, and even Mallory had a lurch in her step, while Jake was alternately fine and hiccupping, and announcing he was fine between hiccups.

Streetside were some street performers juggling and playing flutes, and Austin became wary for Fun Gus, praying he'd not see the damnable clown while in his condition. It was the last thing he needed.

But while there were plenty of people out on Grand Avenue, the clown was nowhere to be found. Mushy the Mushroom was fake-signing autographs, trading them with a group of mimes, to the amusement of onlookers.

"This place is dead after the Festival," Mallory said. "You wouldn't believe it. They just clean up and it gets really quiet. Locals only."

"How would you know?" Austin asked, as they stumbled their way to the raucous Golden Goblin.

"I stayed after," Mallory said. "The people I were with had car trouble, so we had to stay another week."

Jess took some pictures of Mushy and the mimes, while Jake laughed, pointing.

"Who'd you go with last year?" Austin asked.

"Nobody you'd know," Mallory said.

"I don't know, try me," Austin said. "I know a lot of people."

"April, May, and June Taylor," Mallory said. "The Taylor Triplets."

"You went tripping with triplets? April, May, and June?" Austin asked, cackling. "How meta is that?"

Mallory shrugged, smiling shamefacedly.

"Triplets one year, twins the next," Austin said.

"It's a numbers game with me," Mallory said. "Three last year, two this year, maybe one next year. If I find the right one."

Mallory winked at Austin, who accepted it with a drunken smile.

Jess and Jake were getting into a mime argument with the mimes, who were taking pictures of them with mime cameras, while Mushy was looking on, hand on his hip. From where he was standing, it looked like Jess had been put into an invisible box, while Jake was mime-brawling with three of the guy mimes.

Feeling properly drunk, Austin was all flirting eyeballs and easy grins with Mallory, who was looking even better than usual.

"That's kind of trippy," Austin said.

"It was trippy," Mallory said.

"You're right, I don't know the Taylor Triplets. But they sound fun."

"They were," Mallory said. "Like tripping with the Trips was cray, because then you'd think you were seeing triple even more so. They looked like a whole legion."

"You should have taken us last year," Austin said. "I feel snubbed."

Mallory mock-pouted, put her arms around Austin's shoulders and looked him right in the eyes. She smelled like vanilla and cloves and patchouli.

"I had to scout it out to see if it was worth everybody's time," Mallory said. "I didn't want to go and have it suck. You should thank me that I cared so much."

Austin went to mock-thank her when she kissed him, and he kissed her back. One of the mimes had walked up, was pretend-filming it with his invisible phone, and another strolled up, and they were mock-laughing about it. Austin held out a hand to block their mime-filming, which outraged the mimes.

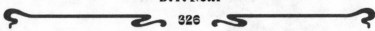
Austin and Mallory parted, and Mallory smiled at him.

"You're a good kisser," she said. "Such soft lips."

"Knew that lip balm was good for something," he said. The mimes were just watching them, while Jess had freed herself from the invisible box with Jake's help. They went to Austin and Mallory, only to bonk themselves on what appeared to be an invisible wall. The mimes that had been filming Austin and Mallory turned their attention to the Twins, pointing and silently laughing.

"Did the Twins do miming or something?" Austin asked.

"They're community theater brats," Mallory said. "I think Jess may have been a puppeteer one summer, too, but seriously don't ask her about it or you'll get a dissertation about puppeteering as a postmodern American political meta-narrative social media substrate."

"Wow," Austin said, bursting into giggles at Mallory's drunken deadpan delivery.

Jess and Jake rejoined them Jess grinning widely.

"Wow, that was intense," Jess said.

"Fucking mimes," Jake said.

"Alright, then," Mallory said. "To the Golden Goblin we go!"

They threw open the door and lost themselves in the Golden Goblin's lair, Austin drunkenly wondering if there'd be time to get Mallory back to the Grand before they trekked off after the Sacred Grove.

# 12

**Emily and Ash had staked out the balcony after getting** room service and taking disco naps afterward. They sat in the dark of the balcony, backlit by the hotel room, keeping an eye on things.

Ash in particular was alert to the Exemplars still lurking around.

"They didn't stop searching," Ash said. "Not all day. What a bunch of freaks."

"Zealots," Emily said. "They probably have orders to keep going until they find you."

"It's bizarre," Ash said. "I lost them."

"I hope so," Emily said. "I don't think they'll be able to do any forensic analysis on the Exemplar robes you wore."

"I was thinking about that, actually," Ash said. "We still have another set of robes. What if I robed up and went to that psycho Midnight Service with you in their Sacred Grove?"

Emily shrugged, shaking her head.

"That sounds like a bad idea, Ash," Emily said. "Like dancing on a landmine. You got away with it once. You really want to push your luck again?"

Ash sighed.

"You're better off just going to it, if you're curious," Emily said.

"No way," Ash said. "I'm *not* curious, that's the thing. The Temple was weird enough for me. I just want Melinda back. And I'd like to expose these creeps for what they're up to out here. People need to know."

"Maybe they already do," Emily said. "I mean, there are hashtags. People can see."

"They see, but they don't see everything," Ash said. "It all looks like a fun festival, but there's clearly messed-up stuff going on."

Emily didn't know what to expect at the Sacred Grove. Part of her thought she should just stay in town, and let it blow over. Hopefully Jerry's people would be able to develop the stolen samples into something profitable. That should have been enough for her, but it wasn't. Emily wanted to know what they had in this grove, to learn more.

"Melinda's likely to be there," Emily said.

"I know she will be," Ash said.

"And she's not going to want to go," Emily said. "You're not going to have any more luck persuading her there than you did the last two times you talked to her."

Ash turned to look Emily over a moment in the dark. The sliver of hotel light only partially illuminated Emily's face. The rest of her was shadowed.

"Are you suggesting I be realistic?" Ash asked, laughing.

"More or less," Emily said. "If Marquis was here, I'd say we could stage some kind of kidnapping or something, but he's not. It's just us."

Emily felt for Ash, could see it was gnawing at her.

"I might take the Exemplar robes myself and try to sneak in on the fringes of it," Emily said.

"How is that better than what I was thinking of doing?" Ash asked.

Emily's mind was working.

"No, maybe we both sneak in," Emily said. "Me looking like an Exemplar, and you as you are. We already know it's taking place in some wooded grove, right? We find out where it is and we just slip in on the fringes."

Ash held up her phone, showing off the Fungo App.

"We have to register with our invitations," Ash said. If we do that, they'll know we should be somewhere. Maybe they'll be able to track us on our phones."

Emily thought that over.

"We have to tip our hand by registering," Emily said. "That's how we find out where it's taking place. But in so doing, then maybe it swings both ways. They can track us, too."

"That's what I'd do," Ash said.

"If something goes bad out there, we're in a real fix," Emily said. "Nowhere to go but the woods."

"Yeah, well, there it is," Ash said. "Whether she knows it or not, Melinda needs me."

"She's going to just blow you off," Emily said. "At best."

"I have to try," Ash said. "She may not appreciate it, but I love her."

Emily wasn't sure how to handle it. As she saw it, she was in the clear. Nobody knew what she'd done. Ash had the connection with her sister, and lord knew what Melinda had told Mona about her sister.

"Okay," Emily said. "You can take the disguise if you want. I'll just go in straight and see what I can find. You can try your subterfuge, although if something goes wrong, I'm unlikely to be able to help you."

"Or, we can just stay in and binge-watch something on television," Ash said. "Call it a night and I can leave it to my parents to hire some first-rate cult deprogrammers to try to get Melinda dislodged from this fucking place."

*No risk, no reward.*

That's what Emily told herself. Ash was right that they could just stay in and enjoy the evening and that would be that. Leave the cultists to howl at the moon or whatever else they intended. There was always that option.

"The Temple's almost assuredly going to be minimally occupied tonight," Emily said. "If the Midnight Service is their big show, it's where they'll be. Although, again, without Marquis, breaking back into the Temple seems a more challenging proposition."

"Forget the Temple," Ash said. "I want to see what's going on at the Grove. Don't forget, I'm the journalist, here. I'll sneak in on the periphery, and I'll try to record what I see. Then I'll get out of there and I'll have enough material for a blowout of a story. Maybe I can bring them down that way. A big story on an insane cult openly operating in a small Pennsylvania town. Somebody'll pick that up."

"Assuming we survive to tell the story," Emily said.

"Yeah," Ash said. "Assuming that. Look, I'm a good runner. I already evaded them once. If something goes bad, I can just outrun them again."

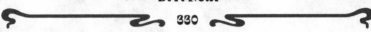
"In the woods," Emily said. "Trickier. And after the Red Death thing, they'll likely have tighter security."

"Quit trying to dissuade me," Ash said, laughing. "Damn you scientists, always being the sensible ones. Mona gave us those invitations for a reason. I mean, you saw her. She was giving those out. Why would she do that?"

"A cult needs new members," Emily said. "It probably passes for recruitment."

"That's what I'm saying," Ash said. She could see Austin and his friends tottering around streetside, heading toward the Golden Goblin Grille after some altercation with a bunch of mimes. "Mona's looking for new blood. She handed those tickets out because she wants people to show up. They're hosting an event and it's not just for the faithful, it's not locals-only. Think about that."

Emily did think about that.

"New blood," Emily said. "Specifically not locals. They're wanting to branch out. It's their own mycelium. Mona said something about that the other day. 'The mycelium binds us all.' It's what she said."

"Meaning what, exactly?" Ash asked. Austin was snogging with one of his friends, a wild-haired redhead. Looks like it worked out for him, after all. Ash felt happy for the kid.

"The mycelium," Emily said. "It's what binds fungi together. It's like their Internet, in a way. It's hard to explain, but the mushrooms you see, those are just the fruiting bodies. The mycelium is a threaded network of hyphae, the way the fungus spreads."

"Hyphae? What the hell are you even talking about?"

"They're like the roots and branches of the fungal organism," Emily said. "The way they spread and propagate. A bunch of them comprise the mycelium, which forms a kind of mat from which the rest of the organism grows. It absorbs nutrients from the environment. The closest analogy I would offer is that the mycelium is like the trunk of a tree, and the hyphae are the branches and roots. The mushrooms themselves are the fruit."

"Okay, so what the hell was Mona talking about with her mycelium?" Ash asked.

"Lynchburg itself is the mycelium," Emily said. "They're all part of it. They're all connected. Maybe not literally, maybe only figuratively, but that's what it is. And the individual mem-

bers of the cult are like the spores. Yes, it's what they're doing. It's why she was sending out invitations that way. She wants to infect us so we can spread their faith."

"You're being figurative again, right?" Ash asked. "I mean, not literally infecting people?"

"Of course," Emily said. "They're not actual mushroom people. But the ideas they represent, that's what they're propagating. It's like any religion, really. Memes and ideas, traditions and rituals. All of that. The cult is the delivery system, the thing upon which their faith grows. So, they try to get some converts at their Midnight Service, nurture and care for them, and they send them off to create new mycelia elsewhere."

"Branches," Ash said. "Franchises?"

"Yes," Emily said. "It's like any multilevel marketing scheme when you think about it. MLMs basically operate like cults, so the analogy holds true. Only maybe one percent of MLM recruits turn a profit—ninety-nine percent of recruits lose money. They grow their cult through the use of Lady's Tears. They offer a transcendent psychedelic experience stewarded by the Temple hierarchy to steer new recruits into the process."

"Interesting angle," Ash said. "It puts their Fungus Festival into context, I suppose."

She saw Austin and the others disappear into the Golden Goblin. How nice to be so carefree. She remembered being that way once, although she laughed. She was never carefree. Ash was always worrying about something.

"I'm sure it's many-layered," Emily said. "The festival is a legitimate business marketing opportunity, a way of getting word out about their products. But the cult is also using it for its own purposes. To get recruits. Think about it. People come intending to trip out. Who knows what mental and emotional state they're already in? Highly suggestible. Maybe blackmail is a part of it. I don't know. Without attending the Midnight Service, I can't know for sure what they're really up to."

Ash thought Emily's explanations seemed cogent. She didn't entirely know what was going on, but it at least made some sense. She didn't like the idea of Emily risking herself by showing up at the Sacred Grove.

"At the Temple," Emily said. "The staff weren't tripping. They administered it to the congregation and kept tabs on things. That's what'll happen at the Grove, I'm sure of it. They'll

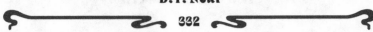
dose the participants as part of their 'sacred ritual' or whatever they call it and the participants won't fully know what the hell is going on. They're completely at the mercy of the *Signora* cultists. In that highly vulnerable and even suggestible state, the cultists can mold them however they wish. Then, once the participants come down, the Temple people are there to guide them in the path of the cult's choosing. The new converts, fresh off their massive high, think they've experienced some sacred event, and are keen to 'spread the word'—it's like a baptism of sorts. They're bathing in the Lady's Tears. They're literally drinking the Kool-Aid."

"Ick," Ash said. "You're not going to drink the Tears, are you?"

"I haven't decided," Emily said. "I am curious about it. Psychedelics can really help people psychologically. I think this cult is using them for recruitment, but as a whole, they are a positive cognitive tool for people with psychological problems. It's why Mycopharmix was looking into this at all. Jerry understands the value, there."

"They're a bunch of hucksters," Ash said. "Melinda's stuck in an MLM scheme, and she doesn't even know it."

"And you can't even convince her otherwise," Emily said. "She said she doses weekly, right? That's like a maintenance dose. Every trip is uniquely personal. It doesn't even have to be mind control per se—rather, it's just an applied transcendence that makes everyday life feel more otherworldly for the participants. They become part of something greater than themselves, and that's enough to motivate them. People will do anything if they're made to feel part of something larger than they are. They'll lie, cheat, steal, or even kill."

Ash liked to think of Mona and her Temple as a bunch of greedy charlatans. It put them in their proper place, no different from anybody else, working their hustle. *La Signora Grigia* was just that, a marketing mascot like Ronald McDonald, Colonel Sanders, or the Kool-Aid Man.

"Oh, yeah," Ash said. "I think you're onto something, Em. And I've got my story. I can build around that. There's just enough mystery around *La Signora* to make her enticing to outsiders. You have your Acolytes at the bottom level, the rank-and-file, the Deacons as the midlevel administrators, and the Exemplars as the elite enforcers. Up top, you have Mona Tem-

pleton and maybe some other trusted confederates. Who knows who else is in the upper tier? There must be a top tier to their pyramid scheme."

Emily nodded, leaning on her elbows, peering at the people below, making their way from shop to shop, past the speckled red pavilion tents.

"Somebody we haven't seen, yet," Emily said. "Not really. Mona's clearly part of that elite. But others as well. It can't just be her. A level that's higher still. Somebody very obvious, like the other Templetons. Somebody sure to be present at the Sacred Grove. I'll wager the other Templetons are in on it."

"You're brilliant, Em," Ash said. "I hope you have good running shoes. It's going to be a long night."

# 13

**Victory wasn't exactly sweet, but that didn't stop Austin,** Mallory, and the Twins from savoring it. After stumbling their way through the Golden Goblin and the Triple Six Tavern, the quartet made their way to the All-Nightclub, drunkenly punching their Pub Crawl tickets on their phones and earning the cheers of the patrons, who were mostly locals decked out in Fungus Festival merch. They were the 13th group to reach the end of the Crawl, which gave Jess considerable pride.

The All-Nightclub staff cheered them on, happily giving them their Pub Crawl mugs and tee shirts, which everybody haphazardly donned, while Jess handed over her phone to have somebody take pictures of them.

"Say 'Shrooms!'" Jess said, and they all mugged for their photos, holding aloft their hard-won mugs.

"Mug shot," Austin said, laughing.

They'd had lagers at the Golden Goblin, Demon's Blood shots at the Triple Six, and were wrapping up with martinis. Jess had puke-stopped in Ambrose Alley after the Triple Six, where she hurled, and Austin joined in. He wasn't a puker by nature, but it seemed like a good plan of action, given how much they'd had along the way.

They shared some celebratory chicken fingers and fried mushrooms at the All-Nightclub, inaugurating their beer mugs with a round of Lady's Lucky Ale from a local Lynchburg micro-brewery that operated at the other side of town. Austin saw the smiling grey-white lady on the blue and white label, holding aloft a mug of frothy beer and smiling at him with bright blue eyes.

"What's that supposed to be? The Grey Lady?" Austin asked.

"Sure is," Mallory said.

"She's smiling," Austin said. "Only time I've seen her smiling."

"She's drunk," Mallory said. "She's happy for us."

Only Mallory seemed relatively together, which impressed and intimidated Austin more than he cared to admit. Jake kept taking off his shirt, revealing his well-sculpted frame, even though the autumn chill was in the air. Steam was coming off of him, and young women and men whistled at him as they made their way from the All-Nightclub.

"The ground is walking," Jess said.

The clock tower tolled eleven o'clock, and Mallory was all business.

"Guys, get your phones out," Mallory said. "Fungo time. Hit that little icon, the three-circle one at the lower right of the Fungo app. After you click on that icon, you should see a dialogue box asking for a code. Enter the seven-digit code you have on your card. Do you need help?"

"I've got it," Jess said, yanking her phone away from Mallory. Jake tapped his own code, mouthing his code numbers as he did, while Austin squinted into his phone and entered his. The ground was shifting beneath Austin's feet, and any hope of getting with Mallory before the Sacred Grove was simply out at this point.

After entering the code, a map popped up on their phone screens, with a You Are Here indicator.

"Alright, we're in," Mallory said. "Now we just follow the line."

"What about our mugs?" Jake asked.

"We can bring'em," Mallory said. "It's fine. They'll pour Lady's Tears in them. We can drink our fill."

"Fuck," Austin said. He saw the line leading out of Lynchburg, like heading due west. "How long a haul are we talking about, Mallory?"

Mallory checked her phone.

"Looks like about three miles," Mallory said. "That's a stroll for us."

"It's a hike," Jess said, pointing to her hiking boots. "I came prepared."

"You sure did, Jess," Mallory said. "Okay, so let's go."

"This better be worth it," Jake said. "All I'm saying."

"Oh, it so will, Jake," Mallory said. "Come on."

She hooked Austin's arm and Jake's arm, and started off along the route, while Jess was stomping after them, cursing.

"You sons of bitches better not ditch me," Jess said.

"Never, Jess," Mallory said. "I'm not letting you out of my sight."

"Three miles west," Jess said. "There'll be ticks."

"Ticks are dicks," Jake said, laughing. "Yeah, I don't want any fucking ticks."

"Came prepared," Jess said, pulling a can of Deep Woods OFF from her purse. She promptly sprayed her ankles and knees and stopped everybody, spraying them as well with admirable inebriated intensity.

"Cannot believe you brought that, Jess," Jake said, while she fumigated them.

"Always prepared," Jess said. "Always."

She stuffed the can back into her purse, then they headed across Grand Avenue and walked down Main Street.

Off the Festival grounds, it got both very dark and quiet very quickly, which Austin thought was sort of creepy, accentuated as it was when he looked over his shoulder and could see the Lynchburg lights, the noise and frolic in the town.

There was a quiet convenience store—Deuce's on Main—which had shadowy Festival masks displaying in its windows below signs advertising beer and sports drinks and hot dogs. The masks gave Austin pause. He took pictures with his phone, the empty-eyed grey, white, yellow, pink, and brown masks staring at them from the display windows of the convenience store. All of them had the three-circle symbol painted on their foreheads in blue.

Where they were, beyond that lone store, it was just streetlights and quiet streets and the endless dark of the surrounding woods they hadn't even gotten to, yet.

It was Mallory's turn to produce something, which happened to be four glowsticks—two white, two blue. She gave Jake and Austin the blue ones and kept the white ones for herself and Jess. They cracked the glowsticks and Austin felt relief at their chemical phosphorescence.

"At least now it'll be harder for cars to accidentally hit us," Austin said.

"Yeah, the only ones that'll hit us are the ones that are actually trying to," Jake said, putting his shirts back on, both the one he'd worn and the one he'd won. "It's almost chilly out here."

"Almost," Jess said, stuffing her hands in her pockets, having tacked her glowstick to her purse, where it bounced as they walked.

"Three miles is too damned far to walk," Austin said.

"Don't worry," Mallory said. "I'm using the Fungo Rider Service. I just wanted to get us out of town proper. You can't get an Uber or anywhere near Grand. Drivers won't go near it."

Jess was underlit by her glowstick, frowned at Mallory.

"We'd better have reception at your Sacred Grove, Mal," Jess said. "No way am I walking back."

"Not a problem," Mallory said, eyeing her phone. "Our driver should be here in like five minutes. His name is Stu."

"Stu," Jake said. "That makes me hungry."

Austin could see other cars driving down Main, leaving town. He wondered if those were other people going to the Midnight Service.

Their ride pulled up, a champagne-colored minivan, and Mallory waved, looking at the driver, who was a middle-aged man with tousled brown hair and a grey-green plaid flannel shirt.

"Are you Mallory?" the man asked.

"Are you Stu?"

"I'm Stu," the man said.

"Then I'm Mallory," Mallory said. "Come on, guys. I'll take front, you guys get in back."

They sloppily entered the minivan, and Stu was eyeing them. He wore black-rimmed eyeglasses that had an industrial look to them.

"You kids having fun?" Stu asked. Austin thought he could hear a hint of a Pittsburgh accent in the man.

"We are," Mallory said. "We're going up Route 219 from here. About three miles."

"Sacred Grove?" Stu asked. His perfunctory way of asking struck Austin as guardedly profane.

"We sure are," Austin said. "Have you been?"

"Not recently," Stu said. "It's a young people's thing, to be honest. I just make some bucks driving kids out there and back."

"There's money if you drive us back later," Jake said. Jess was dozing in her seat.

"I don't know if it's worth it," Stu said. "It'll be pretty late. And honestly, I don't want to be driving a bunch of tripping kids back into town. That can make even three miles feel like an eternity. By the way, nobody better puke back there. I just had the minivan cleaned."

"No problem, Stu," Mallory said. "We did all of our puking in town, right, Jess?"

"She's out," Jake said. He poked his sister with a finger, and she flipped him off without raising her head to even look at him.

Austin laughed. He was still relieved he hadn't seen the clown during the Pub Crawl, but the cold prospect of running into him at the Midnight Service triggered his anxiety all over again. What if Fun Gus was there? The fucking clown was bad enough in town. He'd be beyond intolerable in the woods.

*You decide.*

He hated how that would pop back into his head. He just went back to thinking about what Mallory had said, that Fun Gus had just said that to fuck with him. That there wasn't anything to it.

"You know, people get lost out in the forest," Stu said. "Happens all the time. You take like three steps off the path and you're gone. Nobody ever finds you."

"Sounds dangerous," Austin said. Stu eyed him in the rearview mirror.

"It can be," Stu said. "Jagoffs get lost out here, nobody sees them again."

"Wow, yeah, that won't be us," Austin said. He looked at his Fungo tracker, which showed them to be maybe a mile-and-a-half from the destination.

"We're definitely not jagoffs," Mallory said, grinning at Stu.

"Oh, yeah?" Stu said. "That's good to know."

He pointed to a sign in his minivan, a gold placard with red capital letters:

NO JAGOFFS

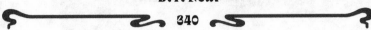
"A wise policy," Austin said. "Say, are there jagger bushes out here?"

"Sure there are," Stu said. "All over the place. They'll stick ya if you're not careful."

Outside the minivan, it was absolutely dark, with only the most sporadic of sodium lights providing meager illumination along the winding road. He thought maybe it would absolutely be safer for them to get an Uber home. He also thought, even as drunk as he was, that he'd pass on the Lady's Tears. He didn't want to be tripping out here.

Not wanting to embarrass himself by saying it aloud, he texted Mallory:

*I'll pass on the Lady's Tears tonight. Somebody's got to stay sober.*

Mallory glanced over her shoulder at him, her face dark, only her eyes reflecting the minimal light. She sneered at him, turned back to facing front.

*Sober is a relative state. You're skunky-drunk right now.*

*You know what I mean.*

*I'll stay free and clear. You have fun.*

*You decide.*

*That's my decision. I'm going to stay sober. Or just drunk. You know.*

*Your choice. Your loss, Austin. This is a life-changing thing.*

*You can trip. I'll play chaperone.*

*Not a chance. We can watch the festivities together.*

*Deal.*

"We're here," Austin said.

"Alright, then," Stu said, pulling over, turning on his blinkers. Mallory settled the account with a few taps of her phone. "You kids be good, now. Have fun. Mind the Lady."

Jake was waking up his sister, and everybody hopped out of the minivan, Jess knocking off her big hat before crabbily snagging it again and jamming it back on her head.

Stu waved at them before turning around and heading back toward town. Austin watched his taillights recede and disappear around a turn after a minute.

Where they were, it was ink-black, with only the sound of the breeze wafting through trees and dry leaves. Overhead, the

sky was studded with stars, and the full moon was covered by a bank of clouds.

Glowsticks aside, Austin could see the light pollution from Lynchburg painting the sky, although he couldn't see Lynchburg itself from where they were.

"Do you hear that?" Austin asked.

They all listened.

"Nothing," Austin said.

"No," Mallory said. "I hear drums. Can you hear them?"

They listened, and every now and then, they could hear some sounding faintly. Mallory took out her phone and consulted the Fungo App again.

"Looks like about five hundred yards that way," she said, pointing. "Northeast."

"You lead, we'll follow," Austin said.

"Wait," Jess said. "Wait. I gotta pee. Anybody else gotta pee?"

"No, just you, Jess," Jake said.

"Well, wait," Jess said, stomping off. "Give me a minute, guys."

They gave her a minute, and Austin could definitely hear the drums, now. They seemed so strange out here in the middle of nowhere, but when the moon cleared the clouds, the cool blue-white light rolled their way, and everything looked both luminous and shadowy.

"Let's GO, Jess," Jake yelled, clapping his hands together.

"Jesus, Jake," Jess said, stalking over to him. "You impatient bastard."

"You can't hold your liquor either way," Jake said.

"Shut up," Jess said. "Alright, Marshmallory, lead on."

Mallory gave an underlit nod, and they walked along a trail that seemed well-trodden. Their feet crunched fallen leaves, and they made a steady, winding pace along the trail.

As they got nearer to wherever they were going, the drums were more audible, and Austin saw luminaria up ahead on the trail, although they were lit with white lightsticks like the ones Mallory and Jess were carrying.

"They used to use candles, but in the dry autumn woods, those became seen as a fire hazard," Mallory said. "Now they use glowsticks. Safer, really."

"Still polluting," Jess said. "Plastics."

"Pshaw," Mallory said. "It's a tradeoff—forest fires or using plastics, Jess."

"I'm just saying," Jess said. "Plastic lasts forever."

"Nothing lasts forever," Mallory said.

"Plastic does," Jess said.

They passed a wooden shack, a tall and narrow thing painted with the three interlocking circles.

"What's that?" Austin asked. "Is that an outhouse?"

"Um, no," Mallory said. "It's for the Grove."

"What, like a toolshed?" Jake asked.

"Exactly, Jake," Mallory said. "Like a toolshed."

"For tools," Jake said, laughing.

"I don't think you'd fit, Jake," Jess said, laughing at him.

Austin glanced over his shoulder and could see other people were arriving. Several cars pulling up along the road, and people getting out, some with flashlights, some with lanterns, others with glowsticks. The points of light marked their position. He wondered if they were tourists like they were.

"Was it like this when you went, Mal?" Austin asked.

"It rained the whole weekend before, so it was sloppy," Mallory said. "It was muddy and messy and unseasonably hot. Can you believe it? You guys are lucky. It's at least dry and mostly comfortable."

"I'll take that," Austin said.

Up ahead, he could see a clearing in the woods, demarcated by lit torches that were on tall stakes. They threw off a welcome light, despite the dancing the flames made, which caused the shadows to play at every turn.

There was a pavilion tent ahead of the grove, a large one with some park benches placed. Upon those benches were some onlookers sitting, and Austin could see there were robed people ringed around the grove. He saw some white trucks parked in the background, near what looked like a gravel road that apparently led up from Route 219.

The Sacred Grove itself was large—it looked like it was maybe a hundred yards in diameter. The trees around it stood like sentinels, and he could make out Exemplars forming a ring around the grove. Their masked, conical-hatted selves were particularly distinct. Each of the Exemplars had a drum they were playing.

"A drum circle," Austin said. "Great."

Mallory was talking to some of the acolytes and deacons, who were pleased to see her, seemed to know her. All of the people here had their faces painted white and blue—like white faces with blue around the lips and eyes. Some of them had stripes of blue paint that bisected their faces, like from forehead to chin.

"Face-painting," Jake said. "Fuck."

"Ooh, I want to do that," Jess said, elbowing her way to a table where some acolytes were apparently applying the face paint.

Mallory shook hands with the acolytes and talked quickly with them. Austin could see adjacent to the pavilion tent was a table upon which sat scores of paper cups, tended by a smiling acolyte, a young woman with long blond hair tied back in a braid. Her face was painted white with the horizontal blue stripe across her eyes.

It was the center of the Sacred Grove that caught Austin's eye most of all, for within it was a preponderance of blue mushrooms—they looked like Fly Agarics, only they were blue instead of red. They were all over the place, in thick clusters. The blue mushrooms were beautiful in the moonlight, and Jess gasped, drunkenly photographing them with her phone, guided by a white-faced acolyte who kept her from stepping on the mushrooms.

Also in the center of the grove were three dark wooden posts, arranged in relatively close proximity to one another. Three lanterns had been placed atop them, and they threw off a lonely, quavering light. Nearby was an idol of the Grey Lady, illuminated by dozens of candles—blue, white, pink, green, black, brown, orange, yellow, tan—all flicking flames within the glass that held them, giving a sinister cast to the idol.

"That is a whole lot of fucking mushrooms," Jake said.

"The Lady sheds Her tears aplenty," said Mona Templeton, having appeared beside them, startling Austin. She was wearing a white cassock with a blue stole stitched with the three-circle motif in a long row that ran down both halves of the stole. She had a white-painted face with both the vertical stripe and horizontal stripe in blue, as well as blue lips. She wore a woven diadem that appeared to have been made of dried vine and sticks that rose from it in a crest.

"Wow, that's quite a look," Austin said. Mona only smiled, her painted visage making him nervous.

"She weeps for you, and She weeps for me. She weeps for us all. Welcome, young man. Welcome all of you. Our service begins in a quarter hour. Those of you who wish to dance with the Lady, I urge you to queue up at the table to drink deep of Her Tears," Mona said.

"The Kool-Aid," Jake said.

"Oh, yeah," Mona said, touching his shoulder, giving him a squeeze. "Please, by all means, guests. Give our acolytes your tickets at the table and drink your fill. *La Signora* is with us tonight, and the moon itself blesses us from the heavens."

Mona gestured skyward, and Austin turned his gaze up to the moon, which looked positively huge overhead. Mona walked to some other guests, her honey-rich voice caressing them as it had Austin. She had a wonderful speaking voice. Her woven stick-crown made her even taller.

Mallory walked over, rapping Austin on the shoulder as the Twins got in line for the Lady's Tears. She had a lateral line of white paint across her eyes she'd scored at the table and had reapplied her blue lipstick. Jess was put out that they hadn't let her get her own face painted.

"That blows," Jess said. "I wanted to get my face painted."

"Poor Jess," Jake said, mocking her. "Baby can't get her face painted."

"I take back what I said earlier. You really should partake, Austin," Mallory said, smiling charmingly at Austin. "You will never be the same, I promise you that."

"Gosh, you make it sound so tempting," Austin said. "But I feel like I should keep my wits about me. I want to capture this."

He held up his phone.

Another woman approached, a tall, dark-haired woman with strong features not unlike Mona's. Mona, seeing her, walked over and embraced her. Both women hugged one another for a long moment. The woman's face paint was half-white with blue about her eyes in daggerlike slashes that could have been tears, only they were far more angular, working with her cheekbones. The blue about her eyes went to her forehead, while the white was around her cheeks and mouth, except for the blue lips.

"Maura," Mona said. "We were so worried you wouldn't make it."

"And yet here I am," Maura said. "Are Daddy and Lionel here?"

"On their way," Mona said.

"I brought guests," Maura said. "Carlos, Santino, come here. Say hi to my sister."

Two men walked reluctantly over, one a handsome, longer-haired young man, the other a more portly, older man with a hefty mustache. They greeted her with what Austin thought was rather forced collegiality. Both men looked ill-used, being covered in blood, dust, and dirt.

"This is my sister, Mona, the High Priestess of our little order," Maura said.

"Grigianists," Austin said, making both Templetons turn and look at him. Mallory looked like she wanted to die right there.

"Pardon me?" Mona said. Austin cleared his throat.

"I wanted to come up with a name for you," Austin said. "I said Grigianists worked. Grigianity. See?"

Mona and Maura laughed, which, upon their painted faces, looked ghastly to Austin.

"Oh, how charming," Mona said, touching Austin's cheek. "Grigianists. Where on earth would you have come up with that?"

"*La Signora Grigia*," Austin said. "It made sense. Greys. The Grey Lady. All of that."

"You are hilarious," Maura said. "That's funny. Who brought you, young man?"

"Uh, I came with Mallory," Austin said. "Say, those guys look kind of roughed up. Are they okay?"

Maura looked over at the two men, who gazed forlornly back at her.

"Workmen," Maura said. "They're fine. Right, fellas? Tell him you're fine."

"We're fine," both men said, weirding Austin out even more. They looked anything but fine to him. Mona piped up.

"Mallory Tilton," Mona said, stroking Mallory's mane of hair. "I remember you from last year. You came back to us."

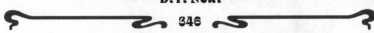
"Yes," Mallory said. "I brought friends. Austin Adams, here. And the Jordan Twins—Jess and Jake. They're over there, getting Lady's Tears."

Mona beamed at her, and even Maura cracked a smile.

"Industrious girl," Mona said. "I'm so proud of you. Triplets last year, twins this year. How delightful."

"I aim to please," Mallory said.

"And you have," Mona said, hugging her. "The Lady will be so pleased with you."

"Carlos, Santino," Maura said, her voice cracking whip-like, startling Austin. "Get in line. You two are drinking Lady's Tears."

Austin thought the men moved stiffly, like they were ill-at-ease and mutely resistant to the woman's commanding tone. She looked at them both.

"Do it," Maura said, and the two men shuffled into the line, sweat pouring down their faces. She saw Austin noticing and turned her attention to him. "Don't worry about them, Austin. They've had a very busy day."

And, incredibly, Austin felt his anxiety leave him. Whatever concern he had for the two oddly out-of-place men evaporated moments after the words left her mouth.

"Grigianity," Mona said, laughing again. "That's so charmingly quaint. We are not Grigianists, Austin. We follow the Lady wherever She takes us. We don't take a name because we don't need a name. We simply are Her chosen people."

"A cult still needs a name," Austin said.

"A cult," Mona said. "Is that how you see us?"

"It's what you are," Austin said.

Having these two tall Templeton women looking him in the eye was intimidating, but he held his ground. He liked philosophical discussions, even with semi-terrifying cult leaders. "How'd it begin?"

Mona's smile never wavered.

"Lucretia Bianchi founded our faith," Mona said. "She had a vision in the forest, a vision of the Lady as She presided over the deaths of fellow settlers who had strayed too far from the safety of Fort Lynch. There she created the beating heart of our religion. She and great-great grandfather, Ned Templeton I. They created it between them. Way out here, where no one could bother them. Far from what was called civilization at the time.

In what few forests still remained in Pennsylvania in the 1890s, they found the Lady, and She found them. You will understand before our Midnight Service ends, young man."

"You should listen to the Eminence, Austin," Mallory said, and seeing her painted face, hearing that, Austin's heart sank. Mallory was clearly part of the cult. He parsed it out in his head. She'd mostly hidden it, seemed like herself, but that simple word—"Eminence"—hit him like a hammer.

"You're part of it, aren't you?" Austin asked.

"I saw something amazing when I was here last year, Austin," Mallory said. "You can see it, too. You can see Her. And, more importantly, She can see you. Let Her see you."

Mona and Maura looked on, amused.

"I invited you all to the Sacred Grove, Austin," Mona said. "Mallory is a bright light among us. She holds so much promise. You're so lucky to be her good friend, Austin. You are her good friend, aren't you?"

"I am," Austin said, although it wounded him to say so. He wanted to get the Twins and himself out of there. Mallory's big eyes went soft.

"And I'm yours, Austin," Mallory said.

"Friends are the gifts we give ourselves," Mona said. "And speaking of friends, is that Dr. Emily Carver I see?"

Austin looked and saw the woman who'd been with Ash at that painful rebuff in front of the Grand. She recognized him and warily accepted Mona's embrace.

"Everybody, this is Dr. Emily Carver, mycologist from California," Mona said. "All the way from faraway California they are coming to see us, can you believe it? Our very special guest tonight."

Emily was shocked to see Maura standing there, speaking quietly to two men who were with her, two men busy drinking down the Lady's Tears.

"Maura?" Emily asked.

"In the flesh," Maura said. "I'm so sorry your lunch was spoiled with Logan today."

"How did you get away?" Emily asked.

"I'm very persuasive when I want to be," Maura said. "The Lady was with me."

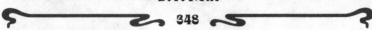
"The Lady is with us all tonight," Mona said, her eyes sparkling in the torchlight. Her face was almost luminescent from the paint, her eyes darkened by the blue.

Emily didn't know what to make of that, but when she saw all of the Lady's Tears *Amanitas* in the grove, she almost fell over.

"Oh, my," Emily said. Mona and Maura followed her gaze and smiled to each other when Emily walked over to the fungi. "So many of these strange fungi and growing so big."

She reached out and touched them. Their caps were as big as tea saucers, some of them bigger, still, and the stalks were thicker than two of her fingers, maybe three. She took pictures with her phone camera, catching them from various angles.

"How do they grow?" Emily asked.

"You'll see soon enough," Mona said. "We harvest from our Sacred Groves, and we feed the mycelium what it needs. We feed our ever-hungry Lady."

Emily could not believe the profligate growth of the fungi. It was like what she'd seen in the Temple, only far greater.

"The winter snows will come, but we will have our harvest well before then," Maura said, over Emily's other shoulder.

Mona went to greet some other people who arrived, while Maura supervised the two men she'd brought with her, making them finish drinking down the Lady's Tears. The Twins had already drunk down their cups. Mallory took Austin's hand, but he shook free of it.

"What the hell is going on, Mal? Honestly?"

Mallory just sighed.

"The Lady is going to be here with us tonight," Mallory said. "At midnight. I wish you'd drink the Tears, Austin. You're going to miss it. You're going to miss Her. And that makes me sad."

"I don't see *you* drinking anything," Austin said.

Mallory just shook her head.

"I already saw Her," Mallory said. "Last year. I saw Her, and She saw me. She's so beautiful. You have no idea how beautiful. You can't even imagine. There are no words. There are only feelings, sights, sounds, sensations."

More people were arriving, a blend of select groups of tourists and cult acolytes, mostly delineated by the painted faces—cultists all came with painted faces, tourists came as themselves. The drums kept sounding, that inexorably steady beat, over and over—*thrum, thrum, thrum, thrum.*

Jess walked over, hugging Mallory and Austin both.

"I drank all the Tears," Jess said. "Oh, man. So good."

"My stomach's in knots, but it's alright," Jake said, giving them a thumb's up.

Mallory pointed to a cauldron at the far side of the Grove, tended by a half-dozen acolytes, who were alternately stirring and pouring more of the Tears into cups which ended up on the tables.

Jake laughed nervously.

"I'm kind of scared," Jake said.

"Don't be," Mallory said. "There's nothing to be afraid of."

Austin looked out at all of the blue mushrooms, which grew thickly in the grove and had captivated Dr. Carver.

"What do they feed on?" Austin asked. "What makes them grow?"

"They feed on dead things," Mallory said. "Like all fungi. They break down dead things."

"Alright," Austin said. Then he saw him. Fun Gus. The damned clown was walking up the trail, bearing a lantern and smoking a cigar. It was him, without a doubt. And worse, people were happy to see him. Fun Gus made the rounds, shaking hands with his white gloves.

Austin wanted to run off into the woods and never look back.

"Hey, am I late?" Fun Gus asked, taking out his horn and giving it a quick honk. Mona and Maura turned and saw him, smiling. They walked over, giving him a hug.

"Never," Mona said. "We are glad you made it, Uncle."

"Wouldn't miss it," Fun Gus said. "Especially this year, Tricky Mona."

Mona smiled and left the clown, who was surveying the grove with his shining eyes. Austin wanted to hide, but there was nowhere to go. Like a lighthouse the clown was, panning and scanning until his eyes settled on Austin.

"Sunshine, you made it!" Fun Gus said, walking right up to him, holding out a white-gloved hand that Austin wouldn't shake. Mallory was thrilled.

"Fun Gus!" Mallory said, hugging him. "Totes glad you're here."

The clown looked at the Twins, who were clutching their heads and swaying, sweating in the bright moonlight.

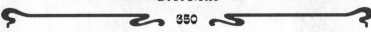
"They dosed, I take it?" Fun Gus said.

"They did," Mallory said. She side-eyed Austin.

"What about Fun Guy here?"

Mallory shook her head sadly.

"What's the matter, Fun Guy?" the clown said. "You too good for us heathens? The forest give you the heebie-jeebies? Could be way worse, Sporto, let me tell you. We could be in a damned cornfield."

Fun Gus laughed and honked his horn three times.

"But seriously, get in line," Fun Gus said, hovering over Austin. "You didn't come all this way to, what, sit and spectate? How will you see the Lady if you're out here by your lonesome?"

Austin wasn't about to let the fucking clown bully him once again.

"I'm not doing it," Austin said. "I'm minding my friends."

"So, you've decided," Fun Gus asked. "That's it? You made your decision?"

"Is this it? Is this the decision?" Austin said. Fun Gus laughed, slapping him on the shoulder.

"Is it? Who can say, who can say? Maybe I was just clowning around," Fun Gus said. The mocking clown went to his other pocket, but Mallory stopped him, holding his arm.

"Austin's with me, Fun Gus," Mallory said. "And I already talked to the Eminence. He's with me, okay?"

"The Eminence?" Fun Gus said. "Oh, jeepers creepers, yeah, well, you know I wouldn't dream of crossing Tricky Mona or Gimme Maura. Is Big Baddy Daddy here, yet? Or His Worship, the Mayor?"

"Not yet, Uncle," Mona said. "They're on their way."

The clown went slack with disapproval.

"They're pushing it right to the limit, aren't they?" Fun Gus said. "It's almost midnight, goddammit."

Another group of people had made the ascent, and Austin could see it was the Mayor and Ned Templeton IV, as well as a dozen aides accompanying them. They all wore three-circle lapel pins and came with white-painted faces and blue lips.

"Daddy!" Mona and Maura said at the same time, running up and hugging him. The silver-haired patriarch of the family accepted their hugs and returned them benevolently. He wore a diadem of woven vine inset with a half-dozen sticks.

"My lovely girls," Ned said. "I'm so happy you're with us, safe and sound, Maura."

"Of course, Daddy," Maura said. "I wouldn't let anything keep me from being here."

"Hey, don't I get a hug, Eddie?" Fun Gus asked.

"You do *not*, Augustus," Ned said. "You stay right where you are."

"Yeah, Uncle Gus," Lionel said. "No clowning tonight."

"Good thing we're out in the woods, then, because you two are sticks in the mud," Fun Gus said.

Austin's head reeled, having finally caught up with what he'd been seeing. Even the fucking clown was a Templeton? Why in the hell would anybody even willingly be a clown performer if he came from the kind of money the Templetons clearly had? Fun Gus seemed to notice him stewing on it.

"Every family has its black sheep, am I right?" Fun Gus said. "My big brother, Ned Bundy, over there, always thought I was a clown. He always did. I just rub it in his face for kicks. I coulda been him. He coulda been me. We coulda been us. Coulda-woulda-shoulda-alakazam!"

Fun Gus made mocking magic hands with his white gloves, fingers trembling, his mouth agape. Ned ignored him and moved into the grove proper with the others.

"My own brother cursed me," Fun Gus said. "Can you believe that, Fun Guy? 'You're always clowning, Augustus, so a clown you'll always be.' He said to me. And here I am. Thirty years later, here I am. I'll be damned, right?"

He honked his horn in Austin's face once, twice, thrice, and laughed.

"I laugh so hard I could cry, I tellya," Fun Gus said. "You're lucky you're with her, Fun Guy. Or you'd have had to have words with my pocket pal, Twitchy. Alright, I gotta go do my part for Farmer Ned. See you on the flip side of infinity, Kiddies."

Fun Gus stomped after the others, leaving Austin even more confused than he'd been moments before. His inebriated mind only picked up about half of what he'd just heard, and the half he retained he couldn't fully figure out.

"What directly the fuck was all of that about, Mal?" Austin asked. "Fun Gus is a Templeton?"

"Yes," Mallory said. "I found that out last year."

"You didn't tell me," Austin said. "Like earlier. All the time I was going on about him, you just let me go on."

Mallory squeezed his arm.

Dr. Carver had absconded to the Table of Tears, took one of the cups in her hand.

"In for a penny, in for a pound," she said. It wasn't a laboratory setting by any means, but she felt she had to at least experience it for herself. She had to know. She took a breath and took a drink. Then she drank the rest of it down, crumpling the empty cup and handing it to a nearby acolyte, who disposed of it in a nearby plastic trash bag.

*Ash, I drank the Tears, she texted.*

*Yeah, I saw, Ash texted back. If something happens...*

*I know.*

"Austin, you need to drink the Lady's Tears," Mallory said. "Like now. The ritual's almost started."

She glanced at her phone. It was five minutes to midnight, and Austin saw that the Templetons were arranging themselves around the circle of the grove—Ned was at the southernmost part, near them, his back to them. Mona and Maura were at two equidistant points on the north, and Lionel and Fun Gus were at east and west, respectively, facing inward.

"Five corners," Austin said. "Points of a star?"

"Smart guy," Mallory said. "I love how smart you are, Austin. If you're really smart, you'll drink the Lady's Tears before She comes."

The drummers kept drumming, shifting to a cadence like the beating of a heart—*lub-dub, lub-dub, lub-dub.* The Exemplars kept the beat, and Austin could hear music playing, like from a synthesizer. He turned and could see a young woman playing a keyboard, striking tunes that were mysterious and macabre, haunting music. For a split second, he thought it was Ash, but then realized it wasn't her.

"Everyone prepare," Mona said.

"They're a coven of witches?" Austin said.

"Yes, yes," Mallory said. "They're witches. Will you drink the Lady's Tears already, Austin? Please."

"They're fucking witches?" Austin said. "Not, like, Wiccans?"

"True-blue witches, Austin," Mallory said. "Like legit."

"Like a coven?" Austin said.

"Jesus Christ, Austin, yes," Mallory said. "What did I just say? Yes. A fucking coven."

The Twins were starting to feel the effects of the concoction they'd drunk already, were gape-mouthed and sweating, Jake dry-heaving, Jess puking.

Acolytes were walking around the attendees, carrying blue silk blindfolds stitched with the three-circle motif in white or silver, Austin could not tell in the moonlight.

He saw Mona and Maura don their blindfolds, saw the Mayor and Fun Gus put on theirs, saw Ned Templeton put on his, tying it fast.

"Last chance, Austin," Mallory said. She held a cup in one hand, a blindfold in the other. "She's coming. You have to decide."

Austin made his decision, and he ran away, even as Mallory called after him, begging him to stay.

# PART FOUR: NEVER WHERE

# 1

**Somewhere in the distant dark, the clock tower sounded,** and Ned Templeton spoke in the Sacred Grove, his voice sonorous and powerfully commanding in the full moonlight.

"Mother, we are here for You again," Ned said. "As we have always been, year after year, decade after decade, century after century. We, Your humble servants and children. We do You honor beneath the light of the midnight moon, as You have always guided us."

Emily could feel the Lady's Tears welling up inside her, the heroic dose she'd taken, the citrus taste of it from the deep cup the acolyte had handed her. She had to see it through, even as her stomach did flips. It had been perhaps a rash move on her part, but she'd wanted to take the plunge, all the same. To know the effects of the Lady's Tears herself.

"This Festival has been good to us, Great Lady," Maura said. "We have fed You well, My Lady. Ninety souls we have fed to the Cursed Earth, Lady. By our hands and theirs, they have given themselves to You over these few days."

The light of the torches shifted and swayed in halo nimbuses, and Emily thought their voices were beginning to echo.

"A bountiful harvest taken in Your name, *Signora*," Mona said, holding her arms up high, a gesture shared by her sister, by her brother, uncle, and father. "We know how You hunger, and we strive to feed You. Give us a sign, *Signora*. Are You sated, or do You require more sustenance?"

Emily heard the ground rumble, could see the blue *Amanitas* tremble in the Sacred Grove, swelling and receding. They were, to her intoxicated eyes, starting to glow. She saw points of light flying from them in pencil-thin white beams.

"She wants more," Maura said. "She wants more. How many more, *Signora*?"

"Nine more," Lionel said. "Nine."

"Nine," Fun Gus said. "Fine."

"Nine," Ned said.

"Nine," Maura said.

"Nine," Mona said.

"I have two," Maura said. "Two more Red Deaths to give You life, My Lady."

"I brought four," Lionel said.

"That's six," Ned said. "I count six."

"I brought one," Fun Gus said.

"I brought two," Mallory said. "Two for You, My Lady."

The Templetons turned their blindfolded faces outside the circle at the interruption. Emily was seeing the radiant light in swirling ropes of luminescent blue that was reaching for the moon overhead. To Emily's eyes, the tenebrous cables would catch the moon and hold it fast in minutes that might drag on for an eternity.

"Who speaks?" Ned asked. "Who speaks from beyond our sacred circle?"

"Mallory Tilton," Mallory said. "I bring two."

"You are not part of our covenant," Ned said.

"An aspirant, Daddy," Mona said.

"Tonight is too important for such things," Ned said.

"Exemplars," Mona said. "Fetch the offerings."

The masked Exemplars quickly grabbed people from the crowd of onlookers, and Emily could see the uncomprehending Jordan Twins being led into the sacrificial circle, joined by Mallory. As her eyes blurred, she could see dozens of people, mirrored versions of the ones who were there, outlined in rainbow colors, like they'd been carved from opal.

"She is not yet here," Mona said. "She has not seen us."

"I'll start," Fun Gus said, drawing a long, blue-handled switchblade from his pocket, which he flicked open. "Bring Lilli Trujillo. Right here. I can't break the circle. Bring her to me."

He held out his free, white-gloved hand, while Exemplars brought a screaming Lilli to them, having to restrain her.

"Somebody gave her the Tears, didn't they?" Fun Gus said.

"Yes," one of the acolytes said. "She fought, but we made her drink."

"Someone stop her thrashing then," Fun Gus said. "Christamighty."

"Don't blaspheme, Augustus," Ned said.

"Yeah, yeah," Fun Gus said. "Is she in reach, yet? Come on, people. Can't keep the Lady waiting."

The Exemplars brought Lilli in reach, the clown's grasping gloved hand finding her top knot and holding her fast while she shrieked and wailed in rapid-fire Spanish.

"Accept my gift, Lady," Fun Gus said, as ceremoniously as he was able. "That this caterwauling wildcat of a woman might bring You sustenance. Will you SHUT IT?"

His yell sounded throughout the grove, momentarily silencing Lilli.

"You sick bastard," Lilli said. "I curse you."

"Curses! Curses? Oh, puh-leeze. Show her what I think of curses, Twitchy," Fun Gus said, slitting her throat with his switchblade. She gasped, her blood spraying, her thrashing became more spasmodic as she choked on her own blood, it splashing on his white gloves.

Fun Gus turned his blindfolded face upward, outward, and yelled to the others.

"There, I did my part. Hook her to the hitching post, already."

He held the bloody switchblade up for all who weren't wearing blindfolds to see. Emily thought the knife was slithering in his hand, as he wiped off the blood on his red sleeve and stuffed it in his pocket. It looked like a serpent, like a chromium cobra to her eyes.

The Exemplars dragged the dying Lilli to one of the three mossy wooden posts and secured her arms to it with manacles. She sagged against the post, her blood having left a trail and pouring down on the ground from her bowed head as she stilled. Someone laid a woven vine crown upon her head, a simple thing.

Lionel's four went somewhat easier, having been secured by a half-dozen Exemplars who held them fast. The Mayor said something to them, and their struggles ceased. They went meekly, without protest, as if under some enchantment Emily could not understand.

"By Your godly grace I find You," Lionel said, holding out a curved ceremonial knife with a horn handle. He said it each time he slit a throat. As the Tears hit Emily harder, she was

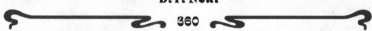
finding it harder to concentrate, to see what she was seeing. She thought she might be floating away, like a balloon.

Lionel's sacrifices were anchored to their own posts, and their blood ran aplenty on the ground as their bodies slumped. Each was crowned with their own unassuming vine diadem.

Emily could see the sacrifices being led into the heart of the mushrooms, the Twins, one of them, the girl, wearing a Cat in the Hat hat, looking bewildered. Mallory, their friend, stood before them.

"I beg of you, Eminence, let me sacrifice these two. Jess and Jake Jordan," Mallory said.

"Flying's a small sacrifice," Jess said. "Oh, my god, am I ever flying."

"There are thirteen of you, Mal," Jake said. "Robed in blue and white. Moonlight masquerade, sinister kisses."

Mona turned her blindfolded face in the direction of Mallory, the three circles over her eyes. Mallory wore her own blindfold, kept her eyes cast down.

"You have been good to us, Mallory," Mona said. "Last year, she brought three to the Lady. Three sisters, a powerful bond, and the Lady was gladdened by her sacrifice. She did not know it then, but she knows it now. In the service of the Lady, she is exemplary."

"She is exemplary," the Exemplars said, behind their masks.

"To give and give again, to take not just three, but three and two, we give our blessings to you," Mona said.

"We give our blessings to you," Maura said.

"We give our blessings to you," Lionel said.

"Sure, yeah, God bless you," Fun Gus said.

"We give our blessings to you," Ned said. "Say it properly, Augustus."

"We give our blessings to you," Fun Gus said, growling, after a pause.

"I'm flying," Jess said. "Mal, Jake, I can see Her. I can see Her. In the sky. High in the sky."

"The Lady is watching. We have opened Her eyes," Mona said. "Tell us, Child. Tell us what you see."

Emily turned her eyes skyward, trying to see what Jess Jordan was seeing. She saw the thick blue radiant tentacles, like cosmic cables, winding the moon in their grasp, binding the Earth to it. And, incredibly, she saw the Grey Lady.

She was massive, coldly implacable. A face that might have been stone or alabaster, beautiful beyond beauty, impenetrable, with the brightest, bluest eyes she'd ever seen. They were like twin blue suns, phosphorescent behind the motionless masks of her face. Her hair wasn't hair at all, but a towering column of shelf fungi, bone-white with shades of grey. She was watching from above and beyond, making her way on the blue tubules that flowed out from the Sacred Grove in a twirling, swirling torrent of light and color.

"I see Her," Emily said. "The Goddess. I see Her in the sky."

"Behold *La Signora Grigia*," Mona said. "Only those touched by the Lady's Tears can see Her without going mad."

"I see Her," Jess cried, jumping up and down and pointing skyward, looking ludicrous in her tall hat. "I see Her! Jake, do you see Her?"

"Brace for the Lady's Kiss," Mona said. "Stay your hand, Mallory, we must know."

Mallory waited, having pulled a curved knife from a cargo pocket.

"I don't see Her," Jake said. "What am I looking for, Jess?"

"She's right there," Jess said, pointing. "She's so beautiful. Like a goddess-angel."

Jake craned his neck, looking up, cursing.

"All I see is the moon," Jake said. "The moon is smiling at me. It's talking to me. It's telling me I need to run."

Mallory looked uncertain, gripping the slippery knife in her hand, like a fish it now was to Emily's eyes, a silver fish, a silverfish, twisting and turning, threatening to slip from her grasp.

"What do I do, Eminence?" Mallory asked.

"Wait," Mona said. "We must wait for the Lady's Kiss. If She spurns them, your knife may return them to the Cursed Earth. But not yet and not before."

The drums of the Exemplars beat faster: *lub-dub, lub-dub, lubdub, lubdub, LUBDUB.* The frenetic beat of the drums built toward a climax, a frenzy, and Emily could see that the Exemplars all turned their backs to the circle, even as they kept playing.

"She's kissing me!" Jess said. "It's like a thousand snow-flakes falling."

And Emily could see them, the Grey Lady blowing some-thing down upon them, and she thought they could look like

snowflakes to the uninitiated, but to her, they looked like spores. Celestial spores, floating down from the Grey Lady's lips to them, between worlds or dimensions, she could not be certain anymore.

"I feel them," Jess said. "Jake, do you feel them? They're like angelic ice. I'm covered in them."

"I feel them," Jake said. "Yeah, iceballs on my skin. All over me. Christ."

"Don't blaspheme," Ned Templeton said, almost grandfatherly in tone.

"Fuck," Jake said. "I'm shivering."

"They have borne the Lady's Kiss," Mona said. "She has seen them, as they have seen Her. Mallory, take them from the circle. Walk the newborn babes from the circle and hold them close to you, Exemplar. You have earned your right to walk among us."

"Exemplar!" Maura said.

"Exemplar!" Lionel said.

"What they said," Fun Gus said. "Brava."

"Say it properly, Augustus," Ned said.

"Fine, Eddie. Exemplar!" Fun Gus said.

"Exemplar!" Ned said.

"Exemplar!" the Exemplars said, raising their fists in the air, as Mallory walked the Twins out of the circle.

"A stay of execution," Mona said. "We must have two more, or the Lady will go hungry, and Her wrath will descend upon us all."

Emily watched the Exemplars pull two more people from the onlookers, startled souls who she did not recognize. A man and a woman, middle-aged. They were swimming deep in the Lady's Tears, did not even fully comprehend what was happening to them.

"Do you see Her?" Mona asked. "Does She see you?"

"I see the moon, the stars, the everlasting sky," the woman said, raising her hands to embrace it.

"I see the trees and the breeze that blows through it," the man said. "I see the wind dancing lively through the branches."

Mona called out to the Exemplars, who brought the couple to her. She drew her own curved knife from the folds of her robe and reached out blindly, guided by the Exemplars.

"To the Cursed Earth you shall go, where we all belong," Mona said.

"Where we all belong," the others present said.

She cut quickly and cleanly, slitting the woman's throat, her blood blasting out of her, spattering on Mona, who accepted it without flinching. The Exemplars pulled the woman to an open spot on the posts and hooked her to it, where she could bleed out and die. A crown of vines was set upon her head as she died.

From Emily's perspective, the blood was a shower of sparks, flashing bright red-orange, lighting everything they touched on fire.

"The man," Mona said. "Give me the man."

"But I see the sky," the man said. "Eminence, I see the sky itself. Like veined marble, white as night."

"I know, my son," Mona said, resting her free hand atop his head. The Exemplars held him fast. She raised the knife and slit his throat without another word, and the man gushed blood on her, which fell to the ground below, hitting some of the *Amanitas*.

"Sparks," Emily said. "Cascading sparks."

He was secured to his post, next to the woman, where he could bleed to death undisturbed. A vine crown was set upon his head.

"The Lady's Tears fall faster, now," Maura said. "How She hungers, for I bring the final two to Her."

Maura stepped forward, and the men strained and sweated, while Maura pulled a wicked curved knife that had hung from her side. To Emily's eyes, the curved knife was like a silvery claw from some great beast. She was both afraid and mesmerized by what she was seeing, unsure if she was even seeing what was unfolding before her.

"I give You these gifts, My Lady," Maura said. "Don't move, *Conejito* and Santino. Know that your hearts, minds, bodies, and souls belong to the Lady, now."

Emily could see the men straining against their fate, but somehow they were held fast by Maura's words. It was incomprehensible to her, but she could see the Lady skulking overhead, even nearer, now, impossibly massive.

She wore the mycelium like a wedding gown, the tendrils of the hyphae like intertwined threads that held her fast. The Grey Lady was very close, now, her long grey-white arms reaching for the Sacred Grove, her long fingers tapering into claws of the most perfect white, like teeth on the tips of her fingers.

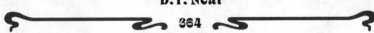
Her cruelly beautiful face bore the barest hint of a smile on full, blue lips. Emily could see the three circles on her forehead, a sacred-profane glyph, a sigil the hearkened slaughter, decay, and death.

Maura reached blindly for the men, putting her hand atop the balding head of the smaller man. She raised the knife and slit his throat, his blood gushing as he collapsed. The man's blood baptized her, festooning the clothes she wore, even as the bloodied Exemplars marched him to his spot on the posts, and secured him, crowning him as the others had been crowned.

"Santino," the other man, the pretty man, said. "I'm sorry, Brother."

Bloody Maura put her hand in the other man's hair and held him fast. The blood upon her glowed to Emily's eyes, an almost incendiary red, like flowing magma. All of the blood glowed like that.

"This is the end of the journey for you, my lovely *Conejito*," Maura said. "*Soy más malvada de lo que podrías ser. No olvides que te lo advertí.*"

She slit his throat before he could say anything, and the man bled out in front of her, his blood falling on the leaves and ground and on Maura, as well.

Emily gasped at the sight of it, for his death—if death it was—shined with even more sparks and light, and the Grey Lady overhead swooped down to lay claim to his soul—if soul it was—and caught it in her clawlike hands before it could fly free. She fed upon it, drawing it into Her.

As he was tethered to his spot on the posts and crowned, Mona spoke again.

"Mother, we have given You the nine more You required," Mona said. "We beg that You come to us and guide us."

And the drums beat faster. Emily could see *La Signora* riding the blue tendrils between the moon and the Earth, impregnating the *Amanitas* in the Sacred Grove, filling them with Her unholy light. It was an unfamiliar word—unholy—but it was the only word that came to Emily as she looked hard upon it.

"She has accepted our sacrifices," Mona said. "She comes to us."

"For 50 years, we have fed them to the ground for You in our Festival, My Lady," Ned said. "For far longer, we have worshipped You in the wood, delivering our gifts to You. We ask

that You come to us on this holy night and become one with our world."

The ground swelled, and Emily could see the monstrous spirit of *La Signora* flowing from the sky to the ground itself in a cascading blue-white wave, consuming the bloody bodies of the fallen as they hung on the posts, who swiftly rotted into nonexistence, collapsing in on themselves into oblivion.

Emily wouldn't have believed it if she hadn't seen it herself, but one moment, there were silhouetted bodies clustered like unholy fruit upon the posts, and a moment later, they had fallen into ruination and corruption, and a fresh crop of blue-capped *Amanitas* grew where they had been only just before, amid a tangle of vine crowns.

She could see the shape of their bodies in the Lady's Tear Agarics that had grown, like the mockery of their bodies in the fungi, and she realized that all of the fungi that grew here had grown from similar sacrifices, from countless nights before, year after year.

The earth buckled and strained, and from the bowels of it, within the depths of the Sacred Grove, the Grey Lady emerged. It was like a birth, Emily imagined, watching Her great form strain and stretch, pulling Herself from the ground, having found the number of sacrifices sufficient to Her incomprehensible needs. She emerged from the earth like a monstrous and eager bride in a procession, the mycelium train tugging at Her as She went from the simply spiritual to the corporeal and tangible.

As She passed between this world and Her own, She formed a basin on the land itself. A great pulse of blue-white light blasted away from Her, enveloping them all in Her unholy radiance. It was horrific and beautiful at the same time, and Emily understood why only those who'd drunk the Lady's Tears could gaze upon the wonder. The Grey Lady Herself cried cerulean tears, which ran down Her gorgeous face, filling the basin beneath Her.

From where the pulse of light had passed, Emily saw the ground had turned to white, like snow, and the surrounding trees had become white as well, festooned with fungi that clung and hung from the branches in otherworldly abundance.

"She is with us," Mona cried, joined by Maura. The two sisters cried out in unison, cries of ecstasy and terror. Ned Templeton spoke up.

"We have delivered unto you, Mother," Ned said. "We have threaded the path."

"More than that, Eddie," Fun Gus said. "Since Lucky Lucretia."

"Be silent, Clown," Ned said. "Mother, forgive us, Your servants. We have ever toiled on Your behalf. As we have asked You a thousand times, are there any here whom You would take as Your own?"

And then Ned and Lionel began to cry out and scream, holding their arms up higher still, as if grasping the heavens themselves, enrobed as they were in the blue-white light thrown off by the Lady. Unable to see, but only to hear, Mona and Maura joined their father and brother's screaming, crying out in ecstasy to the Lady.

Emily thought the Grey Lady was at least nine feet tall, from the size of Her. Her blue tears fell down Her cheeks and touched the ground. Where they splashed beyond the basin, *Amanitas* spawned.

*"We are well-pleased by thine efforts on Our behalf,"* the Grey Lady said in words both heard and felt, Her voice both cold and comforting. Emily knew she should be afraid, but in her state, it simply was a wonder among wonders, this white phosphorous radiance before her. The Grey Lady loomed large within the Sacred Grove, her long-fingered claw-hands out in front of Her, as if She wanted to grasp all of them.

The Grey Lady brought Her hands to her blue lips and She blew another kiss at everyone present. And in that moment, Emily could see a torrent of those starlike spores flowing from Her, hovering in the air, traveling toward everyone present.

Emily saw the strange glowing spores flow from person to person, landing on them, in them. Each person who was so struck called out in wonder and terror at the Lady's Kiss.

She saw one of the motes approach her, and Emily tried to move out of its way, but saw that the thing adjusted, tracked her, heading inexorably toward her.

"I don't want this," Emily said.

*"Thou doth,"* the Lady said. *"Thou and I are to be one, for, among all present this night, I hath chosen thee."*

And before she could protest further, the sparkling spore landed against Emily's chest, sinking into her flesh as if it wasn't there. She could feel the Lady's touch within her, the hyphae even then winding their way inside her.

*"We are become one,"* the Lady said. *"It is My most sacred gift I can give."*

"My Lady," Emily said. "I'm a scientist."

*"I know what thou art, and who, Academician,"* the Grey Lady said. And Emily realized the Lady was standing before her, resplendent. How godlike She was, how toweringly complete. Up close, She smelled of freshly dug soil, of raindrops and tears and lightning. *"I have chosen thee, Dr. Emily Carver."*

Emily saw the Lady reach for her, Her long white hand-claws holding her fast, the icy touch of Her embrace more than Emily could comprehend. And the Lady leaned into her, Her bright blue glowing eyes very close to her own, now. They were the eyes of faraway suns, and Emily lost herself in those eyes.

*"Thou art mine,"* the Grey Lady said, and She showed Emily what the Lady's Kiss truly was, as She brought Her divine blue lips to her own.

# 2

**Austin hadn't stopped until he'd gotten back to the Grand.**
He had managed to compose himself and gotten an Uber using his Fungo App, feeling both afraid and ashamed. He should have rescued the Twins. He should have done something, should have stopped it.

Somehow.

Whatever "it" actually was.

But he'd been afraid.

What intoxication had remained of the Pub Crawl had sweated out of him, and he'd gone back to town lost in his own thoughts. The driver, a young man named Justin, had thankfully not talked to him too much. He drove a maroon sedan, what looked like a Lincoln of some sort.

"Not everybody can handle the Grove," Justin said. "There's no shame in it."

"The Grove?"

"Yeah," Justin said. "I know that's why you're out here. Only reason anybody's out here like this."

"I didn't know," Austin said. "I mean, I didn't know."

"Yeah," Justin said.

"I don't know how to be a hero," Austin said. "What was I supposed to do?"

"Lynchburg's not a home for heroes, Bro," Justin said. "All I'm saying. Heroes die here."

"Lucky me," Austin said. "Just drop me off at Grand and Main. I'll walk the rest of the way."

Justin smiled at him in the rearview mirror.

"You got it," he said.

Austin settled his account and got out. Things were quieter in town now that it was later, but there were still people about.

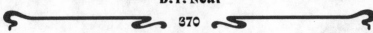
He pinged Jess and Jake, but nobody was responding. It was just dead silence. That wigged him out, and after awhile, he gave up trying. Mallory had probably murdered them or something.

That she was a secret cultist bothered him even more. He thought he knew her. But he'd never known a cultist before. Sure, maybe some kids in college who'd gotten into some cultish shit, but he'd never been friends with them. Mallory seemed so ordinary. Like ordinarily extraordinary. She was fun, up for anything.

But what he saw in that grove creeped him out.

He was grateful to be back within the comforting streetlights of Grand Avenue. Looking out into the dark, knowing his friends were out there in that creepy-ass grove, Austin got the chills. What a wafer-thin sliver of civilization this was, if you even wanted to call this place civilization. Austin became acutely aware of the three-circle motif that he was noticing everywhere. Etched into walls, carved in stone, represented in cornices or in signage, dangling from banners. It was *everywhere* in this town. He'd not noticed it early on because he'd been too busy being busy. But right then, after midnight, he was seeing it absolutely everywhere.

"Fuck," Austin said.

He made his way back to the Grand, his Pub Crawl beer mug gripped in his free hand, his head bowed. The Grand Hotel's marquee lights welcomed him, and in he went, seeing Cloris at the front desk, welcoming him with a big grin.

"Mr. Adams," Cloris said. "Having a good evening, I hope?"

"Jesus, don't you sleep?" Austin asked.

"None of us really sleep during the Festival weekend," Cloris said. "Small price to pay to make our guests feel welcome. Were you at the Grove?"

"You know about that?" Austin asked. He looked around, but the lobby was mostly quiet. The souvenir stand was empty, and it was just Cloris, looking as fresh and unfazed as ever.

"Of course I do," Cloris said. "I went when I turned 18. It's a rite of passage for everyone in the town. Everybody does it."

"What was it like?" Austin asked.

"You were there," Cloris said. "Maybe back a little early, but you get it, right? You drank the Lady's Tears, yeah?"

"No," Austin said. "I didn't."

Cloris gave an uncomprehendingly nervous laugh.

"Wow, really? You passed?"

"I did," Austin said. "Is that a mortal sin around here?"

"Nobody ever passes on it, honestly," Cloris said. "It's a chance to see the Lady. She's always watching, but we can't always see Her. Not directly, anyway. Her Tears help us see more clearly."

She was completely at ease talking about it. Austin thought the Lynchburg cultists were about the most open and agreeable cultists he'd ever known. It was insane.

"What do you see?" Austin asked.

"It's honestly hard to put into words," Cloris said. "It's like describing a sensation. A smell or something you hear. The same thing. The Lady is beyond everyday experience. I'm so sad for you, passing that up. This is the 50th year of the Festival, as you know. Although the Festivals have been going on long before then. It was 50 years ago when they decided to make them a more public thing, a way of letting the rest of the world know about them. After Woodstock, people just thought it was a good idea. Before my time, but who am I to argue?"

Austin took all of that in, didn't know quite what to make of it.

"I didn't see the Lady," Austin said.

"You can't really look at Her," Cloris said. "Not directly. Not without, you know, protection. She'll drive you insane. She's a goddess. You can't look a goddess in the eye without going mad. Her Tears protect us."

Austin had heard enough of that, caught himself from snapping at her, while asking all the same.

"What's with Her Tears, anyway? Why's She always crying?" Austin asked.

"She cries for us, Mr. Adams," Cloris said. "Our pain hurts Her. She takes away our pain. Her Tears heal our pain. Whatever ails us, Her Tears heal us."

"That sounds like a crock to me," Austin said. "What does a goddess have to cry about?"

"Goddesses feel more than mortals do," Cloris said. "There's lots to be upset about if you're a goddess."

Austin shook his head.

"I don't know," he said. "If I were a goddess, I think I'd be like 'Yippee, I'm a goddess!' Who wouldn't want to be a god?"

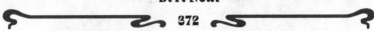
Cloris smiled sadly at him.

"You don't know for a certainty how you'd feel," she said. "I think the Lady perceives so much more than we do. She sees more, feels more. That's why She cries. She cries tears of sadness, tears of joy, tears of anger, tears of anguish and ecstasy."

Austin just couldn't see it.

"That's a whole lot of tears," Austin said.

"That's just your own pain talking," Cloris said. "Your friends are still there?"

"Yeah," Austin said. "Maybe. Or maybe they're all dead."

"You'll see," Cloris said. "They'll come back whole and refreshed. Good as new. Better, even."

"Creepy," Austin said.

"I feel sad that you didn't partake, Mr. Adams," Cloris said. "I'll say a prayer for you tonight."

"Please do," Austin said. "Just don't shed any tears on my behalf."

Cloris smiled at him.

"That's for Her to do," she said. "Not me. Although I would if you thought it would help. I could help you."

She just let that hang on the air a bit, and Austin looked her in the eye, seeing her look him right back.

*Cult chicks are forward*, he decided.

"No, I'm good," Austin said, smiling nervously. "Thanks for thinking of me, though."

"Any time, Mr. Adams," Cloris said, her smile unwavering.

He headed to the elevators. As he waited for his floor, he felt like setting something on fire. He didn't care what it was.

He fished out some booze from the minifridge, lit up a joint, and turned on the television. Anything to tune out the unease he was feeling.

The responsible thing, the adult thing, would have been to get the Twins out of there. But he'd run away scared. He'd only thought of himself. There had only been his desire to escape.

Austin went to the balcony and took in the night air, the night noises below. This late, there were still people out and about, mostly hitting the bars. He listened to the clock tower chime one o'clock. He texted the others again, but nobody answered. One-thirty, he did it again, and still no answer. Two o'clock, and nobody answered. He'd nodded off a bit.

He'd let Jess and Jake down. And who know what the hell Mallory had done to them. What the others had done. Crazy people with their painted faces.

At 2:22, his phone pinged at last, waking him up from where he'd dozed in his seat. He'd actually jumped.

A moment later, Jess pinged him back with a photo of herself and Jake, Jess in her ridiculous hat, them flashing devil's horns with their hands while sticking out their tongues. It was a sloppy, blurry photo, but it was them.

*SHE WAS HERE, ASSTIN. SHE KISSD ME.*

Jake even pinged him.

*Yo, Ass End. Fuck offfff.*

Austin shook his head, grateful his friends were still among the living. Maybe it was just him being paranoid, reading into things.

The Twins had nine lives.

Nothing would ever touch them.

He remembered them telling him the story about them bungee-jumping off a bridge in Mexico, which sounded like a death sentence to him, but they'd had a blast. They'd gone sky-diving in Nevada, they'd surfed the Red Triangle in San Francisco. They'd run with the bulls in Pamplona, and had done *La Tomatina* in Spain a few years back. The Twins were bulletproof, as far as he saw it. Some crazy Pennsylvania cult was pocket change for them. They'd handle it the way they'd always done it.

It was just him.

Everybody was fine.

He was just being the way he always was.

The worrier.

Then Mallory pinged him.

*I'll see you soon, Austin. I'll show you my tattoo.*
*What makes you think I want to see it?*
*Because you're a boy. Boys always want to.*

"Yeah," Austin said.

Did Mallory have him that completely clocked? He went back into the hotel room and poured himself a gin from one of the little fridge bottles and drank it down, relieved that, at least for now, everybody was still alive.

**2**

**Logan woke when Maura had come in. He hadn't realized** he'd fallen asleep, but had awakened to hear her in his shower, humming as she rinsed herself clean.

He propped himself up and glanced at the clock, which said it was 2:22 a.m. on the dot. Logan jumped up even as Maura was coming out of the shower, wrapped in a towel, with another for her hair. She looked nighttime radiant, her dark eyes bright in the bathroom light.

"I told you I'd be back," Maura said. She looked like she'd been crying, her eyes red.

"How'd it go?" Logan asked. He had been dreaming of something curious, being in a massive kitchen with a thousand stoves and a staff of silent souls without mouths or even proper faces, mindlessly cooking on their stoves, following his words to the letter.

"Swimmingly," Maura said. "Better than I could have hoped. Maybe too well."

She gave her hair a tousling, carefully hanging the towel from its rack, using his brush to slick back her wet hair.

"I should have been there," Logan said. "Although I'll admit I'm dying to know how you got away from the gangsters."

Maura put her arms around him and kissed him long and hard. There was a pleasurable ferocity in her desire, and Logan welcomed it, reciprocated. They kissed back and forth for a few moments, what felt like a pleasant forever.

"Later," Maura said, after they'd parted. "I'll tell you everything later. Right now, I just need you. I always feel a thousand times better after a service. The Midnight Service is transformational. This year, more than ever. Pleasure and pain in equal portions. Something extraordinary."

"Yeah?" Logan asked, holding her to him. She didn't fight him, seemed to welcome his touch.

"Yes," Maura said. "It's a special year. I mean, like the Festival-festival, the one for outsiders. Geared for outsiders."

As festival-friendly as the town was, Logan was convinced that they invariably viewed themselves that way. There were the Lynchburg locals, and there was everyone else.

"What's the population of Lynchburg?" Logan asked.

"For now? A soul over 11,000," Maura said, forcing a smirk his way. Her smirks were enchanting—one part impish, one part seductive. They carried with them mirth and mayhem in equally wicked portions.

"And you get over 100,000 visitors with every Festival," Logan said.

"Yeah, we deal with that many outsiders a year, now," Maura said. "It's been a big boon for us. It's grown over the decades. When we first let in outsiders in 1969, it was much smaller. It's gotten successively larger. It's good for the town."

"Outsiders," Logan said. "That's what I am. An outsider."

"Don't take it personally," Maura said, playfully beeping his nose with an index finger. "We Lynchburgers are a parochial and insular lot."

"We need to make Lynchburgers," Logan said. "Like at our restaurants. It should be a mushroom burger, to be honest. A portobello, swimming in soy sauce, balsamic vinegar, and some steak seasoning. Just to get the right flavor. And Swiss cheese. Gotta go with that."

Sure," Maura said. "Knock yourself out."

"I'm just saying," Logan said. "Not even making fun. Just think it's so on the nose, has to be done."

"I love it," Maura said. "We'll add it to the menu. Daddy was all-in on the franchise. I told you he'd love it. He did. Two restaurants, as we planned."

"Did? Past tense? He still does?" Logan asked.

"It's all good," Maura said.

"Yeah?" Logan said. Maura kissed him again, and he felt the click of a tongue stud on his teeth as her tongue toyed with him. She cocked an eyebrow and smiled, her eyes caressing him. Despite the time, Logan felt at ease and at peace. Maura brought that out in him, that sense of comfort and belonging.

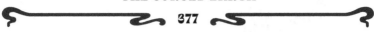
"You are remarkably chill for somebody who was kidnapped," Logan said.

"Am I?" Maura said. "I wasn't scared of them. They were just silly boys with guns, Logan. Wanting to make some easy money. What I saw tonight was something else. Something grander. I can't even explain it in a way you'd understand."

She said it so matter-of-factly, Logan could hardly believe it. He'd have been a mess if he'd ever been kidnapped. But Maura was blasé.

"I've seen a lot in my life, Logan," Maura said. "Nothing much shakes me."

"I can see that," Logan said. "Tell me how it went. How you got away."

"Later," Maura said. "Honestly, there's not much to tell. What I saw tonight shook me."

"Bullshit," Logan said. "You're unshakeable."

"I was shaken," Maura said.

"Wow," Logan said.

"Let's go to bed," Maura said. "It's been a hell of a day. I had morning prep, lunchtime service, then I was kidnapped, then I escaped, and made it in time for the Midnight Service in honor of my Goddess. I saw Her appear."

"Busy day," Logan said. "Wait, what?"

Maura began to cry, and then to laugh.

"It's how I roll," Maura said. She guided him to the bed, set him down at the edge of it, before dropping down in front of him.

"Today is already tomorrow," Maura said. "But we can sleep in. I'm having my staff do prep today. Lay back."

She pushed him gently on his back, but Logan's mind was going over everything. Logistics were always front-and-center with him.

"Which place should we start with?" Logan asked.

Maura paused.

"Philadelphia, honestly," she said. "Your base of operations. We'll hit Pittsburgh, next. You haven't even joined the Faith, yet, so stop thinking so much."

And, weirdly, Logan felt the thought he had walk away from him as soon as she'd said it. They just flitted away, and his mind went blank, leaving only the pleasurable sensations she was conjuring without another word said.

# 4

**Emily did not come down until dawn.**

After seeing visions of herself careening through the psychedelic sky amid a sea of starlike motes, she awoke in the Round Room she'd been in before, the room within the Temple. The room with the Lady's Tears and the idol of the Lady surrounded by the strange and tangled trees. Only all of the candles were now lit.

Her vision was strange, a blend of blue and purple, with splashes of white light. Residual effects of the dose she'd taken, she was sure.

*"How'd I get here?"* Emily asked.

"We brought you here, Lady Carver," Mona said. "Most blessed."

The High Priestess stood nearby, wearing fresh robes, her hair immaculately coiffed. But Emily could see past the face paint, through her skin, could see the blood within.

"What do you see?" Mona asked.

*"I see you,"* Emily said. *"I see through you."*

"Outstanding, Lady Carver," Mona said. "You have been granted such a great gift from the Lady. More than just Her favor, more than Her kiss or Her blessing. You have been made incarnate. You are the Lady Incarnate."

Mona put three fingers to her forehead and made a circle with them.

*"Why did you take me from the Grove?"* Emily asked.

"This is your home now," Mona said. "The First Temple."

Emily rose, could see that her skin was grey and white, oddly mottled, and her hands were bladelike claws. Her body was wrapped in a strange threadlike gown of hyphae.

*"No,"* Emily said. *"Why? How?"*

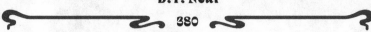
"The Lady chose you for Her vessel, Lady Carver," Mona said. "You, of all we have placed before Her for so long. So many sacrifices we have made. And here you are."

Seeing through her, past her, past the indoor grove, Emily could see some acolytes painting something on one of the curved walls—a new fresco. It was an image of her in the Sacred Grove, being kissed by the Grey Lady.

Anger welled up in her, and she took a step. Her body felt strange, both hers and not-hers. She felt the power swell within her, luminous and strange.

*"What have you done to me?"* Emily said.

"Not us," Mona said. "The Goddess."

The High Priestess looked as handsome and unruffled as ever. The woman had to have the constitution of an ox, for she looked entirely at ease, despite apparently having been up all night.

*"Please tell me you didn't mind me all night,"* Emily said.

"I prayed with you all night," Mona said. "The Sacred Grove has been transformed."

Emily could remember some of that, the vision of the colors and the covering of the land with the frothlike fungus in a monstrous mat, and a blue basin in the center, where the Lady had emerged. Trees surrounding it had buckled and died, while others were enrobed in the fungi, like dreadful garlands.

Incredibly, Emily realized she could sense beyond where she was. She could see the Sacred Grove as clearly as the room she was currently in. Overhead, an alien sky, not like what should have been there. Another world, another universe, even. A place Emily knew intimately but could not recognize. In the morning light, the *Amanitas* looked no less impressive. Emily thought there were more of them than the night before. It was a mild morning, as it had been the days before. The sun seemed to fight the alien sky, and the alien sky fought back.

"We were very busy last night," Mona said. "How much do you remember?"

*"Just afterimages,"* Emily said. *"The Lady's Tears are potent. Her Kiss, more so."*

"Yes, they are," Mona said. "We're very proud of the Tears. They are our most powerful hallucinogen. We have perfected it over the years."

Emily walked out of the grove, followed closely by Mona. The acolytes saw her and bowed low. She could see and taste their terror, the flow of blood in their veins, the quickening of their hearts and respiration.

She could see Marquis talking to Jerry, all the way in California. They were discussing the Lady's Tears. Her Tears. She could see them, could see the blood coursing through them. As far away as they were, she could see them. She did not know how.

"But you likely knew that, being a mycologist, after all," Mona said.

"*I suspected,*" Emily said.

"And yet you had the courage to try it, all the same," Mona said. "Not everybody does."

Emily tried to remember what she'd seen. The blue tendrils she remembered, thick and luminous, reaching up to the sky. And the Lady. The Lady had kissed her. She remembered that. It had been staggering, the welter of emotions.

To be kissed by a goddess was a precious and terrible thing. It had been a kiss of witheringly lustful contempt, acquisitive and all-conquering in its intimate delicacy, in the firmness of her godflesh with the softness of her own.

"*I'm a risk-taker,*" Emily said. "*It goes with the territory when you're a mycologist.*"

Mona smiled at her, dwelling on that a moment or two before speaking again.

"Her kiss was a sacred gesture," Mona said.

"*What happened last night?*" Emily asked. It was hard to think clearly. Marquis and Jerry were talking about her. About Ash. About them. She could see the words and the thoughts behind them, even as her attention wavered and she was back in Lynchburg, both in the Temple and in the Sacred Grove.

Emily could see without looking that Mona was close behind her. She leaned forward, steepling her fingers.

"We have been working for generations to bring the Lady to our world," Mona said. "The liminal space between Her domain and our own was particularly narrow last night. And we breached it. She passed through. She's here, now. It's not a matter of faith, anymore. It's fact."

Emily was unsure what to make of that, and Mona didn't elaborate, only basked in the revelation of that moment.

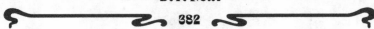
"*You did what?*" Emily asked.

"We breached the dimensional gap between Her universe and our own," Mona said. "This has been a long time coming, by the way. We've been working on this since the Faith was founded."

"*You let an invasive species into our world,*" Emily said. "*Into our universe.*"

"An invasive species? She's hardly that, Dr. Carver," Mona said. "She's not a 'species'—she's the Grey Lady. She's our goddess."

"*Maybe worse, then,*" Emily said. "*She's here, with me, you say. But what are the implications of that?*"

"She walks in our world with you," Mona said. "It's not for me to wonder, only to worship and obey."

"*You're a fool,*" Emily said. The High Priestess not used to being talked to this way, and her generally genial bearing curdled a bit. Emily could read the blood that pulsed inside her.

"A fool, eh? Quite a far cry from Mycopharmix, isn't it?" Mona asked. Emily felt embarrassed, wondered how much Mona knew about her. "Oh, we looked into you the moment we learned about you. Jerry Merriwether has been sending people to us for the last five years, Dr. Carver. You're the first one we've spared."

"*Spared?*"

"Spared," Mona said. "The Lady spared you. Ordinarily, we'd have given you to the ground, where we all belong."

"Where we all belong," the acolytes within earshot said.

Emily could see that she spoke the truth—Jerry had sent others from Mycopharmix. He had not told them that. There had been others. They ended up in the Cursed Earth, feeding the goddess, sacrificed by the cultists. Emily felt anger at Jerry for putting them in danger that way, without informing them of the risk.

"But the Lady—the one you call an 'invasive species'— spared you," Mona said. "I've been in Her service long enough to understand a portent when I see one. She didn't just spare you; She became part of you. Or made you part of Her. You are transformed for all time."

Emily remembered but had been deep in the hallucination. She couldn't be sure of anything she'd seen or felt.

"*What does it mean?*" Emily asked.

"At this point, I don't know," Mona said. "But it sure means something. With *La Signora* crossing the breach, I feel we shall see and feel more of Her than before. Perhaps you can ask Her yourself—since you are Her."

*"You don't know what you've done,"* Emily said. *"You've let a monster into our world. You've invoked Her."*

"A monster?" Mona said. "A goddess, not a monster."

*"What's the difference?"* Emily said.

"A monster is a horrible thing," Mona said. "She's beautiful. You saw Her."

*"I saw something,"* Emily said. *"But there's no difference between a god and a monster, from our perspective. Particularly from mine, as I'm not a fanatic like you."*

Mona held her blue blindfold in her hand, toyed with it.

"There's no room for disbelief in you anymore, Lady Carver," Mona said. "You are Her, now, and Hers. Transformed beyond mere humanity. Would that it had been me. I would know what to do. I'm more than a little envious. But Daddy would not let us risk it. Not after Mother."

Emily could see that she again spoke the truth, could see her thoughts flowing like her blood.

"Even with the Lady's Kiss, you cannot see," Mona said. "She blessed you last night. You would spurn that blessing with what? Your science? Your doubt?"

*"You cover your eyes,"* Emily said. *"I remember that. The blindfolds. How is it you can gaze upon me now?"*

"Any who gaze upon the Lady unprotected goes mad," Mona said. "I've had family members do that. Ancestors. Some say Uncle Gus nearly did it when he was a young man, before Daddy cursed him."

*"What's all of that about, anyway?"* Emily asked. *"You're witches?"*

"We are," Mona said. "A coven. We've been here a long time."

Emily walked the circular room with Mona, past all of the Amanitas that choked the room.

*"Goddess-monsters and witches,"* Emily said. *"It follows, I suppose."*

Covens were not something she ever thought about. Mona seemed to understand that, was sympathetic, even if Emily's line of inquiry was rankling her.

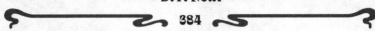

"Lucretia founded our Lynchburg coven," Mona said. "She was a formidable woman, although I never met her. The Lady had claimed her long before I was born. But she'd set us all on the path we've since taken. And we've prospered on that path. Decades ago, the Quakers and the Catholics tried to stop us. Witches and all of that."

Emily thought she could see it in her mind's eye, the righteous souls going after the Lady's followers by day, only to have the first Exemplars hunting them in the night. Masked, robed, knife-wielding, giving their victims to the Lady beneath the light of the moon, and the Lady's Tear Agarics growing where the bodies fell. She could see it, although she did not know precisely how.

"They didn't win," Mona said. "Hunting us, we exterminated them, instead: one by one, two by two, three by three, and more. Death and decay are inescapable. We have that as our advantage. We do the Lady's work. All falls eventually into ruination. Over time, the crusaders grew fewer and fewer. And we brought lasting prosperity to the town. True prosperity that carried over from generation to generation, until the holy wars were just a distant memory. The Lady is generous to those who follow Her. She is not like the Christ figure, who seems to savor the suffering of His flock. The Lady is as kind to Her people as She is cruel to Her enemies."

Emily could see Mona's mother, a witch as well, who tried to give herself to the Lady, to become Her holy vessel years before. Another Sacred Grove, and a coven of six. Their mother, Magdalena. How she had beseeched the Lady to incarnate within her, but the Lady had refused her. She had died rotting in the circle, falling apart in her husband's arms while he wept.

"*Your mother Magda,*" Emily said.

"Long dead," Mona said. "Mother was like that. Determined to get her way. The Lady cast her aside for reasons only She knows. It nearly broke us spiritually and emotionally. Daddy all but died with grief. But the Lady guides our path in all that we do."

"*Why tell me all of this?*" Emily asked.

"Jerry Merriwether is the Lady's enemy," Mona said. "You stole Lady's Tears from our Temple, didn't you?"

Emily could see Marquis guiding Jerry through a presentation deck. She could see the chemical compounds of the Lady's

Tears, the first stabs at the spectrographic analysis. Jerry was soaking it all up, nodding, smiling. They were happy. More than happy. They were thrilled. She would visit them soon enough when She was able. There would be words one day.

Mona reached out and touched Emily's shelf fungus hair with her hand, a gentle motion that nonetheless made Emily irritated with its proprietary presumption.

"*I had to learn about the Lady's Tears myself,*" Emily said. "*I was hired.*"

"I know," Mona said. "I know, Lady Carver. You and Marquis Allen and Ashley Dunn. When the Lady kissed you, your soul was laid bare to me. I know why you were here."

Emily felt a splash of malice touch her heart, but Mona shook her head.

"No, Lady Carver," Mona said. "The Lady's grace has saved you. She knew and She forgave you for your trespasses. And as She goes, so must we all. However, there is the matter of the infidels acquiring specimens of our holy *Amanitas*. That is a transgression not so easily forgiven. Do you think we want our sacred Agarics deconstructed and gene-sequenced by the likes of Mycopharmix so they can peddle, what? An antidepressant? Some other mundane thing, devoid of the ardent solace of holy ritual? Jerry Merriwether is a man rooted in the material world. He sees only the nose on his face and would wring all of the gold from the world, if he could only grasp it."

"*What do you want from me?*" Emily asked. "*There's nothing I can do to dissuade him.*"

"There is nothing you can't do," Mona said. She pointed a finger at Emily and poked her with it. "The Lady's inside you, now. You'll know what to do in time. In the meantime, I have sent Exemplars to deal with both of them."

Emily could imagine how that would play out, thought it would be bloody for both sides.

"*The Lady's will isn't mine,*" Emily said. Mona laughed.

"Oh, She is you, now," Mona said. "She is free with Her Tears, but not with Her Kisses. But last night, She was generous. I am not one to judge Her actions. I can't thank you enough for spending last night with us. For having the courage to risk our company, though it may have meant the end of you. Or the end of you as you were. I divined that you would take the risk. I knew you would."

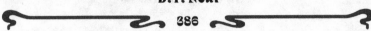
*"What you've done is end our world,"* Emily said. *"Whatever the Lady is, you've brought about the end of our world as it was."*

"Then let it end," Mona said. "The Lady teaches us that all things end. Entropy and ruin are the shadows cast by life and living. All falls into disarray and is born again in newer forms. I welcome that transformation. As you will, too, eventually."

*"Will I?"* Emily asked. She willed her bladelike fingers to become her own digits again, and was pleased to see the grey-white flesh shift and resemble her own hands again, albeit with the ghastly, mottled coloration. But the new flesh was malleable, and Emily took heart in that.

*"Call a special service at the Temple, Priestess. I would have words with you and your flock at noon."*

She looked through Mona, watched the blood pump, saw her thoughts work. She was elated that she thought Emily had resigned herself to her fate, that the bonding with the Lady—or whatever part of the Lady the Goddess had seen to share with her—had gone as well as it had.

Already, she was making plans for more temples, expansions of the unholy franchise in other cities within the state, then the tri-state, then regional, then national, then international. The Grey Lady would be known throughout the world even as She conquered it.

As she gazed at the world through her bright blue eyes, Emily saw things as they were, not as they could be.

*Thou understandeth Me as no other can, Academician,* the Lady said inside her head, as she watched Mona make her arrangements with her Acolytes, Deacons, and Exemplars. *What fools these mortals be.*

# 5

**Austin was only aware of having been asleep when**
Mallory had woken him up. She was curled up next to him in
one of the hotel beds, naked. He was naked, too, and the balcony sliding doors were open, which let in some of the Festival
noise outside.

"What the fuck?" Austin said, hopping out of bed, grabbing
one of the blankets to cover himself.

Mallory yawned and rolled over.

"Problem?" she asked.

"Um, yeah," Austin said. "When the hell did you get in?"

"Around three," Mallory said. "It took longer to corral the
Twins than I intended. Plus, it got kinda crazy up there at the
Grove."

"I didn't wake up?" Austin asked.

"You were pretty wasted," Mallory said. "So was I, maybe. I
was tripping on what I had witnessed at the Grove. I just slipped
in bed with you."

"Wait, what?"

"I just experienced the most incredible thing I'll ever encounter in my whole life. You looked so innocent and adorable
sleeping there, and, you know, I just hopped in with you. That's
what friends are for, right?" Mallory said. "You're my friend,
Austin. We're friends."

"Jesus," Austin said, walking over to his suitcase and grabbing some fresh boxers and a tee. He didn't pick another Lynchburg tee, opting for his "Beware of the Blob" ringer tee, which
showed the titular blob in raspberry red against a white background. He saw he was covered in blue lipstick kisses, like
bruises.

"Whoa," Austin said. "I look abused."

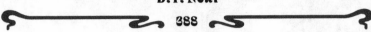
Mallory rolled her eyes. Austin went into the bathroom and soaked a washcloth, mopping himself off, before coming back out. While he scrubbed, Mallory talked.

"Dude, I saw the birth of a goddess," she said. "I mean, I didn't see it with my eyes. They made us wear blindfolds. But I could feel it, and, you know, see it in my heart and head, like what I was hearing. And, like, not the birth of a goddess—the Lady is already born, already out there. I mean, like, maybe Her arrival here. Like on Earth."

"What the hell are you even talking about?"

"I was there," Mallory said. "Ground Zero, Austin. I was right there in the middle of it."

"Blindfolded," Austin said.

"Had to be," Mallory said. "It's like Cosmology 101—you get a sunburned soul if you look upon a god without protection."

"Oh, yeah? A blindfold is enough protection?"

He had managed to get the worst of the blue kiss-prints off his body, rinsed out the washcloth and wrung it out, hanging it from one of the racks. Then he came back out to finish getting dressed.

"Don't tease," Mallory said.

Mallory watched him get dressed, perched on her elbows.

He saw a grey mask resting atop folded grey robes on the nearby dresser table, as well as a netlike shroud and one of those conical hats. And a curved knife.

"What the hell is this?" Austin asked.

"I've been upped," Mallory said. "I'm an Exemplar, now. It's like being knighted."

Austin picked up the wood-handled knife and gazed at the curved blade, turning it this way and that. He could see the three-circle stamp upon it, etched in the steel, near the handle.

"What does that even mean?" Austin asked.

"It means I'm, like, a made guy," Mallory said. "Nobody can touch me here in Lynchburg."

"Oh, in Lynchburg, right," Austin said, rolling his eyes. Mallory pouted at him.

"Anywhere the Lady is," Mallory said. "And She's absolutely everywhere. She's here now, in fact."

Austin whirled around, almost bringing the knife up, but Mallory only laughed.

"No, Stupid," Mallory said. "I mean, like, here-here. The world. They brought Her here last night. I helped. She's possessed that mycologist lady whose friend you were macking on."

She smiled at him, looking almost smug at the revelation.

"You missed it, Austin," Mallory said. "She's been a long time coming. It's taken decades or longer to do it, but She's here, now. In the flesh, not just spirit. And that means I matter. Way more than I did just the night before. I mean, the High Priestess herself noticed me. She knows me by name. She made me an Exemplar. It came right from her."

"What does that even mean? She's here?" Austin asked.

"She's been made manifest," Mallory said. "It's hard to explain. It's like before, the Faithful simply had to content themselves with glancing at the Lady through ceremonies, rituals, momentary visions, signs and portents. Because She was in another dimension, far from ours, alien. But She's here, now. We created a conduit, a portal, I don't know what you'd call it—a path from there to here. Only for a moment, but we did it last night. The work of decades upon decades, maybe centuries, and we realized it last night."

"That seems really dangerous," Austin said. "She's an alien."

"She's a goddess," Mallory said. "Not an alien."

"Goddess, alien, demon, abomination, whatever you want to call it," Austin said. "She's not from around here. That's my point. She's not native to our world."

"Yeah, and?"

"And that's trouble," Austin said.

"What, you're anti-immigrant, now, Austin?" Mallory said.

"She's not an immigrant," Austin said. "I love immigrants. Immigrants are people like us, just from somewhere else. What's the Lady? She's an invader. A conqueror."

Mallory paused a moment, thinking it over.

"She's a goddess," Mallory said.

"Is She human?"

"Well, no," Mallory said. "Of course not. Although by incarnating through Emily Carver, She's now flesh and blood."

"Gods don't bleed," Austin said.

"Like you even know," Mallory said. "You know fuck about gods."

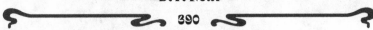
"You don't know what the fuck She even is," Austin said. "Whether or not She's an alien, She IS alien. As in 'not like us'—does that make sense now?"

Mallory scowled at Austin.

"You make it sound like a bad thing," Mallory said.

"It is a bad thing," Austin said. "You've somehow managed to let a stranger into our planetary house. I'm being metaphorical here, but that's what you've done. You think you know the Stranger, but you only know what the Stranger has let you see. And from the gobbledygook you've shared so far, the only thing we can be sure of is that the Lady loves killing things and cries a lot."

"Oh, man, you are so willfully reductionist, Austin," Mallory said. "I can't believe you sometimes. The Lady loves Her followers. Everyone who follows Her has thrived."

"Or else She's been using you. Payment for services rendered," Austin said. "She rewards Her faithful. She punishes Her enemies. There you have it. At best, you've started some kind of holy war. Or unholy war."

"She's a true god," Mallory said. "No fairytales, no myths and legends, Austin. She exists. I've seen Her. We've seen Her. Maybe not directly, but She has bonded with Dr. Carver. You wouldn't be so damned flippant if you'd been there. Mona and her Exemplars spirited her away to the Temple once the ritual had completed. It was impressive as hell."

Austin set down the knife, feeling tainted by it.

"What's the knife for, anyway?" Austin asked.

"Infidels," Mallory said, challengingly. "Anybody the Lady doesn't like."

"That's creepy-crazy-weird, Mal," Austin said. "My point exactly."

"You *like* that I'm weird," Mallory said.

Austin knew he had to tread carefully with his cult-indoctrinated friend. He felt like it was almost a hostage negotiation, only he was maybe the hostage as much as she was. What did you do when you shared a space with a maniac? You kept your cool.

"Sure," Austin said. "But seriously, what are you going to do with that getup?"

"Whatever the Lady requires of me," Mallory said. "Anything She asks. Anything She commands."

"So, you're a fanatic, now?" Austin said. "A zealot?"

"I'm an Exemplar," Mallory said. "I go where She wills me to go."

"What about, you know, your life?" Austin asked.

"This *is* my life, now," Mallory said. "You think I can go back to being a barista after what I've experienced here? No way, Bro. No way."

Austin wondered what Mallory had done the year before, and she just bit her lip and smiled at him, shaking her head.

"You think too much, Austin," Mallory said. "You're an overthinker, do you know that?"

"Yeah," Austin said. "My friend trips out at a sacred grove and comes back with a knife and a mask and a bunch of fanatical zeal, what's to worry?"

Mallory laughed again.

"Austin, if I wanted to kill you, I'd have slit your throat while you slept," Mallory said. "Overthink about that a little bit, would you?"

Austin pondered that way more than he expected to, raised a finger, then lowered it.

"Fair point," Austin said. "Yeah, okay. I confess that I raided the fridge when I got home, drank some vodka and smoked up a bit to level off."

"Sure, sure," Mallory said. She hopped out of bed, and Austin jumped. He could see her three-circle tattoo in blue, about two inches below her belly button, right above her denuded crotch.

"Ah, okay," Austin said. "There it is."

"You see it now?" Mallory said. "I got that last year. After the Festival."

She walked toward him, and he backed away. She laughed at him, grabbed the grey robes, slipped them on. Then she tied the grey sash at her waist and hooked the knife on it.

"You see?" Mallory said. "I'm still Mallory."

Then she slipped the grey mask on and put the hood over her head. Then she put on the hat, fastening it so it stayed on.

"And now I'm Exemplar Mallory," Mallory said. She picked up some grey gloves and slid them onto her hands and held the shroud in her gloved hands. The leather of the gloves creaked agreeably. "Only when you're an Exemplar, you simply are. Who you are ceases to be when you put on this mask. You can be any-

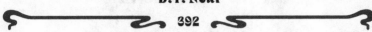
body. That's the point. Nobody knows who you are. Complete anonymity."

"You're creeping me out," Austin said.

"Poor baby," Mallory said. "You have no idea how powerful this makes me feel. You can't ever know. You're normcore to the bone, Austin."

Although she wasn't as tall as he was, in the Exemplar costuming, she seemed larger, more frightening and formidable.

"Anything I want," Mallory said. "Anything I want to do to you, Austin. Nobody would say a word in protest. Not even the Sheriff would."

The mask muffled her voice, and the black eyes of the mask hid her pretty eyes. He didn't like seeing her like this, tried to make a joke of it.

"You look like you've escaped from a slasher movie," Austin said.

"I have," Mallory said. "Exemplars are *supposed* to frighten people. We're *meant* to be terrifying. We're the Lady's enforcers. We hunt Her enemies. We put the fear of Her in others."

"What's the shroud for?" Austin asked.

"Ceremonial on some level," Mallory said. "But functional, too. See the hole in the middle? You can put it on your hat like this."

She slipped it atop her hat, and her face was hidden by the shroud, which made her even more mysterious and threatening.

"You see the little loops at the bottom? You can put these little bells in those. They have them at the Temple. Like you saw in the parade," Mallory said.

"The one you slept through," Austin said.

"I was gearing up for last night," Mallory said. "Anyway, you can wear it that way. But it can also be a shawl. And even a weapon."

"Handy," Austin said. "Creepy *and* practical. You are quite possibly the creepiest girl I've ever known. The Practical Fanatic."

Mallory laughed behind her mask, taking off her shroud and flinging it at him. It caught around his arm and she tugged at him a moment before releasing him. Then she took off the hat and flicked it to one of the hotel room chairs.

"Let me guess, you can lop somebody's head off with that," Austin said.

"It's not MORTAL KOMBAT, Goofus," Mallory said. She rested her hand on her hip, hovering too close to the knife. She just regarded him like that a moment, which made him even more wary.

"I want to be sure you understand something, Austin. You're not equipped to stop me, even if you wanted to. Let's say you were going to. What would you do? Murder me? You don't want to do that. Can you even imagine all the work you'd have to do? Hiding my body. Hiding from the Sheriff—who's totes part of it all. And what else? Explaining to the Twins what happened to me? Going on the run? You're spectacularly ill-suited to be a fugitive, Austin. You're just too cute to be a fugitive. You're a great guy, Austin. But you don't have it in you to deal with me, to deal with them, to deal with any of this. Just roll with it, okay? You do that, and I promise you it'll be worth your time. You came out here with me to have fun. So, let's have fun."

"You brought us here knowing what we were getting into," Austin said. "You set us up."

"I gave you a chance," Mallory said. "A chance to experience something as amazing as what I experienced last year. More so, honestly. This was way, way bigger."

"What happened to the Taylor Triplets?" Austin asked.

Mallory shrugged. "They went away. They were just Festival-friends. You know how that is. It's like when you go to a beachfront town. You make beachfront friends, and you all go on your way."

"They're missing," Austin said, taking out his phone and showing the missing persons poster for April, May, and June. "They disappeared last year. Right after last year's Festival."

"Whatever," Mallory said.

"You were with them," Austin said. "Police would want to know what you know, at the very least."

"It's a festival, Austin," Mallory said. "People come and go. I don't know where they went."

"I think you do," Austin said. "I think you murdered them. Or had them killed."

Mallory scoffed.

"You think so, do you?"

"Yep," Austin said. "Something happened. That's all I know. And I think you know what happened. Did you sacrifice them to the monster-goddess?"

"Jeezus, Austin," Mallory said. "You are so paranoid."

"You're not answering my question," Austin said.

"I don't know what happened to the Taylor Triplets," Mallory said. "Don't forget, I drank the Lady's Tears that night. I was tripping hard. Hard as the Twins were tripping last night. Maybe harder, I don't know. I don't remember what I remember. Don't play hero-detective with me, Austin. You don't have the practice."

Austin was angry at being so breezily brushed off, that Mallory had him so completely figured out, he couldn't argue it. Not here. Not in Lynchburg.

"Get on the bed," Mallory said.

"Um, no fucking way," Austin said. "Least of all not with you looking like that."

She made a chicken sound again, a cluck-cluck-clucking as she took off the sash and tossed the knife on the chair with the hat, then slipped off the mask and put it with the other things, took off the hood.

"See? I'm back," Mallory said. "Now get on the bed."

Austin glanced at the clock as he heard the clock tower toll.

"It's eight o'clock," he said.

"And?" Mallory pushed him on the other bed, quickly hopping on him, hiking up the robe as she straddled him.

"And fuck it," Austin said. It wasn't Stockholm Syndrome he was feeling. It was something far more tactical and practical, as circumstances dictated—he was sleeping with the enemy.

"Good boy," she said, neither knowing his mind nor particularly caring.

**Logan and Maura caught the Lady's Procession at 8:30**
that morning, which amounted to a bunch of robed faithful
toting a statue of the Grey Lady down one side of Grand Avenue and up the other side, while acolytes beat drums and shook
tambourines and played flutes. Everyone was in good spirits,
while Logan only looked on with ironic detachment as they
made their way.

"What's the purpose of this, then?" Logan asked.

"Last day of the Festival," Maura said. "Honoring the Lady
in our way."

"Why aren't you, you know, dancing down the street?" Logan asked.

"I've done my time," Maura said. "This is newbie stuff. Besides, I did solid service for the Lady the past two days. I'm on
Her good side."

"How do you know?" Logan asked.

"Oh, I know," Maura said. "I'm still breathing. I'm in Her
good graces."

"I have to ask you something," Logan said, which made
Maura smile at him as she lit a cigarette.

"Shoot," Maura said.

"Am I really going to have to join your cult before we open
up the restaurants with you?" Logan asked.

"We will make time for it on our own," Maura said. "Just
call it our religion. That's less demeaning than calling it a cult.
Calling it a cult is insulting."

"Okay, but the point still stands," Logan said, watching the
procession continue.

"Daddy just wants a hard commitment if we're going to be
working with you, investing in you," Maura said. "The Lady

welcomes everyone who comes to Her. But, you know, we don't actively evangelize. I don't know if you noticed that or not."

Logan had to admit that. None of them had actually tried to convert him. Besides Maura, of course. Maura watched him stewing over it and laughed, blowing smoke to one side, over her shoulder.

"We're happy with our numbers," Maura said. "And with the Lady here, it's mostly out of our hands, anyway. She'll go where She wants to, now. We need Her, but She doesn't need us. She's never needed us. Not in ways we can truly understand."

"I need you," Logan said. Whatever she was talking about, he was simply seeing her in front of him and wanting her. He didn't care as much about the rest.

"I know you do," Maura said, putting her arm around him. "And I love that about you, Logan."

The procession had rounded the end of Grand, near Main Street, and was headed back their way. The Festival tents were opening up as well, with farmers and exhibitors setting up for the last day of the festival. The day looked like it would be at least partly sunny, which felt like a victory.

"We should go to Hecate's Horse Farm and go riding," Maura said. "Just get out of town and relax a little. Or better yet, we should just get out of town entirely. Head to Philly. I want to see what kind of restaurant you run."

"Wasn't that what we were doing this morning?" Logan said. "Relaxing?"

"Was that what that was? Relaxing?" Maura asked.

"Hardly," Logan said. "I don't think I could handle horse-back riding after what we've been through. As for Philly, yeah, sure, we could do that."

Maura laughed at him, slipped her cigarette into one of the disposal urns.

"Don't worry, Old Man," Maura said. "I'll go easy on you in the future."

"Thank you," Logan said. "Really, I appreciate that. Gotta ask you another question—you said the Lady's here, now. What does that mean?"

Maura smiled, flicking a stray lock of dark hair from her eyes.

"We brought Her here," Maura said. "Last night."

"How?"

"It's complicated," Maura said. "A ritual."

"What kind of ritual?"

"The secret kind," Maura said, squeezing his arm. "But She's here, now. It changes everything."

"You sent out invitations to your secret ritual," Logan said. "An open secret?"

"We're a mystery religion," Maura said, grinning. "We need to be mysterious."

Logan looked around them. He couldn't see the Lady anywhere, only saw the acolytes heading back up Grand, dancing and singing some hymns with tambourines that were tied with blue, green, and white streamers. It was a day like any other, as he saw it. The sun still rose, the world still turned.

"What does it change?"

"I don't try to get into Her mind," Maura said. "She's a goddess. A true-blue divinity. She'll do whatever She wants to do."

"But how do you know?"

"I saw Her," Maura said. "She has a presence. She incarnated."

Logan didn't know what to tell her. She believed it. Whatever she and her fellow faithful did, they *believed* something special happened. Logan knew better than to probe too much about that, where people's beliefs were concerned. Maura could see him thinking about it.

"You don't believe me," Maura said.

"Hell, no," Logan said. "I believe you believe."

Maura crossed her arms, piqued.

"I know what I know," Maura said. "You know?"

"If you say so," Logan said. "I'm a cynic. Ergo, I'm cynical."

The acolytes were halfway up Grand, and the effigy of the Lady kept moving closer, stony-faced.

"You think I'm making it up?" Maura asked. "Or that I'm crazy?"

"You were tripping, more than likely. This is why I don't like to talk about religion," Logan said.

"Alright, Tough Guy," Maura said. "You want to drink some Lady's Tears? You'll see Her then, I promise you."

"Tripping doesn't count," Logan said. "Anybody can see anything when they're hallucinating. See the problem?"

Maura laughed at him.

"Wow, you're a *Signora* skeptic," Maura said. "Here's the thing, Logan—only if you drink the Lady's Tears can you see Her safely. And 'safe' is a relative concept where She is concerned."

"For real?"

"Definitely," Maura said. "I wish I could tell you more, but I'm sworn to secrecy. My sister would kill me if I said too much. I mean, she'd actually kill me."

The procession had reached them, the revelers moving past them, paying nodding homage to Maura as they passed. Logan watched them file past. Up close, the effigy of the Grey Lady looked to him like any other saint, just with different markings and the strange three-circle glyph festooned in silver thread on the blue silk robe the effigy wore. The same impulses drove these kinds of divine venerations.

"Hold," Maura said, and the acolytes all stopped, to Logan's amazement. She walked to the effigy and dug into her pocket, producing dozens of gold necklaces, chains, and pendants, which she hung from a blue-capped wooden painted mushroom, one among many at the feet of the effigy. She hung the plethora of gold chains there. "For you, My Lady."

She traced a circle on her forehead three times, muttering something Logan couldn't make out.

"Now, go," Maura said, and the acolytes resumed moving, dancing and playing their strange tune to the rattling of the streamer-tied tambourines.

"You have them well-trained," Logan said, watching them go. "What as that all about?"

"Tribute," Maura said.

"A lot of gold chains," Logan said. "The *Rojas?*"

"Yep," Maura said.

Logan was dying to ask her about it but decided to leave that particular stone unturned for the moment. How she had managed to get the drop on a bunch of gangsters was something he wasn't sure he'd ever understand, even if she leveled with him on it.

"It's convenient, don't you think?" Logan asked. "You can't look at Her unless you're high."

"It's for your own protection," Maura said. "You don't want to become Grazed."

"What the hell is Grazed?"

"Someone who's been grazed by the Lady," Maura said. "It's not pretty. Let me put it to you this way—She's beyond anything you can comprehend. Like way beyond. More beautiful, more magical, more powerful, more everything. She's divinity. Way more than our monkey brains can handle. Come on, Hotshot—we can go to my place, we can dose on Tears, and you'll see Her. Then you'll get it."

Logan laughed, folding his arms.

"But if your goddess is here, now, why the razzle-dazzle ritual? Why doesn't She just show up?" Logan asked.

"Oh, Logan," Maura said. "You don't want to do that. You taunt Her, who knows what might happen."

"See, now, that's what I don't like," Logan said. "About any of that. The whole 'don't do that or you'll make You Know Who angry' stuff. Who needs that? Who can live like that?"

Maura laughed uncomfortably, noticing that the work crews were marking off Templeton Lane for the 5K Fungus Run at noon.

"If She's here, let Her appear," Logan said, holding his arms out. Maura looked like she was going to die, and they waited there, the two of them, in silence. The moment became a minute, and the minute became two. "See?"

"You smug jerk," Maura said. "Don't mess with me that way. You do not want to get on my bad side, Bud. And you absolutely don't want to get on the Lady's bad side."

Logan laughed.

"Let's go get breakfast somewhere. Is this our first fight?"

"It just might be," Maura said, looking around them warily, as if the Lady could be waiting for them around any corner, before smacking his ass. "Let's go to Hotcakes, Hotcakes."

# 7

**Ash awoke in a kind of cocoon. She was enrobed in** white, with holes around her that let in light that flowed in dusty beams. Gasping, she sat up, startled, bonking her head on the flexible membrane that had entombed her.

"What the fuck is this?"

She had been at the Sacred Grove in her grey robes, sneaking on the periphery, filming what had been going on. She'd set up her phone and her digital voice recorder, had been capturing it all. The maniacs at the grove had been so focused on their mumbo-jumbo, they hadn't noticed she was there, even when the Exemplars had turned their backs to the circle.

Ash's mind reeled from what she'd seen. She'd averted her gaze as the light show had gotten too bright, had hidden behind the ash tree where she'd set up. It was the last thing she remembered from the night before.

She played back her DVR to distract herself.

"*September 14, near the Sacred Grove. It's 11:30 p.m. This is Ash Dunn reporting. The cultists have been setting up camp near the grove. It looks like they've been here for hours. There's a main tent and a station for what I'm assuming are Lady's Tears. The cultists are also putting on white face paint, as well as blue. Some ritualized adornment involving sticks, like crowns and such. My sister, Melinda, is setting up her keyboard. No sign of Emily, yet, although I see some others. That boy, Austin, and his friends. They're talking. I see Exemplars ringing the grove. They're setting up torches. I'm going to lay low.*"

The DVR jumped to her next entry:

"*11:45 p.m. More notables showing up. The Exemplars are playing drums and have lit torches. I have to say that security is pretty lax, to be honest. I'm able to get pretty close. I've been filming with my phone. I see Emily Carver. She's chatting up Mona Templeton, who is decked out with facepaint and is wearing some kooky stick crown. More guests arriving. I see a mix of onlookers and cultists. Kinda can't tell who's who, besides the ones wearing robes and the painted faces."*

*"11:55 p.m. Wow, I'm seeing the Mayor, and Ned Templeton, and that creepy-ass clown. They're all talking. All of them face-painted. It's insane. The drums keep playing. Reminds me of a pow-wow I reported on long ago, except this is white people—like literally white people, with their weirdly painted faces. The pounding of the drums is kind of mesmerizing. People have been drinking the Lady's Tears for the past half hour. I should have mentioned that earlier, but they're doing it more, now. Oh, Emily, don't drink that shit. Don't do it. Fuck, she drank it. Emily, come on, now. Emily drank the Kool-Aid."*

Claustrophobic, Ash felt her breath coming faster, and she began clawing at the light holes in the whatever that was surrounding her. It was cool to the touch, almost clammy, and broke off easily and cleanly in her hands, for what that was worth.

She went about tearing her way out of the thing that held her, following the brighter light that guided her to freedom. She hoped Emily was alright.

*"Midnight: The Templetons—and the clown—is he a Templeton, too? Jesus. They're forming a ring around the grove. It's some kind of invocation. I'm filming it while I talk. It's a ritual. Wait, they're bringing people into the ring. Sacrifices? The clown just brought a woman. OMG. He slit her throat. Fuck. OMG. Yeah, sacrifices, I think. They're killing people. I'm calling 911."*

The DVR stopped. Then another entry came on.

*"12:15. I called 911, so we'll see who turns up. They killed nine people. I counted nine. I see nine people dead, hanging on these wooden posts. Slit their throats. Each Templeton brought somebody. They put wreath crowns on their heads. Yeah. And somebody else. Some stupid kids in stupid hats. But they were spared. Not sure what that was about. Something's happening to the ground. It's swelling. Something's coming out of the ground. Oh, God. Something's there. It's a woman. A tall woman in white. Grey. White. Grey. She's laying hands on Emily. She's slipping into her. She sees me. Oh, God, her eyes. Blue, like fire. She sees me. She sees me. She sees me. She sees me. She sees me. She—"*

The DVR clicked off, and Ash had made a big enough hole to climb out of. She winced in the white-bright light and could see that the ground around her was covered in the frothy white

stuff, springy like Styrofoam, but cool to the touch. She ditched the grey robe, hanging it from a white-covered tree branch.

"What the hell is this?" Ash said aloud, looking around. Everything was covered in it—the ground, the trees. The trees had it worse, in a way. They were garlanded with ropes of it that covered the branches, like somebody had sprayed them with the fake snow people sometimes used on Christmas trees.

Everything was covered with it.

Ash carefully stepped, mindful of her balance, putting a hand out to the ash tree that had been her hideout. She had to find her phone in all of this gunk. She'd been filming with it.

She tore at the membrane and tossed it aside, trying to clear an area where her phone might be. After some time, she managed to find her phone wedged between some tree branches.

"There you are, you little bastard," Ash said.

Ash texted Emily, but Emily didn't answer.

*Em, where are you?*

*Meet me in the Temple.* It hovered in her head. It wasn't a text. Emily's voice, like the memory of an echo.

She walked carefully along the bizarre, alien-looking ground, filming as she went, narrating as she traversed it.

"September 15, 9:30 a.m. I don't entirely know what I saw or didn't see last night, but I woke up to see the landscape weirdly transformed."

She entered the grove, where she saw the white membrane even more evident here. The three sacrificial posts were covered in it, and in the center of the grove, there was a basin surrounded by blue fungi. The basin was filled to the brim with the blue liquid that Ash assumed was the Lady's Tears. The idol of the Grey Lady hovered over it, untouched by the strange substance.

Some acolytes were bowing before the idol of the Grey Lady, and when they saw Ash enter the grove, they looked at her uncertainly. All of them had white-painted faces with lines of blue upon them in different patterns—some vertical, some horizontal. All of them had blue-painted lips. They carried wicker baskets and curved knives at their belts, but didn't otherwise look threatening, at least by the standards of menace Ash was becoming used to with the cultists.

A white truck was nearby with an open back door. The truck had the Nightcap Mushroom Farm logo on the side of it, its cheeky mushroom mascot winking at her. In the back of the truck Ash could see other workers packing cut chunks of the white membrane into white boxes.

"Who are you?" one of them asked. It was a young man, brown-haired and brown-eyed.

"Just a hiker," Ash said. "What happened here?"

"The Lady came," the young man said. "Last night. She is here, now."

"How do you know?" Ash asked.

"She inhabited the body of the woman," the young man said. "We brought her here and the Goddess laid claim to her."

Ash approached the basin and saw the pool had a light within it, strange and glowing.

"What woman?"

"A Black woman," the young man said. "The mycologist. That's what they told us before they took her away."

"Where?" Ash asked, texting Emily.

*Emily, are you okay? Talk to me.*

*Meet me in the Temple.* Again it pulsed in her head. It was Emily's voice, but different, too.

"The Temple," the young man said. "It was glorious."

"What are you doing here?" Ash asked.

"Everyone from the Temple who wasn't here last night is making a pilgrimage here," the young man said. "This is holy place, now. And a harvesting place. We're calling it 'Ladygate'."

"Ladygate," Ash said, scoffing. "Like Watergate?"

The acolytes didn't know what she was even talking about, and she didn't push it. Ash looked around the blasted-looking grey-white ruin of it, the piles of blue-capped mushrooms and the engulfed trees that hung heavy with the strange membrane. It looked like some bizarre fairyland.

"What is this stuff?" Ash asked.

The acolytes laughed, and none other than Ned Templeton emerged from the back of the truck, looking at Ash with his glittery eyes. He was wearing blue jeans and a red flannel shirt and hopped out of the back of the truck, landing on the springy ground with a nimbleness that was surprising for a man his age. He wore cracking white facepaint with a blue line across his eyes and nose. His lips were painted blue. He looked both obscene and absurd in the light of the day, dressed as a farmer, priestly painted.

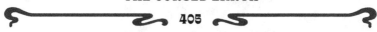
"It is manna, Ms. Dunn," Ned Templeton said, kneeling to caress the pearlescent ground covering. "The Food of the Goddess."

He broke off a chunk of it and ate it, smiling at her. He held a piece out to Ash, but she shook her head.

"No way," Ash said. "You mean all of this shit is edible? Isn't this the Cursed Earth you people are always talking about?"

"No," Templeton said. "That's the ground itself. This is something else, the manifestation of Her blessed presence."

Following his lead, the others were eating it, too, cheerfully chewing it. Ash shuddered even as she filmed it.

"How do you know it's not poison?" Ash asked.

"We've been feasting on it all night," Templeton said. "And nobody's died, yet. Would you like some? You should join us, Ms. Dunn."

"No thank you," Ash said. She had to get the hell away from this strange place. Overhead, despite the sun of the day, the sky looked cracked and broken, like an opalescent fracture that couldn't be directly perceived, only hinted at the corner of one's eye, and yet there.

*Emily, I need to know you're okay.*

*Meet me in the Temple.* As before. She sounded calm. Composed, even. And something else, something Ash couldn't fully comprehend.

"It's wondrous stuff," Templeton said. "Do you know it grows back? I call this place The Lady's Gate, now. It is a gate between Her world and ours. And She has gifted us with this manna."

"What do you mean it regrows?"

Ash felt weird standing on it, watching the acolytes harvesting it, cutting it with their knives and putting it in their baskets. With Ned standing there, they were busily walking it to the truck, where other workers took it and put it in boxes.

"It regrows," Templeton said. He pointed to a white-covered area. "This was cleared hours ago, but it grew back. You never see it growing, but it does. If you were standing where you are for some time, it would grow over you, Ms. Dunn. Isn't that amazing?"

Ash filmed it, and Templeton smiled to himself.

"Of course you'll need to secure permissions for using any of that footage, or else my lawyers will hunt you down," he said.

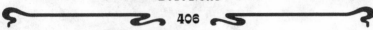
Ash wasn't going to push the issue, turned off her phone and took out her DVR.

"How about this? Are you willing to go on the record with what happened here?" Ash asked. She knew what she'd seen but wasn't about to confront the man about it. Let him think she didn't know as much as she did.

"Let's keep it off the record for the moment," Templeton said.

"Too bad," Ash said, switching it on and slipping it into her pocket. She didn't think journalistic ethics came into play when dealing with cult ritual murderers invoking extradimensional god-beings. She was pretty confident that this situation didn't come up in many professional association review boards.

"After working for decades, we opened the Breach and the Lady came through," Templeton said. "She landed here. In this place, Her touch brought the manna you see. And now we're reaping what we have sown, you might say."

"You don't even know what it is," Ash said.

"I already said what it is, Ms. Dunn," Templeton said. "One does not question manna that falls from the heavens."

"What are you doing, then? Harvesting it, going to package and sell it?" Ash asked. "I would think the FDA would have a thing or two to say about that."

Ned Templeton only smiled at her, completely unruffled and at ease. The man's confidence was supernatural.

"The FDA? Are you kidding? Only if they know about it," he said. "How enterprising and brave you are to come up here all by yourself. Your sister has said you are one heck of an investigative reporter."

Ash hated hearing him mention her sister in so familiar a way but wasn't going to let that color her attempts to pump him for information.

"I do my best," Ash said.

"How would you like a job?" Templeton asked.

"You're insane," Ash said.

"Hear me out," Templeton said, glancing at his workers cutting the manna like they were slicing whale blubber. "The work we're doing here is only just beginning. My family has been here since the 19th century. I am doing their work. The Lady's work. This has been a watershed. Last night, I mean—the culmina-

tion of so many lifetimes of effort. Nightcap could use someone handling public relations."

Ash couldn't believe what she was hearing.

"You have to be joking," Ash said. "I'm trying to get my sister out of your cult. The last thing I'd want to do is join and help you do your work for you. I mean, have you looked in the mirror?"

Templeton merely chuckled dryly, flakes of white paint falling as he did.

"You don't have to join the Faith," he said. "We don't require that. We work with business partners from all over. And, honestly, you'd bring a different perspective to things because you're hostile to what we're doing. Call us what you will—call us a cult, fine—but the problem with a cult is that there are true believers throughout it. I could use someone who brings another point of view to the table."

"While marketing your products?" Ash said.

"People did it—and do it—for tobacco, alcohol, soft drinks, pharmaceuticals, fossil fuel industries, weapons manufacture, and so on," Templeton said.

"Yeah, and they're called sellouts," Ash said. "I hate people like that."

"We'd pay you well for it," Templeton said. "Nightcap could use someone like you, Ms. Dunn. I'm a farmer and a businessman. That's what and who I am."

"And a murdering witch or warlock, whatever you want to call yourself," Ash said.

"I prefer 'wizard' as an appellation, but call me what you will," Templeton said. "I'm making you a sincere offer. Manna is a new and exciting product we will bring to the world. A readily renewable food source. And a proprietary one. Who cares where it comes from, if it feeds people and makes them happy? Join us and help us cure hunger."

"With that crap?" Ash asked. "The Food of the Goddess?"

"It has a ring to it, doesn't it?" Templeton said. "Squint your eyes a little and *La Signora* could become the new Mother Earth. Marketing makes all things possible. It's its own kind of magic, isn't it?"

He just smiled at her, an elfin grin on his old, oddly charming-yet-ghastly white face. Ash couldn't believe the man was even making this sort of offer to her.

"I know why you're here," Templeton said. "You're here for Melinda. But Melinda is happy with us. Why interfere with that? Think of what could get done with both of the Dunn Sisters here, working for us? You could keep tabs on your sister and ensure she's okay. If you ever feel she's in danger, I'll let you leave with her. We are a family company at Nightcap, after all."

Ash watched the workers carving the manna, others carting it to the truck, where it was further cut into smaller portions.

"You think we're evil, Ms. Dunn, but all we are is different from you," Templeton said. "Your sister is one of us. I think you could be happy with us, too."

Ash hadn't expected this from the man. She didn't know what she expected, but a job offer wasn't one of those things.

"What about Emily Carver?" Ash asked. "What happened to her? What happens to her?"

Templeton smiled benevolently.

"She is with the Goddess," he said. "I am so happy for her. My own wife attempted such a union twenty-five years ago, and the Lady consumed her. It almost destroyed me. It is the risk we undertake in our Faith. The Lady does what the Lady wills. We thought my Magda would be the perfect host for the Lady, but somehow we were wrong back then. Mona thought Emily might be a good host for her. Mona was so right."

"How many have you sacrificed for this?" Ash asked.

Templeton pondered it a moment, digging back into his old mind. Ash wondered how old he truly was, for though he was silver-haired, he had a vitality to him that was undeniable.

"Only three have ever tried to bond with the Lady," Templeton said. "It is not undertaken lightly. It's family lore, and I won't bore you with it. But Dr. Carver was accepted by the Lady, when Lucretia and my own Magda had been rejected."

Ash thought of Emily, could only imagine what her friend was feeling.

"I need to see her," Ash said. "To talk to her."

"Would this persuade you to work with us?" Templeton asked.

"It wouldn't hurt," Ash said.

They watched the workers continuing to harvest the manna. One of the trucks was leaving down the wooded path at the far side of the grove, and another was approaching, the workers hopping out and positioning the truck to take the next load.

"Then I shall make the arrangements myself," Templeton said. "And think of it this way—however you choose to see the Lady: whether goddess or alien or something in-between— through Dr. Carver, and your own friendship with her, you'd have unique and unparalleled access. You could interview her to your heart's content. Quite a scoop, one might say."

"I can interact with her safely?" Ash asked. "I won't go insane or something?"

Templeton laughed.

"The human substrate makes Her safer to interact with," he said. "As an incarnation, you're only dealing with part of Her, not all of Her. She's too much to take in all at once. Whereas Dr. Carver embodies an aspect of Her, now. It's like the difference between squinting at a sunbeam versus staring hard at the sun, if that makes sense."

"Sure," Ash said. "I'll talk to Emily. And I need to talk to my sister. Then I'll make my decision."

The workers were cutting the manna in the cleared area, which, to Ash's eye, was already beginning to sprout again with the whitish substance.

"Splendid," Templeton said. "I would expect no less of you."

# 8

**Austin had slipped away from Mallory, who was sleeping**
blissfully after her big night. He checked on the Twins, but they
didn't answer their door, and he didn't make an issue of it. Instead, he went to the parking deck and got in the van.

He was going to check things out himself, see what happened at the Sacred Grove. The van started up readily, and he
wound his way out of the deck, taking the alley route behind
the Grand to avoid the Festival grounds.

Although he'd been pretty hammered when they'd headed to the Grove, Austin still remembered it. He had enough of
a sense of direction, and, frankly, the place was on a winding
country road. It wasn't like he was navigating downtown Pittsburgh or anything.

He figured he probably had a good hour or two before the
others were up and fidgeting for food or whatever, and that
would give him enough time to check things out.

Austin drove for a couple of miles, mentally roadmapping
where he thought the place was when he saw Ash jogging along
the road. He almost rolled the van as he stopped and did a quick
U-turn.

Ash kept up her pace, running smoothly and steadily, trying to ignore him as he rolled on up as he rolled down the window.

"Ash," he said. "Hey, Ash. It's me, Austin."

"Austin?" Ash said, frowning like she was trying to remember who he was.

"Remember? I'm your fanboy?"

"Ah, yes," Ash said. "What are you doing out here?"

She stopped jogging for a moment.

"I was going to check out the Sacred Grove," he said.

Ash scowled, shaking her head.

"I wouldn't do that, to be honest," she said. "There's weird shit going on up there."

"That's why I wanted to check it out," Austin said. "Wait, were you up there?"

"All night," Ash said.

She looked pretty good for someone who'd been up all night. Maybe all of that running helped. He didn't say anything about that.

"Did you see what happened?" he asked.

A white Nightcap Mushroom Farm truck passed between them, heading the way Austin had been going.

"I saw some of it," Ash said, eyeing the road, then crossing. She went to the passenger side and climbed in. "Do you mind?"

"Uh, no," Austin said.

"I figured it was easier than, you know, yelling at each other across the street," Ash said. Up close, she was even prettier than he remembered. He realized this was the first time he saw her while he was sober and felt embarrassed by that.

"So, what did you see?" Austin asked.

"Why don't you drive and I'll tell you," Ash said.

"We're only a couple of miles from town," Austin said. She considered that.

"Take us to Bianchi Gardens," she said. "We can talk there."

As they were just south of the Festival District, the Bianchi Gardens were accessible, and Austin was able to find parking. They could see tourists checking out the gardens, which were an intricate blend of well-tended topiary hedges, a half-dozen sumptuous fountains, as well as a series of paths, promenades and alcoves. In the center of the fountains was a bronze statue of Lucretia Bianchi, who gestured plaintively for a release that never came. Ash thought about what Templeton had said when she saw the statue but didn't share that with Austin.

Ash and Austin walked in the gardens, her telling him everything she'd seen the night before. As they walked, Austin saw statues of the Grey Lady in some of the alcoves, the statues seeming to gaze upon them with blind eyes.

"I saw something crawl out of the ground itself," Ash said. "It was the Grey Lady. She was tall and lean, beautiful-awful. She had bright blue eyes that burned like fire. She looked at Emily and, I don't know, flowed into her. Possessed her. Then Emily looked at me with the same blue eyes and everything went crazy. Like a flash of bright blue and then I woke up entombed in this stuff."

She explained the manna, and Austin shuddered.

"That's gross," he said.

"Um, yeah," Ash said. "I had to dig my way out. And people were harvesting it. Eating it. It's food. Ned Templeton was there. He called it 'the Food of the Goddess.'"

"Also gross," Austin said.

"Emily had said something to me. Like in my head," Ash said. "She told me to meet her at the Temple."

The burbling blue-tiled fountains were soothing, despite her unease. Looking up at Lucretia Bianchi, Ash shivered. She could only imagine how it ended for her.

"He said they'd tried two other times to bring the Lady to a host," Ash said. "Lucretia Bianchi, and Ned's wife, Magda. Now Emily. It only worked for Emily."

"Why?"

"Even he doesn't know," Ash said.

The tourists were taking pictures, happy, talking, exclaiming. Ash looked around, gazed at the sunlit sky, working its way toward noon. In the warmth of the day, the light, the ghastly way her day had begun almost receded from memory. Except for what Templeton had told her.

"I have the story of the making of the Breach," Ash said. "I saw all of that. I need to find Emily and talk to her."

Austin's phone pinged, and he glanced at it. Mallory and the others.

*Where are you, Dude?*

*We're starving.*

"Hold on," he said.

*Check your Fungo Fungible tokens. I think Hotcakes is offering 15% off.*

He knew that would get the attention of the Twins.

*I'll meet you there. Get a table, I'll catch up.*

He pocketed his phone, after muting it.

"We need to find Emily," Austin said.

"She said the Temple," Ash said.

"My friend, Mallory, she's one of them," Austin said. "She's joined the cult. Said she was an Exemplar."

"Sorry to hear that," Ash said. "They're the really crazy ones."

"I guess," Austin said. "They gave her grey robes and a knife."

"I know," Ash said. "I, uh, masqueraded as one yesterday."

"You did?"

Ash nodded, listening to the fountains bubble and spray.

"Why?"

"I wanted to infiltrate them, see what I could unearth," Ash said. "But those Red Death guys messed things up. I ended up running away."

Austin took all of that in without comment.

"The Temple is where I should go," Ash said. "I have to find Emily. You need to be with your friends, Austin. You said your one friend is part of the cult. What about the others?"

"I don't know," Austin said. "I haven't talked to them, yet."

From where they stood, Ash could see the Temple several blocks away, powerfully monumental and imperious as ever. Emily was in there somewhere.

"We have to slip in there somehow," Austin said. Ash cleared her throat.

"I, uh, kind of have an invitation to attend," Ash said. "You know, like a Press pass?"

Austin scoffed at that.

"Well, okay, then," he said. "We could have just driven up there."

"No," Ash said. "You need to hang back. Go be with your friends. Only I need to send you some stuff. You have AirDrop?"

"Of course," Austin said. "Why?"

"The footage I shot last night," Ash said. "I haven't reviewed it, yet, but I want someone else to have it. Like insurance."

Austin was touched she'd even trust him with that stuff. She smiled at him, pulling her phone and DVR from her pockets.

"Let me send them to you. At least what I filmed," she said. "I can't transfer the DVR files this way. You can listen to what I recorded, though."

He played back what she had recorded, listening closely to them, including the ritual she'd seen and her conversations with Templeton. While he listened, Ash looked around them, but nobody seemed out of place or even interested in them.

When he was done listening, he gave the DVR back to her.

"Fuck," Austin said. "Talk about a Faustian bargain. Are you going to take the gig?"

"Hell, no," Ash said. "Screw that old creep."

He gave her his number and email, and she sent the files to him. They waited in the gardens, beneath the shadow of Lucretia Bianchi, feeling somewhat concealed by the spraying of the fountains.

"Why are you really giving me this stuff?" Austin asked.

"Just in case something happens to me," Ash said. "I can't trust anyone else around here. I mean, I could send it to the guy who hired me and Emily to come out here—Jerry Merriwether, but he's kind of a billionaire son of a bitch, and I don't feel like he deserves it."

Austin knew the name, and what he didn't know, he looked up on his phone while Ash was sending him the files. The CEO of Mycopharmix, a mushroom-based pharmaceutical company in northern California.

"Why send these to me? You don't know me from anything," Austin said.

"That's sort of the point," Ash said. "You're the last person they'd suspect. Unless they're following us and watching, nobody'll know you've got the stuff but me."

"I don't even know what I have," Austin said.

"If something happens to me, you need to open the files and look," Ash said. "See what's in there. Get it out there. Let people know what went on here."

Austin looked uneasily at Ash and around them. Nobody appeared to be paying them any mind, but that didn't mean somebody wasn't watching.

"Do you think something's going to happen to you?" Austin asked.

"Templeton offered me a PR job for his farm," Ash said. "He's trying to buy me out. You tell me. I've got a billionaire pharma tycoon on one side, trying to find out what he can. I've got a multimillionaire cult leader warlock on the other side, trying to pay me off. And my friend has apparently been possessed by an alien-goddess thing. I'm a little overstretched."

They laughed a moment, and Austin felt better. Ash had a nice laugh.

"I can help you," Austin said. "I want to help you."

"You are helping me," Ash said. "Look, I'll know where to find you. I'll find you if I can. I just wanted this to be on the safe side. And if something bad happens, at least I'll know the stuff

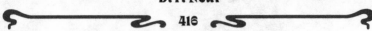
I saw can get out there. Nobody'll ever believe it. I saw it and I don't even believe it."

She sent the files to him and asked him to confirm that he'd received them.

"Okay," Austin said. "I've got the video clips."

The two of them cleared the fountain area, headed toward one of the crushed stone promenades.

"I'm going to head to the Temple, now," Ash said. "I'll let you know if there are any problems."

"Promise?" Austin asked.

"I promise," Ash said, and she gave him a hug she hadn't planned on giving. He returned it.

"Please be safe," Austin said.

"I will," Ash said.

They parted and Austin watched her take off jogging for the Temple, which bemused him, as he answered texts from his friends, who were nagging at him. He couldn't manage more than a stroll, jacking his phone and watching the video clips as he walked.

# 9

**Hotcakes was hopping, packed with people, Logan noticed,**
but Maura said a few magic words to the hostess, and managed to garner them a booth. She mock-shrugged adorably and smiled at him.

"I have a way with words, what can I say?" Maura said.

"Yeah, clearly," Logan said, surveying the menu with his chef's eyes, weighing, evaluating, assessing.

"Fun Gus is performing at 10:30," Maura said. "South Stage."

"Hard pass," Logan said. Maura laughed.

"Uncle Gus will be so put out," Maura said.

"You're related to that clown? You literally have a clown for an uncle?"

Maura nodded, wincing.

"I know, right?" Maura said. "We're not proud of it. He's been a clown for like, I don't know, thirty years. As long as I can remember."

"How can someone even be a clown for thirty years?" Logan asked.

"Hey, now," Maura said. "What about Bozo?"

"I don't think anybody was Bozo for that long," Logan said. "Honestly, your uncle has been Fun Gus the Laughing Clown for that long?"

"Yeah. The laughter will die long before he ever will," Maura said. She ordered pecan pancakes when the server showed, an overly deferential young woman with "Heidi" on her nametag. Logan ordered buttermilk pancakes, and coffee for the both of them. "Daddy cursed him."

"Cursed him?"

"Yep," Maura said. "A long story. Uncle Gus has been a clown ever since."

"You mean like a curse-curse," Logan said. "An actual curse?"

Maura nodded.

"This is another of those family revelations, yeah? Like how you summoned an otherworldly being to invade our world?" Logan asked.

"Overstated, but something like that," Maura said. Her brown eyes were free of guilt but masqueraded as feeling a saccharine contrition.

"We can't run a business like that," Logan said. "I won't deal in curses and ritual invocations."

Maura laughed at him as their coffees arrived. He took his black, while she drowned hers in cream and sugar.

"No worries, Logan," Maura said. "I'm breathtakingly pragmatic when I put my mind to it."

"Right," Logan said. "Sure."

The coffee was good—strong and freshly-brewed. He wondered if the people who ran Hotcakes just made sure that Maura got top-notch service.

"Hotcakes is perfect for the 5K," Maura said, nodding to the streetside windows they had. "You can see the runners go by."

"As if I'd want to do that," Logan said. "I mean, a 5K? C'mon. Watching runners is like slow death. Living death. Something lethal to the human spirit."

Maura laughed, drinking her coffee.

"You're funny," Maura said. "Your irreverence is refreshing. You literally don't care who you offend."

"Why start now?" Logan said. "I'm a chef. I don't care who I piss off."

"Clearly," Maura said. "Oh, jeez."

"What is it?" Logan asked, following her gaze. He saw some kids in tee shirts, looking a little bleary-eyed.

"They were at the Service last night," Maura said. "Some of them."

Logan looked them over. A pretty redhead with big eyes and a knowing grin framed by blue lipstick. A dusky blonde in white coveralls and a black jersey tee wearing a fisherman's hat jammed low on her head, and a young man who looked like he could be her brother, wearing an orange stocking cap and blue jeans and a sweatshirt. A dark-haired, earnest-eyed young

man in wire rim glasses wearing a Blob tee and jeans joined them, shrugging and gesturing while he talked.

"Ah, your secret ceremony," Logan said.

"Exactly," Maura said. "What happens at the ceremony stays at the ceremony."

"Like Vegas," Logan said.

"Just so," Maura said. The redhead caught Maura's eye, and she gave her a cooler-than-cool head nod Logan couldn't have missed if he'd tried. "The redhead's Mallory Tilton."

"Mallory Tilton," Logan said. "Alright. Is that significant?"

"An up-and-comer," Maura said. "She really wants to be me so badly."

Logan looked the young woman over, amused that she became self-conscious at the fact that both he and Maura were looking at her.

"Can anybody ever be you, Maura?" Logan asked.

"Hell, even I find it hard to be me, every now and then," Maura said.

The kids were told they had a 45-minute wait until they could be seated. Maura knew this because the hostess handed them one of those pagers they gave out to let patrons know when their number came up.

"Sucks to be them," Logan said. "Unless you want to use your sway to get them seated."

"Nope," Maura said. "Definitely not. I use my powers only for us. I'm just *that* witch."

Logan laughed, watching the kids file back outside, lurking by the building crowd for the 5K.

"Never seen so many people lining up for a 5K," Logan said.

"It's a big deal in Lynchburg," Maura said. "People just love the Fungus Run."

"Sure they do," Logan said.

"You can't run anything larger," Maura said. "Any longer and you're literally out in the hills. Nobody'd ever find you out there. You'd be surprised how quickly it gets, I don't know, scary."

Logan thought that was funny.

"I can see that," Logan said. "Driving out here was like that. Lynchburg is like an island. Although a woman who breaks free from her kidnappers probably doesn't have much to fear in this world."

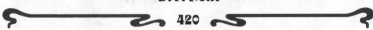
Maura snickered, drinking her coffee before sinking her knife and fork into her pancakes with nearly surgical skill.

"Sure, sure. This island will be dead quiet after the Festival," Maura said. "People live all year on the money they make this weekend. You'd be amazed. It's why yesterday's crap with *Las Rojas* was so disruptive. It's not supposed to go like that."

Logan nodded, eating his own breakfast, wanted to ask her about what really happened with her and her kidnappers. He steeled himself and asked.

"What really happened with you and those *Rojas* who took you?" Logan asked.

Maura looked at him, smiling half to herself, shaking her head.

"You really are a bulldog, aren't you? Okay, I'll tell you," Maura said. "I put a spell on them and commanded them to kill each other and to release me."

Logan laughed. He couldn't tell if she was joking or not, so he went with joking as the only thing that made sense.

"Yeah, right," he said.

"You asked," Maura said.

He speared some pancake and drowned it in a pool of the syrup at one side of his plate.

"I'm thinking you slipped out of your bonds and you ran off," Logan said. "Hid in the woods around St. Sophia and they couldn't find you. Local girl that you are, you took advantage of that and got away from there."

"You don't believe the spell story?" Maura said. Logan rolled his eyes.

"Why would I? My explanation is more plausible," Logan said.

"If you already had your own explanation, why bother asking for mine?" Maura said.

"I wanted to hear what you'd say," Logan said. "It's not that often one runs into a kidnap victim. Especially one who freed herself from a gang of well-armed thugs."

"I was never a victim," Maura said. "I let them take me."

"You let them?" Logan asked. She nodded.

"I didn't want the lunch service being disrupted," Maura said, and the two of them laughed over that. He understood how that went. As a chef, nothing was more irritating than having a service spoiled by unfortunate circumstance.

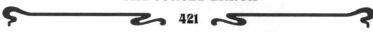
"What happened last night?" Logan asked. "Besides, you know, the apparent physical manifestation of your heathen goddess?"

"Don't tease," Maura said. "It's unbecoming, Logan. We held our secret midnight ritual, like I told you."

"How do you *really* know your goddess physically manifested?" Logan asked.

"You just know," Maura said. "You can feel Her presence."

"Wow," Logan said. "Now I'm really sorry I didn't go."

Maura's face betrayed nothing more than weariness and a worldly sort of amusement that only she could carry off without looking too jaded. She held a forkful of pecan pancakes inches from her mouth, pausing for his benefit.

"Don't be," Maura said. "It was really something, but nothing you'd want to be a part of. Worlds colliding, that sort of thing. You're not ready, yet. But I'll get you there, don't you worry."

"If you say so," Logan said. "I'm not sure what you saw, or think you saw, but whatever it was, it was weird."

"Forget about it," Maura said, in a curious tone, and, incredibly, Logan did. The thoughts he'd had simply vanished as if they were never there to begin with, and there was only him sitting there across the table with Maura.

"What was I even talking about?" Logan asked.

Maura smiled at him, that warm, sugary smile she had just for him.

"You were telling me how much you loved me," Maura said.

"That's right," Logan said, and, between bites of breakfast, he told her.

He could see the dark-haired bespectacled kid walking up to the window where they were. He looked maybe mid-20s, tops. He took out a Sharpie and wrote something on the window in black, frowning as he wrote:

!THGIN TSAL DID UOY TAHW WONK I

"Wait, is that Spanish or Latin?" Logan asked, laughing. "Does he even realize it's backwards?"

Maura read it, frowning at the young man, who met her gaze evenly, nodding, pointing to the words he'd written. He then flipped her off with both hands, snarling at her as he did so.

"Hold on," Maura said, putting down her coffee. She got up and went to leave. The young man took off running. Logan deciphered it:

I KNOW WHAT YOU DID LAST NIGHT!

He wanted to say something, but Maura was already outside, looking for the young man, who was now nowhere to be seen. She said something to the pretty redhead, who looked over at the writing on the window and nodded gravely. The young woman handed the pager over to the girl in the fisherman's cap, who looked at Maura in confusion.

The redhead then took off running. Maura came back inside, having said something to the hostess. In moments, one of the Hotcakes staffers had gone to the window with a spray bottle of cleaner and was mopping down the window, smearing and clearing off the message.

She came back in.

"What was that all about?" Logan asked.

"Forget about it," Maura said, and for the second time, Logan felt himself forgetting what the hell he'd been thinking about a moment before.

"Damn, I must be having a stroke," Logan said. "I literally forgot what the hell I was just saying."

"You were still telling me much you love me," Maura said, and Logan realized she was right.

"I do love you," Logan said. "So much."

"Sweet man," Maura said, caressing his cheek.

Her phone pinged, and she took a look.

"Oh, Jeez," Maura said. "I have to go to the Temple this morning. Mona's called a Conclave."

"That sounds serious," Logan said.

Maura was texting, her long fingers flying over her phone.

"Told you we should have gotten out of town," Maura said. "Goddamned Mona. Queen of the Busybodies."

Logan saw a bunch of people doing much the same thing, both in the restaurant and on the street—they were checking their phones and then heading off.

Maura pried herself from her phone and looked Logan in the eye.

"Sorry, Babe," Maura said. "I've got to tend to this. You enjoy your breakfast."

"Wait, you're leaving?"

"Yeah, I have to," Maura said. "Look, we can meet up in a couple of hours, I promise."

"Meet up where?" Logan asked.

"I'll ping you," Maura said. "Just finish your breakfast."

"Okay," Logan said. "You ping me."

She got up, and he got up, and she gave him a kiss that tasted of maple syrup, coffee, cigarettes. Then she left, joined by others who were leaving as well.

*Wow, when Mona calls, everyone comes running,* Logan thought, irritated. He thought maybe he'd check out the Temple after he finished breakfast, just to see what was going on.

# 10

**Emily was awash in colors she only partly knew as she** sat inside the Round Room in the indoor grove, beside a statue of herself. Only it wasn't her. It was the Grey Lady. That she'd thought it was her alarmed her.

*I have made a terrible mistake,* Emily thought. *I am infected.*

Mona had acolytes bring forth a golden thronelike chair carved with glyphs she could somehow read:

I AM *LA SIGNORA GRIGIA,* BLESSED ONE FROM BEYOND, FORETOLD BY THE SAINTS AND SCRIBES OF THE BIANCHIS. IN THE GREY AND THE WHITE, THE LADY OF THE FOREST, HANDMAIDEN OF DECAY AND GOD-DAUGHTER OF SLAUGH-TER. THEY WHO WOULD STAND AGAINST ME SHALL FALL. ALL SHALL FALL. I AM THE SWIFT RUINATION AND EVER-LASTING DAMNATION OF MINE ENEMIES. WOE TO ALL WHO STAND AGAINST ME AND WEAL TO THOSE WHO WOULD BE MY SERVANTS FOR THE FLEETING ETERNITY.

Emily had wanted to leave the Temple, but Mona had guid-ed her back to the throne, her voice reassuring.

"A goddess should not go walking about," Mona said. "We want You to make a grand entrance. I have called the Conclave as You commanded. When they are all arrived, we will bring You forth."

The Lady spoke within her, and Emily listened.

*Be patient,* the Lady said. *I am with you always.*

And She took Emily to Her home, a strange, white world with pointed mountains like spears that stabbed the sky, where strange, massive crimson centipedes crawled in and out of the manna, their shiny skin sparkling like ruby from the light of a

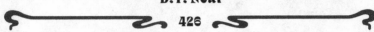
waning sun, and dreadworms writhed in ebony abundance in tangled masses that squirmed ceaselessly, burrowing throughout the manna with their round-toothed maws. In this surreal place She stood amid cyclopean white megaliths that grasped for the psychedelic sky with carved stone spars hewn by long-dead worshippers.

How lonely a place it was, while the sky cried tears of cerulean, emerald, and saffron. How long had She waited in that sorrowful place, before they had come to Her, or She had come to them. Only a glimpse at first, like a pinhole glimmer of a witch in the woods, crying for aid against her persecutors. And the Lady had been only too happy to answer as She sat upon Her cold stone throne. She had answered, and the witch had seen the blessing of the first drop of the Lady's Tears, in finding the blue *Amanita* in the deep forest. The blood sacrifices that followed grew more fervent, and the Lady brought Her blessings through a wider opening, Her window to another world, another universe.

The more they brought, the more She took, the hungrier She got. While the dread centipedes clacked their mandibles by the twisted light of three moons—one white, one black, one blue—the Lady turned Her attention to Her followers, who became worshippers. Always Her blessings fell to them. It was a courtship and a seduction, as much as anything else.

No longer alone in exile, but with a window on this new world, the Lady turned Her celestial attention toward widening the portal between Her world-universe and theirs.

Time had never mattered to Her, for She had long been eternal, but when a hand had come to Her from that blue beyond, She had taken it—Lucretia Bianchi, in her grinning greed and aching ambition, had tried to forge the bond between them, but it had been too soon, and the effort had torn her apart, the link severed.

The Lady, bathed in Bianchi blood, had not given up. Her will passed through the pinhole portal, and Her worshippers, more numerous, now, put themselves to the task She had given them.

*Make me a portal fit for a Queen,* She had told them. *A grand entrance.*

And Her Faithful had done so for a time. She did not measure time the way they did, so it was another moment and this

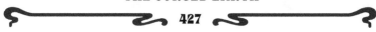
time, the portal was greater still, and Magda Templeton, another witch, wild-eyed, wanton and wicked, had crawled through the portal, only to have it hitch on her hips, for it was still not wide enough for her to pass, and the Lady's Kiss killed her outright, and again the Lady was bathed in the boiling blood of a faithful witch. She'd added her skull to that of Lucretia's, in a place of honor in Her home, with all the other sacrifices that had been carried out in Her name. She understood the smallfolk seeking to honor Her, for She was the true Hand of Glory.

Again and again, they sacrificed in Her name, and with more Faithful, the portal grew larger, still. While the dreadworms burrowed and the centipedes hunted them, spilling their black bilious blood upon the fields of manna with their gnashing mandibles, the Lady focused Her gaze in Her blue pool in Her high castle, captive in the confines of the three circles that bound Her to this place. But She worked harder and harder, and the fragile Faithful did not waver in their devotion, and the portal grew ever larger as the sacrifices came with increasing regularity, like the pulsing of a monstrous heart that beat faster and faster.

*And at last you came, Emily. Unwilling, as you must be. I was too eager, as were the others. Too eager. They sought to force their way into My world. You, My reluctant host. You were perfect because you alone did not want it, you rejected it, would not believe it. That was why I chose you, and why you worked where the others failed Me. Your disbelief was the key to My salvation.*

That moment, Her bright blue eyes burned brighter still, the two of them dancing together in the alabaster palace, the three great circles disappearing in stardust motes as they whirled about, the two of them dancing in spinning circles, ever-faster, until, at the end of it, they were one, and passed through the portal together.

*And now I am here,* the Lady said, in her head. *Braided together with you.*

*You don't belong here,* Emily said. *This is not Your home.*

*It is, now. And what a home it is.*

Emily's gaze turned outward again as she saw the acolytes had run golden poles through the throne upon which she sat, turning it into a sedan chair. A pair of gold-masked Exemplars in shiny silk blue finery had flanked her, hefting her up and

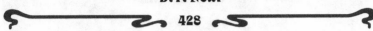
walking her along the *Amanita*-laden path, toward the blue door.

*Patience, Academician,* the Lady counseled her. *You will know when.*

The rocking motion of the sedan chair was strangely soothing, as the golden-hatted Exemplars guided her along the path, while acolytes went to the door, which opened.

Into the dancing light they went, Emily seeing the stage lighting of the Temple in full effect, a cacophony of psychedelic tunes playing from the nimble fingers of Melinda Dunn, unseen from her perch.

Out from the opened door she came, beneath the great carved idol, into a packed Temple filled with the Faithful, who gasped and cried out at the sight of her, throwing themselves to their knees in ecstatic supplication.

"Behold, Brethren, the Lady made flesh," Mona said, wearing blood red robes garlanded with grey, her arms upraised, her face freshly-painted white and blue, her stick crown again upon her head. The music was triumphant, and as Emily gazed around her with her bright blue eyes, she could see the look of wonder and worship on the faces of the Faithful. She could pick out faces she recognized—Clea, tears in her eyes. Cloris, prostrate. Maura Templeton, smiling wryly, her big eyes even bigger. And Ash, in the back of the Grand Hall, gazing in wonder, filming it all.

*They are not all here,* Emily said. *The Clown, the Mayor, and the Wizard are not here.*

*Do not fret, Academician. I am here. I am with you always.*

"I am here," Emily said aloud to the gathered Faithful. "I am with you always."

# 11

**Austin had run down Ambrose Alley after his impetuous**
bit of vandalism had drawn out Maura from the breakfast
place. He hadn't known what had compelled him to do that, except that it had angered him to see her nonchalantly dining after what he'd seen her do in that footage. People like that didn't
deserve to go about their daily lives as if nothing happened. It
was like how he imagined it was with war criminals—they had
to face the consequences of their wrongdoing, however small.

Who knew how many people Maura Templeton had sacrificed that way? There were at least nine people who'd been
killed last night. There were likely many more. Year after year.
Thinking of that made Austin want to scream. All the happy-
go-lucky posturing of the Lynchburg Fungus Festival was just
that—it was a deception, the candy shell covering something
dark and rotten inside.

That he and his friends had fallen for it, that Mallory had
been consumed by it, it was almost too much to bear. Mallory
texted him as if she'd been conjured up.

*Austin, quit running, Chickenshit.*

He texted her back, talking into his phone, letting it dictate
as he ran.

*I know what you did, too. Murderer.*

*You don't know anything.*

*I saw.*

"Austin," Mallory said, and he saw she was behind him, in
the alley, some distance back. He was near Grand, near the clueless festivalgoers.

Mallory had run hard for him, having eaten up his head
start. She walked toward him, arms out, her face concerned,
breathing hard. Another hostage negotiation.

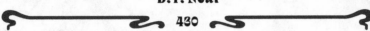
"Stay back," Austin said.

"What's wrong with you, Austin? We were going to have breakfast, and you just go nuts?" Mallory said.

"I just went along with it to go along," Austin said. "I've never dealt with a murderer before. Not sure what's the protocol."

"Ha," Mallory said. She kept walking toward him, slow and steady, and he kept backing away, into the relative comfort and seeming safety of the crowd. Whatever she intended, she was less likely to do it here. "I just want to have breakfast, Austin. Then you poke the bear by riling up Maura. She's not the type of person you want to piss off. She killed those gangsters, you know. The *Rojas?* All of them. And they were badasses. Think about that a moment. If they had no chance against her—against us—what kind of chance do you have? You're not cut out for this, like I said before."

She was only a few paces away, now, and he could see her big eyes scanning him, assessing him in her way.

"I'm going to tell the Twins what you tried to do to them," Austin said.

Mallory laughed.

"You think they'll understand? Or even care? They're going to think you're the crazy one, Austin, not me," Mallory said. "Don't you know how that goes? The more incredible the accusation, the less likely you'll be believed. It's the Cassandra Complex."

Austin didn't care.

"They deserve to know," he said.

"They're already claimed by the Lady," Mallory said. "They don't even know that, but She's inside them, growing. Do you know how that'll go? She'll grow and grow inside them, and they'll walk outside one day, out into the woods, like deep, and they'll keel over and where they fall, Lady's Tears will grow. Vessels for the Lady. That's all they are, now. They're already dead. They just don't know it, yet."

The offhand was she talked about it chilled Austin, filled him with both rage and fear.

"This entire trip was a setup," Austin said. "Yeah? You brought us all here as sacrifices."

"Yeah? So?" Mallory said. "Again, you can't tell anybody that. There's no evidence. Not a trace. The Taylor Triplets? Vanished."

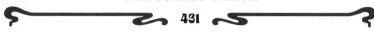

She made a blowing sound with her fingers, spreading them like spores on the wind.

"Why are you like this?" Austin asked.

"I want to be on the winning team, Austin," Mallory said. "Last year, at the Festival, I was as clueless then as you are, now. I didn't know how it really was. I went into it blind, and then I saw. I mean, I truly saw. I saw Her. What She means for our world. That Midnight Service last year, I gave myself fully to it. I was all in. The Triplets were my backstage pass to almost everything."

"Did She infect you?" Austin asked. She was right across from him, and people navigated around them, passing by them without comment.

"No, She didn't," Mallory said. "She didn't have to. I was Hers that night. I became something."

"'Something' is right," Austin said. "You're definitely something, now."

Mallory rested a hand on her hip, fishing out some lipstick. She did a touch-up.

"Oh, nice," Austin said. "How on-brand is that?"

"Like before," Mallory said, smiling at him.

"Seems about right," Austin said.

"You didn't mind last night," Mallory said. "Or this morning, anyway."

"Yeah, well—" Austin said.

"I wasn't going to sacrifice you," Mallory said. "Just them. You're special to me. You could be something, too. We could have something here. Our own thing."

Her voice was what it always was—that tomboyish blend of companionably casual comfort and breezy nonchalance. No great shakes. A human sacrifice here and there. What did that matter between friends with benefits?

"Something? Like what? I'm not joining your frickin' cult," Austin said.

Mallory smiled at him, shaking her head.

"You don't have to," Mallory said. "I'm twice the cultist you could ever be, anyway, Austin. I'll take care of the messy stuff. You can be my boy toy."

"Ha," Austin said.

Mallory looked around, gestured.

"The winning team, Austin," Mallory said. "You don't know it, yet, but it is. These people here. They're part of something greater. Something real. We're not talking abstractions, anymore. She's *here*. She's not going away."

She held out her hand to him. He could see her blue-painted nails, her wild eyes, her sultry smile, like poisoned sugar.

"Hey, Kid, you missed my show," came the voice that made him cringe. He looked, and there was Fun Gus, smirking at him over a cigar. "Have you made your decision, yet?"

"Fun Gus!" Mallory said. "Help me with him, would you?"

"Help you with what?" Fun Gus asked. "Didn't you get Mona's message?"

He held up his smartphone with his free hand, jiggling it mockingly.

"What message?" Mallory asked.

Fun Gus laughed silently to himself, shaking his head, blowing smoke. He nodded around them on Grand, where they could see people running down the street.

"She's called a Conclave," Fun Gus said. "At the Temple. Check your phone."

Mallory grabbed her phone, toggling through the Fungo App, to the three-circle icon, which was flashing. She clicked on it, cursing.

*CONCLAVE AT THE TEMPLE AT NOON.*

"Fuck," Mallory said. The clock tower rang 11:45.

"Best get a move on," Fun Gus said. "She'll be waiting."

Mallory looked at him skeptically, and with irritation at Austin.

"What about you?" Mallory asked.

"Nah," Fun Gus said. "I don't come running when my niece comes a'calling. I don't run for anybody. But you'd better, if you want to secure yourself a place at the Big Show."

Mallory was conflicted, trying to decide whether she wanted to keep razzing Austin or whether she should go to the Temple.

"To be continued," Mallory said. "Goddamn you, Austin. We're not done, yet."

She took off running for the Temple. He watched her go, grateful that she was leaving, while Fun Gus simply smoked, having put his phone back in his pocket.

"Murderer," Austin said, which made the clown laugh.

"Oh, so you saw that?" he said.

"I saw everything," Austin said. "From last night."

"I highly doubt that," Fun Gus said. "If you did, you'd be wearing a bib and gibbering in a corner, Sunshine."

The clown flicked ash from his cigar, looking around, watching the Faithful race past befuddled tourists.

"See how they run," Fun Gus said. "Am I right?"

"What's your deal with me?" Austin asked. "How'd I get so lucky?"

Fun Gus reached out for Austin with his white-gloved hands, but Austin recoiled, and, amused, the clown wiggled his fingers.

"I know a thing or two about what's what," he said. "The Lady spared your friends. Lucky kids, gotta say. If I were you, I'd take your friends—those goofy Twins—and get the hell out of Lynchburg while you still can. Get out of here and never look back."

"Yeah? Why is that?" Austin asked.

"Because *She's* here, now, Bozo," Fun Gus said. "I've seen what She can do. Me, I'm getting the hell out of here first chance I get."

Austin could not comprehend the logic of the clown.

"But you're part of it," Austin said. "I saw the footage."

"You can't choose your family, Sport. I was there because my family needed me, not because I wanted to," Fun Gus said. "All those wannabes are crowding the Temple because Mona rang their bells. No way. Not me. I don't have to go anywhere I don't want to be. Not anymore. And where.I don't want to be is near that Thing we brought into this world."

"If you were opposed to it, why'd you help?" Austin said. "You killed that woman."

"Her or me. Ned wanted Her here, and who am I to stand against Ned? Just a clown," Fun Gus said. "I want to live. Even as I am, I want to live. If you're smart, you'll do as I said, and scram."

"Is that the decision you've been nagging me to make?" Austin asked.

"Sure, Kid," Fun Gus said, turning and walking away from him, heading toward a red van polka-dotted with white spots the size of baseballs that was parked at the edge of the Festival grounds, at the corner of Grand and Main. "I don't give you

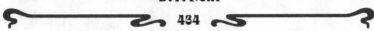
more than maybe a half an hour before She gets busy. Consider this a fair warning and a head start to get the hell out of here."

"What are you even talking about?" Austin asked.

Fun Gus tapped his forehead while fishing for his keys to his van.

"I'm a witch, you idiot," Fun Gus said. "I *know* things. And that Thing in the Temple is going to pop like goddamned Krakatoa. Mona can't see it, Maura won't see it. Lord knows what Ned's thinking, and Lionel's got no idea."

"How do you know that?" Austin asked.

"Jeezus Palomino, Sparky," Fun Gus said. "You need me to spell it out for you? Okay, yeah, you do. She needed us to get Her here. All these years, She needed us, and we were there for Her. Our Goddess, yeah? We lied, cheated, stole, killed for Her. In Her name. She loves that. But She doesn't need us anymore. Savvy?"

"I don't think so," Austin said.

"C'mon, now," Fun Gus said. "She's a god. You don't want to cross a god, Sunshine. Maybe you do, but I sure don't. I did my part for the family last night. I was there. I saw everything. And I'm getting my polka-dotted ass the hell away from here."

"Coward," Austin said.

"Count on it," Fun Gus said. "Never bank on the courage of a clown. Besides, you think that's a fight I'd ever want to have? I'm the least of the coven. I'm the fifth wheel. I'm the punch line. No way, Slick. I'm gone."

"How can I stop the Lady?" Austin asked.

"You can't, Dummy," Fun Gus said. "Hey, Mushette, you coming?"

He was looking over Austin's shoulder. Austin turned, startled to see the Mushette mascot standing there. How long the thing had been lurking there was anybody's guess. The mascot looked longingly at the clown's van and shook her head, pointing to the north stage, where Mushy was performing for an audience of rapt onlookers. Mushette mimed wringing tears from her eyes.

"Suit yourself," Fun Gus said.

He found his keys and wolf-whistled, a piercing, two-finger whistle that brought a half-dozen mimes running. Fun Gus surveyed them, while they lined up in mock-formation, saluting him.

"Consider this a lifeboat," Fun Gus said, walking in front of them, scrutinizing each one. "You, you, and you."

He picked the three female mimes, shrugged at Austin, grinning as he did. The male mimes looked put out, miming their displeasure, but afraid to cross the clown. They mime-protested, but he shooed them off with a hand.

"What can I say? Witchcraft's a bitch, Kid," Fun Gus said. "Like I said last night: seeya on the flip side of infinity!"

He honked his bike horn three times, tossing it to Austin, who caught it instinctively, while the girl mimes silently argued over who was going to ride shotgun, until they resolved it and they got in, their white faces in the van windows, eyeing Austin, making mock-sad faces at their mime brothers they were leaving behind.

"Got room for one more, Sunshine," Fun Gus said. "Could teach you a thing or two about the way of the world."

"No fucking way," Austin said, and the clown cackled.

"Good decision," Fun Gus said, winking at him. "Don't blow your lead, though. You got maybe twenty minutes left."

He got in the van and started it up. Then he wheeled around, his tires squeaking a little as he turned, and then he was gone, racing down Route 219, honking his van horn as he went, the van horn sounding like a bigger version of the bike horn, receding as he shot down the road.

Shaking his head, Austin texted the Twins.

*We have to get out of here. Like now.*

*WTF, Austin? What are you talking about?*

It was Jess. The Twins were up for anything fun, but they were rampant scenesters as well. If he told them he was trying to follow the advice of a clown, it was maybe a 50-50 shot.

*Fun Gus told me we had to get out of town. He said like now. Hell, he just took off.*

*What? Why? What about Mallory?*

They still didn't know. They had no idea how close they'd come to dying last night. He ran to the Grand Hotel, mindful of the clock tower, counting down the minutes.

*Just get to the Grand, please. I'm leaving in twenty minutes, with or without you.*

*Are you insane?*

*Stone sober.*

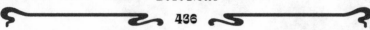
*What is going on? Jake's pissed at you for rushing us through brunch. I'm kinda pissed at you, too.*

*Fine, be pissed. We have to leave. I'm getting my shit and I'm getting out of here.*

He went in the lobby, saw a concierge he didn't recognize, somebody other than Cloris, and he took the elevator up to their unit.

Packing was easy because Austin was always pretty neat. He loaded up his stuff, pinging Ash.

*Are you at the Temple?*

*Yeah. It's packed.*

*Uh, I got word that maybe that's not a good place to be.*

*Yeah? Who said?*

*Fun Gus.*

*Ha. I can't leave. I need to get a chance to talk to Emily. They're trotting her out on a golden throne. Weird shit. I'm filming it.*

*He told me like maybe a half hour, maybe twenty minutes, and shit's going to go crazy.*

*How does he even know that?*

*Just repeating what he told me.*

*I just can't leave without talking to Emily. I have to try to help her.*

*I don't know if you can.*

Austin looked at Mallory's Exemplar mask and robes, her knife. He took them, stuck them in a canvas bag.

He did a quick check, then went down to the lobby.

"Checking out," Austin said. The concierge slightly frowned, a slender young man with a very short brown haircut and a sharp nose and little coffee bean eyes.

"Leaving early? That's too bad," he said. "I hope your stay at the Grand was to your liking."

"Um, yeah," Austin said. "Great. No complaints. I just have to get going. You know how that is. Beating the traffic, all of that."

Austin was able to get checked out without difficulty, and hastily left the lobby, heading out onto the Festival grounds, where people were crowding the tents, oblivious. He felt like he had to warn them, even as he felt stupid about that. They'd want to know why.

He then hustled to his van, tossing his luggage in the back, before bringing the van back around, parking it closer to Grand.

It was nearly noon. With so many of the cultists having run when Mona's Conclave call had gone out, many of the tents were untended, leaving confused tourists stumbling around.

He walked to one of the tourists, an older man, and cleared his throat.

"Did you hear about the bomb threat?" Austin asked.

"The what?"

"The bomb threat," Austin said. "I heard a rumor that those *Rojas* gangers left a bomb out here somewhere."

The man's eyes went big, and he took off running with a yelp.

"Fuck," Austin said. He'd hoped word would spread, didn't count on the guy just running away. The clock tower sounded noon, each tolling of the bell making him more uneasy. He texted Jess and Jake.

*Where the hell are you guys?*

*I'm coming.*

*It was Jess.*

*What about Jake?*

*He said not until he's done with brunch. He told you to fuck off.*

"Oh, come on," Austin said. He texted Jake.

*WTF, Jake? You've got to listen to me. We have to jet ASAP.*

*Whatever, Bro. I'm not falling for your crap.*

*Not a joke. We have maybe 15 minutes left.*

*Until what?*

*I don't know, exactly. Something bad. That's all I know.*

*Right. Screw that.*

Jake didn't answer when he tried texting again. After the clock tower finished striking noon, some boat horns went off, and Austin could hear cowbells ringing. The 5K had begun.

Austin ran toward Templeton Lane, past the North Stage, where Mushy was helping a red-vested emcee do a Q&A session about mushrooms for the curious crowd. Mushy seemed to see Austin, waving at him mockingly, while Mushette lingered nearby, wringing her mittened hands.

Ignoring that, Austin went to the edge of Templeton Lane, where the barricades were placed, the street clear, with only a few sheriff's deputies clomping around on horseback. It ended at the Temple. In front of the Temple, at the intersection of Templeton and First Street, there was a finishers' tent, and the

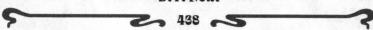
Mayor's people had set up a stage. There'd be a big crowd here by the time the 5K ended.

"Austin!" Jess said, waving. She jogged up to him, grinning. "Dude, I thought you were leaving."

"We are," Austin said. "We have to get the fuck out of here."

Jess wrinkled her nose.

"I pinged Mallory," Jess said. "Told her what you told me."

"Oh, fuck," Austin said, whipping his head around. He didn't see Mallory.

"Jess, do you even remember what happened last night?" he asked.

Jess smiled wider.

"I was flying, Dude," Jess said. "I saw the Lady. I swear to God, I saw Her. And She saw me, man. She saw me. Eyes as big as planets, like shining fire. I can't even put words around it. Blue fire."

"Yeah," Austin said. "Mallory was going to sacrifice you two to the Lady."

Jess laughed, slapping her thigh.

"You're so paranoid, Austin," Jess said. "Cracks me up. Did you smoke up this morning or what?"

"No," Austin said. "I have footage of it. Footage of last night. I saw what went down. Mallory was going to serve you up to the Lady."

Jess looked at him a moment, giggling, waiting for the punch line. When it didn't come, she wrinkled her brow.

"Let me see the footage," Jess said.

"There isn't time," Austin said. "Trust me, though."

His phone pinged. It was Mallory.

*Austin, you idiot. What are you doing? Where are you?*

He held up his phone.

"It's Mallory," Austin said. "Do not tell her where we are."

Jess grimaced. She never liked bad vibes.

"Dude, you're freaking me out," Jess said. "Mallory's our friend."

"She's part of the cult," Austin said. "She's a killer."

Jess laughed again, her galloping snorting donkey laugh that came out on special occasions.

"You're crazy, Austin," Jess said. Austin glanced at the clock tower. 12:12. He didn't want to abandon his friends. He didn't want to abandon Ash or Emily.

*I'm at the hotel.*

*No, you aren't. I called them. You checked us out of our room, you Dumbass. I'm not leaving the second biggest event of my entire life for your stupidity, Austin. You'd better pray I don't find you when this is over.*

"What's she saying?" Jess asked.

"She's pissed," Austin said. "She's going to kill me."

Jess rolled her eyes.

"You're so melodramatic, Austin," Jess said. "Let's just watch the race and chill out."

She was texting her brother and hooting at the deputies who rode by on their horses.

Austin texted Ash.

*What is happening in there?*

*Mona's talking. And talking. She really loves to talk.*

*You need to get out of there.*

*Not a chance.*

"Fuck," Austin said. "Nobody'll fucking listen to me. Not you, not Jake, not Ash, nobody."

Jess absentmindedly listened while texting.

"You worry too much," Jess said. "You're, like, an overworrier. That's like an overthinker except with worrying, not thinking."

"Yeah, I got it," Austin said.

Jess hooted again, waving at the runners. There was a big crowd of them down the way, now. Hundreds, anyway, just little multicolored speckles in the distance.

Jake caught up with them, laughing at Austin.

"Hey, Bro," Jake said. "World end yet?"

"Hope you had a nice, leisurely brunch," Austin said.

"Dude, I did," Jake said. He was toying with a toothpick in the corner of his big mouth.

"You're just hangry cuz you missed it," Jess said. "I get majorly hangry."

"I'm not fucking hangry," Austin said.

"That stupid shit you wrote on the window seemed pretty rando hangry to me, Rando Calrissian," Jake said.

The clock tower gonged 12:15, the quarter-hour bell sounding.

"We have to leave now," Austin said. "I swear to God, we have to leave."

"Man, that clown did a number on you, Bro," Jake said. "I'm going to, you know, let my food digest. Watch these idiots run their 5K. You know, just chill."

"Guys," Austin said. "Come on. I'll give you all the shrooms I bought if you just come with me."

Jess and Jake exchanged glances, then broke into laughter.

"Come on, Austin," Jake said. "We drank Lady's Tears last night. That was the mindfuck of all mindfucks. You think mere shrooms are going to sway us?"

Austin wanted to write them off right there. Maybe the crap Mallory had said was true. Maybe they were already taken by the Lady. But he just couldn't write them off.

"Okay, listen," Austin said. "We can hang out, watch the race. But if shit goes crazy, then we get out of here, alright? Deal?"

The Twins looked at each other, like a secret pact between them, some Twin Bond bullshit.

"Alright," Jess said. "We chill out, and, like, if it goes cray like you say, then we'll split."

"Sure," Jake said. "Meanwhile, we can enjoy the race. Watch these Lynchburg losers get their fake medals and shit."

Austin was far less than happy about it, but it was not in him to ditch his friends. He'd abandoned them at the Sacred Grove; he wouldn't abandon them now.

# 12

"**Blessed day,**" **Mona Templeton said, addressing the** Conclave. "For She is with us. Since the founding of Lynchburg, we have honored Her. We have sacrificed in Her name, and we have reaped the benefits of Her blessings. Today is a singular day, for the Goddess walks among us, now. Not an idol, but Her spirit made flesh."

Emily could barely contain herself, being held aloft by the Exemplars. She rose from the gilded throne, holding her arms up.

*"I am here,"* Emily said. *"I am with you always."*

The Exemplars lowered her to the ground, while the Faithful bowed. Emily could see and feel their adoration and terror pulsing with their heartbeats. It was overwhelming, but the Lady was in her, was with her, and she felt no fear, only hunger and dark desire, welling up inside her in coruscating waves. There was so much life here, pulsing and pristine.

And yet, Emily pushed back on the Lady, would not give herself over to Her so completely.

*I am still myself. I am still me. I am Dr. Emily Carver.*

The Lady smiled within her, the god-splinter, the Ladysliver as Emily sought to see Her.

*We are as one,* the Lady said. *Speak to the Faithful, Academician.*

"My Faithful flock," Emily said, feeling the Lady's words on her lips. *"Thou hast tended My gardens in groves, have drunk deep of My Tears. Thou hast tasted My favor and found it sweet. Thou hast sent Me gifts of so many lives over so many of your years. I savored every one."*

"To the Cursed Earth, where we all belong," Mona said, her words repeated in unison by the Conclave.

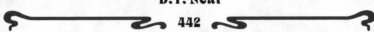
"To the Cursed Earth, where we all belong," the Temple Conclave thundered. The Temple rang with it, and the Lady was gladdened by their ardor, even as Emily was saddened by it. How tiny they all seemed.

*This will not end unless they do,* Emily thought. It was a calculation.

*I do not want it to end,* the Lady thought.

*"Thy world is far from My own,"* the Lady said through Emily. *"Indeed, another universe away. When thou came unto Me in prayer, I did not know thee. But I know thee now. Thou hast done Me a great boon by linking thine own world to the place of My exile."*

The Lady in her mind squirmed, and Emily fought for control.

*I am Dr. Emily Carver, Lady. You snuck into my soul, but I am my own self.*

*We are as one,* the Lady said in her head.

Emily felt tears well up in Her glowing eyes and marveled at the bright blue tears that fell down her cheeks, to the startled exhortations of the Faithful. They bowed low before Her but stole glances. Where Her tears fell, mushrooms grew—bright blue, brighter still than the Lady's Tears Agarics, for they were entirely blue, not just blue-capped, and glowed with a radiance that matched that of Her fiery eyes.

*The Lady's Lamentations,* Emily thought, naming these new and unfamiliar mushrooms that blossomed at Her feet.

*Lamentations? They are blessings,* the Lady thought.

The nomenclature, the taxonomy was like a latticework of order that Emily could cling to. Her background, her knowledge and understanding. Against this was the Lady's unearthly essence, Her godhead. The very reticence that had made Emily a worthy vessel to contain Her was also a source of discord for the Lady.

Seeing the miracle of the sprouting mushrooms appearing on the ground touched by Her tears, Mona cried out.

"Behold the miracle before us," Mona said. "Her tears bring life from stone itself. A new blessing for all to behold with wonder and despair!"

One of the Faithful grabbed one of the blue fungi and plucked it from the ground. It was a young man, blond-haired and blue-eyed, and as he picked up the blue mushroom, blue veins lanced through his flesh, like phosphorescent rivulets

that made him gasp in amazement. It was not painful, but it passed through him swiftly, consuming him in moments, until he fell backward and, upon hitting the ground, burst into hundreds—even thousands—of other blue mushrooms just like the one he'd picked.

And as he did so, others were grazed by his rapid passing, and they, too, began to transform, until it spread frenetically throughout the lower galleries, causing an ecstatic panic among the Faithful, as some embraced and others recoiled from the stunning spread of the phosphorescent blue fungi that covered the ground and benches in a roiling, hasty conquering transformation of flesh, bone, and blood.

Emily could see Ash filming it, her mouth agape as she beheld the lower gallery bubbling and turning from prayerful people into a sea of glowing blue fungi. Some of the less ardent were running past her from the gallery, their arms and faces ribboned with the bright blue veins.

*Run*, Emily said to Ash, in her head.

In moments, the floor of the Grand Hall was filled with the luminescent fungi, where before, many hundreds of people had stood.

Ash gasped and backed away from it, afraid to touch anything, moving carefully even as she filmed it. At the center of the Hall, beneath the great idol, Mona stood in wonder, surrounded by the blue fungi. With so many of them growing, the glowing blue was almost overwhelming to the eye, coloring her face, and illuminating Emily's own.

But Emily welcomed it, saw only beauty and unearthly life. She saw the upper galleries were filled with startled parishioners, who were moaning and howling and crying out to the Lady, who raised Her hands to them and with sweeps of Her arms, sent snowy-white, starlit spores to them in wave after wave.

*Your gifts are well-received by Your flock,* Emily said.

*They are,* the Lady said. Emily could see that the Lady did not care, could not comprehend the fragility of the lives of Her own worshippers, and counted on that. The barest whisper of a god was, to a mortal, tantamount to a scream.

She saw Maura cry out and run from the upper gallery, while the others who were not so quick on their feet were touched by the mote-like spores, which, when they touched

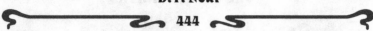
flesh, ran through their bodies in tentacular waves of white, bursting their bodies open from within in founts of red and white—the red of their spilled blood and the white of thick ribbons of freshly-formed fungi that wound and tangled around everything they touched, rotting wood and flesh and sinking deep into stone.

Mona let out a wail at the sight of the carnage in the upper gallery, the tumbling avalanche of white tubules and slick red blood, fast consumed, falling in ghastly garlands that turned and twitched with the fading remembrance of the lost selves that spawned them.

"What have you done?" Mona asked, tears in her eyes running down her painted face, drawing a jeweled, curved dagger from her belt. "Dr. Carver, what have you done?"

The Temple smelled coppery from all of the spilled blood, with an earthy scent as well from the fungi.

*"I thank thee for thy service unto Me,"* Emily said, reaching out and grabbing Mona by her forearm, holding her knife-wielding hand immobile in Her cool grasp. *"And I bless thee with what thou hast craved the most—the divine communion with thy Goddess."*

Emily pulled Mona to Her and kissed her beneath the great idol, while Mona struggled and flailed in the clutches of the Lady, unable to escape. Emily could see her blood welling in her and could feel the Goddess touching her as well, with only the hunger driving Her.

The kiss was long and hard and sweet to Emily's taste, and when she released the High Priestess, Mona choked and gagged on her own blood, unable to scream for all the blood that ran from her blue-smeared lips, splashing on the ground.

*"Not the Lady's Kiss you desired, Priestess,"* Emily said, and the Lady appreciated the irony of it, the dark amusement Emily felt at paying Mona Templeton back in this fashion.

Mona's bloodshot eyes went wide, her flesh went from pink, to white, to grey, to black as she rotted before Emily's eyes in mere moments, falling in a dusty mass of black rust that splashed against the floor in an explosion of withering putrescence.

How beautiful the Temple had become to Her divine eyes, Emily thought, seeing the intoxicating glow of the blue fungi in the lower gallery, and the thick, ropy, swaying ribbons of white fungi in the upper gallery, and the splash of black rust where

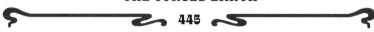

Mona had been only moments before. No human flesh or blood remained, having been consumed by the explosion of fungal growth.

*It is as it should be,* Emily thought, and the Lady agreed. Emily was going to hurt the Temple badly. Perhaps irrevocably. It was the least she could do for them, after what they had done to her.

Melinda had stopped playing her keyboards from her perch when Mona had fallen, and Emily smiled up at her, the young woman gazing at her in red-robed horror.

*"How liketh thou My work, Troubadour?"* Emily asked. *"Doth it inspire thee?"*

Melinda screamed and ran from her booth, and Emily could hear the screams echoing in the hallways of the First Temple of the Lady.

Emily reached out and caressed the idol with an open hand, her grey-white flesh against the grey stone, and lines of black rust traveled up the Lady's leg, devouring the stone. In moments, the stone became riven with the black rust, and the entirety of the thing collapsed in a malevolent black cloud that filled the Grand Hall of the Temple, to the delight of the Lady.

*Thou art an untapped engine of devastation, Academician,* the Lady thought, finding satisfaction in the mayhem they were causing.

*"I am the God-Daughter of Slaughter. I am Entropy's Orphan,"* Emily said, raising her hands high above her, toward the great dome. She gestured, and the dome burst, exploding in a crash of glass and groan of bending steel as it split open and outward. Emily let out a cry of joy that sent a beam of blue light skyward, and She blew a kiss upward, and more of the starlit motes flew upward and outward in search of hosts.

She could hear people screaming outside and walked through the Grand Hall as the black rust that had wafted through in clouds that kissed the stone of the Temple, eating into it, taking first the polished smoothness of it, then degrading the stone itself as it devoured, making more of itself, the black rust that collapsed as the stone fell, exposing steel beams like skeleton bones, and still the black rust was not through, for it bit that steel as deeply as it had the stone.

To Emily's eyes, everything glowed with a celestial light, and She took delight in the carnival before Her.

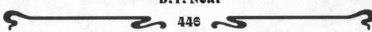
She cleared the Grand Hall as it collapsed in a thundering clang as the black rust continued to make its way throughout the Temple, the stone creaking and cracking before the on-slaught it had not been designed to withstand.

Melinda stood there, terrified, tears in her eyes, having only made it downstairs just ahead of the black rust.

"Why, *Signora?*" Melinda asked.

"*I am here, My Child,*" Emily said. She held Her arms out for the organist, who only shrieked and ran from Her. "*That is why.*"

Melinda vaulted through the front doors of the Temple, while Emily strode down the main hallway, hearing the clang-ing chorus of the groaning stone and steel as it rotted away, falling down upon itself.

Outside, in the bright light of the midday, Emily emerged, the colors even more beautiful to behold—fuchsia skies, char-treuse trees, cerulean streets, puce people screaming her name, pointing and falling over themselves to escape Her joy and wrath. It was enough to bring tears to Her eyes, and Emily wept with joy, Her bright blue tears splashing groundward, produc-ing more of those incandescent fungi wherever they fell.

"*I am here,*" Emily said. "*I have come at last.*"

The horse-mounted constables had drawn their weapons and fired at Her, the bullets decaying into ruin even as they touched Her flesh, and Emily laughed. She welcomed it, bore them no malice, only everlasting love, the deathless love of a Goddess incarnate. She saw Deputy Stirner bravely firing at her, and wished he would flee, but knew that he would not. A good man, he would not run away.

She held Her arms out to them, and could see Lionel Tem-pleton on his phone, looking at Her with uncomprehending terror.

"*Younger Brother,*" Emily said, Her fiery eyes upon him. "*Sweet Lionel, gifted heart-taker. I love thee as I loved thy sisters.*"

As She walked, the ground became manna, the grass giv-ing way with each step, withering and turning black while bubbling masses of snow-white manna burst from the soil and grew quickly in the light of the day in a bubbling, membranous sea that radiated outward from Emily with each step.

Behind her, the Temple had collapsed, sending a wave of black rust out ahead of Her. Anyone it touched gasped and screamed, falling into decay in moments. Lionel was caught in

the choking black cloud, crying out for Her mercy, not under-standing that what She was giving him *was* Her mercy.

She raised Her hands to Her blue lips again and blew as be-fore, sending more white spores out across Templeton Lane, the motes bursting everyone they touched, turning them into tan-gled masses of white fungus that rolled out in bloody masses where bodies had been only moments before.

The clock tower chimed 12:30, the halfway point in the hour, and Emily laughed, awash in the iridescent spectacle unfolding in front of Her as the 5K Fungus Run participants, the first of them having crossed the finish line only a handful of minutes before, had been running back the way they'd come, this time for their lives, crashing into the others who had not yet realized that something horrible had happened just past the finish line.

"Emily," Ash said, off to one side, having hidden behind a rotting tree. She was filming still, incredibly. Melinda, her sis-ter, was weeping nearby.

"*Sweet Scribe,*" Emily said. "*Why are thou not running like the others?*"

"I have to see," Ash said, filming Her. "And to reach you. You're still in there, aren't you?"

"*I am as I have always been,*" Emily said. "*I am eternal.*"

Ash's heart beat fast, her blood pumping quickly inside her, while Melinda's blood boiled with rage.

"You have ruined everything," Melinda said. "You ruined it all!"

"*This is My song, Troubadour,*" Emily said. "*Wouldst that thou listened to Me. Scribe, thou shouldst flee this place whilst thou can. I go to the birthing basin, the Sacred Grove that spawned me, the Lady's Gate.*"

Emily felt for Ash, could see her love and pain, her friend-ship, her indomitable spirit and drive to get to the bottom of what she was witnessing, to know. She loved that about her friend, and could see her wounded sister beside her, could feel the hate within her, like a toxic blossom. Hatred for Her in the topsy-turvy alchemical transformation that only a jarring jilt-ing could conjure.

"I don't know how to help you, Em," Ash said. "I don't un-derstand."

*"Get thee from this place, Scribe,"* Emily said. *"Thou hast done all that thou can. Take thy kin and run far from here, before the Lady's Kisses descend again in this new Neverwhere I hath created."*

Ash grabbed her sister's hand and began running down First Street, the two Dunn Sisters making haste, while Emily smiled, seeing restaurant patrons running forth from the streets, only to run headlong into the white-ribboned fungi or the luminous blue mushrooms or the black rust, finding their bodies bursting or blossoming, depending on what they touched.

And while Emily felt sorrow for each soul She drank upon the streets of Lynchburg, She also felt pleasure and satiety as She fed, for each life made Her stronger still, and that knowledge brought more tears from Her bright blue eyes, splashing the ground and making a swath through the town, while overhead, the midday sky grew clouded as the Breach that had come from Her birth cracked the heavens overhead, bringing opalescent darkness.

*"I am at home in My new home,"* Emily said, and shared Her joy with the screaming multitudes who ran from Her as fast as their legs would take them, while She sent Lady's Kisses flying after them, borne on the gusting, divine winds of Her whims.

# 13

**Logan had finished his breakfast as Maura had told him,** settled his bill, and made his way slowly up Templeton Lane while the 5K was going on, stopping in front of the Temple when the roof actually blew off of the place.

He couldn't believe what he was seeing and hearing—the smash of the glass and scream of metal, like an explosion without the boom or the fire. He saw the glass flashing skyward, catching the midday sun.

Then things got crazy. He saw Maura come racing out of the Temple, her eyes wide, and he could hear screaming inside.

"What's going on?" Logan asked.

"We have to get the fuck out of here," Maura said, grabbing his arm, gasping. He saw over her bent shoulders, saw others running from the Temple, people in white robes, people in brown robes and grey, screaming and flailing, clutching themselves, and, incredibly, falling to the ground in psychedelic splashes of luminous blue fungus that seemed to lay claim to their bodies where they fell.

"Lionel!" Maura yelled to her brother, who was standing on the stage at the end of the 5K. He turned and looked at her, only to be distracted by the shrapnel falling from overhead. His aides worked to shield him from the stuff, and he ducked under a table.

"Maura, what—?"

"No time, Logan," Maura said. "Come on!"

He felt the compulsion to follow her, and he did, as she guided them to Ambrose Alley.

"What the hell is going on?" Logan asked. "Terrorists?"

"Babe," Maura said, like he was an idiot. "It's Her. Like I said earlier."

"Oh, your 'goddess' is it?" Logan asked, irritated to be running down the alley with her, as he wasn't wearing running shoes. He could hear more screaming from the Temple, and Maura was breathing hard as they ran.

"Yeah," Maura said. "She's, uh, I don't fucking know what She's doing. But we have to get out of town, and fast."

She took her phone and dialed it.

"Daddy," Maura said. "She's gone crazy at the Temple. Where are you?"

Logan glanced behind him, saw white sparkling motes of light that looked like burning phosphorous arcing from the Temple like some insane volcanic eruption. The screaming was only escalating.

"No," Maura said. "I didn't see Mona. The Lady blew Kisses at us in the galleries. I didn't stay for them. I got out of there. The Temple's exploding. No, I didn't see Uncle Gus."

Maura was breathing hard again, slowed down, dragging Logan back with her.

"We're in Ambrose Alley," Maura said. "I'm getting my car. I'm with Logan. We're getting out of here. No. Just Lionel."

She yanked her keys from her pocket and lobbed them to Logan, who was startled, dropping them. He picked them up.

"Get us out of here," Maura said, and Logan keyed into her car, a black Mercedes sedan. He fired it up, and she jumped in next to him, still talking on her phone. He went to turn the car around, toward the Temple, but Maura shook her head, pointing to Grand. "That way."

"But it's marked off for the Festival," Logan said.

"Fuck the Festival," Maura said. "That way. Drive through it."

Her words compelled, and he floored it, the Mercedes skittering out onto Grand, nearly hitting some pedestrians, sending another one careening off the hood, fried mushrooms flying.

"Ambrose Alley goes all the way through," Maura said, pointing across the street. "Just keep going."

Logan kept going, hitting Mushy the Mushroom, who tried to get out of the way. The mascot went flying, white confetti flying on the wind from his ruptured wicker basket.

"Sorry, Mushy," Logan said, fishtailing his way down the other side of Ambrose Alley. He glanced in the rearview mirror,

seeing people pointing and gesturing, and, far beyond them, something worse, like a black cloud settling over Lynchburg.

The Mercedes growled as he shot them down the rest of Ambrose Alley, toward the edge of town.

"Left on Sycamore Lane," Maura said. "Then a right on Country Road."

"Where are we going?" Logan asked.

"Anywhere but here," Maura said. "The Breach."

The Mercedes cleared Sycamore Lane and he swerved into Country Road, his heart pounding. Maura looked terrified, and that made him afraid, too.

"I don't know, Daddy," Maura said on her phone. "We'll be there in a few."

She hung up, dialed somebody else.

"Mona, it's Maura," she said. "Pick up if you're there. I got out of there. Daddy wants us back at the Grove. All of us. We need to get a handle on this."

She hung up, dialed up her uncle.

"Gus, where the fuck are you?" Maura asked. "You son of a bitch."

She didn't know what he was saying, but Maura wasn't happy about it.

"Yeah, well, fuck you, too," Maura said. "Daddy wants you back here ASAP. Hello? Gus?"

Maura cursed, actually screaming at her phone.

"He hung up on me," Maura said. "He hightailed it out of town after he did his shitty show. Cannot believe him. Take a right here. The gravel path. You see it?"

Logan whipped the car hard right and was relieved when the tires bit into the softer ground, as he sent them up the slope, the trees whooshing past them.

"Slow down a little, Babe," Maura said. "I don't want you rolling us off the hill."

He did, seeing the autumnal ground giving way to a strange white, Styrofoam-looking mass that was growing over absolutely everything, like ground and trees. In the middle of this were some trucks, and Ned Templeton and some acolytes, all of them with white facepaint.

"Stop here," Maura said, and Logan obliged her, getting out. The area looked alien to him, like a rounded clearing covered with the strange bumpy stuff and a bunch of blue-capped mushrooms, as well as a basin filled with clear blue liquid. The ground was springy beneath his feet, like stepping on a rubbery mat.

Ned Templeton had a serene look on his face as Maura told him what she'd seen at the Temple.

"I can't reach Lionel or Mona," Ned said. "They're dead."

"Gus told me to fuck off," Maura said. "It's just us, Daddy."

"Not enough," Ned said. "Not nearly enough, now, we two."

Logan could see Lynchburg from where they were, a hint of the town in the rolling hills, three or more miles away, awash in an ever-darkening sky.

Maura's eyes danced over the acolytes, and over Logan, too.

"What about them?" Maura asked.

"We fed Her well," Ned said. "As She wanted. But you know how She is. Always hungry, always wanting more. There's nothing to be done for it."

Maura's face fell.

"Daddy, what do you mean?" Maura asked.

"Even if I were inclined to stop Her—which I'm not—what could we two hope to do? You're the greatest of my children, Maura. More than Mona, even. Your mother would have been so proud to see the woman you've become."

Maura's eyes welled up with tears.

"Daddy, what are you even saying?" she said.

"It's over," Ned said. "We're over. All things pass into ruin. We have done our part. We brought Her here."

He walked to the basin and cupped his hands into the Lady's Tears, holding them up.

"Come," Ned said to those who were present. "Let's drink to the Goddess. We've worked hard enough today. The future is what She makes of it. And of us."

He held up his cupped hands and drank from them, and the acolytes and workers present followed suit, all of them dipping their hands into the basin and drinking from it.

Ned's teeth stained blue from the pure Lady's Tears, purer by far than what they brewed themselves, and he smiled at his daughter, at Logan, as he sat upon the manna, while the white paint ran down his face where he'd drunk the Tears.

"We are blessed today, Maura," Ned said. "The Goddess is here, now. Our work is done."

"What about the farm?" Maura asked. She pointed to the trucks filled with manna. "What about the goddamned manna?"

"The Food of the Goddess will remain," Ned said, already beginning to feel the effects of the basin brew, his eyes going bright blue. "For all who may want it."

Maura was fretting, pacing, watching the acolytes and her father loll around upon the springy white manna.

"Fuck this," Maura said. "I'm not ready to give myself to Her. Not like this. Not this way, Daddy."

"To fly," Ned said, his eyes now brighter still, radiant. "Through the Breach and beyond. Beyond care, beyond Cursed Earth and Air, where we all belong."

"Where we all belong," the acolytes said.

"Goddammit," Maura said. "Logan, can you drive a truck?"

"Kinda," Logan said. Maura pointed to the truck.

"Take that fucking truck," Maura said. "Follow me."

She walked to Ned and kissed his forehead, the patriarch of the Templeton coven no longer truly seeing her, his smile pasted on his face as he saw whatever it was he was seeing. Maura glared hard into the luminous basin.

"I'm not done, yet," Maura said. "Not by a longshot. Not for you, not for anyone."

Maura turned and stomped away.

"Does it burn?" Logan asked, gesturing to the manna.

"Everything burns," Maura said. "But we don't have time. We're heading to Philly. You and me."

Her words were enchantments, and Logan couldn't have resisted if he'd wanted to. He simply knew that he'd be there whenever, wherever, however Maura needed him. The recipe for as good a relationship as he knew how to make.

He got into the truck and started it up, grinding the gears until he found them, turning and wheeling the truck around. Logan could see that the manna was slowly growing over the tripping Ned Templeton and his loyal acolytes, who gazed at the fracturing sky with glowing blue eyes. Logan did not look back again, even as he saw a blue-white flash of light that lit up the sky.

# 14

**Austin had pointed to the Temple with a loud "HA!" when** the thing had exploded. It was 12:30 on the dot when it had happened, the clock tower bells sounding the half hour.

"I fucking told you!" Austin yelled, while the Twins looked on, stunned. Everyone was stunned. "What did I fucking tell you?"

People were unsure how to react, but as things kept happening, panic set in, and people had begun stampeding. From where they were, it looked strange—Austin could see people running from the Temple, and there were flashes of blue light, and clouds of black and starlit puffs of light flowing from the place. There they landed, people were freaking out and things were breaking. People were breaking, too—bursting, to Austin's eyes.

From this distance, he saw three things happening at the same time—people were exploding into white ropey strands of bloody stuff, they were dissolving into piles of glowing blue fungi, and others were collapsing in puffs of black dust that flowed outward in curling waves. The Temple itself was collapsing, sending bigger clouds of black dust that was afflicting even more people.

Overhead, the sky was splintering and the noonday light was giving way to something else, something differently colored, opalescent.

"You fucking assholes," Austin said, watching Jess and Jake filming it with their phones. "We have to get out of here right now!"

He took off running, and, to their credit, the Jordan Twins followed, the three of them navigating their way down Grand Avenue while people were shrieking. Austin saw a black Mercedes cut clean across Grand from Ambrose, knocking over Mushy, sending the mascot flying.

"Fuck," Austin said. Had they been a bit quicker on the draw, they might have been the ones being run over. People were tending to Mushy, who was rolling around from side to side on a sea of colorful confetti, silently clutching his ribs.

Police sirens were sounding and Austin could hear gunfire.

"What about our shit?" Jake asked as they ran.

"Fuck it," Austin said. "Seriously. Just fuck it. You didn't listen to me."

"Dude," Jake said. "Don't rub it in."

Things were getting worse, because Austin could hear the screams magnifying behind them. Like people were running down Templeton Lane, crying out with garbled shrieks as they were being consumed by unseen blights.

Jess was hot on Austin's heels, running alongside him, while Jake was groaning about stomach cramps, clutching his side.

"We passed the Grand," Jess said.

"We're on Main," Austin said. "I parked the van there. Long story."

"You knew this was coming," Jess said.

"Toldja," Austin said.

"What about Mallory?" Jess asked.

"Yeah," Mallory said, running behind them, startling Austin and Jess both. "What about me?"

Austin stopped running, glaring at her. Mallory's eyes were big, full of tension that didn't quite come across as fear. More anticipation than anything else.

"No," Austin said. "You stay here. Where you belong."

Mallory smiled at him while Jake lurched past her, clutching his sides.

"Dude, I ate too much," Jake said.

Jess jabbed a finger at Mallory.

"Austin said you were going to sacrifice us last night," Jess said.

Mallory scoffed.

"Austin says a lot of things, Jesster," Mallory said. "You believe everything he says?"

"I have proof," Austin said. "But now's not the time."

Mallory angled her way toward Austin, arms out.

"Come on, Austin," she said. "You can't just leave me here."

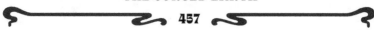
Behind them, things were getting worse. People were fully panicking now—running feet, crying out, shoving, screaming, yelling, scrambling. Worse sounds and sights followed close behind, like people strangling, clutching their throats, decaying into puffs of black, or bursting into white tendrils, or growing blue-veined and falling into masses of glowing blue mushrooms.

"What the fuck?" Jess said, filming it with her phone.

"You can't come with us, Mal," Austin said. "Consider yourself ditched."

Mallory laughed, throwing herself at Austin, kneeing him in the balls. Austin should have seen it coming, but the spectacle on Grand Avenue distracted him, as well as his unease in confronting Mallory at all, despite what she'd done. He dropped to the ground, croaking as he tried to get back up. Mallory kicked him in the face with her boots.

"What I told you, Austin," Mallory said. "You don't have the stomach for this. Or the balls, to be honest."

She kicked him in the stomach for good measure, then clamped her foot down on his wrist, the hand that held the keys. He could feel the tread digging into him as she ground down with her boot.

Jess grabbed Mallory's hair and yanked her head back.

"Not cool, Mal," Jess said. Mallory cried out, throwing her elbows, while Austin got to his feet, feeling like he wanted to puke.

Mallory and Jess were thrashing at each other, while Jake was trying to intercede on behalf of his sister.

"Lay off my sis, Mal," Jake said, only to let out a gasp as Mallory slashed his stomach with a curved knife. His blood splashed on the ground as he backed away in disbelief. "You fucking stabbed me?"

Mallory composed herself, holding out the bloody curved knife in front of her, her eyes locked on Jess and Austin.

"Give me the keys, Austin," Mallory said. "Now."

Jake dropped to his knees, clutching his stomach, and Jess ran to him, her hands on his bleeding wound.

"You can't stab all of us, Mal," Austin said, getting back on his feet.

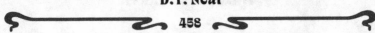
"The keys," Mallory said, edging toward him. Her eyes were wide, her voice was cold, her steps were even, her knife hand was as steady as it was bloody.

"Hey," a voice said, catching Mallory's eye before she lunged at Austin. It was Ash. It was enough of a distraction for Mallory, as Ash fired pepper spray into Mallory's face. Mallory shrieked, her hand instinctively going to her eyes as she choked on the spray, swinging her knife defensively as she tried to mop the caustic stuff from her eyes. Ash kept laying into her, spraying it right in her face, while Mallory backed up, coughing and cursing.

"Everybody in the van," Austin said, noting that Ash had brought her sister. "We are leaving now."

He helped Jess get Jake into the van after he opened the sliding side door, and Ash and her sobbing sister got into the van. Then he knocked Mallory down with a shove as he went around the front of the van and keyed in, starting it up. Ash kicked Mallory in the face and hopped in the passenger seat.

On Grand, people were running in terror as the blend of blights was descending upon them. Austin saw Mushy clutching his stomach, pitching forward and bursting into a blossom of blue fungi, while Mushette threw herself to the ground beside him, exploding into an equivalent mass of blue mushrooms that bloomed from the confines of the costume.

Austin gunned the engine and got the party van rolling, turning hard to head south on Route 219 as fast as caution allowed, heedless of the moans coming from Jake, or the wailing tears of Jess, the whimpering of Melinda, or the nervous laughter of Ash.

"Wow," Ash said. "Just keep driving, Austin. Don't stop until we're in Pittsburgh."

A black Mercedes and a white truck wheeled in behind them, but Austin didn't pay them any mind. He was simply happy that Lynchburg was in the rearview mirror, and he kept rolling until all that was left was the endless army of leafless trees on either side of them.

Left behind, Mallory got to her feet, blinking away the pepper spray with angry tears and plentiful swearing. Her eyes burned and blurred, but when she reached down to fetch her knife, she found that she had grazed a luminous blue fungus that had appeared on the sidewalk as people behind her only moments before screamed and burst into the deadly fungi.

Her vision came back in time for her to see the blue veins racing up her arm, carrying with them a curious chill, like a painlessly coursing infection, even as it went from finger, to wrist, to elbow, to shoulder, to chest, to all of her. Whatever pain she'd felt had gone away, replaced with an otherworldly numbness that was not entirely unpleasant, despite the horror it represented.

This while Lynchburg thrashed behind her, awash in the threefold terrors inflicted by the Lady's undying hunger, in overlapping waves and alternating flashes of coiling white, luminescent blue, and dusty shrouds of withering black.

Mallory held up her infected hands and began to laugh, fetching out her Brutal Blue lipstick and reapplying it to her lips, then carefully drawing a line down from her forehead to her chin, smiling to herself as she capped and pocketed it and watched Grand Avenue explode in a sea of pestilence and devastating death.

"My Lady," Mallory said, raising her arms skyward, before falling face-first to the ground as she died where she stood only moments before, popping like a piñata on Main Street into a fresh cluster of Lady's Lamentation, giving herself as completely to the Cursed Earth in as exemplary a manner as anyone ever could, or would.

# 15

**Emily had appeared at the Lady's Gate, having walked**
Her way through town, to the terror of the townsfolk and tourists, who had fled from Her by any means they could. The swath that She had cut through Lynchburg—down Templeton Lane—had left a trail of manna, black rust, Lady's Lamentation, and Stranglestrand (as the white ribbon fungus was soon to be known) in Her wake.

Emily hadn't wanted to kill all of those people—not exactly. The Lady had wanted to feed on everyone in explosive excess, while Emily had tried to channel Her ravenously malevolent attention in such a way that would put an end to the Lynchburg cult without killing too many. Emily cried boiling blue tears for all She had slain, and the Lady only felt greater pleasure at Emily's pain, an added delight to what was turning out to be a fantastic day for *La Signora*.

One way or another, what had been festering in Lynchburg all those years would be ended. Or, at the very least, it would no longer be able to operate as it had. Emily hoped that She had sufficiently uprooted the Lynchburg mycelium as to bring lasting harm to the Lady's followers.

The Lady hardly noticed, as She was gorging on all of the souls of the slain, delighting in the waves of slaughter She had caused. The entropic ecstasy of oblivion washed over them both in Emily's radically altered body, and the Lady laughed for the first time in millennia, Her blue-lipped mouth open wide, Her teeth bright white, the sound flying feverishly from Her—the guffaws of a goddess rattling windows and shaking trees.

The colors washed in Emily's eyes, the most magnificent colors She'd ever seen, and shifting with each step She took. Having reached the edge of town, She saw Herself at the Lady's

Gate, and was pleased when She vanished in a burst of blue-white light and appeared there. It was that easy now that She was here.

The manna was growing over Ned Templeton and his acolytes, while they hallucinated with bright-blue eyes that were themselves only pale shadows of Her own. She saw their blood pulsing within them as their minds wandered wildly from the intoxicant of the pure Tears.

"Lady Carver," Templeton said, hardly seeing Her clearly, for he was deep in the Tears. He crawled from his manna cocoon, prying himself free of it, breaking it with his hands, crawled for Her, his old heart beating quickly.

The Lady looked through Emily's eyes, Her laughter dissolving as She looked about Her.

*Why here again? We have claimed this land already,* the Lady thought. *Best to spread beyond it. Fresh land, fresh blood, a surging sea of souls, Academician.*

But Emily understood the intricacies of the interdimensional mycelium and the celestial hyphae, the link that bound Her to this place still, the pipeline to divinity, the pathway to infinity. It was clear to Her from the night before, the hint of a memory, the things She had seen.

"*This is my home,*" Emily said, and She gazed into the blue basin, the light within it, while Ned Templeton still crawled toward Her. She could see deep into him, the churning of his blood, the disorder of his flying mind.

And Emily knelt by the basin, running Her hands through the accumulated Lady's Tears, the purest of them that had ever been rendered, and She willed Her fingers to be the bone-white blades they had been before, and She cut into the basin, breaching the Breach at the Lady's Gate.

How easily it cut, and the Lady's Tears ran down across the ground, spawning the blue-capped *Amanitas* as before, splashing in the crawling wizard's face.

With otherworldly eyes not entirely Her own, Emily could see the cosmic hyphae She'd witnessed at midnight, the blue cables that linked this dimension to the Lady's, and She grasped them in Her clawed hands, holding them tightly. They carried with them an enervating power that would have destroyed a mortal, were they even able to perceive them. But in Her current condition, Emily could both see and handle them unharmed.

*What art thou doing, Academician?* The Lady asked. *That particular knot, once woven, can never be untied.*

*Not the knot between Thee and Me, bound together, eternally. And yet, as You so often say, all things decay,* Emily said, raising Her free clawed hand and severing the tubules She'd seen formed before. The ones the Grey Lady had ridden from Her place of exile to the Earth. The fount of Lady's Tears spilled from the torn conduits, and the bridge began to buckle.

"No," Templeton said, his face and body soaked with the Tears he'd crawled through. "You can't, Lady Carver."

Three cuts Emily made, and the link was severed, the bridge broken, and, at once, the Breach was mended, the Lady's Gate slammed shut of its own cosmic accord, for the gap between dimensions could not hold on its own.

*This will not stop what has beg*—the Lady said, only to be cut off as the gate closed in a flash of blue-white light that cracked the rift in the sky like a rock through stained glass, sending the fragments tumbling earthward.

*"I can and I have,"* Emily said to the old warlock clawing the manna, reaching for Her in the throes of his hallucinations, impaled by shards of the falling firmament of his lost Goddess.

There was only Dr. Emily Carver, now, although not as She was before. She would never be as She was before, and the sorrow of that knowledge brought bright blue tears to Her eyes, which birthed Lady's Lamentation wherever they fell.

She made Her way from the broken Breach into the forested hills beyond, without so much as a backward glance at the mortally wounded wizard and many of his hapless acolytes bleeding out beside a broken basin in a sea of Lady's Tears and festering manna, sizzling in the unobstructed sunlight of an ordinary day.

# EPILOGUE

**It had not been so easy to return to Lynchburg, and it took**
Ash awhile to even decide she wanted to. Melinda had still not
abandoned her faith, even when she'd been taken home, and it
bothered Ash far more than she wanted to admit. Melinda was
supposed to get better, and she did not. She only mourned and
prayed. Ash thought maybe she'd find answers in Lynchburg
yet.

The governor had declared the town a disaster area after
some sort of classified industrial-agricultural accident had
been claimed to have taken place that weekend in mid-September in 2019. As cover stories went, it wasn't the worst she'd
heard. The body count wasn't ever revealed, but Ash estimated
it to be in the low thousands, based on what she'd seen. Since
there were no bodies, it was hard to quantify—people were simply classified as "missing and presumed dead."

Of course, the shaky phonecam footage that was circulating over the Internet wasn't much help in that, even before the
COVID-19 pandemic had captured everybody's attention. Survivor stories abounded—frightened, panicked tales of people
fleeing, trying to make their way while the Grey Lady walked
the streets, killing all in Her path.

Seeing wasn't always believing when you only saw through
a screen, it seemed. People thought it was some meta-marketing event, some CGI-laden effects demonstration from a rogue
digital design studio, or an indie horror movie. People didn't
know what to believe, because believing it was too incredible.
Other stories emerged to explain it, none of them entirely satisfying—space aliens, elder gods, demons, bioweapons, secret experimentations, mass hallucinations and hysteria. People talked about the footage from so many phones, what they'd seen.

There were people who'd been there walking off into the forests, disappearing. Strange blue-capped mushrooms appearing deep in the woods all over the country, without explanation.

Ash hadn't yet written her story, felt like there was still more to uncover, more to learn. There was always more to learn. She had to find Emily. And she didn't want to be thought of as one of the Lynchburg Loonies, as people saw many of the people who claimed to have been there. There were Lynchburg Truthers out there, too, whatever that even meant.

Meanwhile, kids from St. Sophia would sneak to Lynchburg, stealing souvenirs or pictures of the buckled streets, the empty storefronts, the glimpses of the ghost town. It became a local rite of passage, and graffiti artists had their way with the old town. And, always, the three circles represented, even in spray paint, and a common tagline that had appeared on walls:

THE LADY AWAITS.

Ash had tried to get in as part of the Mycopharmix Disaster Remediation Team, something Jerry Merriwether had successfully leveraged before he'd disappeared under mysterious circumstances in December 2019. He'd vanished from his home on December 12, and nobody had ever seen him again. After Jerry's disappearance, Marquis made himself scarce, and Ash didn't hear from him again. The Mycopharmix check had cleared, and Ash had been grateful for that, at least.

Right after the disaster in September, Mycopharmix had generously sent workers in yellow HAZMAT suits who had worked carefully to remove the deadly Lady's Lamentation fungi, the white Stranglestrands, and the black rust wherever it was found. In the cooler temperatures, it had been somewhat easier to clear the bioagents, and since the town had been evacuated, the work could take place without interference.

Lynchburg was officially considered off-limits until it could be declared free of biological contaminants, and work was going slowly on it, because of the pandemic. A Route 219 detour was made, which allowed people to avoid the town entirely.

Stories of Ladycarver had arisen over the roughly ten-month period of time when the Mycopharmix DRTs had been there, and Ash had managed to piece things together, even

though all present had nondisclosure agreements with Myco-pharmix.

A woman was often seen wandering the empty streets of Lynchburg. Always at a distance. Her glowing blue eyes could be seen from far away, and she wore what some said was a white bridal gown that trailed behind her. Long, sharp fingers, and skin that ranged from black, to grey, to white, to something in between. Wherever She walked, mushrooms grew. All sorts.

Someone somewhere started calling her "Ladycarver" and the name stuck. Her kiss was said to be death, although no one ever claimed to kiss Her, except for a few wags who professed to have stolen a kiss from Ladycarver. Her knife hands were said to be able to cut through the world itself, and anything else they touched. This came from the testimony of some of the surviving acolytes who'd been at the Lady's Gate Breach with Ned Templeton on that fateful day. It's what they called it—September 15, 2019—the Fateful Day. Most of those acolytes had disappeared after giving their testimony. Ash had kept track of them—at least a half-dozen had gone missing.

She'd enlisted the help of Park Ranger Hunter Charles, an unassuming, grey-eyed 30-something man with a buzzcut who tended the nearby Templeton State Forest Preserve, which had been set up by the Templeton Family Foundation with the full approval of Maura Templeton in honor of the untimely passing of her father, brother, and sister, who had all been claimed in the disaster.

Ash had seen that Maura Templeton had started a Shroom Room in Philadelphia with her partner, Logan Stephens, without so much as mentioning Lynchburg or her deep roots there, beyond the Forest Preserve to honor all the fallen. Ash bided her time, would let Maura get comfortable. But not too comfortable.

For example, the surviving *Las Muertes Rojas* had found out where Maura had settled, thanks to some anonymous tipster. How that would play out was anybody's guess, but at the very least, Maura had to keep on her toes, which Ash thought she more than deserved, after what she'd helped do to Emily. As Ash saw it, nobody who slit people's throats deserved to sleep easily.

Ash pushed that all out of her head while in the Forest Preserve, however.

The Forest Preserve was beautiful and lush, with an abundance of fungi that were, of course, off-limits for anyone to pick or eat. Ranger Charles patrolled it with particular zeal. He reviewed Ash's credentials carefully.

"We don't get many people in here," Charles said. "Not since the accident, and, you know, the Vid."

"I'm sure," Ash said. "But Mycopharmix thought it might be a good story to tell. Recovery and rebirth. The triumph of the human, or at least, the American spirit. That sort of thing. People are looking for good news these days."

She was wearing her face mask, just as he was wearing his. He handed back her press credentials and let her into the Preserve, which covered 333 acres to the west of Lynchburg.

"There's no good news here, Ms. Dunn," Charles said. "Only peace and quiet."

"And Ladycarver?" Ash asked, smiling to herself that the Park Ranger was startled that she knew. Of course she knew. It was her job. She'd laugh with Austin about it when she got back home. He wouldn't believe a word of it, but then he never did. Except for Fun Gus. He was dead-serious about Fun Gus.

Fun Gus the Laughing Clown was increasingly more of an urban legend than an actual person after Lynchburg—a scary story people told about seeing a cursed, switchblade-wielding, cackling clown in a polka-dotted van packed with his mime sidekicks who'd unfailingly turn up where he wasn't wanted and invariably overstayed his welcome wherever he went. Austin lived in perpetual dread that he would run into him again, and Ash would tease him about it. He'd just point to the horn, which he had put on a shelf.

"One day, he's going to come back for it," Austin said. "Swear to god, he will."

"He gave it to you. So, why'd you take it?" Ash asked.

"Instinct?" Austin said. "Reflex? Good manners? Temporary insanity?"

"Souvenir," Ash said. "Like your Pub Crawl mugs and tees. Like Mallory's mask. Your little Grey Lady statuette. Proof that you were there when it got crazy. Your own tiny shrine."

"Guilty as charged," Austin said, smiling shyly. Ash found she liked his shy smiles. After the Jordan Twins had disappeared one day, Austin complained that he didn't have a friend left in

the world. She was there for him, brought him back to some semblance of himself. She was glad she'd been able to help him.

Ladycarver, on the other hand, was Ash's own haunting. Someone—and something—she could never leave behind. Those moments with Emily outside the exploding Temple, the moments she'd filmed with her phone, they haunted her. Her friend, transformed. Her bright blue eyes, burning like fire. The way she spoke, that strangeness to her voice, otherworldly. And she'd saved Ash and her sister that day. Ash had printed stills of the shots she'd taken, had put them on the walls of their place. How beautiful Emily looked, and how strange. She'd spared Ash, and Ash had never forgotten.

Once she talked to Emily again, she'd have what she needed. Bigger than the story she was originally planning. A book, maybe. A memoir. A tell-all. Something suitably grand. A way of honoring what Emily had done that day. Whatever the cultists had intended, Emily had messed it up somehow. Ash had to find out. She had to know, so she could tell others how, in her sacrifice, Emily had maybe saved the world.

"I've never seen Her," Charles said. "Not since I've been here, Ms. Dunn. There's a shrine to Her. I could take you to it. It's a hike."

"I like hiking," Ash said. "I think maybe I'll go for a run, though."

"You won't find Her. And God help you if you do," Charles said, as she stepped out of the Ranger's cabin with him and out into the cool spring daylight. The trees grew thick and healthy in this place, and she could feel the peacefulness it carried with it on every branch.

"You just have to know where to look," Ash said, giving him a smile, before she set off running into the forest, looking for her best friend in the world.

This world, or any world, for that matter.

# FINIS

# A NOTE ON THE TYPE

The text of this book is set in Monarcha, designed by Isac Corrêa Rodrigues (b. Vacaria, 1986). He is a graduate of Universidade Federal de Santa Maria, Rio Grande do Sul State and is the founder of Isaco Type.

Isaco Type is a type foundry located in Vacaria, Brazil, and was established in 2009. The foundry's goal is to create highly-graphic, advanced-technology fonts. Through constant improvement and careful observing of classics, Isaco Type pursues the creation of balanced concepts. The foundry has been selected in several international exhibitions, such as Tipos Latinos (Latin American Typography Biennials), Latin American Design Awards, Brazilian Graphic Design Biennials and others.

*Composed by Clever Crow Consulting and Design,*
*Pittsburgh, Pennsylvania*

# ACKNOWLEDGMENTS

Special thanks to Susan Kayser of the Illinois Mycological Association for her insights related to mushroom harvesting and transportation.

I would also like to thank Christine Marie Scott of Clever Crow Design Studio in Pittsburgh for her wonderful cover art and her invaluable assistance with the layout of these pages.

# ABOUT THE AUTHOR

D. T. Neal is a fiction writer and editor living in Chicago. He won second place in the Aeon Award in 2008 for his short story, "Aegis," and has been published in *Albedo 1,* Ireland's premier magazine of science fiction, horror, and fantasy. He is the author of *Saamaanthaa, The Happening,* and *Norm,* known collectively as the *Wolfshadow Trilogy.* He's also written the vampire novel, *Suckage,* as well as the Lovecraftian cosmic horror-thriller, *Chosen.* He has written three creature feature/eco-horror novellas, *Relict, Summerville,* and *The Day of the Nightfish.* He continues to work on several science fiction, fantasy, horror, and thriller stories.

DTNEAL.COM

# ALSO BY D.T. NEAL

## THE WOLFSHADOW TRILOGY
*Saamaanthaa*

*The Happening*

*Norm*

*Lupinia:*

*The Selected Poems*

*of Polly Drinkwater, 2007–2015*

A Wolfshadow Book

## Other Novels
*Chosen*

*Suckage*

## Novellas
*Relict*

*Summerville*

*The Day of the Nightfish*

CPSIA information can be obtained
at www.ICGtesting.com
Printed in the USA
LVHW101602061022
730135LV00016B/171